THE WATCHFUL CORONER

THE WATCHFUL CORONER

BOOK SIX OF THE
FENWAY STEVENSON MYSTERIES

PAUL AUSTIN ARDOIN

For Chris Dehlinger

TABLE OF CONTENTS

I attempted to rise, but was unable to stir: for, as I happened to lie on my back, I found my arms and legs were strongly fastened on each side to the ground... In a little time, I felt something alive moving on my left leg, which advancing gently forward over my breast, came almost up to my chin; when, bending my eyes downwards as much as I could, I perceived it to be a human creature not six inches high, with a bow and arrow in his hands, and a quiver at his back. In the meantime, I felt forty more of the same kind (as I conjectured) following the first.

—JONATHAN SWIFT, GULLIVER'S TRAVELS

PART ONE

SUNDAY

CHAPTER ONE

Fenway had always hated this room.

Odd for a former literature major to hate her father's library, full of handsome, leather-bound tomes of Western literature. But it smelled strange. Not bad, exactly, but strange.

She sniffed, hoping Charlotte wouldn't notice. Slightly tropical, maybe an undercurrent of bleach. Then it hit her. How does a room with so many classics not even *smell* like books?

She switched her mimosa to her left hand and ran her finger along the shelf at her shoulder. She closed her eyes for a moment, and the image flashed in her mind: her father lying at her feet, blood pouring from his chest, as the smoke swirled around her and the EMTs burst in—

She opened her eyes, the image fading. She focused on the shelf in front of her.

There.

That book looked like it had been opened some time in the last decade.

She set the champagne flute on the side table and pulled the book out. Gold lettering on the spine, vellum pages, a weathered leather cover.

The book fell open to the first chapter, and an illustration stared back at her.

Gulliver, tied down by tiny men.

It was her father.

"What is it?" Charlotte said, crossing the room and peering over Fenway's shoulder.

"Take a look." Fenway raised the book. "Doesn't that remind you of Dad?"

Charlotte recoiled. "Ugh. With the IV drips and oxygen tubes?"

Fenway winced. "Oh—no. I was thinking of all the Lilliputians swarming all over him like the board of directors trying to keep him down. Before they were indicted, anyway."

Charlotte walked away from Fenway and took a long drink of her mimosa.

Fenway ran her finger lightly over the image. The page was thick and smooth. She wished she knew what to say. "Tiny men trying to bring down a giant," she muttered, lifting the book back into its place.

"Don't put it back," Charlotte said. "I think he'd like you to read it to him."

"*This* book? I can't take it to the hospital. It's got to be a hundred years old."

"Books were meant to be read, weren't they?"

Fenway nodded.

The doctors thought Nathaniel Ferris would wake up from the surgery that had removed the bullet lodged near his heart. For the first few days, Fenway had sat at his bedside in silence. She'd perused the medical journals about the positive effects of talking to comatose patients and had seen success when she'd worked in the ER. But she hadn't uttered a word.

What would she say? Would she tell him about her first few dates with McVie? Would she discuss the interview process for her new assistant? Maybe McVie's decision to start his own private investigator firm?

Then the week of Thanksgiving, she bought a book to which her father had constantly referred: *Endless Crude*. The insider's look at the oil industry had spent a few weeks at the top of the bestseller lists and seemed like an anecdote-filled take on the journey from crude to use. She'd sat down at his bedside and read the first few chapters out loud. It wasn't exactly conversation, but it was something. Fenway was pleasantly surprised that, while filled with jargon, many of the stories were engaging. She even suspected that her father was one of the anonymized players in Chapter Sixteen.

The first weekend in December, she'd brought *The Immorality Amendment Act*, a memoir written by a South African comedian who'd been raised by a Black mother and a white father in Johannesburg before the end of apartheid. His parents' relationship had been illegal, and while many of the stories were hilarious, Fenway had put the book down the day before: she'd gotten to a chapter in which, two weeks apart, his mother had been beaten to death and his father had been shot in the head by his white wife, who didn't approve of his Black mistress or his intent to attend her funeral.

Fenway had looked across the book face down on her lap, then raised her eyes to the crisscross of tubes and wires, the sentries of softly-beeping machines, spitting out numbers and flashing yellow lights. The comedian had not been able to visit his own father in the hospital because his skin was the color of Fenway's. Hadn't been able to say goodbye.

"I hope you make it through this," Fenway had whispered, feeling a tear slide down her cheek.

Fenway blinked and came back to the present, to her father's library, stepping over to his grand mahogany desk and setting *Gulliver's Travels* down.

"I think brunch is almost ready," Charlotte said. "Let's go see."

This early in January, the sun struggled to peek through the clouds even though it was almost noon. The hallway was dim, and Fenway stifled a yawn. She felt odd taking the seat at the head of the table.

Lemon-ricotta crêpes and croissants with what appeared to be home-made marmalade. "This looks great," she said, draping the napkin onto her lap and pushing down the plunger of the French press in front of her.

"I'll tell Sandrita," Charlotte said, though her voice was far away. "Oh —I forgot. You like lattes, don't you? I can ask—"

"No, please don't," Fenway said quickly, realizing that Charlotte hadn't asked her to brunch at the mansion to be friendly. Something was on Charlotte's mind.

"Did you visit your father today?"

"Yeah," Fenway said through a mouthful of lemon and ricotta. Oof—this was good. A bite of this might have even been worth whatever Charlotte wanted.

Charlotte glanced briefly up at Fenway, then her eyes went back down to her plate. "Still reading that oil book?"

"*Endless Crude?* No, I finished that a while ago. I'm reading *The Immorality Amendment Act.*"

"By that one comedian? The one who grew up in South Africa?"

Fenway nodded.

Charlotte chewed thoughtfully, then swallowed. "It's interesting. First you tried to understand him. Then you wanted him to understand you."

A flash of annoyance. "I guess."

"Did you like *Endless Crude?*"

Fenway shrugged. "I didn't really expect to, but some of the stories were interesting."

"Which one was your favorite?" Charlotte's tone was oddly casual.

"Hmm. I guess I'd have to say the trend in specialty fuels. All the equipment you need to produce it and how expensive it is if you don't have things set up. I had no idea that some companies literally made their fortune undercutting bigger suppliers just because they could control their systems." Fenway heard the enthusiasm build in her voice and quickly took another bite of the crêpe to mask it.

Charlotte laughed. "You know, Nate saw that trend five years before *Endless Crude* was published. It's one of the reasons Ferris Energy grew so quickly." Charlotte set her fork down and rested her chin in her hands, elbows on the table. "Interesting that you both saw the possibilities in that."

"Uh... like father, like daughter, I guess."

"Maybe it's more than that."

Fenway set her fork down as well. Her stepmother's eyes keenly took Fenway in. Fenway suddenly felt underdressed: Charlotte's powder-blue wrap dress looked elegant and professional yet somehow effortless, while Fenway's half-zip pullover and concert tee were designed for lounging around on a lazy Sunday. "I have a feeling you have something to ask me, Charlotte."

"Yes." Charlotte hesitated. "I need a sounding board."

"A what?"

"A sounding board. I need someone I can trust."

"And—you're asking *me*?"

"Yes."

Fenway sat up straight, her skin prickling with worry. "You don't have anyone you can trust? How about the controller? Or one of the company lawyers?"

Charlotte shook her head. "Look, I didn't expect to be thrust into the CEO position, and I haven't spent the years your father did building relationships with the different departments. Or like the board members did while they were all jockeying for position. No one is on my side. And everyone—" She stopped and dropped her hands to her lap. "Everyone is hoping I'll fail."

"You're doing a great job," Fenway said.

"I'm keeping the lights on, which in the current environment is hard enough. But I need to make a lot of tough decisions in the next couple of weeks, and I know myself too well. I'll be full of self-doubt, second-guessing everything, overthinking every tactical move, seeing threats where none exist. You can keep me on track."

Fenway's eyes widened. "I hardly know anything about the oil industry."

Charlotte shrugged. "Nine months ago, you didn't know anything about being an investigative coroner, but here you are." She smiled. "And if your interest in specialty fuels is any indication, you'll be a quick study."

Fenway's jaw tightened.

"We haven't always gotten along, but I know you'll treat me fairly." Charlotte picked up her fork again. "And you won't have any problem telling me something I don't want to hear. You're no yes man."

Fenway leaned back. She'd wanted to focus on the coroner position now that she was no longer an interim coroner or a coroner-elect. This had the potential to be a huge distraction, not only from her professional goals but from her personal life as well.

But Charlotte wasn't asking.

"Is this a paid position?" Fenway said.

"You'll be well-compensated."

"I'll have to see if it's a conflict of interest with the coroner's office."

"Of course."

Fenway folded her arms. "I don't know about this, Charlotte. Surely someone at Ferris Energy knows more about the business than I do. I can't just read one book about the industry and expect to give you decent advice."

"I can teach you the basics," Charlotte continued. "I've attended enough golf outings and fancy business dinners with your father." She smiled as she raised her mimosa glass. "He calls me his secret weapon. He'd excuse himself from the table, and then all the dealmakers would discuss business in front of me, thinking I didn't know what they were talking about—or wasn't interested enough to care."

Fenway set her mouth in a thin line. She hadn't been the only person who'd underestimated Charlotte. She'd have to say yes.

She wondered how many more tiny men would try to keep her father down.

Fenway drove her Accord down the winding road in the darkness, the leather-bound edition of *Gulliver's Travels* on the passenger seat. She got onto the freeway and almost passed the San Clemente Street exit before remembering she was going to McVie's apartment.

She exited the freeway and drove the six blocks to the neatly maintained but outdated apartment complex, where she found an uncovered visitor's space.

Applying her makeup in the rearview mirror, she sighed at the mess her hair had become in the constant drizzle. She put on a dark red lipstick, striking against her light brown skin. Her large eyes needed just a hint of liner and mascara.

Her stomach rumbled as she exited her car. Ever since her father had caught the bullet for her, she hadn't had much of an appetite, and she'd only finished half of her crêpes at brunch. She figured she'd lost at least ten pounds the last six weeks.

Maybe the gurgling was a sign that she was coming out of her funk.

It helped that she was finally dating McVie openly, now that he'd signed the quickie divorce papers in Vegas so Amy could get married again.

McVie opened the door, and an easy smile came over his handsome, lightly freckled face. "Hey, Fenway. You made it."

"Well, yeah. I said I'd come by after I saw my dad in the hospital."

"I know. I wasn't sure you'd still be up for it. How's he doing?"

"No change."

McVie shifted his weight. "Sorry to hear it. Have you eaten?"

Fenway didn't respond, but a slow grin came over her face.

"Really? Dos Milagros again?" McVie laughed and shook his head.

"I think I'm getting my appetite back," Fenway replied.

McVie rolled his eyes. "I knew when we started dating that eating at Dos Milagros was part of the price of admission. I didn't realize it would be so often."

"I keep telling you to try the burritos. Just because I get the lengua tacos every time I go there doesn't mean you have to get tacos too." Fenway looked out of the corner of her eye at McVie. "Besides, the carnitas are maybe the only disappointing thing on the menu. You really need to get the lengua."

McVie made a face.

"Or the carne asada."

"Fine, fine, I'll have something besides the carnitas," McVie said. "I can drive."

On the short drive to Dos Milagros, Fenway leaned against the passenger side door and looked at McVie in profile. His striking face, square jaw that wasn't too hard, and kind eyes made a certain type of woman look at him twice when he passed. Not for everyone, maybe, but certainly for Fenway. "So," she said, "I think I should be your first client."

McVie stopped at a red light and turned his head toward Fenway. "Oh, no you don't. I don't want to be a pity hire."

"It's not a pity hire. I know you're a good detective." She reached across and elbowed him in the ribs. "And I definitely know that Piper is fantastic at what she does. I hope you're paying her enough."

"I'll pay her more when we get clients."

"Well, that's where I come in."

McVie harrumphed. It was almost cute. "What would we be doing for you?"

Fenway hesitated. She liked McVie—she might even have a real future with him. But she hadn't discussed what she wanted McVie to investigate yet. She'd wanted to, but something always got in the way. They got interrupted, or they ran out of time, or Fenway decided they needed to make out at the end of the movie instead of talking about her mom.

Now the moment had come.

"So," she said, "I've got a mystery I need you to solve."

McVie pulled into a parking space right in front of Dos Milagros. "Look at that," he said. "Rock star parking."

Fenway nodded as McVie turned the car off and opened the door. "Can we talk about the mystery after we order?" he asked. "I'm famished."

In the short line inside, McVie studied the menu intently.

"No carnitas," Fenway said.

"No lengua either. I'm not ready for tongue yet."

Fenway pointed to the specials board. "Get the Mariscos Yucatán. That sauce is amazing."

"What's mariscos?"

"Seafood. It's a recipe traditionally from the Yucatán. That's where Cancún is."

"I know where the Yucatán Peninsula is, Fenway. I went on spring break in college."

"You got your ass from Fresno State all the way to Cancún?"

"My junior year. That's where I fell in love with carnitas."

"If you tell me it was at Señor Frog's, I'm leaving you."

The couple in front of them finished ordering and Fenway stepped forward. "An order of Mariscos Yucatán for the gentleman, and I'll have—"

"Dos tacos de lengua, bien picosos," said the cashier.

"Sí," she said, holding up three fingers, "y un taco de carne asada."

"Not going all tongue tonight?" McVie said, handing the cashier his credit card.

Fenway smirked wickedly. "Maybe I'll go all tongue later."

McVie chuckled and slipped his arm around Fenway's waist.

After he signed the bill, McVie sat with Fenway at an open table. "So," McVie said, stretching his long legs out and staring up at the ceiling, "what is this mystery you have for me that has nothing to do with you feeling sorry for the town's newest private investigator?"

"It's my mom," Fenway said.

McVie's head snapped forward. "Your mom?"

Fenway nodded. "Piper hasn't told you about this?"

McVie set his mouth in a line. "You've told Piper but not me?"

"Well—she was there when I found out. But then my dad got—" Fenway swallowed hard. "He went to the hospital, and we really haven't talked about it since."

McVie narrowed his eyes into a hard stare, affixed on Fenway, then looked down at his hands. When he raised his eyes again, his gaze was softer, his voice mellower. "What did you find out about your mom?"

She paused. "I'm not really sure I want you to know. I'm kind of—it's embarrassing."

"Embarrassing?"

"Right." She hesitated, then plowed on. "So you know how I don't—I didn't get along with my dad very well."

"Yeah. I've got eyes."

"Did I ever tell you the reason?"

"I assume it's because he pretty much abandoned you until your mother died."

Fenway touched her nose. "See? You're already making me glad I'm going to hire you."

"Is there something more?"

"Well—I mean, my dad has always been super-rich. I got postcards from him of all the exotic locations he traveled, and then I saw this twenty-three-year-old beauty queen he was dating, and the mansions and cars and private jets."

McVie nodded.

Fenway folded her hands and stared down at them. "Meanwhile, my mom and I had nothing. I can't even tell you how many nights I went to bed hungry because we didn't have any food in the house." Fenway looked up at McVie. "You ever go to bed hungry when you were growing up, Craig?"

He paused, then shook his head.

"I was nine years old, and there were nights I went to sleep knowing I wouldn't be eating until free breakfast at school the next morning." She pursed her lips. "I didn't know any different, but trying to go to sleep ignoring your hunger sucks." She leaned back. "Anyway."

"Your dad didn't give you or your mom any money?"

"I'm getting to that. See—I never thought he did. I always assumed that with his team of high-priced lawyers and with Mom stealing me away in the middle of the night, he had all the leverage. Maybe he agreed that he wouldn't press kidnapping charges if she agreed to go without alimony or child support. I don't know—I was a little kid. I knew he was rich and powerful, and I just figured he could get away with it. Maybe I made up stories and told them to myself so many times I believed it was the truth."

"Sure."

"But then I found out that my father *had* been paying. Not a ton, compared to his income, but he sent my mom ten grand a month to support me."

"That's not a lot for someone with his salary or net worth."

"Well, yeah, but like I said, he had his team of high-priced lawyers and leverage over my mom because she took me over state lines without an agreement."

McVie nodded and leaned forward. "Why didn't your father have her arrested? Why didn't he just throw her in jail and take sole custody of you? I bet the courts would have agreed with him."

"Well—I don't know. I guess I never thought about it. Maybe I could ask Charlotte." Fenway made a face, then shook her head. "Nope, I don't think I really want to ask her. Maybe I don't want to know."

"So—you want me to find out what happened to that money?"

Fenway leaned back in her chair and closed her eyes. "That's why it's taken me so long to ask. I've got good memories of my mom. I thought she was always there for me. I thought she was trying her best in a bad situation." She opened her eyes and stared at the festive orange pendant light hanging above their table. "I mean, I've thought the worst. I thought she was using drugs. Maybe pills, since I think I would have noticed a smell or a change in behavior if it was heroin or cocaine. Or maybe it was gambling. There was a casino about forty-five minutes east of Seattle. We didn't have a car, but she took the bus to her swing shift job at the grocery store. But maybe she wasn't going to the grocery store at all. Maybe she was going to the casino. Or the racetrack. Something like that."

McVie hesitated, then sat up straight and put his hand over Fenway's. "I'm really sorry you have to go through this," he said. "It's bad enough that your father is in the hospital, but for you to have to wonder what happened to your mom—well, it sucks. I'm sorry."

"So you'll take the case?"

The cook called out their number, and McVie got up, returning with an orange plastic tray full of their food.

He set down the tray as he sat, then put his elbows on the table. "Are you sure you want to hire me?"

"Yes."

"What if you don't like what I find?"

Fenway turned the tray around so the tacos were closer to her and the seafood plate was in front of McVie. "I'm a big girl. I can take it."

"Okay, then I guess I can accept."

"How much?"

"What?"

"How much do you cost? What's your hourly rate?'

"Oh. Uh—don't worry about it."

"No, no, I most definitely *will* worry about it. I've got money. One of the last things my dad did in that courtroom was give me a check to cover my college loans."

"And he just cut a check? Just like that?"

"He said he paid my mother years ago—but it was like if a hundred-dollar bill fell out of your pocket before you went out to dinner. You'd still have to pay. So that was him making good on his promise."

"Wow."

"After the shooting, I wasn't sure I should use the check, but Charlotte insisted. No more college loans, so now I have a lot more money every month. And the elected coroner position pays more than the interim position did. So I've got money."

McVie stared into space for a moment. "Friends' price is forty an hour."

"Cool. I'll hire you for a week and see where we are on Friday." She unscrewed the cap on the hot sauce and shook several drops onto the taco closest to her. "Are you sure that covers your expenses?"

"When I'm starting out? No, but it gives me some momentum. You can give me a nice review on Yelp if we find what happened to that money."

"We?"

"This is a forensic accounting thing. I'm definitely having Piper look into it."

Fenway nodded. "I'm honored to be your first client."

McVie looked down at the table.

Fenway grabbed one of her lengua tacos, took a big bite, and looked thoughtfully at McVie as he pulled the Mariscos Yucatán toward himself.

"This looks great, Fenway. How come you never suggested this dish to me before?"

"What am I, your mother?" she said playfully through a mouthful of taco. "I get it now. You're a platter guy, not a taco or burrito guy."

"Maybe I am a platter guy," McVie said, putting a forkful of whitefish and red sauce into his mouth.

Fenway swallowed. "You have any other potential clients out there?"

"One or two."

"Anyone I know?"

McVie shrugged.

"Oh—client confidentiality. I got it." She took another bite.

"No, it's not that. It's a personal connection, and I'm not sure how comfortable I am with it."

Fenway looked up at McVie's face as she chewed. *Not sure how comfortable...* "Oh, hang on. Amy?"

McVie nodded and took another bite.

"Really? The ink is still drying on your divorce papers and she's asking you for a favor?"

"It's not a favor. It's a legitimate thing people hire private investigators for."

"Wait—she got married the weekend after Thanksgiving, didn't she? She's barely back from the honeymoon. And she wants to hire you?"

"You've got to remember, Fenway, my daughter lives in that house too. It's not like I can just turn my back on her. It's not that easy."

Fenway frowned. Being reminded that Amy would never be completely out of McVie's life set her teeth on edge. "So you said yes?"

"Well—look, she came to me just before Christmas, and I sent her to another P.I. You know Darren Ellsworth, right?"

"I don't know. The name sort of sounds familiar."

"He's popular with parents who are worried their kids have gotten into drugs. He does a lot of cheating spouse cases too. Darren's pretty typical."

Fenway squinted. "Did you think that's what you were getting into when you hung out your shingle?"

"I was hoping I'd get more missing person cases, sure, and I knew I was going to get the occasional cheating spouse. I just didn't think Amy would want me to follow Rick around a month after their wedding day."

"So you directed her to Darren Ellsworth?"

"Yes. I mean, at the time, I hadn't even officially ended my term as sheriff yet. It's not like I could have done anything right away."

"And what happened?" Fenway asked.

Her phone rang. Fenway dug it out of her purse.

"Oh, look at that," she said. "My first call from Sheriff Donnelly."

A wistful cast shaded McVie's face.

Fenway answered. "Hi, Sheriff."

"Good evening, Coroner," Gretchen Donnelly said in her overly formal tone. "I hope I'm not interrupting you."

"I'm just at dinner."

"Listen, I hate to bother you on a Sunday night, but I wanted you to be prepared. Mayor Klein is asking to speak with you regarding, uh, your new hire."

"What? It took me four months to find a replacement for Rachel."

Gretchen took a breath like she was starting to speak, then hesitated.

"What is it, Sheriff? Did something come up in the background check?"

"Uh..."

"Never mind. If he just wants to be a pain in my neck, that's not your fault. Thanks for the heads up."

"Sorry about this, Fenway. See you tomorrow."

Fenway clicked off and stared at her tacos. She really didn't want Mayor Barry Klein micromanaging her personnel decisions.

"Everything okay?" McVie asked, then took a bite of his mariscos.

"We'll see," Fenway replied. "Barry Klein is on the warpath again." She sighed. "I don't think he's going to be happy until I'm gone."

McVie shook his head. "You would think that with your—" Then McVie stopped talking through his bite of taco, chewed carefully, and swallowed.

"With my what?"

"Nothing."

Fenway nodded and folded her arms. "You meant to say that since his hatred of me has more to do with my father than with me, he'd mellow out now that my father's in a coma."

"I'm sorry. That's a horrible thing to say." McVie looked down at his food. "Which is why I stopped talking before I said it."

"That's just not how Barry Klein thinks," Fenway said. "He got it into his head that I wronged him, and now he's out for blood. When he was just on the county board of supervisors, I used to think cooler heads would prevail. Now that he's mayor, he's really unleashing the crazy." Fenway picked up her second taco and took a huge bite.

McVie laughed lightly. "I may deeply regret running for mayor against him and not staying sheriff, but I'm glad I'm out of his orbit." He took another bite.

"These tacos really hit the spot," Fenway murmured.

"I think it's the first time in a few weeks you're actually tasting the food," McVie said. "You've been pretty down since the courtroom."

Fenway nodded. "You, uh, want to come over to my place tonight? Maybe we can watch a movie?"

"And fall asleep on the couch again?" McVie's eyes sparkled.

"Maybe."

McVie wiped his mouth with his napkin. "I think that sounds pretty good."

———

They didn't turn the television on when they got to Fenway's apartment. Instead, McVie took Fenway in his arms as soon as the door closed behind them and covered her forehead with gentle kisses.

The wave of exhaustion hit her, her shoulders tightened, and McVie —kind, understanding McVie—got Fenway's pink fuzzy pajamas out of the drawer, and while Fenway was taking off her makeup and brushing her teeth, he washed the dirty dishes from the day before and wiped off the counters. Fenway was too tired to feel mortified. Or maybe too comfortable with him.

About twenty minutes later, McVie switched the bedside lamp on and the overhead light off before taking off his shirt and climbing into bed. She'd already started to doze off, but she turned toward him, then laid her head on his chest, listening to his heartbeat, and fell asleep.

Fenway's phone on the bedside table rang, and she jolted awake. The side of her face was sweaty from where it had rested on McVie's bare chest. How long had she been asleep? Ten minutes? Fifteen?

Her clock read 4:51 A.M. She exhaled loudly, her heart thumping in her ears, and looked at her phone. It was Sheriff Donnelly again.

She answered. "Sheriff," she croaked, "Mayor Klein better not be summoning me at five in the morning."

"I apologize for the early call, Coroner," Donnelly said. "There's a dead body at the Phillips-Holsen Hotel."

PART TWO
MONDAY

CHAPTER TWO

The Phillips-Holsen Resort Hotel was the nicest hotel in a beachfront town full of nice hotels. One of the few truly independent hotels left in California, the Phillips-Holsen prided itself on exceptional service and over-the-top luxury. Fenway's father often suggested it to his rich friends from out of town.

Fenway pulled her Accord up in front of the French bakery next to the hotel. It wasn't open at five thirty, but the pastries were calling her name already.

She got out of the car, and the doorman opened the grand cherry-wood door with the inlaid glass panels. The door itself looked heavy. The doorman tipped his hat to her as she walked into the lobby.

Marble floors stretched the length of the fifty-foot lobby, and matching cherry countertops throughout the lobby shone with varnish. Bouquets of fresh flowers stood in crystal vases, giving the large room a fresh but not overpowering scent. She looked up at the ceiling; in the corners, several small cameras painted the same color as the walls were mounted unobtrusively.

An officer stood at the entrance to the elevator and nodded to Fenway. "Good morning, Coroner. You'll want the penthouse suite."

She stepped into the elevator and pushed the PH button. Classical music played at a low volume over the speaker. A string quartet—Fenway recognized Schubert's "Death and the Maiden." How oddly appropriate.

The elevator opened to a short hallway, and the hotel room door to the right of the elevator was open, leading into a suite. Dez, dressed in her black sheriff's uniform, still with her jacket on, stood several feet inside the doorway. A stout white woman, about sixty years old, sat slouched in a straight-backed white leather chair at the dining table, her head bowed. She wore the light-blue uniform of the Phillips-Holsen housekeeping staff.

Dez looked up and caught Fenway's eye, then motioned with her head to join them.

"Good morning, Sergeant Roubideaux," Fenway said.

"No need to be so formal, Coroner," Dez replied. "Jessie here was just collecting herself before giving us a statement." She pointed at Fenway's feet. "Bootie up, Fenway."

"Right." Fenway noticed the pack of disposable shoe coverings at her feet.

"I'm sorry," Jessie said, her head still bowed. "I—I just haven't ever seen a dead body before."

Fenway tilted her head as she put the booties over her shoes, then took a pair of blue nitrile gloves from her purse.

Dez stepped closer to Fenway and lowered her voice. "Room was in the name of Frederick Ginn."

"Frederick Ginn?" Fenway said.

"Getting information was like pulling teeth." Dez folded her arms. "The woman at the front desk wouldn't give me the name on the credit card on file, which got me thinking that Frederick Ginn is a fake name. It also made me suspect that our decedent is a regular customer of the Phillips-Holsen. Looks like I was right thinking it was a fake name—the name on the driver's license in the wallet on the dresser is Richard Tonnick."

"Oh, I get it. Tonnick. Ginn." Fenway paused. "I wonder if it's the same Tonnick as the Lexus dealership."

"And the Ford dealership, and the Subaru dealership, and the Toyota dealership in Paso Querido. In the commercials, he goes by Rick."

"Ah. Local celebrity. I suppose we'll have to use some discretion."

Fenway paused again, turning the name over in her mind. *Rick Tonnick.* "You know, McVie said that Amy's new husband—"

"It's him," Dez said. "The guy was clever enough to use a fake name on the hotel reservation, but doesn't look like he was real bright otherwise."

"Why do you say that?"

"Go ahead into the bedroom," Dez said. "That's where all the cool kids are anyway—they got here about ten minutes ago. I'll take Jessie's statement."

As she snapped her gloves on, Fenway stepped further into the penthouse suite, her booties crackling with each step. The sumptuous black leather sofa against the wall on the other side of the room sat underneath a large modern oil painting of shapes and splotches. She thought she might like the painting had she been able to stop and study it.

Past the sitting room was a short hallway. An open door on the left led to a large bathroom, light and airy, decked out in glass and buttery tan marble tile. A large elevated Jacuzzi tub stood as a focal point of the room next to a shower that was larger than the entire bathroom in Fenway's apartment.

At the end of the hallway, a half-closed door. Fenway pushed it open with a gloved fingertip. Both Kav Jayakody and Melissa de la Garza from the San Miguelito Crime Scene Unit were in the room. Kav stood back while Melissa took pictures with a large SLR camera.

The dead body of a white man with bronzed skin and salt-and-pepper hair lay face up in the bed, eyes closed. He wore no clothing, and he had a tribal tattoo around his right bicep and a tattoo of a Celtic cross on his left pectoral. The top sheet, blanket and comforter were under his left arm and covered his left leg, pelvis, and most of his right leg, leaving his hip uncovered. Melissa leaned over the body and took several close-up pictures of the dead man's face, tattoos, and where the covers met his skin.

A bottle of Macallan Rare Cask, about a third full, sat on the nightstand next to the brushed silver lamp. A highball glass sat next to it, about an eighth of an inch of liquid in the bottom, faintly amber in color.

"Expensive whisky," Fenway said to Kav.

Kav nodded. "I'm not much of a scotch drinker, but I figured."

Kav crouched down and moved his slender frame forward to look under the bed. He reached out a gloved hand and pulled out a prescription bottle. "Zoeszoplon," he said. "Downing a couple of these pills with whisky is asking for trouble."

"Death?" Fenway asked.

Kav pursed his lips. "Death is not unheard of," he said thoughtfully, "but it would have to be a lot of zoeszoplon, and compromised health is usually a contributing factor. This guy, on the other hand, looks to be in good shape."

"Does he match the photo on his driver's license? Richard Tonnick?"

Kav gave Fenway a slight smile. "I'm surprised you don't recognize him from his commercials."

Fenway shrugged. "I don't watch a lot of TV."

Melissa stepped back. "You wouldn't have seen them anyway. He stopped doing those ads a couple of years ago. Now the ads look more slick. Got some agency in L.A. doing it now." She looked up. "My brother-in-law used to work for the local agency that produced those ads."

The wheels in Fenway's mind started to spin. The victim was a rich guy—who stood to gain from his death? Then she looked back at the scotch and the pill bottle still in Kav's gloved hand and clenched her jaw. She shouldn't be thinking murder until the evidence suggested it.

"Does this look like an overdose?" Fenway asked.

"No," Kav said. "There isn't the skin discoloration I'd associate with overmedication."

"He looks like he's familiar with a tanning booth," Fenway said.

"That might be hiding the discoloration," Kav mused. "Still..." He turned his head toward Melissa, who was walking toward the bathroom. "You photographed everything in here?"

"Unless you think I missed something."

"Did you get the scotch and the bottle of pills?"

"The pills under the bed? Yep."

Kav took a step forward and opened the nightstand drawer. "Ah," he said. "Take a photo of this, please."

Melissa walked up next to Kav. Fenway craned her neck to look over their shoulders between their heads.

An open twelve-pack of condoms sat in the bottom of the drawer next to the Bible.

Fenway shifted her weight. "I never met the guy, but I understand he's Craig's ex-wife's new husband."

Kav nodded. "I've heard that too. You never met him?"

"Craig wasn't invited to the wedding. I didn't really think anything of it at the time—it's Amy's second marriage and this guy's, what, fifth?"

"Something like that," Melissa said.

"They've only been married a month," Fenway said.

"Guess the honeymoon is over," Melissa said.

Kav turned and glared.

"Sorry. Just slipped out." Melissa put the camera up to her eye and snapped three pictures.

"So he was expecting a romantic evening," Fenway said. "And since this is a hotel, and he checked in under an assumed name, I guess we can conclude that it wasn't his wife."

"Not necessarily," Melissa pointed out. "They could have some sort of roleplay thing. Spice things up a little."

"I suppose," Fenway mused, "but a guy on his fifth marriage?"

"I'm just saying, him cheating isn't the only possible explanation." Melissa took a few steps back, then went into the bathroom.

Kav leaned over the body and gently opened Rick Tonnick's eyes, first the left one, then the right. "Possible damage to the capillaries," he said. He tilted his head, looking up the dead man's nose. "I'd have to run some tests back in San Mig to be sure, but I believe Mr. Tonnick was asphyxiated."

Fenway hesitated. She'd thought murder at first, too. Maybe it had been the position of the body, or that he was clearly naked in bed. "That couldn't have been from the scotch-and-sleeping-pill cocktail?"

Kav picked up the glass on the nightstand and sniffed. "I'd have to run tests on this to be sure as well. The scotch is potent, but—well, here, smell for yourself." He put the glass under Fenway's nose, and she sniffed. The smell of the whisky was strong, as Kav had said, but there was something else.

"Black licorice?" Fenway asked.

Kav nodded. "I'm not familiar with this whisky, so maybe I don't know what it's like, but when zoeszoplon is crushed, it gives off a scent of black licorice."

Fenway set her mouth in a line. "You're saying someone spiked his drink? And then—what, waited until he passed out and put a pillow over his face?"

"Like I said, we'll have to wait until we get some results from preliminary testing, but so far I find that scenario probable."

"Hmm. Could it have been anything else? Heart attack? An erection lasting more than four hours and he didn't call the doctor?"

"Sorry to disappoint you, but I found no medication to assist with erectile dysfunction," Kav said, gently opening Tonnick's mouth. "If I find evidence that suggests anything more likely than asphyxiation, I'll let you know."

"Could it have been an accident?"

"An accident?"

"For instance, if he had confused his Adderall and the zoeszoplon, and then passed out, rolled over, and suffocated himself? Then his would-be lover comes out of the bathroom, rolls him onto his back, finds him dead, panics, and gets out?"

Kav looked skeptical. "I suppose that's technically possible."

"I counted at least three security cameras in the lobby," Fenway said. "I'm sure the elevators and the hallways have a couple as well. We'll be able to see who's come and gone."

"If the cameras aren't just for show," Kav said under his breath.

"Ritzy hotel like this?" Fenway asked. "My father puts up his VIPs here when they come into town. I can't imagine the cameras are just for show."

"And the richer the clientele, the more they'll squawk about their privacy," Kav murmured.

"Someone woke up on the wrong side of the bed today."

"Just being realistic."

"If you and Melissa have the forensics taken care of, I'll see if they've got video for the time in question." Fenway turned to leave, then stopped in her tracks. "Guess it would be good to narrow down the time frame."

"I haven't taken the liver temp yet," Kav said, "but with the temperature of the room and lividity, I'd say the time of death was somewhere between one and four this morning. I should be able to give you a more precise window later."

"Can you text it to me?"

"Sure."

Dez was still with Jessie, now sitting in the chair next to her. Fenway caught Dez's eye and pointed to the door. Dez gave a slight dip of her chin in assent as Fenway reached down and slipped her booties off.

A thought came to her, and she turned around. "I'm sorry," she said, "you might have already answered this, but isn't it awfully early to be cleaning the room? I got the call at almost five this morning."

"Mr. Ginn is a regular client of ours," Jessie said. "And he's always out early. Usually four or four thirty. I clean the room right after he checks out." Her voice caught. "When the door opened with my key, I just assumed he'd already left."

"With your key?"

"Yes, ma'am," Jessie said. "Mr. Ginn likes his privacy—but the deadbolt and chain weren't on. Just the automatic lock. As I told Sergeant Roubideaux here, I came right in."

"I see."

"I can give you a rundown later," Dez said.

"Right—sorry to interrupt." Fenway turned and went out the door. As she pushed the down button at the elevator, she mulled the scene over.

She remembered the conversation about Amy McVie—oops, Amy Tonnick—asking Craig to tail her husband. She tried to recall the name of the P.I. McVie had recommended—Darren somebody. Perhaps he could shed some light on the women Tonnick was involved with.

The elevator dinged, and the doors opened. She stepped into the empty elevator car, folded her arms, and leaned against the back wall. Rick Tonnick certainly had all the signs of meeting someone for a tryst in the hotel room. How many people was he seeing on the side? Was it just one person who had met him the night before? Or were there multiple people?

If she could talk to the private investigator, she might be able to get a better sense of the crime. The killer might have been his lover, or it could have been a jealous husband.

Oh crap—jealous husbands.

McVie might be a suspect. Maybe she'd have to recuse herself from the case because of that—certainly if Fenway was called to provide McVie's alibi.

But so far, there was no clear reason to leave the case. Dez was leading the interviews anyway. And Fenway had never met Rick Tonnick before. Besides, she was probably one of the few people in town not familiar with his local celebrity status.

The elevator stopped at the lobby, and Fenway walked to the registration desk. The two people behind the counter were assisting customers with checkout, so she meandered to the concierge.

A brunette woman appeared at Fenway's side. She was about Fenway's age, dressed in a smart, well-pressed tan business suit and an ascot in colors that matched the burgundy and navy blue in the Phillips-Holsen logo.

Fenway looked at her out of the corner of her eye.

The woman wore a lot of lipstick, a fire-engine red that didn't flatter her skin tone. "Hi there," she said in an overly chipper voice.

Ugh. A morning person.

Her silver nametag read *Brianna* in an elegant typestyle. "Can I help you with something?"

"I hope so," Fenway said. "I'm Dominguez County Coroner Fenway Stevenson—"

"I'm sorry, did you say Fenway?"

"Like the ballpark for the Boston Red Sox, yes. My father's a big fan."

"Ha!" she said. "I'm from a long line of Yankees fans, myself. Hope that doesn't put me in your crosshairs." She giggled and snorted slightly.

Fenway paused. Had this woman not heard of the death yet? Did she not know what a coroner's job entailed? "Brianna," she said carefully, "what is it you do here at the Phillips-Holsen?"

"I'm one of the property managers."

"And what are your responsibilities?"

Brianna smiled, showing straight white teeth that starkly contrasted with her lipstick. "I run the day-to-day operations here at the hotel. I make sure everything having to do with the property itself is running smoothly—the lobby, the pool, the gym, the sauna, the landscaping, the parking garage."

"Housekeeping?"

"Not the maintenance of the rooms or the guest check-in process, and not the food, but just about everything else."

"What about security?"

"The security team doesn't report to me, but I might be able to answer some of your questions." Brianna tilted her head. "I take it this has to do with the unfortunate guest in the penthouse suite?"

Fenway nodded.

Brianna put her hand over her mouth. "Oh—you must think I'm horrible for not being more sad."

Fenway blinked rapidly and tried to figure out how to respond.

"You mustn't think that," Brianna said, putting a sympathetic hand on Fenway's arm. "It's the hospitality world. You're never allowed to show anything but enthusiasm and a welcoming attitude. I've gotten very good at it—maybe too good, if I can't even turn it off when there's been a death in the hotel." She set her mouth in a straight line, but her effort at abandoning her smile was apparent.

"I understand," Fenway said. "My job can make someone a little jaded, too. I've been known to be a little insensitive." She cleared her throat. "Anyway, I was hoping I could take a look at your security footage from last night."

Now Brianna's lack of a smile turned genuine. "I'm so sorry, Coroner, but we have strict policies in place at the Phillips-Holsen. As you can probably surmise, we have many clients who take their privacy quite seriously here."

"Like Frederick Ginn."

Brianna smiled. "That's correct. And he's not the only one."

"Miss—uh—"

"Harlow," Brianna said.

"Miss Harlow, I'm not a private investigator trying to get his wife a better divorce settlement. I'm the county coroner. I'm trying to establish the facts in this case."

Brianna paused. "I'd assumed that Mr. Ginn had a heart attack or—well, how shall I put this—"

"A drug overdose?"

"A misadventure," Brianna said evenly.

"We're still trying to determine the cause of death," Fenway said. "And if we can establish whether or not he had a visitor during his stay—"

Brianna shook her head. "We have a policy that we don't turn over any customer information, including our security footage, without a warrant or a subpoena."

"You don't even want to check with the security team?"

Brianna folded her arms. "I get paid to make sure that all our team members are focused on their duties. That includes not wasting their time when I already know what our policies are."

Fenway sighed. "All right."

"I apologize I can't be more helpful, but I can't undermine our policies."

"I understand. We'll be back with a warrant." She cocked her head. "I understand Mr. Ginn was a regular customer. Do you know who was with him last night?"

Brianna shook her head. "I didn't start my shift until six this morning."

"Do you have any idea who it might have been? Maybe"—Fenway thought of Melissa's theory—"he and his wife were here together?"

Brianna put her hand in front of her mouth, her eyes dancing. "Oh my," she said. "His wife. I'm sorry. Of course, I can't answer your question."

Fenway nodded, mentally crossing Melissa's theory off the list.

"All right," Fenway said. "Sounds like I'll be seeing you later today."

"Sorry I couldn't be of greater assistance." Brianna smiled widely again and turned away.

Fenway's phone rang in her purse, and she dug it out. Charlotte was calling. She tapped ANSWER.

"Hi, Charlotte."

"Fenway—hi. Is this a good time?"

Fenway watched Brianna disappear around a corner into the back office area. She'd have to get Dez, or maybe Sheriff Donnelly, to find a judge to sign off—though she was confident she'd be back within a few hours, approved warrant in hand. "Your timing's pretty good. Just finished talking to a potential—uh, witness, I guess."

"What? You have another murder?"

"We're not sure yet. Anyway, I've got some time. What's up?"

"You're aware of the vacancies on the board of directors."

"I am."

"I called a meeting so that we could convene to address the vacancies. The remaining directors agreed to meet later this afternoon, and fortunately we have a few candidates to discuss."

Fenway widened her eyes. "I hope you're not asking me to weigh in on candidates for the board of directors, Charlotte."

"No—no, no," Charlotte said quickly. "But we've had another resignation. Not one of the directors. This time it's the community liaison."

"The community liaison? What's that?"

"It's a position that advises the board of directors on how its decisions will be received in the community."

"You want me to recommend someone? Or do you have someone in mind who I know?"

"I want to nominate *you*."

"Me? Why on earth would you think I'd be qualified for that?"

"You don't have to have experience in oil and gas. Or energy."

"Did the guy who just quit have experience in oil and gas?"

"Well—yes, but I think that was part of the problem. He was thinking about community relations from the perspective of an energy company, not the perspective of a community leader."

"And I'm a community leader?" Fenway scoffed.

"Of course you are. You hold a very important elected position in the county. How can you say—"

"Okay, fine, yes. I suppose I'm a community leader. But certainly there have to be other people who are more qualified to be the Ferris Energy community liaison than me."

Charlotte was quiet for a moment. Then she took a deep breath and spoke. "Fenway, you will not hesitate to tell me and the board when something is a bad idea. If Nate had appointed you community liaison when you first moved to Estancia, he'd never have gotten into the trouble he was in."

Fenway closed her eyes and saw the image of her father's body from November, lying in front of her, the wound in his chest spreading blood.

"I don't—" Fenway said, and her voice caught.

"That's not what I mean," Charlotte said. "He wouldn't have made some of those errors in judgment. He's always had a killer instinct and great negotiation skills. But the last year or so, he's overreached. He's made some poor decisions because he thought he could become more influential in politics."

"I assume Barry Klein had something to do with it. He's been fighting Dad forever."

Charlotte clicked her tongue. "Your father doesn't falter very often, but Barry Klein got under his skin, that's for certain."

"Do I need to be there?"

"Well—if you're in the middle of an investigation, I don't want you to give that up. But if you can. The meeting is at two thirty."

"Two thirty. Got it."

"Maybe we can meet for lunch to go over a few things."

Fenway hesitated. "I'm not sure I can meet for both lunch and a board meeting this afternoon."

"Don't you have people you can delegate to?"

Fenway sighed. "Yes, I do."

"Just because you enjoy the investigations doesn't mean you have to micromanage everything, you know."

"I don't micro—" Fenway caught herself in time. "Yes, you're right. And I know this company is important to Dad. I'll be there."

"Thank you, Fenway," Charlotte said. "I—I didn't mean that you micromanaged your team."

"That's okay." Fenway paused.

"Let's go to that place you like."

"The taquería? Dos Milagros?"

"Right, that one. As long as you don't make me eat tongue."

"It's really delicious. Life-changing." She didn't mention she'd eaten dinner there the night before—she was just starting to get along with

Charlotte, and eating at the same taquería two days in a row might have made her stepmother clutch her pearls.

"Still no."

Fenway paused for a moment. "Charlotte, if I'm going to be your sounding board, can I ask you something?"

"Sure."

"Why are you doing this? You and Dad are rich enough. If you get bought out by the remaining shareholders, you have more than enough for the rest of your lives. And if—when—Dad wakes up, you'd have plenty of money to invest in other businesses. You could just view this like the Ferris Energy exit strategy."

Charlotte sighed. "I have to keep the company from sinking until your dad comes back. I think one of the reasons that his marriage to your mother didn't work out is that she never wanted to be part of the Ferris Energy world. She wouldn't attend any events with Nate—not the golf outings, not the business dinners, not even the Christmas party. Your dad loves sharing that part of his life—certainly with me. Probably with you, if you'd let him."

Fenway was silent.

Charlotte cleared her throat. "Anyway, I'll let you get back to your investigation."

"Okay, Charlotte, thanks."

She clicked off and sat down on one of the black leather couches in the lobby, and she watched the elevator doors open and close, releasing men and women in business suits, some pulling their small wheeled suitcases behind them, some putting their plastic room keys into the collection box in front of the elevators, some heading to the registration desk to check out and get paper copies of their receipts.

Surely the camera had captured whoever had visited Rick Tonnick's penthouse suite.

And been the last person to see him alive.

CHAPTER THREE

Fenway went to the French bakery for a croissant and coffee and sat for a few moments thinking about the murder, but her mind kept jumping to the community liaison position. She drove the short distance to the city center parking structure and arrived at the coroner's office suite shortly after eight. As she opened the door, a blonde woman of indeterminate age behind the high desk sat up stock-straight. Fenway almost jumped out of her skin.

The platinum hair, the sharp features—oh. Fenway's brain put everything together.

"Holy crap," she said, her heart beating fast, trying to remember her new assistant's name. "I—I guess I didn't remember today was your first day."

"I'm so sorry," the blonde said in a rich contralto. "Your look made me worried I'd come into the wrong office." She shook her long, straight tresses away from her face, and the gold-plated bangles on her wrists tinkled. The woman had on an aquamarine sweater that made her gray eyes stand out.

"We had a death at a five-star hotel downtown," Fenway said.

"The Phillips-Holsen?"

"Right. You know it?"

"I do."

"Dez and I have been there since before six." Fenway paused. "Migs is on vacation this week—how did you get in?"

"Migs?"

"Our paralegal."

"Oh—well, fortunately, Sergeant Trevino arrived just a few minutes after I did," the blonde said. Fenway blinked. She searched her brain for the name of her new hire—her first and last name began with the same letter, she was sure of it. And the last name was something bright and lively—Springtime? Sunbeam?

"Oh, good." Fenway nodded.

"He said to tell you he was helping out over at the sheriff's office with the New Year's burglaries."

"Gotcha."

The phone rang. The woman looked down. "That's your line, Miss Stevenson."

"Go ahead and get it. I'll go into my office."

The blonde picked up the receiver, and her voice went up in pitch. "Coroner's office, Sarah speaking. How may I direct your call?"

Sarah. Sarah Summerfield, that was it.

Sarah pulled the receiver away from her ear. "Yes—I understand. I'll see if she's in." With a deft hand, she placed the call on hold. "It's Mayor Klein."

Fenway rolled her eyes. "I can't believe he's calling me already. The new term has barely started, and he's already crawling up my ass." She looked out of the corner of her eye at Sarah.

"I can tell him you're out of the office."

"You don't need to lie to cover for me, Sarah. He might have camped out in the amphitheater waiting to see my car pull into the parking garage."

Sarah laughed.

"Oh—no, I'm not kidding. He has it out for me."

"He has it out for you?"

"He has it out for my father, and that means he has it out for me too."

Sarah leaned forward. "Anything juicy?"

"No. Well, probably, but you can get the story from someone else and then never ask me about it." Fenway grinned.

"Oh." Sarah leaned back.

"Tell him I just walked into the office and I'll be right there."

She walked into her private office. She wanted to redecorate but hadn't had the time or energy. The dark wood and black leather were both too sterile and too masculine for her taste. Fenway walked around the desk to the large leather chair, set her purse on the floor next to the bookshelf, and sat.

The cold leather felt like ice, even through her trousers. The January day was blustery, and a storm was coming down from the Gulf of Alaska. She shook her head. Ordinarily, after having lived in Seattle for twenty years, she would have laughed at anyone who thought fifty degrees was chilly. Now she wondered if the California coast was already spoiling her.

She looked at her desk phone, its red light next to the LINE 1 label blinking impatiently.

"Like ripping off a Band-Aid," Fenway muttered.

She picked up the phone. "Good morning, Mayor."

"What is this I hear about a dead body at the Phillips-Holsen?"

Why, yes, I did have a nice weekend. Thanks for asking how my father is. "I don't have a lot of details yet, Mayor," Fenway said. "The CSU team from San Miguelito are doing a full workup of the suite—"

"The suite? At the Phillips-Holsen?"

"That's correct. It was the penthouse suite."

Mayor Barry Klein groaned. "So much for keeping this out of the media. I haven't even been in office a week, and already people are dropping dead on my watch."

"Well—" Fenway began, intending to remind Mayor Klein that he'd actually taken office right after Election Day due to the vacancy, but then she bit her tongue.

"Was it a tourist? Someone from L.A.? Not a famous actor or musician, I hope. That's not the kind of publicity this town needs."

"Rick Tonnick."

"Rick—but Rick's a local. What's he doing at the..."

Fenway waited for the mayor to finish his sentence, but he didn't.

Barry Klein cleared his throat. "Was there anyone with him?"

"The evidence would suggest that he was not alone in his hotel room."

Klein groaned. "If it gets out that he had a prostitute in his room—"

"Oh!" Fenway said. "Did you know him, Mayor?"

The mayor paused, then cleared his throat. "It's not what—uh—we've had the occasional dinner together. He is a pillar of the local business community, after all."

So is my dad, but that doesn't mean the two of you ever shared a meal. "Since I haven't even lived here a year yet," Fenway said, "I only recognized his name from his dealerships." She turned over her question in her head, trying to phrase it as delicately as she could. "What makes you say he might have had a prostitute in his room?"

"Oh," Mayor Klein said, "well, uh, there were rumors a few years ago." He hesitated a beat. "And his third wife made some things public in the divorce proceedings."

"Got it," Fenway said. "His third wife—is she still in town?"

"I don't know," Klein said gruffly. "I want you to keep this out of the papers, do you understand?"

"Spin isn't my thing, Mayor," Fenway snapped. "I'm going to try to find his killer—"

"Wait, killer? No one said anything about this being a murder."

"We don't know for sure, Mayor, but the initial evidence—"

"Miss Stevenson," Klein said, seething, "I'm sure I don't have to tell you that we had more murders in this county last year than in the previous five years combined. We're fast becoming the laughingstock—"

"The best way to keep this county safe is by catching the people who kill other people," Fenway said.

"Just don't—"

"I'm an elected official, Barry," Fenway said. "I won't tell you how to run this city if you don't tell me how to catch killers. It'll be really difficult to find this murderer if you want me to categorize it as an accidental death just to score you political points."

"Listen, Miss Stevenson," Klein said. "You may not have your father's last name, but you both share a penchant for trying to make me look bad."

"I'm not your errand boy," Fenway said. "You don't do anything to contradict the facts, you don't try to blame people who aren't to blame, and we won't have any trouble working together."

"I better not see this on the *Courier*'s website later this afternoon."

"Of course not."

"Your friend Rachel better keep a lid on this, too."

"The public information officer only exists to make you look good, Barry. There's no need to threaten anyone."

"It's not a threat. This is for the good of this city."

Neither of them said anything for a moment, then the pause stretched into an awkward silence.

Finally, Fenway spoke. "Was there anything else?"

"Yes," Klein said. "I seem to remember that Rick Tonnick got married at the beginning of December."

"He did," Fenway said, her stomach dropping.

"The ex-wife of the former sheriff, my mayoral opponent, if I'm not mistaken."

"You are not mistaken."

"And your current beau."

"You are, once again, correct."

Another pause. "Are you in a position where you'll have to recuse yourself?"

"No," Fenway said.

Another pause, this one just as long and perhaps more awkward.

"Are you sure about that?"

"If McVie becomes a suspect at any point in time," Fenway said, "I'll have to give him an alibi, and that will constitute a clear conflict of interest. We've done this before, Mayor. When my stepmother was accused of murder, Sergeant Roubideaux took over the case and reported directly to Gretchen Donnelly. We can follow that protocol again." She sighed. "I have work to do, Mayor. Was there anything else?"

"Yes, in fact. I know you still have an opening for your assistant, and I've got a niece who just moved back—"

"No," Fenway said. "I've filled the position. You just talked to her. Sarah Summerfield. She started today."

"The one I just talked to? With the low voice?"

"We can't all be delicate flowers, Mayor."

Klein harrumphed. "Sarah Summerfield? What kind of name is that? Sounds fake. Maybe she's in witness protection."

Fenway narrowed her eyes. "She doesn't really look like a mafia informant."

"She's not a temp?"

"Filled out the permanent employee paperwork on her myself."

"And she's qualified?"

"A little overqualified, if you ask me, but she was excited about the work. Nice to have someone who wants to be here."

"Well, if Miss, uh, Summerfield doesn't work out, you let me know. My niece was a public policy major at Nidever. She's sharp."

"I'll keep that in mind, Mayor."

The silence between them grew again.

"Well," Fenway said, "if there's nothing else, I've got an investigation to get to."

"Don't make this a black mark on Estancia, Coroner."

"You have a nice day too, Mayor."

Fenway hung up.

Sarah opened the door and stuck her head in. "Everything okay, Miss Stevenson?"

"Please call me Fenway."

"Of course. Anything I can do?"

"Sure." Fenway leaned back in her leather chair. "I've got a dead rich guy in a fifteen-hundred-a-night suite at the fanciest hotel in town, and it looks like homicide."

Sarah's face grew tight. "Rich guy?"

"He owns a string of car dealerships. Apparently, he's a pretty big deal."

"Car dealerships?" Sarah gasped. "It's Rick Tonnick, isn't it?"

"I'm not going to have you investigate anything," Fenway said quickly. "We've got a new person in the IT department. Patrick, I think his name is. Replaced someone who used to be really good with forensic accounting. Reports to a guy named Jordan Daniels. Think you can set up a meeting with him?"

"With the new IT person or with Mr. Daniels?"

"The new guy. We'll see if he's as good as the last person in the position."

Sarah paused. "What exactly do you need to find out?"

Fenway hesitated and looked in Sarah's face. Piper Patten had showed a similar optimism when she first started doing forensic accounting for Fenway. "I need to figure out who benefitted from the death," Fenway said.

"Understood. I'll get right on it."

Sarah vanished as quickly as she had entered and closed the door behind her.

Fenway stared at the closed door for a moment, then rifled through the papers on her desk until she found Sarah's résumé.

Though in the right light, Sarah could have passed for twenty-five, she'd listed her college graduation as fifteen years earlier, putting her between thirty-five and forty. Sarah had worked as a network administrator for five years until a gap of about eighteen months in her job history. It coincided with the big recession, so it wasn't that worrisome. But when Fenway had tried to locate anyone who'd worked with her back then, she came up empty. She'd called Human Resources, who promised to look into it, and two days later, they'd assured her that everything had checked out.

"But I want to talk to one of the people who worked with her when she was a network admin," Fenway had said.

"You've got three references for much more recent jobs," the HR administrator had said. "How important is it to dig up people who worked at an application service provider that got purchased almost a decade ago? She wasn't even in a relevant position."

It was technically true—Sarah had moved from network admin to administrative assistant. And her references were all glowing. Just after Thanksgiving, Sarah had left Ishikawa & Knapp, a law firm that Migs assured her was run by a pack of rabid wolves. "They don't care about anything but the bottom line," Migs had said. "I'd be more concerned if she'd stayed on there. If they laid her off, it probably means she has a conscience." Fenway had been interested in Sarah's technical capabilities, even if the knowledge was a decade old. She supposed that she wanted a replacement for not only Rachel—whose work as public information officer was putting Estancia back on the map—but for Piper Patten as well.

It was impossible to deny that Sarah had nailed her job interviews. She impressed everyone on the team, and even the new sheriff, Gretchen Donnelly, had given her the thumbs up. She seemed to take a great deal of care in her appearance—not unlike the faux-chipper Brianna at the Phillips-Holsen Resort Hotel. But Fenway had no complaints—and no other candidates even came close. She was lucky that Sarah had been laid off around the holidays because Fenway was sure that Sarah only accepted because of the uncertain job market. Now it would be Fenway's responsibility to keep Sarah engaged and interested enough in the position to make her stick around.

Her phone buzzed, and she reached down to pull it out of her purse. It was a text from Kav.

Got liver temp – probably closer to 3 A.M. than 1:30 or 2

At least that was something.

Fenway went online and began to research the dead man.

Rick Tonnick had no problem making the news. Whether it was a splashy story about one of his many ex-wives or one of his many female lovers—he'd been caught with several women, and yes, had been arrested six years earlier for soliciting a prostitute—he found a way to get into the headlines.

Tonnick Auto Sales owned a string of dealerships too, and while the organization was privately held, Fenway pieced enough information together to conclude that Tonnick was worth tens of millions of dollars, perhaps even hundreds of millions, depending on the talent of his lawyers to avoid alimony. Three of his ex-wives had married again, and his two children—one from his first marriage, one from his second— were grown. Fenway nodded—if this is what the former Amy McVie had wanted out of a marriage, no wonder she and Craig couldn't make it work.

A little bit of sleuthing in some publicly available tax documents— Piper had taught her some useful things—revealed that Tonnick Auto Sales was much more valuable than its namesake.

Hmm. Tonnick had been in the business a long time, but he was only in his fifties—late fifties, but it wasn't like he had one foot in the grave. He was fit, he was vain enough to get a fake tan, and he had a new wife a decade younger—and who looked two decades younger. Perhaps he hadn't made out a will, in which case Amy would get everything.

But Tonnick was probably smart enough—given his four ex-wives— to get a prenuptial agreement. And if he'd gotten a prenup, he'd probably gotten a will or a living trust established as well.

She read a few more articles and discovered that Tonnick Auto Sales had been sued by several families over the past several years. The Ford dealership had been accused of not performing necessary safety recall procedures for its airbag problems, which had resulted in three fatal accidents—and six deaths—in Dominguez County in the span of three months.

The lawyer who had defended Tonnick Auto Sales was Raymond Ishikawa. In one article, Ishikawa had successfully lobbied the judge to move the civil trial outside of Dominguez County. Another article from a few months later breathlessly revealed that a few witnesses for the plaintiff hadn't been able to travel—or at least, they hadn't made it to court on time.

The judgment had been returned in favor of the plaintiffs—but for just over two million dollars to be split between the three families, rather than the tens of millions of dollars they had originally sought. In one crash, a family of four had perished, all dying before reaching the hospital. The other two drivers had incurred hundreds of thousands in medical expenses before they passed away—the settlement would have barely covered it.

Ishikawa.

She opened a browser window and began to search. Yep—it was the same Raymond Ishikawa who was the managing partner of Ishikawa & Knapp. She wondered if the same firm managed Rick Tonnick's personal affairs.

Just then, the door opened to Fenway's office, and Sarah stuck her head in again. "Miss Steve—uh, Fenway?"

"Hi, Sarah. Any luck setting up an appointment with IT?"

"The employee you want to meet with," Sarah said efficiently, "is in training until Wednesday afternoon."

Fenway sighed. "All right."

"But," Sarah said, "while I was waiting, I called my contact at the law firm that handles Mr. Tonnick's affairs."

"You used to work there."

"Yes. And I looked at your calendar. If you're still free, I set up a ten o'clock with Gordon Knapp. The law firm is over on Santa Barbara Street."

The offices of Ishikawa & Knapp were light and airy, all cream-colored tile and whitewashed ash. In the mild summers in Estancia, the lobby must have been gorgeous. On the wet, rainy January day, however, mud streaks on the light floors and the damp cloudy sky set a pall over the whole building.

Fenway and Sarah sat in aluminum and leather straight-backed chairs in the cavernous lobby close to the wall of glass that served as the first-floor entrance. Knapp was already five minutes late, but Sarah assured Fenway that his tardiness was to be expected.

At a quarter after ten, a white door opened on the far side of the lobby, and a white man in a black turtleneck sweater and khaki clamdiggers with loud red-and-blue paisley socks and tan boat shoes strode through the lobby. He was balding but not yet gray, and his turtleneck did nothing to hide his small beer belly. His round face was clean-shaven, and his eyes crinkled heavily, as if smiling was his default position. Fenway stood, and Sarah followed, smoothing her A-line skirt, her five-seven frame tottering on aquamarine heels that matched her sweater.

"Sarah!" Gordon Knapp opened his arms for an embrace.

"Gordon!" Sarah nimbly sidestepped the wide arms and side-hugged Knapp. "I'd like to introduce you to Fenway Stevenson, the county coroner."

"Oh, yes, of course," Knapp gushed as Sarah stepped back. "I've heard quite a bit about your escapades since you arrived." He leaned forward and winked. "I voted for you, you know."

"I appreciate that," Fenway said.

"You're awfully tall," Knapp pointed out.

Fenway looked down at her feet, then back up at Gordon Knapp. "Thanks. I worked hard at it."

Knapp cocked his head, then guffawed. "Oh—of course. Silly, silly. Come on back, now, and we can talk about poor Mr. Tonnick." He lowered his voice to a stage whisper. "I expected that man to outlive me," he said. "So sad. And if he had just—well, I suppose it is what it is."

Fenway shot a quizzical look at Sarah, who shrugged.

Knapp led them through labyrinthine corridors and then into an open workspace with about twenty casually dressed employees.

"I guess I expected suits," Fenway said.

"Everyone expects suits," Knapp said. "If we have to go to court, we put on a suit. Otherwise—it's casual. This is a law office, true, but we must be as comfortable with the law as we are with our friends."

"Oh," Fenway said.

"Excuse the mess," Knapp said. "We're working on some big cases right now."

Fenway looked around but didn't see any mess that Knapp could be referring to. Files were in small, neat piles on top of filing cabinets. Two thick hardbound tomes were open on a desk.

Knapp led them to the elevator, taking them to the fourth floor, then into a corner office with *Gordon J. Knapp, Managing Partner* in neat block letters on the window next to the door. Fenway stepped into the office, which felt more like a day spa than a law firm. Tropical plants—the large leafy greens of areca palms and banana leaf trees, as well as the orange and red hues of birds of paradise and bromeliads and the white blooms of azores jasmine—sprang from three corners of the office. Floor-to-ceiling windows covered the two outside walls. The scent of jasmine was powerful, almost knocking Fenway back. The furniture, what there was of it, was set at a forty-five-degree angle. A small desk made of light wood was set about five feet back from the outside corner where the two full-length windows seamlessly met. A sleek, tiny laptop sat in the middle of the desk, and a modern mesh task chair was unexpectedly on the room side of the desk, not on the window side.

"Beautiful view," Sarah said.

"Oh, that's right, Sarah, I don't think you've been in my office too much, have you?" He looked out the windows, where the ocean was visible through a line of palm trees. "If you're going to live somewhere this beautiful, why spend ten hours a day cooped up in a windowless office where you can't enjoy it?"

Knapp turned to Fenway and, catching the look on her face, smirked. "Not what you expected from some high-powered attorney, is it? Well, once I went into business with Raymond, I decided to do things my own way. No stuffy suits. No hoity-toity Harvard grads looking down their noses at our clients. And no typical power offices. Instead, I work in the middle of a tropical paradise, where we can have some real conversations that keep things in perspective, so we can have a human touch—so it's not just about percentages and dollar signs."

"It's refreshing," Sarah offered.

"And I'm so sorry we weren't able to keep you here," Knapp said, his tone bordering between sympathetic and patronizing. "But I'm glad you've landed on your feet."

"Perhaps I worked for the wrong side of the business." Sarah's tone was light, and she chuckled after saying it, but Fenway detected a darker undercurrent in her words. Knapp didn't seem to pick up on it.

"At any rate," Knapp said, taking a seat in the task chair at the desk and waking up his laptop, "I'm happy to cooperate with your investigation. If we get into any areas of attorney-client privilege, I'll have to demur, of course, but I can certainly tell you who benefits the most from the will."

Fenway looked around the room. Near each of the tropical oases were three chairs in a medium wood that matched the color of the palm and banana tree bark. For the *real conversations*, apparently. Fenway picked up a wooden chair and brought it closer to the desk, placing it about three feet from where Knapp sat. Sarah did the same, and both women sat, looking at each other as Knapp typed and clicked.

"Here we are," he said, picking up the untethered laptop and spinning around in his chair. "Rick rewrote his will at the beginning of December, just before he and his new bride went to Aruba. He moved some of his assets around his fourth wife got remarried in September, so we took those assets out of some foreign investments." Fenway wanted to cringe at the tricks to hide the assets, but she plastered a smile on her face. "And over the summer, he invested in the businesses of each of his children—a little over a million each—so he asked to rewrite the will to leave the bulk of the estate to his wife."

"The bulk of the estate?"

"Yes. His stock portfolio, all his investments, the house and most items—the children have specific things set aside—and his liquid assets. Oh, and of course the chalet in Aspen and the condo in Maui both go to her."

"His children were cut out?"

Knapp laughed. "Oh, no, not at all. The Tonnick children have already gotten their inheritance as it is—Rick put quite a bit of money into Grant's restaurant business and Noreen's software company." Knapp leaned forward. "Their houses are. paid off as well. They know they weren't getting much more."

"So Amy gets it all," Fenway murmured.

"He's left instructions in place regarding the auto dealership group's controlling interest, and both his wife and children will begin to get an annual profit share. Not private-jet money, but more than enough to live comfortably."

"What about the management of the dealerships? Those must be worth millions."

"They are. He's had a second-in-command for the last ten years or so." Knapp laughed. "Thomas Kinsella—everyone calls him Tommy. Screwed around in high school. Starting fixing cars at Tonnick Ford after he graduated by the skin of his teeth. Rick saw something in the kid, maybe. Worked his way up fast. Managed the service department before he was twenty-three, then the sales floor, then spearheaded the buyouts of the Subaru dealership and Paso Querido Toyota. It was Tommy's idea to start the Lexus dealership. Made money hand over fist." Knapp looked down at his laptop and shook his head. "I remember Tommy coming in here just sick over the whole recall kerfuffle. He wanted to do something more for those poor families. I couldn't say anything about it, of course—that was Raymond's case."

"So he's litigation, and you're family law?"

"Well," Knapp said, "we don't have clear-cut guidelines like that, but we do divide the Tonnick account that way."

"And Mr. Kinsella doesn't just get the entire dealership group?"

"He gets a decent chunk of it—and he becomes the president and chief executive officer. But the profits are divided up between him and the remaining family members."

"Still," Fenway muttered. It was a thriving business, and Rick Tonnick had been perhaps the richest man in the county besides Nathaniel Ferris.

"Where can we find Mr. Kinsella?"

"He's usually in the corporate offices. It's that big purple monstrosity out where Broadway hits Ocean Avenue."

Fenway smiled. "I'm surprised you can't see it from your window."

Knapp barked a laugh. "You can see it from Raymond's window. That's why I took *this* corner office. His might be bigger, but mine has a view that isn't ruined by the architectural version of Barney the Dinosaur."

They sat for a beat or two, Knapp looking at them expectantly. Fenway stared out the window, feeling Knapp's eyes on her. There was something else, surely, that they could discuss. After a moment, Knapp turned to Sarah.

"How was your Christmas?" Knapp asked.

She shrugged. "Quiet. Most of my friends were with their families."

"Oh," Knapp said, and took a breath as if he were going to ask something else, then decided against it.

Fenway piped up. "I heard that Mr. Ishikawa did quite well when he defended Tonnick from the recall allegations."

Knapp nodded. "Even though the jury found for the plaintiff, Rick was more than satisfied with the amount he was required to pay."

Knapp was certainly loose-tongued for ten in the morning. It made Fenway wonder if Knapp's love of the casual extended to more than office dress and tropical plants. She looked to the jasmine flowers, overflowing their pots in the oases in the corners, and wondered if she could get close enough to Knapp to sniff him. The clamdiggers, in particular, looked like a fashion choice one would only make while high. "Really?" Fenway said. "It was over two million dollars, wasn't it?"

Knapp scoffed. "That's nothing compared to what he would have had to pay to actually *fix* those vehicles. Yes, he would have been reimbursed for the parts and labor, but the dealership group was on the hook for purchasing special equipment, running training programs for mechanics—not to mention the courtesy vehicles and all the lost revenue taking those mechanics off the job. Tonnick was going through his third divorce at the time, and he just didn't have the liquidity to cover it." Knapp smiled. "Plus, when the verdict went against him, we were able to lower the alimony amount. It was a real win-win for him."

Fenway plastered on her smile again. "Any problems with any of the plaintiffs after the judgment?"

"You'd have to ask Raymond," Knapp said, standing. "And the poor suit-wearing bastard is in court today, I'm afraid."

He tilted his head toward Sarah. "It was great seeing you. I hope our paths will cross again."

Sarah's smile looked as artificial as Fenway's felt. "Thank you, Gordon. I really appreciate you seeing us on such short notice."

"Don't mention it," Knapp said.

He walked them to the elevator. The silence was awkward between them as they waited for the car to arrive, then Fenway was surprised that Knapp got in with them.

As the doors closed, Knapp said, "Are you still commuting from Paso Querido?"

"No," Sarah said, "I've got an apartment here in Estancia now."

"Oh—whereabouts?"

"Near downtown. Makes the commute a lot better."

They arrived on the first floor and all stepped out.

"Great seeing you again, Sarah," Knapp repeated.

"Thanks, Gordon. Give my best to Mr. Ishikawa."

Fenway felt Knapp watch them as she and Sarah traversed the long, bright, tile-floored lobby. They pushed the glass door open into the blustery January morning.

"That was a little weird," Fenway muttered. "You never reported him to HR?"

Sarah turned her head to Fenway and pursed her lips. "I didn't want to put myself in that position."

"But I—" Then it dawned on Fenway—the gap in employment, the snide comments from Barry Klein. She felt the heat rise to her cheeks but kept walking, hoping Sarah wouldn't notice. "Of course you wouldn't want that. I wasn't thinking."

"I don't want to make a big thing out of it," Sarah said. "In my experience, HR isn't going to be on my side."

"Right," Fenway said, a dozen questions running through her head that she immediately tamped down.

"I don't mind if people know I'm trans," Sarah said, "but it doesn't define me. If they know before they meet me, sometimes it's a little weird." She blinked quickly a few times. "I had a good feeling about you in our interview. You treated me like just a regular applicant."

They approached the Accord, and Fenway unlocked it with her key fob. The lights blinked, and the Honda emitted a soft beep. "You were the best candidate we had."

CHAPTER FOUR

BACK IN THE CORONER'S OFFICE, DEZ GAVE FENWAY HER NOTES ON the hotel staff interviews. Jessie only served to bookend the time the body was found—about four thirty, though she wasn't sure if it was ten minutes in either direction. Dez had dropped off Rick Tonnick's cell phone with Jordan Daniels. Piper Patten's replacement would work to get information off it when he returned from training.

Fenway filled Dez in on the will and on Amy's windfall. Dez pursed her lips and shook her head but didn't say anything before going back to her desk.

Sheriff Donnelly had asked for a report, and Fenway delegated that to Sarah, who typed up both Dez's and Fenway's notes. Kav texted again and said that it would take several days for the toxicology report, but that the glass had tested positive for zoeszoplon. The techs discovered that one of the pillows in the room had blood and saliva in the center of it but nowhere else, making it the likely murder weapon. The lab was backed up—it seemed like it was *always* backed up—and the test to see if it was Tonnick's blood and saliva wouldn't be available until the next week.

Fortunately, Fenway had enough to go on to officially classify the death as a homicide. With the right footage from the hotel cameras, the killer might be identified shortly after the warrant was signed. That would certainly make the new mayor happy.

Fenway sighed. She wondered how McVie's ex-wife had reacted when she found out that her new husband was dead.

A light knock, then her door opened and Sarah popped her head in. "There's a woman here to see you. Amy Tonnick—I believe she's the widow."

"What?" Fenway asked. "Wasn't she notified? I thought Dez would have told her."

"I bet it was Knapp," Sarah whispered, stepping all the way in and closing the door behind her. "He can't keep his mouth shut."

"Crap. I'm not ready for this. We should have her over in the interview room in the sheriff's office, not here. How can I get her over *there*?"

"I don't know. She's here now."

"Okay." Fenway's mind raced. "Tell Dez to come in here, then send Amy in."

Sarah opened the door and left.

What in the world should I say? Fenway ran through the first time she met Amy—then known as Amy McVie. Fenway and Dez had gone to her office to tell her that her lover, one of the men she was cheating on Craig with, was dead. Fenway and Amy had barely spoken since—and not at all in the eight weeks since Election Day, when Fenway and McVie had started dating. McVie hadn't been invited to the wedding, but he was far more relieved than annoyed. Fenway strongly suspected that Amy and Rick Tonnick had been seeing each other long before the ink was dry on her divorce papers.

Fenway shook her head, trying to clear her mind. *Treat this just like a normal next of kin notification. Sympathize, nod, listen. Don't treat her like a suspect. Don't think of all the millions of dollars that are now hers since her husband was killed. There will be time for all of that later. If she tries to push my buttons, treat her just like the people who lash out at the bearer of bad news. Professional.*

The door opened, and Dez came in.

"Didn't we notify Amy?" Fenway whispered.

Dez nodded. "I did it this morning, right after leaving the hotel. Amy and Megan were both there."

Fenway set her mouth in a line. "Then what's she doing here? I wanted to question her, but I'm not ready yet."

"I don't like this," Dez said as she stepped behind Fenway's desk and stood, her arms crossed. "I never trusted her when she and McVie were married, and I sure as hell don't trust her now."

"What can we do, though?" Fenway asked. "If we ask her to go over to the sheriff's office, she'll know she's a suspect."

"I'm worried about what she'll say to you. She'll try to make this personal."

"Great," Fenway said. "'Hey, remember when we told you your new husband was found dead in a hotel room under an assumed name? By the way, where were you last night?'"

"What could possibly go wrong?" Dez said.

Fenway cleared her throat. "Okay, let's get this over with." She pushed the intercom button on her desk phone. "Sarah, would you send Mrs. Tonnick in here?"

"Right away," Sarah's voice buzzed. A moment later, the door opened, and Sarah ushered Amy Tonnick into the room.

Amy wore a red-and-white silk jersey wrap dress with three-quarter sleeves and a hem just above the knees. Her blonde hair, shoulder-length the last time Fenway had seen her, was longer now. Her large green eyes, although slightly bloodshot and puffy, had a glint of determination, her body leaning forward as if she had to take on the world.

"As if I didn't have enough going on with Rick's death," Amy Tonnick snapped, "I got a message from Rick's lawyer that you had something important to talk to me about. Knowing it came from you"—Amy shot a rueful look at Fenway—"it can't be good."

Fenway motioned to the chairs in front of her desk. "Would you take a seat?"

Amy's mouth was set in a line. "Don't tell me you need me to make a statement *now*."

"I'm sorry," Fenway said gently as Amy sat. "We were going to wait to talk with you. We did see Mr. Knapp this morning. Perhaps he thought you didn't know yet."

Amy closed her eyes. "Rick didn't come home last night."

Fenway hesitated.

Amy leaned forward and put her elbows on Fenway's desk, then put her head in her hands. "I knew this was coming," she whispered. "I knew it." Her shoulders started to shake slightly, but Amy stayed silent. Fenway pushed the box of tissues in front of her.

A minute passed, then another. Amy turned her face away from Fenway and Dez and grabbed a tissue. She dabbed and wiped, then cleared her throat and turned around to face Fenway.

"Where did it happen?"

"He was found at the Phillips-Holsen Hotel."

"What was he..." Amy's voice trailed off. She leaned back in her chair, then folded her arms. "Who was he with?"

"We don't know yet," Fenway said.

"I didn't ask you this earlier," said Dez, "but we need to know—"

"Where I was last night, right?" Amy blinked a few times, her tears drying up. "Home. I had dinner by myself around seven thirty, then I watched some TV. Talked to Megan about applying to college, which she didn't want to hear, then I watched some more TV and started getting ready for bed around ten o'clock. I was annoyed that Rick wasn't home yet, so I got my iPhone and read some web articles and did some social media stuff until about half past eleven. Then I turned the light out and figured I'd yell at Rick in the morning."

"Can anyone confirm this?"

"Megan can probably tell you that she and I fought about college around nine," Amy said. She looked at Fenway and shook her head. "And I bet Craig, the little goody-two-shoes, told you about me coming to him about following Rick around."

Fenway nodded. "You suspected he was cheating?"

Amy frowned. "I guess so."

"Anything in particular set you off?"

"He'd been restless when he got back from our honeymoon."

"Restless?"

"I recognized the mood."

Fenway sensed that dangerous territory lay ahead. "Listen, Amy, there are a lot of questions we probably should ask you that will help us find out what happened to your husband. But I'm willing to bet that you'd rather tell someone else besides your ex-husband's girlfriend."

Amy's eyes widened. "His—his what?"

Fenway shifted uncomfortably in her seat. "Uh… Craig and I have been dating for a couple of months."

"A couple of months? And he didn't think to tell the mother of his daughter?"

Fenway frowned.

"And of course he didn't let you know that he didn't tell me, oh no. That would be too scary and confrontational for him." Amy stood up. "I wouldn't have even come in if I had known you two were dating." She shook her head. "You're half his age!"

Fenway remembered Amy's past dalliances with younger men but didn't say anything. "Well, maybe he wants to be sure it's more serious before he tells you."

"Are you there when Megan comes over?"

"I don't—"

"Tell me, dammit!" Amy growled. "Are you there when my daughter stays with her father?"

Fenway hesitated and tilted her head. "I'm happy to have this conversation with you, Amy, but in my office, when we're discussing an investigation, is not that time." She sat back. "We'd be happy to walk you across the street to give a statement to the sheriff."

Amy stood up. "No. Not now. I—I don't know why I came down here. I've got some arrangements I need to make. Please make sure I get regular updates on the investigation." She paused. "But not from *you.*"

She left Fenway's office, closing the door firmly behind her.

Dez and Fenway stared after Amy for a moment. Fenway stuck out her arm and showed her middle finger to the closed door.

"Now, Fenway," Dez said, "be kind. You know she doesn't handle grief well."

Fenway nodded. "How do you think she'll handle my foot in her ass?"

Dez cackled. "Remind me not to have you staff any hotlines. Listen, about the updates, do you want me—"

"Get Mark to do it," Fenway sighed. "She doesn't hate him yet."

Judge Didi Miller was no-nonsense, punctual to a fault, amenable to the argument that discovering what happened to a murder victim presented a more compelling state interest than the privacy of most individuals, and, perhaps most importantly, was eating an early lunch at Le Jardin, a French bistro only a block away from Dos Milagros.

Fenway parked in front of Dos Milagros in the same parking spot that McVie had gotten the night before. She grabbed the folder with the warrant, walked the block to Le Jardin, and entered the tiny restaurant at 11:28 A.M.

Judge Miller, waiting in front of the host station for her lunch companion, saw Fenway enter and groaned.

"Now, Judge Miller, don't be like that," Fenway said, walking up with the folder in her hand. "You're waiting for your lunch companion anyway, and this will just take a moment."

"I'm doing well, thank you for asking," Judge Miller said dryly. "Fancy meeting you in a place like this."

Fenway opened the folder and showed the judge the warrant. "It's for the Phillips-Holsen. Just to compel them to show their security footage. We believe there was someone else in the room when the death occurred, and the footage should allow us to recognize and question them."

"Ah, yes, the Phillips-Holsen," Judge Miller said, taking the folder from Fenway's hands and putting her glasses on. "They can afford good lawyers who never met a smooth course of justice they didn't want to derail. I hope you crossed your t's and dotted your i's."

"I hope so too," Fenway said, handing the judge a pen. Sarah had started the process, and it might not have been a good document to assign to the first-timer. Fenway's pulse raced as Judge Miller read the warrant.

"Everything looks to be in order," Judge Miller said. "Good call, limiting the scope of the warrant just to those cameras where the visitor was likely to have been. That will minimize the risk of their lawyers fighting it." She signed the warrant and handed it back.

Fenway nodded. "Thank you, Your Honor," she said, then quickly turned her back and strode out of the bistro just as a middle-aged Latina woman entered, raised her arms, and exclaimed, "Didi!"

Fenway squeezed past her and went out into the street. The rain and wind had stopped for the most part, and the sun peeked out from behind the clouds, shining off the wet asphalt of the street and blinding her for a moment. She walked toward her car again. The interaction with Judge Miller had been so fast that she might have to wait for Charlotte at Dos Milagros.

She texted Dez to meet her at the Phillips-Holsen at one o'clock—she wanted to be armed with the warrant.

To her surprise, Charlotte was already seated at a high-top at Dos Milagros, sipping a diet soda from a can and looking lost.

"Hey," Fenway said, walking up to Charlotte. "You're here early."

"I can't believe this is your favorite place to eat," Charlotte said. "They've barely started their lunch service, and the whole restaurant has —I don't know, a smell to it."

"Cilantro and lime," Fenway said. "Have you ordered?"

"I was waiting for you," Charlotte said. "Can you—can you just get me something that's not scary?"

Fenway rolled her eyes. "Chicken tacos okay with you? Mild sauce?"

"That sounds delightful."

Fenway stood in the short line, debating whether or not to get the lengua tacos she'd gotten the night before, or if she was going to be adventurous. Maybe she'd get the Mariscos Yucatán like she'd recommended to McVie. He'd definitely enjoyed that.

She ordered two chicken tacos for Charlotte and decided on two carne asada tacos for herself. The big seafood platter wasn't a great lunch choice. Plus, she had to be nimble to catch things on the video—she didn't want a big meal to put her to sleep. She got a medium horchata for herself and sat down with Charlotte.

Her stepmother looked put-together and cover-model beautiful as always, but her shoulders were tense, and her brow was knitted.

"How's Dad?" Fenway asked.

Charlotte nodded. "Nothing's changed, really. Same as he was last night. And the night before that. And the month before that." Charlotte smoothed her dress down. "I'm in over my head with this, Fenway."

"Oh." She should have guessed that Ferris Energy was the problem.

"The members of the board that are left are willing to give you more time."

"I don't think our competitors are. That's the issue. We've got suppliers who are asking about our long-term viability."

"What? That's crazy! We've got plenty of cash on hand to last us well into the next decade."

"Not if our orders significantly decline." Charlotte paused. "I think a couple of our competitors are sowing seeds of doubt without Nathaniel at the helm. And if we're not careful, soon those rumors are going to be taken as fact. You're right, we have quite a bit of cash on hand, but you know as well as I do, Fenway, that one big customer or one big supplier ceasing to do business with you—well, the whole house of cards can come tumbling down."

Fenway nodded, taking a sip of the horchata. "So," she said after swallowing, "do you have a plan?"

"Not much of one. The only thing I can think of is for you to be more visible. Appointing you as community liaison should be perfect."

"Me to be visible?"

"You won the election in a landslide."

"Against a racist."

"And you've got a one-hundred percent close rate. The television cameras when you came out of the hospital after your dad was shot—not a dry eye in the county."

"I wasn't faking that."

"I didn't say you were—oh, Fenway, no, I don't think you were at all. You have a real gift."

"A what?"

"A real gift. When you're genuine, you really come across as genuine. People fall in love with you when you're on camera. You're human."

"I was a complete mess. I looked horrible."

"You looked vulnerable and real, and you looked like you cared about the people of this county. When you asked them to turn the cameras off and then you asked about Judith Cygnus getting her medication—"

"People thought that was staged."

"*Two* accounts on Twitter said it was staged, and they were Russian bots. It was real. You explaining to the staff about the seizure—"

"Every privacy violation known to man," Fenway said. "That wasn't good. I should have—"

"Fenway, would you please shut up when I'm giving you compliments?"

Fenway looked down at the table. "Sorry."

"You're going to be good at this role precisely because Ferris Energy needs someone who's compassionate and real and genuine."

Fenway chuckled.

"What?"

"It's just," Fenway said, "I guess those aren't qualities most of the leadership has. An MBA can only teach you so much."

"I don't have those qualities either," Charlotte said. "I'm better than I used to be. I've learned what I need to do to be empathetic. But it's not in my nature." She shook her head. "I know what you think of me."

"*Thought* of you," Fenway said. "Past tense. I've seen the way you two stood with each other when both of you were falsely accused. I've seen how both of you fall apart without the other one there for support. I didn't want to believe it. Maybe I never wanted anyone to replace my mom."

"Or maybe I was a real bitch to you at first," Charlotte said softly.

"I suppose."

The four tacos appeared on the counter, and the cook nodded at Fenway. She picked them up and set the chicken tacos in front of Charlotte, who eyed them suspiciously.

"That's good old-fashioned spit-roasted chicken," Fenway said. "Come on, don't pretend you need champagne and caviar at every meal. You shoot stuff. You own guns. Your Louboutins only get you so many entitled-prick points before the real you starts sticking out the sides. Pick up the taco and eat it."

Charlotte grinned in spite of herself, then raised the taco to her mouth and bit into it with a soft crunch.

"See?" Fenway said. "You didn't die."

"Yet," Charlotte said through a mouthful of taco.

"I know you don't mean that," Fenway said. "You love it. You wish Sandrita could make tacos this good."

"I suppose I could have her try," Charlotte said.

They ate in silence for a moment.

"So," Fenway said, "what else does the community liaison have to do?"

"You'd help coordinate the public face of the foundation," Charlotte said. "Ever since I got arrested, they put the foundation work on hold. No new charities—just the financial commitments. And they completely stopped fundraising for it."

"Oh," Fenway said. "There's the rub."

"What's the rub?"

"You want me to start cold-calling people to ask them to give money to the Ferris Foundation."

Charlotte shook her head. "No, no, no. I want you to get out in front of the cameras so people will start associating the Ferris family with positive things again."

"Do you really think people associate me with the Ferris family?"

"Some people do."

"Well, some people will never get over me and my dad having different skin tones."

"It's still the best shot we have at saving the company," Charlotte said. "If we don't do some serious rehabilitation of our image, our competitors will be sowing uncertainty in all of our customers and all of our suppliers. I can't let it come to that. Your father's going to wake up from that coma—maybe not tomorrow, maybe not this week, but I bet it'll be this year. And if I can't keep the company alive for his return, I don't know what I'll do."

"I'd really like to hear a professional opinion on this," Fenway said. "You're a beauty queen who can shoot straight, and I'm a nurse practitioner who fell into this coroner position, and we're trying to run an energy company." Fenway thought for a moment as she picked up her second taco and ate it. She swallowed slowly, then picked up her horchata and drank until the straw sucked air loudly.

Charlotte still had her shoulders hunched and looked down at the table, not touching her second taco. Fenway started to chuckle.

Charlotte glanced up.

"You *did* get a professional opinion on this," Fenway said. "You talked to one of your fancy public relations people, and they recommended some crisis firm, and that crisis firm spent an hour convincing you how relatable and genuine I am, and how I'd be a real asset to rehabbing Ferris Energy's image. Did they have binders? I bet they had binders."

Charlotte shook her head, and then she began to laugh too. "I'm sorry for not telling you. I thought you wouldn't want to do it if it was some five-hundred-dollar-an-hour Beverly Hills psychoanalyst marketing firm telling you what to do."

"You believe that I'm the right person for it, though?"

"I do," Charlotte said. "I'm still not sure it's going to work. We might be too late as it is."

"Still worth a shot?"

"You know I think it is," Charlotte said, wiping her hands with three paper napkins.

"Okay," Fenway said. "I have some footage to review in about an hour, but I should be done in plenty of time to be there at two. If you can get my appointment to be accepted, I'll get behind the microphone as much as my day job will let me. Maybe between the two of us, we can figure out just enough to save the company."

"Good," Charlotte said, standing from her barstool. "I'm glad. So I'll see you at two?"

"Yes." Fenway looked at the uneaten chicken taco in Charlotte's basket. "You didn't even finish your second taco."

"I assure you, the first one was delicious. I've got to get going." She walked past Fenway, giving her shoulder a gentle squeeze, then walked out the door.

Fenway reached for Charlotte's uneaten pollo asado taco and took a bite. "The lengua is better," she said to no one in particular, setting the taco back in the basket and wiping off her hands. Her phone dinged in her purse. Piper had texted.

I need some info on your mom if you can swing by

Fenway still had almost an hour before she had to meet Dez at the Phillips-Holsen. She asked Piper if she wanted lunch from Dos Milagros and walked out five minutes later with a veggie burrito.

Fenway walked five blocks away from City Hall until she arrived at a nondescript two-story brick building with an athletic shoe store and a restaurant called Gateway of India. After she opened the glass door between the two first-floor businesses, she read the plastic sign on the wall in front of the staircase: MCVIE INVESTIGATIONS / SUITE 202. The stairs were carpeted in a dark green with tan and gold flourishes around the edges, and every speck of dust and lint was visible. The deep green color had faded in the middle of each of the stairs, and the banister creaked as she placed her hand on it. She pulled it off quickly—whether from the old varnish or a new soda spill, the banister was sticky.

She arrived at the top of the staircase. Three plastic numerals, 202, were glued to the wooden veneer of the door. Between the forest green of the carpet and the wooden doors, Fenway was reminded of a cabin in the woods that had been decorated a few decades previously. She knocked.

Piper opened the door, and Fenway held the bag with the veggie burrito in front of her. In spite of the bleariness of the day, the small office was sweltering, with the small window in the back letting in cold air and the wafting smell of garam masala, cumin, and coriander.

"Thanks, Fenway, this smells great."

"No worries." How Piper could smell anything except the Indian spices was beyond Fenway's comprehension.

"I've got a couple of questions about your mom," Piper said. "You sent me her bank account information and her social security number, her birthdate, and a few other things."

"Right. Have you been able to get any information yet?"

"I already told you she withdrew cash."

"Right—almost nine grand a month, a day or two after receiving the check from my dad."

"I've narrowed it down to a couple of wire transfer places in the neighborhood where your first apartment was in Seattle. The customer records don't go all the way back to the late nineties, but I have a guy working on it for me."

"And you think you'll be able to tell who the money was wired to?"

"Or at least an office. Maybe the geography will lead us to the recipient." Piper paused. "Did your mother ever go by another name?"

"Another name? I don't think so. I mean, she changed it when she was married, but as soon as she could go back to Joanne Stevenson, she did. Why?" Fenway had heard of people having completely different identities, even having multiple families who didn't know each other.

"Because," Piper said carefully, "I can trace Joanne Stevenson back to Estancia. Her name first appears on an apartment lease in April 1986. Everything checks out—her name, date of birth. She'd gotten a job selling classified ads at the *Estancia Courier*. A family friend recommended her to the editor. She'd supposedly moved up from Los Angeles."

"Supposedly?"

"Yes," Piper said. "Because here's where things get a little strange. Before April 1986, Joanne Stevenson doesn't exist."

CHAPTER FIVE

Fenway wrapped her thin coat around herself as she walked the eight blocks to the Phillips-Holsen. She kept turning the new information over in her mind.

Her mother had existed as Joanne Stevenson for about a year before she met Fenway's father. But before that—nothing. Piper had shown her the listings for all the Joanne Stevensons in the greater Los Angeles metropolitan area—as far south as the Mexican border, as far east as Victorville, as far north as Bakersfield and Santa Barbara. If her mother had been in the Los Angeles area in the mid-1980s, she hadn't used that name.

But "Joanne Stevenson," both name and social security number, belonged to a girl who'd been born on the same day as Fenway's mother. Or at least, the same day that Fenway's mother *said* she'd been born. Piper had shown Fenway the birth certificate: Joanne Leticia Stevenson, born July 14, 1962, to Ray and Roberta Stevenson of Ladera Heights, California. Piper had shown Fenway the short newspaper article and the death certificate, too: all three Stevensons died when their Dodge Dart had been struck by a tractor trailer at the intersection of Rodeo Road and La Brea Avenue during a hailstorm in November 1969.

Fenway didn't have any pictures of her mother with family members.

She'd said her parents had died just after she graduated high school, and the pictures had all been lost. Fenway knew her mother was quiet, reticent about her past, but when Fenway was young, she had thought that was how *all* mothers were, and when she was older, she'd assumed that Joanne Stevenson was simply gun-shy about her failed marriage to the rich oil magnate who was supposed to be the answer to all her problems.

But this? Fenway had never expected anything like this. Everyone had secrets, but very few had false identities. And her mother, of all people.

The day was cold, and the wind blew frigid off the ocean. She shook her arms from shoulder to wrist to get her blood pumping again. She was only a block away from the Phillips-Holsen, and she had to be on top of her game.

She took the folder with the warrant out of her purse as the doorman held the heavy door open for her.

Dez was already in the lobby, sitting on a plush armchair next to a bar-height circular side table. "Judge Miller sign the warrant?"

"No problem."

Dez and Fenway walked to the concierge desk. A tall, skinny olive-skinned man in a black pinstripe suit and small square rimless glasses appraised them as they walked up. "Good afternoon," he said, his accent thick and possibly European. "Can I be of assistance?"

Fenway nodded, placing the folder on the counter between them. "Yes. I spoke to your property manager this morning, Brianna Harlow."

"Ah, yes, Miss Harlow. Did you have a question for her?"

"This morning, I asked to see the video footage from last night."

"It is about the unfortunate incident with Mr. Ginn, is it not?"

"That's right." Fenway opened the folder. "Miss Harlow told me how much you value customer privacy here at the Phillips-Holsen and asked us to return with a warrant to view the video recordings."

"I can take you to see Miss Harlow," the concierge said, and he glided around the side of the counter, hurrying down a hall next to the registration desk. Dez fell into step behind him. Fenway grabbed the folder before following Dez down the hall.

After a confusing series of turns, the concierge stopped at an office door with a placard reading *Property Manager*. "Is there anything else I can do for you?" he said, folding his hands and tilting his head to the side.

Fenway stepped forward and knocked. "No, I think that will do, thank you."

He stood there as if he expected a tip, then when the door opened, he glided off the way they had come.

Brianna Harlow stood behind the door. "Ah, Coroner Stevenson. And Sergeant Roubideaux. Good to see you again. Back with a warrant, I assume?"

Fenway held the folder out. Brianna took it, opened the folder, and looked over the warrant. She nodded. "Everything seems to be in order." She closed the folder and nodded to the large copier in the middle of her office. "You don't mind if I make a copy of this for our legal team, do you?"

"Go right ahead," Fenway said.

Brianna opened a cabinet at her feet, where she took out a ream of paper, opened up the printer's paper tray, and put the ream in. The office smelled of glass cleaner. "Make yourself comfortable," she said, gesturing at a computer workstation with three wheeled task chairs, two of which looked out of place in the office.

"Were you expecting someone?" Dez asked.

"You," Brianna said, closing the copier and pushing the START button. "It's not hard to convince a judge that you need to see our security footage." The copier shuddered slightly as it worked. Brianna put the warrant back in the folder and then handed it to Fenway. They all sat, Brianna in the middle chair in front of the computer keyboard.

"Okay," Brianna said. "Here we go—we use a cloud-based recording system. You said the incident happened around two in the morning?"

"Probably closer to three, actually."

"The gentleman checked in last night at about ten thirty," Brianna said. She clicked, and the registration desk showed onscreen.

Fenway leaned forward. The clock behind the registration desk showed a couple of minutes before ten thirty. Brianna clicked, and the recording sped forward. She stopped when a man in a blue dress shirt and jeans appeared, carrying a duffel bag.

"That's Rick Tonnick," Dez whispered.

Fenway nodded. "Almost looks like he just came from the gym."

They watched as he checked in, received two keys, then walked briskly to the elevator.

"He arrived alone," Fenway said.

Brianna nodded.

A few more people came and went during the next forty-five minutes, but they all checked into their own rooms. Brianna sped up the recording again, but the lobby was empty except for employees coming and going. Fenway stifled a yawn.

The clock flitted past 1:00 A.M., then 2:00, then 3:00. After four, a few smartly dressed business travelers went through the lobby. One checked out. At 4:18 A.M., Jessie—the woman who had found Rick Tonnick's body—came in through the side hall where the concierge had taken them.

"There's an employee entrance?" Fenway asked.

"Yes."

"Can guests get in and out, too?"

"Well, I suppose so," Brianna said. "A guest would need a valid key card to get in."

"How often do guests use it?" Dez questioned.

Brianna didn't speak right away.

"Ah," Dez said, "this is the famous celebrity entrance. When a big star comes up from L.A., they come in through the back way. That way, they avoid being mobbed by fans. Or businesspeople who are in the news, so they can avoid protestors."

"Does Mr. Tonnick use that entrance?"

Brianna hesitated, then nodded. "Mr. Ginn has been known to use it quite a bit in the past."

Fenway squinted at the screen, but the hallway between the registration and concierge desks gave no additional information. "For guests he wants to have in his room—but doesn't want to use the front entrance?"

"Yes. It's kind of an open secret around here." Brianna sighed. "He tips well and expects us to act as if nothing is happening."

"There are cameras in the hallway of the top floor, too?"

Brianna hesitated again.

"No cameras up there?" Fenway said.

"We had a problem a few years ago with one of our security employees selling a recording to a tabloid," Brianna said. "After a lot of arguing, we disconnected the cameras from the private penthouse elevator and from the floor with the penthouse suites."

Fenway leaned back in her seat. "So no camera on the side entrance?"

"No," said Brianna.

"And none in the elevator."

"Not the one Mr. Tonnick used with his guests, no."

"And no cameras on the penthouse floor."

"That's correct."

Dez sighed. "I'm really glad we waited to get that warrant."

"Well, hold on," said Brianna, tapping her fingers on her chin. "I bet there's something else." She clicked around on the screen. "Here we go."

Fenway leaned forward. The screen was mostly dark, with some amber-colored walls of what looked like cement, as well as shadows. A few dim out-of-focus lights—were those street lamps?—were in the center of the screen. "What are we looking at?"

"It's the parking garage."

"Where are the cars?"

"They're not in view. This camera is behind the front gate, looking out to the street."

Fenway blinked. "Oh—there's the gate arm."

"Right. This camera will catch cars driving in as well as people who exit from the garage to the elevator."

"The back-alley, super-secret elevator?"

Brianna shook her head. "No, the main elevator, so you probably won't see anyone going between their car and the employee entrance. But maybe you'll get lucky and see the car."

They waited for a few moments as Brianna cued up the correct recording for ten thirty.

"Look," she said, "there's Mr. Tonnick driving in."

A large Ford pickup truck, front license plate visible, pulled up to the gate. The driver's face wasn't visible, but the gate rose, and the truck drove past the camera. A minute later, Rick Tonnick walked in front of the camera in the same dress shirt and jeans.

"And now we wait for his guest," Brianna said.

Two other cars pulled in, but they were the same people who had checked in after Tonnick. Fenway grew impatient and shifted in her seat. Finally, when the recording read 1:46 A.M., a red Ford Mustang convertible, its top up, drove into the garage.

Fenway took a notepad from her purse and fumbled with her pen. "Pause it—" she started, but Brianna had already frozen the recording, the license plate clear.

The Mustang's brights were on, and as it drove past the camera, the glare prevented the driver from being visible through the windshield. Fenway squinted. Was that hair blonde? The shadows made it hard to tell.

"Can you see the driver at all?"

"She has blonde, maybe light-brown hair, a little past the shoulders," Dez said. "And from her hand on the steering wheel, she looks white to me."

Fenway nodded. "Me too."

Brianna nodded. "Should we wait and see if she crosses in front of the camera?"

"Yes," Dez said.

They waited as the minutes on the recording ticked by. No one appeared.

The timestamp moved to two thirty, then three. At 3:24 A.M., the Mustang convertible drove out on the other side of the lane.

Brianna clicked STOP and turned to Dez and Fenway.

"We'll need a copy of all these recordings," Fenway said.

"Certainly," Brianna said. "Just leave me an email address—I can have the video company share their files with you."

"One more thing," Fenway said. "Did you happen to notice anything unusual?"

Brianna shook her head. "I didn't start my shift until six o'clock."

"Oh—that's right. Still, did you find anything out of place? Any chance that you went by the secret entrance or the private elevator? Anything unusual on the floor?"

"What, like rat poison or a note saying 'I did it'?" Brianna chuckled.

Fenway nodded, smiling through her annoyance. "You never know.

We've gotten lucky before." She paused and didn't make a move to rise from her chair.

Brianna rolled her eyes. "You know, if I had a nickel for every private investigator or police officer who asked me to provide the name or description of some of the people who visit our guests, I'd be able to retire by thirty-five."

"This isn't about more alimony. It's about finding a murderer."

Brianna shook her head. "I've seen quite a few women—and men—come in and out of the private elevator. I haven't seen anyone leave in a red Mustang convertible."

Fenway nodded.

"Okay," said Dez, standing up. "We'll get out of your hair. Thanks for seeing us."

"Any time, Sergeant."

Dez took the lead out the door of the property manager's office but turned the other direction.

"What are you doing, Dez? We came from this way."

"Yes, but we didn't pass the secret-squirrel entrance, did we?"

Fenway nodded and followed Dez.

The hallway emptied out into a small foyer with tiled floors. Signs on the wall pointed to the pool and the workout center straight ahead, as well as the parking garage to their left. Fenway craned her neck to the right and saw an elevator in an unassuming corner—probably the penthouse elevator—then a hallway with a sign pointing toward registration.

She followed Dez out to the left, and Dez pushed a door, much less elegant than the heavy wooden door in the front of the building. She stuck her head out, and Fenway stepped behind her. A concrete staircase led down to the left into the parking garage, and a tiled path jutted to the right and out to Fourth Street.

"Really, anyone could have come in this way," Fenway said. "It wouldn't have to be the driver of that Mustang."

"We got a good look at the license plate," said Dez. "Let's see who the car is registered to, and we'll see if their defense attorney can successfully argue that the 'real killer' entered from an unlit footpath from Fourth Street at two in the morning." Dez pushed the door open all the way. "Come on, Fenway. I don't feel like staying around this hotel any longer than I have to." She turned down the tiled footpath, and a minute later, they were on the sidewalk, walking down Fourth Street.

———

Dez's car was parked closer to the hotel, and she was already at her desk by the time Fenway returned to the office.

"Hey, Dez," Fenway said as she entered, "let me know when you've run those plates."

Dez shot her a worried look from her desk.

Fenway blinked, then noticed that Sarah was turned away, typing furiously, her hair covering her face. She turned her head to look at the door to her office. It was closed.

Fenway never closed her door when she was out.

"Is the mayor in my office?" Fenway whispered to Sarah.

Sarah nodded.

"Did that asshole say something to you?"

Sarah didn't say anything but kept typing.

Fenway grunted. "I don't know what he said to you, but I'm sorry he said it."

She turned and strode to the door, throwing it open.

Barry Klein sat in Fenway's leather chair behind her desk, his feet up next to her phone.

"Get your feet down and get out of my chair."

"I don't think so," Barry Klein said, "until you tell me why you think you can embarrass me."

In a sudden, fluid movement, Fenway reached over the phone and swept Klein's feet off the desk. He lost his balance and almost fell out of the chair.

"You can't—" he squeaked.

"Get out!" Fenway said. "You are not my boss. You do not control what my department does! You do not control how we conduct investiga—"

Barry popped up to his full height, a few inches shorter than Fenway. "When I get calls from the media asking about who Rick Tonnick screwed last night—"

"I am not responsible for that," Fenway growled, leaning into the mayor's face, "and if you're going to come in here and insult my employees—"

"Your employees. As if you didn't hire *that* one just to be another source of embarrassment for me."

"Get out of my office—and get out of the building, Barry."

Klein pushed past Fenway around the desk. "I may have to work with you, Coroner," he said, "but I don't have to make it easy for you."

Dez appeared in the doorway. "Leaving so soon, Mayor?" She moved as if she was going to take him by the arm to usher him out, but Klein shook off Dez's hand and walked past Sarah's desk, opening the door and leaving the office suite.

Fenway let out a long breath when the door closed behind him.

"He makes everyone so happy when he goes away," said Dez. "I'm going to make sure he leaves the building." Then she, too, was out the door.

"You okay?" Fenway asked Sarah.

"I'll be fine," Sarah said, her voice strong.

"Okay." Fenway turned to go back to her office, then hesitated. "You know, about six months ago, Barry Klein said something to me that hurt me more than just about anything. I was sobbing in the bathroom for twenty minutes."

Sarah looked up. Her eyes were red but dry. "You? You always seem to —I don't know, have it all together."

"You've known me for half a day," Fenway said.

"I voted for you," Sarah said, "and I did my research."

"Maybe I look like I'm in control of everything," Fenway said, "but I assure you, I'm always about sixty seconds away from losing my shit." She smiled. "So, yeah, the mayor is an asshole, and we're not supposed to let him bother us, but he does. I won't beat myself up over him pushing my buttons, and I hope you don't either."

Sarah nodded.

Fenway gave Sarah a smile, then walked back into her office and closed the door.

She took a seat in her leather task chair—it was still slightly warm from the mayor sitting in it—and leaned back.

Klein was taking everything about the Rick Tonnick case personally. Each reporter's call insulted him, and his first thought was that Fenway wasn't doing her job.

She picked up the phone and called Rachel's office.

"Public information office."

"Hi, Emma. Is Rachel in?"

"Oh, hi, Miss Stevenson. Yes, I'll put you through."

A click turned into City Hall's hold music, then the sound of a phone receiver being picked up.

"Hey, Fenway! You calling because you're finally up for happy hour tonight?"

"Oh—no. Not tonight. But soon. Maybe after this case."

Rachel sighed. "Is the mayor up your butt about the Tonnick murder too?"

"Of course." Fenway paused. "So you've heard that the preliminary findings are that it's murder."

"Yep. I'm on the need-to-know list."

"Right. Well, I was calling to see if the mayor was treating everyone badly about the Tonnick case or if I was the lucky one to get the special treatment."

"It's everyone. He screamed at Emma this morning too."

"Screamed at Emma? She's the nicest person I've ever met."

"I know, right?" Rachel laughed. "I expected her to cower, but she stood up and told him off. I opened the door after I heard them yelling, and he turned to me and said, 'Are you just going to stand there and let her treat me like this?'"

"And what did you say?"

"Ha. I said, 'She just said what everyone else is thinking.'"

"Has he left you alone since then?" Fenway asked.

"He sent an email telling me not to talk to any reporters about the Tonnick death."

Fenway paused. "He must be worried about something."

"I know—that's the only thing that makes sense." Rachel hesitated. "Do you think he's had some sort of shady business dealing with Tonnick?"

"I don't know," Fenway said. "He seems much more concerned about Tonnick's private life. Like who he had in the suite."

Rachel snickered. "It would be such a Barry Klein thing to do for both him and the murder victim to be having an affair with the same woman."

"Or paying the same prostitute."

"And it's classic Barry Klein for him to be more concerned with his own reputation than with catching his friend's murderer."

"You're assuming that Barry has any friends."

A giggle gave way to a snort. "It's a shame, really. Such a nice guy. He's just misunderstood."

"Obviously," Fenway said.

"Do you think that's really what it is?" Rachel asked.

"What—that Barry Klein is having an affair with the woman who killed Rick Tonnick?" It was Fenway's turn to giggle. "Wouldn't that be a hoot?"

"And imagine how much it would bother him if you kept up that line of inquiry."

"Tonnick has quite the reputation," Fenway said. "He was a regular at the hotel, and it sounds like the staff kept everything hush-hush for him." She leaned forward and scratched her head. Her fingers caught in her hair, frizzy from the damp weather. "The property manager told me that an employee was fired over leaking some information. Maybe I can find who's been fired and see if they'll tell me as well as the tabloids."

"I bet the tabloids paid better for the story than you will."

"Truer words have never been spoken," Fenway said.

"Okay," Rachel said, "I'll see if I can reach out to my contacts at the hotel and get any names for you too."

"Think we'll find any dirt on the mayor?"

Rachel laughed. "A girl can dream."

CHAPTER SIX

Fenway hung up. While it was fun to fantasize about getting Barry Klein out of their hair, even if they were successful, it wouldn't lead to a good working relationship with the mayor. In fact, it would probably worsen it.

She looked over her notes. From the discussion with the lawyer that morning, she knew Rick Tonnick's two grown children—the ones who weren't getting much of anything from the will—were Grant and Noreen. Waking up her laptop, she logged into the database and in short order had work addresses for both of them. Neither one of them had a red Ford Mustang registered to their name, but Fenway didn't expect them to. A part of her hoped the Mustang belonged to Barry Klein's lover.

She looked at the clock on her computer. A little before two forty-five. Grant's restaurant would either be on a lull between the lunch and dinner services, or, if it just was just open for dinner, employees would be prepping the menu for that evening.

She tilted her head. Two forty-five.

Oh no. Charlotte. She'd completely missed the start of the two thirty board meeting. She squeezed her eyes shut. How could she forget?

She was just kicking Barry Klein out of the office at two thirty. She smacked the top of the desk with her open hand. Just when she was getting along with Charlotte, too—now her stepmother would think that nothing had really changed between them.

Except when Fenway had missed an appointment before, she'd never truly apologized. There was always a reason why Fenway didn't want to issue Charlotte a genuine apology. She called Charlotte's mobile number, but it went right to voicemail. She apologized profusely, then hung up, grabbed her purse, and rushed out the door.

She ran halfway to the parking garage when she got a text message from Charlotte.

Don't bother
The board accepted your nomination as community liaison
We're onto other items now

Not too much forgiveness in the tone of that text, but if Charlotte was in the middle of the board meeting, brevity was to be expected. Fenway texted back.

Sorry. See you at the hospital about 6:30

She slowed to a walk. She hadn't even remembered her coat, thin and ineffectual as it was against the chill of the January day. She looked up at the gray sky. It smelled like rain, and Fenway shivered now that she wasn't running.

Java Jim's was less than a block away. Perhaps she needed an afternoon latte to clear her head.

A new cashier was behind the terminal, and Fenway felt her stomach tighten. Yet another new person who would need to be taught that yes, Fenway was her real name.

The cashier greeted her, and Fenway stepped forward. "Large latte, please."

"Whole milk okay?"

Of course it was okay. That was one reason she came to Java Jim's instead of the impersonal chain coffeehouses. Fenway nodded.

"Can I have your name?"

Fenway hesitated. "Joanne."

The name tasted bitter on her tongue as she said it. *Joanne* had been her go-to barista-cup name since her sophomore year at Western Washington, when she grew tired of all the Red Sox jokes, or worse, the endless requests to spell it. Joanne was easy. Sometimes with an E, sometimes without, but always simple to read and pronounce.

But now?

Now that wasn't even her mother's name. Fenway had had a critical part of her identity taken away from her, and she didn't know why—nor did she know what to replace *Joanne* with.

She looked up. The cashier stared at her expectantly. "Oh," Fenway said, "I'm sorry. Off in my own little world. What was that?"

"Four twenty-five."

Fenway handed the cashier a five and didn't wait for change, moving next to one of the overstuffed chairs in the corner with a sightline to the espresso bar.

She turned things over in her mind. Amy was suddenly a very rich woman, one who could more than afford to pay Craig the alimony she owed him. She would be able to quit her real estate job if she wanted to —although Amy seemed to relish everything about it.

Neither Grant nor Noreen would be getting much money in comparison to Amy—although by Fenway's standards, a million dollars was still quite a bit of cash. Enough to kill for, certainly.

She hadn't remembered the addresses. She'd have to go back and get them. The barista poured the steamed milk into the cup, and Fenway took a few steps forward.

"Joanne?" The barista looked up and handed Fenway her latte with a smile.

Fenway gazed longingly at the overstuffed chair in the corner, but she walked out the door, back toward the office. She wondered what Grant and Noreen thought about their new stepmother. Perhaps they thought she wouldn't last more than a couple of years—after all, Rick Tonnick's recent marriages hadn't had a long shelf life. Maybe they didn't even have an opinion of Amy—or of Megan, for that matter, who was seventeen, probably going away to college in a year and a half.

She walked into the office, nodding at Sarah in greeting. Dez was back at her desk and raised her hand to catch Fenway's attention. Fenway walked around the counter, and Dez turned in her chair to face Fenway.

"You're not going to believe who the red Mustang belongs to," Dez said.

"Barry Klein?" Fenway guessed.

Dez chortled and shook her head. "Though that would please me a lot more than what the right answer is."

Fenway felt the bottom fall out of her stomach. "Amy."

Dez nodded.

Fenway's knees went weak. She stepped to the side chair next to Dez's desk and, holding the arm of the chair for support, sat.

"I know," Dez said. "It doesn't look good. She gets pretty much the entire Tonnick fortune, her car is in the parking garage, arriving just before Tonnick gets killed and leaving right after."

"But we never saw the driver's face."

"What are you saying?"

Fenway hesitated. "It could be someone else who had access to the car."

"Like who? You're not suggesting Megan had something to do with this? That's McVie's daughter you're talking about—"

"No, no," Fenway interrupted. "Not Megan. I was thinking one of the grown kids. Maybe Grant, maybe Noreen."

Dez shook her head. "Neither of them live with Rick and Amy and Megan."

"Just because they don't live together doesn't mean they don't have access," Fenway insisted. "When I lived in the dorms at Western, I still had a key to my mom's house. I bet lots of adult children have keys to their parents' houses."

Dez leaned back in her chair. "But this is Amy's car we're talking about, not Rick's car."

The gears in Fenway's head continued to turn. "If they had a house key, it wouldn't be that difficult to go into the house and get Amy's Mustang key. It's the best of all worlds: Grant and Noreen get their small share of the money now, and then when Amy gets convicted of Rick's murder, that money goes to them too, since Amy can't profit off the killing."

Dez cocked her head. "Okay, Miss Getting-Ahead-of-Yourself. That's a nice theory, but do you have any evidence to back it up?"

"I'm just proposing an alternate theory of the crime. Just so we don't automatically assume that it's Amy."

"No," Dez said, "but the evidence all points to Amy so far." She pursed her lips. "You don't even like Amy. You don't like the way she treated McVie. You don't like that she slept with other men when they were married. She's not a nice person. So why are you defending her?"

"Because," Fenway said, "she managed to hide her cheating from one of the best police officers I know. Someone who's a good investigator. It doesn't make sense to me that she'd be so oblivious that she'd let herself get caught on camera. I mean—look, she was having sex with a guy half her age last year. And they only got caught because of a parking ticket."

"Oh, yeah, that's right."

"So I don't think Amy would decide to kill her husband by driving into a hotel parking garage, walking in, putting sleeping pills in his whisky, then smothering him with a pillow and walking back out. It's just —" Fenway stopped.

"It's just what?" Dez asked.

"It's not her style," Fenway said. "Yes, she can be obnoxious, but when she wants to slide under the radar, she does."

"She managed to avoid every security camera except the one in the parking garage."

"But don't you see?" Fenway said. "She'd be savvy enough to park a few blocks away and walk along that stone footpath so that she'd be sure she never got on camera at all."

Dez shook her head. "Could have been a mistake. Amy makes them, you know. Just like she didn't hide her affair very well from Megan."

"All right. But we need to find more evidence." Fenway paused. "Can you ask Mark to get a warrant to search Amy's Mustang?"

Dez nodded and pulled her phone out.

"Great. I'm going to see Grant and Noreen. I know Amy is the most compelling suspect right now, but something doesn't feel right to me."

"It's worth talking with them," Dez said, setting her phone down. "Because look at this."

She moved her mouse, and the screen woke. Two pictures of Grant Tonnick, one front facing, one in profile, under a Maricopa County board with his name and a case number. He looked solid and strong.

"Maricopa County—is that Phoenix?"

"Yes. He mixed it up with another fan during a spring training game. Both arrested for assault. The other guy got a black eye and a bloody nose."

Fenway squinted at the screen. "Does that say six-six?"

"He's a big guy. Tall, and if he still looks like his mugshot, built like a linebacker."

"When was this?"

"About a decade ago."

"Nothing since then?"

"No." Dez folded her arms. "But at the very least, we should establish his whereabouts—or maybe a lack of an alibi." She grabbed her Impala keys off the desk. "I'll drive."

Grant Tonnick's restaurant, Cantle & Pommel, wasn't in the row of trendy eateries on Broadway downtown. Instead, it was a converted barn out on Highway 326 just as it crossed the city limits. When Dez parked her Impala in the lot, the Pacific Ocean stretched out before them. The barn was further back from the road but closer to the cliff. Fenway opened the passenger door.

"I bet the food is crap," Dez said, getting out of the car. "A place like this, you pay for the view, not for the quality of the chef."

"You must be an awful date," Fenway said, stretching her arms above her head as she pushed the door closed with her hip.

"Heh," Dez said. "I do all right. Don't you worry about me."

The barn was rustic, with ironwork along the whole front of the restaurant. The façade was constructed of redwood that had weathered to a brownish gray.

Dez grabbed the door handle, fashioned to resemble a pickaxe, molded into the burnt orange metal door. The pickaxe had a logo with "C&P" in script lettering etched into the metal head.

Fenway stepped inside. It was warmer, and the waiting area had a homey, earthy feel to it without feeling cheap or dirty. The maître-d' station had the same C&P logo just below the lectern.

"Oh, hey," a Latino man said, walking toward them. He was dressed in a black T-shirt and faded blue jeans under a forest green apron with the restaurant logo. He saw Dez's black police uniform and stopped in his tracks. "Something I can help you with, Officer?"

"We're looking for Grant Tonnick," Dez said.

"He's around here somewhere," the man said. "We're prepping for dinner service tonight—I'm not sure this is a great time."

"It'll just take a minute," Fenway said.

The man nodded and turned, going around the maître-d' stand to the left, then out of sight around the corner of a plank wall.

Dez walked up to the stand and pulled a menu from behind the lectern. It was on thick paper, probably meant to be replaced every day as the menu changed. She perused the front.

"Anything sound good?"

Dez harrumphed. "It's a steak house that wants to pretend it isn't fancy, but you can't get a steak for less than fifty bucks." She turned the menu over once, then back again. "And that's a la carte."

Fenway stared at the C&P logo. "Cantle? Pommel? What are those? Gymnastics terms?"

Dez guffawed. "Parts of a saddle, you tenderfoot." She pointed to the menu. "You and your dad like pheasant, right?"

"Mostly him, but yeah."

"Mostly him? Okay, whatever. Anyway, they have a section on wild game, and they've got grouse. That's *almost* pheasant, right? Pan-seared with chestnuts and thyme." Dez rubbed her chin. "Actually, that doesn't sound half bad. Don't know if I'd pay fifty-seven bucks for it, though."

The man returned and gestured for them to follow.

They rounded the corner and walked through a swinging door into the kitchen. A large white man, easily six-foot-six and three hundred pounds, stood at a stainless-steel counter, artfully carving steaks off a rib roast.

"Grant Tonnick?" Fenway said.

"Who wants to know?"

"I'm Fenway Stevenson, Mr. Tonnick."

"Is that name supposed to mean something to me?" Grant finished with a steak—a bone-in ribeye, from the mouthwatering looks of it. Grant raised his knife to begin another cut.

Fenway swallowed hard. "I'm the county coroner."

Grant paused, then put down his knife.

"Is Ellen okay?"

Dez nodded. "This isn't about your wife—it's your father."

Grant grabbed a thin cloth towel and wiped his hands. "My father. He's dead?"

"I'm afraid so," Fenway said. "I'm sorry for your loss."

Grant set the towel down on the counter. "Well, you don't have to be sorry. I hated that son of a bitch. Treated my mom like shit."

"I hear he invested in your restaurant." Fenway pulled her notepad out of her purse.

"And was looking over my shoulder every minute of every day," Grant said. "He actually told me that he wanted to do inventory with me today. I arrived here about nine. I would complain about him not showing up, but I was relieved, frankly. I worked on a couple of sauces."

"You didn't get along with your father?"

"Not even close. He always lorded everything over me. How he was a millionaire when he was my age. How the restaurant business was stupid." Grant looked across the room, and his eyes glazed over. "He's really dead?"

Fenway took a small step forward. "We do need to ask you where you were last night between one and three thirty in the morning, Mr. Tonnick."

Grant turned his head sharply. "You mean—he didn't die of some kind of stress-related stroke? Someone actually did him in?"

Fenway cleared her throat.

"Right—one and three thirty, you said? We close at ten on Sundays. I was here with the staff. Ricardo, Queenie, Al... and I think Jackie was here, but she might have left by midnight. I got out of here at about one thirty."

"Then where did you go?"

"Home," he said. "Ellen's a cardiologist at St. Vincent's. She had an early procedure scheduled, so I got a few hours of sleep before I took the kids to school."

"Can anyone confirm that you went straight home after leaving here?"

Grant raised his eyes to the ceiling. "Uh, not that I can think of. Ellen was asleep when I got home. I was a little wired, so I watched some TV before I went to bed."

"What did you watch?" Fenway said.

"Sports Rewind."

"Highlights, stuff like that?"

"Right."

"What do you remember?"

"From the highlights? Uh... one of the announcers was doing an analysis of Notre Dame's strength of schedule and whether they deserve to be in the championship. I was waiting for a report on the winter meetings."

"Baseball?" Fenway said.

Grant smiled. "Red Sox your team?"

"My dad's. What about you?"

"Dodgers, baby."

"Any news? They extending Majorca's contract?"

"I didn't see any baseball news at all. It was all basketball highlights."

Fenway nodded. "Not a Lakers fan?"

Grant shrugged. Clearly, trying to get him to open up by talking about sports wasn't working. But it seemed truthful. Enough details that she thought he'd actually watched it, but not so many details that it sounded rehearsed.

"So," he said, "you're asking questions where it seems like someone finally had enough of his bullshit and took him out. What do you think it was? Jealous husband? One of the customers he'd screwed over?"

Fenway hesitated.

Grant pointed at her. "Ah—you hesitated. You wouldn't have done that if it was just a simple business disagreement."

"Do you—" Dez started, then looked at Fenway, who shrugged. "Do you," continued Dez, "know the names of any people besides his wife with whom he was romantically involved?"

"Oh, that's quite clever," Grant said, smiling. "Nicely phrased. Leaves it open so that it might not just be a woman he was seeing on the side, but doesn't come right out and say it in case I'm one of those 'My dad is *not* gay' people. Bravo."

"Thank you," Dez said. "Can you answer the question?"

"The last woman—last person I know he was cheating on his wife with was Amy McVie." Grant leaned forward. "Look, Victoria wasn't my mother—they'd only been together a couple of years, anyway, but I don't think anyone deserved that." He shook his head. "And I know she was the sheriff's wife—but I don't think he knew either. I wouldn't have known if I hadn't walked in on them in the back office of the Toyota dealership in P.Q."

"So you don't have a great relationship with your stepmother," Dez said.

A look of confusion crossed Grant's face. "Victoria?"

"No, Amy."

"Oh, don't call *her* my stepmother," Grant spat. "She's, what, only ten years older than me? She was after the lifestyle. Going out to fancy restaurants every night, vacations in the Caribbean. First class, of course, even though she used to be delighted at flying economy-plus. Not that she has great taste anyway—any car in the world could be hers, and she picks a Mustang convertible." He shook his head and pantomimed a phone call, holding his thumb to his ear and pinkie to his mouth. "Hello?" He held the fake receiver out. "Amy! 1985 called, and they want their car back!"

Fenway closed her eyes, fighting hard to suppress a giggle.

"Listen, I don't know what my father was thinking. Divorcing Victoria for Amy McVie was one of the worst decisions in a series of increasingly bad decisions."

Grant took a step back, seeming to find himself. "Anyway, I'm sure my father is—was—still screwing any woman he could. But I don't know anyone he was seeing besides Amy."

"Do you know how much money you'll inherit?"

Grant laughed. "Inherit? I suspect it's nothing." He folded his arms.

"I got in credit card debt after college. When you have a rich father, the banks give you a lot of rope to hang yourself." He blinked. "Sorry, poor choice of words."

"And your father bailed you out?"

"And he gave me startup money for the restaurant."

Fenway nodded. "If we looked at your finances, do you think we'd find a reason you'd want what he *is* leaving you?"

Grant shrugged. "The restaurant costs a lot to operate, but we made a small profit last year, and this year looks like it'll be better. I would have given Dad a percentage of the profits due to his investment."

"And what about the regular payments you'll start receiving from the auto dealership group?"

"Regular payments? I don't have anything to do with that. As far as I know, he's leaving the entire business to Tommy Kinsella."

Fenway nodded. "So Ishikawa and Knapp haven't gotten in touch with you yet?"

"For what?"

"The will."

Grant exhaled loudly. "Ugh. No. I hope it doesn't cut into the restaurant time."

"I'll let you get back to your prep," Fenway said. "I appreciate your time."

Grant turned his frame toward the side of beef, and Fenway took a step back, then paused. "Oh. One more thing."

Grant looked at her out of the corner of his eye.

"You were arrested for assault in Arizona."

"A decade ago," he said, tapping his fingers on the stainless-steel counter. "I was wondering if you were going to bring that up. Look, I'm not going to deny anything. I got drunk at the stadium. There was a Giants fan mouthing off. I told him to shut up, and he told me to make him." Grant shrugged, smirking. "I don't know why the cops were so upset. I was just doing what he asked me to."

Fenway glanced over at Dez, who set her lips in a tight line—it was no smoking gun.

Fenway closed her notebook and put it in her purse. "Thanks, Mr. Tonnick. I'll let you know if we have any more questions for you."

"Any time," Grant said. He began to cut another steak off the side of beef.

Fenway and Dez walked out of the restaurant into the suddenly bright day. The sun glinted off the wet sidewalks, and Fenway's eyes watered at the brightness. Dez squinted at the bright sun and sneezed.

The phone buzzed in Fenway's purse. She dug around for it for a few seconds as they walked toward Dez's red Impala, and Fenway read the name in spite of the glare.

"Hey, Piper."

"Are you at work?"

"No—we're about ten or fifteen minutes away. We just finished an interview."

"Can you come over here for a few minutes? I found some information, but I wanted to tell you in person."

"You can't tell me over the phone?"

"Not really."

"Why not?"

Piper hesitated. "I—I found out who your mom is. Who she *really* is."

CHAPTER SEVEN

Fenway hung up and looked at her phone, and she stopped in her tracks.

Dez took another few steps before she turned to see where Fenway was. "You okay?" She took a few steps back toward Fenway. "Did something happen with your dad?"

"No, not my dad." Fenway knitted her brow. "Piper told me that she found out who my mother is. Her real identity."

Dez exhaled. "Listen, I've been through some of these things before. People finding out someone they loved was hiding stuff from them." She reached out and put a hand on Fenway's shoulder. "It doesn't matter what your mom hid from you. It doesn't change the fact that she loved you, or that she wanted what was best for you, or that she thought—however wrong she might have been—that she was doing right by you."

"Even with giving all our money away? Even with the years where I went to bed hungry? Where we lived in a rundown apartment in a shitty neighborhood?"

Dez squeezed Fenway's shoulder. "Yes. Even then." She dropped her arm to her side. "Look, I understand that this is hard to hear, or that you can't possibly think of a reason your mom did what she did." She took a step back. "Just be aware that you don't know the whole story."

Fenway nodded.

"Want me to drive you over there? McVie's new office, right?"

"Right. Have you been?"

"Yeah, I went and saw it before he moved in."

"What do you think?"

Dez smirked and unlocked the doors to the Impala. "We all have to start somewhere."

Fenway fidgeted in Dez's passenger seat for ten minutes. Dez glanced over at her as they exited the freeway. "Maybe you should have gone easy on the coffee."

"I don't know if I'm ready for what I'm about to find out." Fenway clicked her fingernails against the seat belt and looked out the window.

Dez stopped at a red light, and Fenway opened the door.

"Hey—what are you doing?"

Fenway swung her legs out of the Impala. "Thanks, Dez, but I think I'll walk from here. I need—I need a little time to process this first."

"It's supposed to rain."

Fenway stood. "The light's green, Dez. I'll see you back in the office a little later, then. Maybe an hour." She shut the door and hurried to the sidewalk.

Fenway crossed the street with the light and began walking toward McVie's new business. She shuddered, thinking about the possibilities. Did her mother witness a mob murder? Was she a drug kingpin's girlfriend? Or maybe a former prostitute who slept with a powerful politician who tried to have her killed? Each thought sent Fenway down a rabbit hole, and every possibility was less plausible than the one before.

Raindrops splattered on her head, and she looked up at the sun, which beat a hasty retreat behind gray clouds as the light rain began. She huddled close to the sides of the buildings and hurried from awning to awning. She finally made it the eight blocks to Gateway of India and pulled the door next to it open. McVie was coming down the staircase as Fenway was going up.

"Hey!" McVie said. "Fancy meeting you here."

Fenway nodded. "I didn't see you earlier."

"I was meeting a potential client."

"Oh, cool, another potential client?"

"Right." McVie and Fenway landed on the same step, about five from the bottom landing, and McVie awkwardly put his arm around her shoulders and pulled her in for a kiss. Surprised, she offered a chaste kiss on the lips. McVie pulled back from it almost immediately. "Is everything okay?"

"Sorry," Fenway said, "it's just—well, I don't know how to prepare myself for what I'm about to find out."

"Oh," McVie said, "right. Piper's been working really hard, getting a lot of information. More for one morning than I expected."

"I'll make sure to mention that in my Yelp review," Fenway said.

McVie smiled and continued down the stairs.

"Where are you going now?"

"To P.Q.," McVie said. "Apparently my ex-wife is dissatisfied with the service she's gotten from Darren Ellsworth."

"Wait," Fenway said, "you're going to see Amy?"

"I'm meeting her at her real estate office," McVie said, pushing the door open. "I guess it can't wait till she gets home. Don't worry, I'm not planning on taking her case. I've got a couple of other recommendations for her."

"Hold on."

McVie stopped, half in and half out of the door. "What?"

Fenway bit her lip. What was the protocol here? Should she tell him that Amy was the lead suspect in the case? Should she tell McVie not to go over to try to help? Should she tell him that Rick Tonnick was found murdered in his hotel room this morning?

Why not? His lawyer was telling everyone.

"Rick Tonnick," she said.

"What, he's got a problem with me now?" McVie chuckled. "I didn't make a big thing about it when I wasn't invited to the wedding. I've barely said ten words to him."

"He was the call this morning."

"*Who* was the call this morning?"

"Rick Tonnick. He was the body in the hotel room."

"No." McVie's face fell.

"I'm kind of surprised you haven't heard by now."

McVie took a step inside and closed the door. "I'm not the sheriff anymore. Who would have told me?"

Fenway dropped her eyes. "Me, I guess. I'm sorry, Craig." She grimaced. "And one more thing—Amy came to see me."

"You?"

"She came into my office."

"Is she okay?"

Fenway snapped her head up. "What?"

"Is Amy okay? Her husband was just murdered."

"Why—" Fenway bit her tongue. Of course McVie, ever the Boy Scout, would be concerned about his ex-wife's state of mind.

He squinted and crossed his arms. "There's something else. Are you thinking she's a suspect?"

"I—uh—"

McVie held up his hands. "Sorry, sorry. I know you can't answer that. Forgot that I'm a civilian now."

"Given that, I'm not sure you should be going there."

McVie narrowed his eyes. "Why not?"

"Well—it might not look good if my boyfriend talks to me, then speeds over to her office."

McVie shook his head. "I don't care how it looks. Amy's ex-husband was just murdered. Even if I hadn't planned to see her, I'd probably go over there. I may not get along with her, but she's Megan's mother, and I need to make sure she's okay."

Fenway felt a pang in her chest as McVie turned and left. She watched the door swing back and close firmly, then slowly went up the stairs.

Pushing open the door to suite 202, Fenway saw Piper at her computer, scrolling through what looked like a database of names. Piper turned around at the sound of the door opening.

"Hey, Fenway. Figured that was you."

Fenway nodded. "So you've found out who my mom is?"

"It's not like I have DNA evidence, but I've got a pretty good idea." She clicked away from the database and pulled up an article from the *Los Angeles Times.* "So," Piper said, "I can't find any records of Joanne Stevenson—your mom, that is—before April of 1986. And I knew that she'd used the social security number and the name of a girl who'd been killed about twenty-one years earlier."

"Right."

"I'm working off a couple of basic assumptions," Piper said. "The first is that something happened before April 1986—but not too far before then—to make your mom take on this new identity. Think that's a reasonable assumption?"

"Probably," Fenway said. Her fingers were starting to grow numb, which ordinarily she'd think was just from the chilly day—was she really acclimatizing to California this fast? But her breath came short and shallow, her muscles tense. Her body was on high alert, as if this were an attack, and she couldn't figure out if she wanted fight or flight as the response. "Maybe she disappeared for a while first, though. Went underground or something."

Piper shook her head. "I think this is the way she went underground."

"Did that lead you to anything?"

"Not at first. A lot of African-American women around your mom's age went missing in early 1986. But most of them turned up, one way or another. Then I found *this*." Piper clicked on a window and a *Los Angeles Times* article popped up. Two photos of just faces, one man and one woman, appeared alongside the text. Fenway gaped.

"It—it's like looking in a mirror."

"Your cheekbones are higher, but yeah, I can see the resemblance." Piper enlarged the window. "This article is from October 1985. String of burglaries in Ladera Heights and the surrounding communities. Described by witnesses—in only one or two cases where they found witnesses—as a man and woman working together, late teens or early twenties, both African-American."

"Ugh," Fenway said. "My mom robbed convenience stores?"

"Residences," Piper said. "In fact, it looks like it wasn't the same M.O. at all the burglaries."

"Which means what?"

"Well, it means that I really doubt your mom was involved. She may have been seen driving the getaway car, but from what I saw in the police report, she may not have even known she was the getaway driver."

Fenway folded her arms. "Are you just saying that to make me feel better? Because I'm a big girl. My mom's been gone for almost a year. I can take it."

"Well," Piper said, "there's nothing to suggest that she was involved in any more than what I just mentioned." She put her hands up, palms facing down, in front of her. "But I'm getting ahead of myself. So— there's a string of burglaries. The police get a sketch artist, and they find this nineteen-year-old kid in Ladera Heights named Edward Drake."

"Edward Drake? Sounds like he should be a yacht owner, not a burglar."

"Goes by Eddie to his friends. The word on the street is that he's trying to make a name for himself."

"The word on the street?"

"It was mentioned in the police reports," Piper said. "Not computerized back then—now it's all in PDFs, but nothing's searchable. Kind of a stroke of luck that I found it. He kept trying to get the cops to call him 'E-Money' during his interview."

Fenway peered over Piper's shoulder.

Suspect Arrested in String of Residential Burglaries

The article was only about two column inches, no more than seventy-five words.

"That's it?"

"As far as local media goes, yes," Piper said. "But it doesn't look like they could get anything to stick. Eddie never gave up the names of any of his friends, and the public defender did her job. The eyewitness couldn't be sure it was him, so they let him go."

"You got the court transcripts too?"

The corners of Piper's mouth curved into a smile. "It's all public record."

"Get to the point, Piper. Who is my mom?"

"Oh—sorry. I think her birth name was Samara Godwin. She was interviewed by the police, and the reports have Eddie saying they lived together."

"That's why you think she was driving the getaway car?"

"Yes."

"Guys like that—they sometimes have women they're seeing on the side. Could have been one of them."

"Could've been," Piper agreed.

"So—what? Is that the only evidence you have that she's driving the getaway car? Does something happen during the next burglary?"

Piper shook her head. "In fact, the burglaries die down. But then the last week of February, I come across this gem in the *Times*." She clicked on another window, and a small article appeared.

EDWARD JONAS DRAKE passed away on Saturday, February 26, 1986 at the age of 20. To forever cherish his memory, he leaves his parents, Lawrence and Jewel; his brothers, Lawrence Jr. and Michael; and his sisters, Constance and Alannah. Services will be held on Wednesday, March 2, 1986 at 12:00 P.M. at Calvary Baptist Church, 4911 West 59th Street, Los Angeles. The family will receive friends from 11:00 A.M. until time of service. Pastor Ernest Johnson, officiating; Pastor Rodney Chavez eulogizing.

"No mention of Samara Godwin."

"That doesn't necessarily mean anything," Piper said. "But after February 26, 1986, Samara Godwin ceases to exist."

"Just like Joanne Stevenson didn't exist before April 1986."

Piper nodded.

Fenway looked into Piper's face. "Twenty years old is awfully young to die."

"Yep," Piper said. "I'm going to dig through more police reports. I don't know if your mom—Samara Godwin—had anything to do with the death of her boyfriend."

"How do you know it's her?" Fenway asked. "I mean, okay—so you've got the dates worked out, but two months is kind of a long time to wait between when you disappear in one place and appear in another."

"True," Piper said, clicking again, and a photo came up onscreen. "Maybe this will help."

Fenway gasped—it was a black-and-white picture of a woman. The woman was beautiful and radiant, smiling shyly into the camera, wearing a black off-the-shoulder wrap and standing against a cloud-covered background. The woman had the same eyes as Fenway, though slightly different cheekbones—but Fenway recognized her mother.

"Samara Godwin's senior photo, class of '84," Piper said. "I found an online yearbook, too. She was the president of Art Club." She paused. "Does that look like your mother?"

Fenway stared in fascination and fought an urge to reach out and touch the screen.

"How—how did she get to Estancia in April? How did she become Joanne Stevenson?"

Piper nodded. "I have a couple of ideas about that. Samara's father was the lead pressman at one of the biggest print shops in Los Angeles. Access to a lot of equipment. And in 1992, an employee of the print shop was investigated for manufacturing fake IDs."

"My grandfather was arrested?"

"Another employee," Piper said. "Still, if Maurice Godwin—that's the name of Samara's father—worked at that print shop and thought his daughter was in danger..." She shrugged.

Fenway was about to burst. "Is he still alive?"

Piper winced. "Sorry. I'm not there just yet. I thought you'd want a name. And the photograph."

Fenway leaned forward, grabbing onto the desk for support. "Thanks, Piper. I—I didn't even know what I was missing. I have grandparents. Maybe my mom—maybe Samara had brothers and sisters." She looked up at Samara's high school portrait again. "You know, when you grow up a certain way, you just assume everyone is the same as you. Not that the way you're growing up is weird or unusual. My mom never had a lot of friends. She never talked about where she grew up. I just figured that when you were an adult, you kind of left behind where you came from."

Piper was quiet.

"So." Fenway cleared her throat. "What's next? Are you going to try to find out why Samara left Los Angeles?"

"I can." Piper nodded. "I could also try to find Samara's relatives. Your relatives. Which do you want me to prioritize?"

Fenway leaned her five-ten frame over Piper, sitting in her chair, and gave her an awkward hug. "Thank you, Piper. Thank you for finding this for me."

"Oh," Piper said, reaching up her hands to pat Fenway's arms. "Um, you're welcome."

"I've never really had a family before. It was just me and Mom. And now—well, now, I might have some history. I might be able to figure out where I come from. What I am."

"I'll prioritize finding Samara's family, then," Piper said. "I'll let you know when I have something."

"Thanks." Fenway released Piper from the awkward hug and stood up, smoothing down her slacks. "Um—do you guys have a bathroom?"

"Down the hall to the right. It's all the way at the end."

"Thanks. I'll see you later." Fenway picked up her purse and turned to leave. "Hey, is there any way you can email me that picture?"

"Sure." Piper smiled.

Fenway left the McVie Investigations office and found the bathroom. She entered and locked the door, almost immediately feeling the tears run down her cheeks. She expected to be—what? Embarrassed? But her mother had been nineteen in February of 1986, when her boyfriend, or maybe ex-boyfriend, had died. Fenway was sure that Eddie Drake had gotten involved with the wrong people in "trying to make a name for himself," as Piper had delicately put it. And the people who had killed Eddie might have had it out for Samara, too.

She turned the name over in her head. Samara. So much more elegant than Joanne, and somehow, so fitting for her. Samara was an artist's name. Fenway found herself smiling in spite of the tears. She pulled a paper towel out of the holder and dabbed at her eyes and her mascara.

Fenway looked in the mirror. She had the same eye shape as her mother, but more of her father's sturdy build—and his height. Her mother had always been a little more delicate. Shorter, too. She wondered what Maurice Godwin was like. Maybe she had his hair. Did Samara have brothers and sisters? Eddie Drake certainly did—what was he, one of five?

She'd been used to having dead grandparents all her life. Her father had been in his mid-thirties when Fenway was born—her mother had only been twenty-one or twenty-two during their courtship. Nathaniel

Ferris apparently liked younger women, even when he was a slightly younger man. Her paternal grandfather had died young, though she was never quite clear what it was from. And she didn't remember her paternal grandmother either—was she dead, or did Nathaniel Ferris just act like she was?

With a start, Fenway had a horrible thought. Her grandmother might not have ever met her or her mother because she didn't want to. Because Nathaniel Ferris had married a Black woman.

She studied her face in the mirror. Did she have any of her paternal grandmother's features?

No Christmas cards from her. She struggled to even remember her name.

Evelyn. That's what it was. Evelyn Ferris. Where did she live? Back east somewhere, maybe.

Fenway shook her head. She was telling herself stories based purely on conjecture. There could have been a zillion other reasons why Evelyn Ferris had broken off contact with her son.

She pulled her phone out of her purse. A little past three forty-five.

Hmm.

Amy Tonnick had hired the other private investigator to follow her husband. What had he found? Why had Amy fired him?

Maybe Darren Ellsworth's office was near downtown Estancia too. She brought up the browser on her phone and searched. Sure enough—it was only about a mile away. Not close enough to walk, but close enough that she could make a detour before going back to the office. She could ask Darren Ellsworth herself why Amy McVie Tonnick had fired him.

A little voice in her head whispered that she hadn't fired him. That she really just wanted to get close to Craig again. That the divorce was the worst mistake she'd ever made.

Ugh. Fenway would have to get that anxiety out of her head. She washed her hands thoroughly and decided she was okay with just a quick touch-up of her makeup. She pulled out her makeup case and spent about a minute cleaning up around her eyes. Then she drew herself to her full height, gathered her purse, and strode out of the bathroom.

Despite being open for more than two decades longer than McVie Investigations, the offices of Ellsworth Investigative Services showed no signs of a thriving business. The building was located in the warehouse district, and the entrance was next to a cargo bay door. Inside was even less impressive. The office was smaller than the outside would lead the viewer to believe, and the carpet was threadbare. The computer, sitting on a desk clearly made of particle board with scratched and chipped oak veneer, was at least seven years old. Next to the computer keyboard sat three plastic CD cases and what looked like fake bullets, one gold and one blue, with three large X's printed on the side. Fenway frowned and looked around the small room.

Two side chairs made of aluminum, each with a ratty beige seat cover, sat on either side of the tiny office, one next to the front door and one next to the back door, whose wooden paneling looked as if it had been designed in the seventies.

As if on cue, the back door opened, and a white woman around forty in a green knee-length dress with long sleeves—and were those shoulder pads?—walked behind the desk and stopped short when she saw Fenway.

"Oh," she said, startled, "hello. Do you have an appointment?"

"I don't," Fenway said.

"Well," she said, "Mr. Ellsworth doesn't see—"

"I'm the county coroner, ma'am," Fenway said. "I'm investigating the death of a man I was told Mr. Ellsworth was following. I just need a minute of his time."

"What did you say your name was?"

"I said I was the county coroner. Fenway Stevenson is my name."

"Fenway?"

"Yep. Like the baseball stadium. My dad's a huge Red Sox fan."

The woman nodded and left through the back door again, closing it behind her.

Fenway heard the muffled voices of the woman and of a man—presumably Darren Ellsworth. But she couldn't understand anything they were saying. The man grew increasingly agitated, and then they were both quiet. Nothing happened for a moment.

Fenway looked at the side chair near the front door. She was dying to take the seat next to the back door, but that wouldn't get any conversation with Ellsworth off on the right foot. She sauntered over to the chair next to the front door and took a seat.

Finally, the door opened, and the woman beckoned her. Fenway got up and crossed the tiny office, following the woman in the green dress inside.

The back office was a mess. Three overstuffed bookcases lined the wall on Fenway's left. The far wall was entirely glass with a cheap-looking swinging door out into the rear parking lot, where a blue Toyota pickup was parked next to a dumpster. The wall on the right contained framed certificates, and two chairs identical to the ones in the waiting room sat in front of a metal desk at a ninety-degree angle to the wall.

On the desk were a monitor and keyboard, beige and tan and discolored, which may have been even older than the computer in the front office.

And behind the desk, adjusting the nameplate reading *Darren Ellsworth, Private Investigator*, a heavily tanned white man sat in a denim long-sleeved shirt and a cowboy hat.

The hat looked too big for the man's head, but blue eyes burned intensely from the shadow the brim cast on his face. The wrinkles around his mouth pulled the sides down, and an 1890s-style blond city-boy mustache, obviously waxed and curled at the ends, conflicted in style so much with the cowboy hat that Fenway's eyes started to water.

"Darren Ellsworth," he said, standing and shaking Fenway's hand. The man was lean, trim, and fit, and stood about six-foot-one, just slightly taller than Fenway.

"Fenway Stevenson." She took the rightmost chair, which squeaked noisily as she sat. The whole office gave her the creeps. "I understand that Amy Tonnick engaged your services a couple of weeks ago."

Ellsworth looked up at the woman in the green dress before talking. "Well, I don't like to discuss clients. They expect a certain amount of discretion."

"That's okay," Fenway said. "She's not your client anymore."

Ellsworth blinked. "No—no, she's not."

"And the subject of your investigation was found dead in a hotel room this morning."

"I'm going to my desk," the woman in the green dress said, turning and opening the door.

Ellsworth nodded, not taking his eyes off Fenway, as the door closed gently behind the woman.

"You've been at this a long time," Fenway said. "Private investigators don't enjoy the same client communication privilege that attorneys do."

"There's an expectation—"

"Not according to the Supreme Court." Fenway leaned forward. "You could let me know what Amy Tonnick hired you for, and I'll be out of your hair in, what? Ten or fifteen minutes, tops?"

"Or I could make you come back with a warrant."

"You could do that. It would delay my investigation. You probably know that the first forty-eight hours are the most critical, though."

"That's not my problem." Ellsworth shrugged. "I don't have anything to hide."

"Here's the thing, though, Mr. Ellsworth." Fenway stood, towering over the seated private investigator. "Every judge in the state will see my photographs of the cocaine paraphernalia on your assistant's desk and let any search I want to do in here stand."

Ellsworth blanched.

"I personally don't have any problem with a couple of, uh, consenting adults who want to partake of recreational drugs, as long as they don't drive when they're high, and as long as they don't do anything stupid to burden our already-overtaxed medical system. But," Fenway continued, "if you make me call some of my co-workers to come back with a warrant, I'm not sure what *they'll* be willing to overlook and what they won't." She looked around the office and lowered her voice. "If I can just be out of here in ten minutes, though, you and Miss Tight Green Dress can continue to spend the afternoon on your teambuilding exercises."

"You know," Ellsworth said, "as it happens, I have the Amy Tonnick file right here." He pulled a file drawer out at his feet and hefted a folder onto the desk. "She came to me last week and told me to follow her husband, see if he was seeing anyone on the side." He shook his head. "I saw the wedding announcement in the paper. They just got back from their honeymoon."

"I guess the fifth time wasn't the charm," Fenway said, taking her seat. "Did you find anything?"

Ellsworth nodded. "He likes the Phillips-Holsen. He goes there a lot. I can't believe anyone would pay five hundred a night to stay there if they lived in town." He smiled; his front lateral incisor was crooked. "Unless they're using the hotel to have an affair." He leaned back, took the cowboy hat off with one hand, and ran his other hand through his thinning yellow-and-white hair. "I followed him in twice last week. He checked in and was given the penthouse suite, but no one I saw came to the front desk asking for him. I stayed in that lobby until five in the morning, and then he came down and checked out. Twice I did that, and nothing."

"You didn't check the back entrance and the private elevator for the penthouse?"

Ellsworth's jaw dropped. "The back—no, isn't that for employees only?"

"No," said Fenway.

"And you said that Mr. Tonnick is dead?"

"Killed at that hotel," Fenway said. "When did Amy Tonnick fire you?"

Ellsworth's nostrils flared, and he paused for a moment. "She didn't fire me."

Fenway rolled her eyes. "When did you part ways, then?"

"Yesterday," Ellsworth said. "She called my cell phone on a Sunday, can you believe that? After I was up all Friday night following her husband, and she says she's not renewing my contract for another week."

Fenway shook her head. Semantics must have been important to Ellsworth—it sure seemed like that was the equivalent of a pink slip. The gears in her mind turned. Did Amy fire Ellsworth so she wouldn't have any witnesses when she used the back entrance to murder her husband? Or did she realize Ellsworth's laziness and incompetence, and the timing with the death was just odd?

Fenway looked at the desk where Ellsworth was busily tapping a pen on the notepad next to the mouse. No, this almost sealed Amy's fate. Woman hires P.I., woman fires P.I., woman exploits the security flaw that the P.I. didn't catch to murder her husband. It was circumstantial evidence, sure, but the license plate on the Mustang convertible? That was hard to fake. She couldn't see any way Amy wasn't getting arrested—and soon.

"So you don't know any of the possible visitors that Rick Tonnick might have had."

Ellsworth shook his head. He looked displeased, perhaps realizing that Rick Tonnick had outsmarted him, costing him a client. "I know he's cheating on her," he said, "but he's had so much practice at it and he's got so many resources at his disposal, I guess I'm not surprised he pulled one over on me."

"You have any photographic evidence at all?"

Ellsworth hesitated. "I took pictures of him at work, going to his dealerships. I saw him hit on a few of the women who were looking at the cars. Seemed to work with one of them—I thought I might be seeing her in the hotel lobby."

"You got pictures of them together at the dealership?"

"A few. I got pictures of him going into the Phillips-Holsen hotel, too, and coming out."

Fenway nodded. "Another thing, if you don't mind."

Ellsworth's eyes darted around the room. "No trouble at all, Coroner. I have all the time in the world."

"You said he 'pulled one over on you.'"

Ellsworth's eyes narrowed.

"That implies that you've got a give-and-take, a back-and-forth between the two of you."

Ellsworth grunted. "Maybe you're reading too much into that."

Fenway shook her head. "I don't think I am." She tapped her fingers on the aluminum arm of the chair. "If I went back to my office, where I've got a whole legal database at my disposal, what do you suppose I'd find if I put in your name into the database and hit search? Would it show me any sort of legal action either you or Mr. Tonnick took against the other? And if I found *that*, Mr. Ellsworth, how do you think I—"

Ellsworth raised his hands. "All right, all right, I give up, Miss Stevenson. I've been a private eye in this town for over two decades now, and I've got a good reputation for sniffing out cheating spouses. Rick Tonnick's second wife hired me, and I caught him cheating with the woman who became his third wife. Then Rick hired me to catch his third wife cheating—Noreen's calculus teacher, if you can believe it. And then his fourth wife paid me to catch Rick and Amy together. All of 'em caught in hotels, one person arriving, then about twenty minutes later, the second person arriving."

"The Tonnicks are really keeping you in business."

"They were until Rick changed things up."

Fenway leaned back in her seat. "Tell me, what hotel did you catch Rick and Amy at?"

"The Phillips-Holsen. I guess Rick thought that a ritzy hotel like that wouldn't let some low-life P.I. just hang out in the lobby taking pictures." Ellsworth grinned, the crooked tooth sticking slightly to his lower lip before letting go. "A fifty-dollar bill will get most anyone to look the other way. Doesn't matter how fancy the hotel is."

Fenway rested her forehead on her fist. The thoughts were coming one after the other. Finally, she lifted her head. "Mr. Ellsworth," she began slowly, "the customer that Mr. Tonnick flirted with—did she end up buying a car?"

Ellsworth nodded. "A Subaru Crosstrek. A new one, with that new kind of paint that looks flat. Sort of an eggshell blue."

Fenway nodded, digging in her purse before pulling out a business card. "Yeah, I know the color you mean. Can you send those photos to my email?"

"Certainly." Ellsworth frowned as he took the card from Fenway, who looked at her phone.

"That only took thirteen minutes, Mr. Ellsworth," she said, rising from the chair. "I'll let you get back to your afternoon activities." She stepped toward the door and opened it. "Though I would really appreciate those photos before you get too far involved in your work."

"Understood," Ellsworth grumbled.

"And," Fenway said, "perhaps hanging up a CLOSED sign and turning the deadbolt would be a good idea." Crossing the front office, she glanced at the woman in the green dress, whose ears were turning scarlet. Fenway turned the handle of the door and exited into the rain.

CHAPTER EIGHT

Her hair was a mess, but Fenway was buzzing with the information she'd learned from Ellsworth. The walk was invigorating but cold, and the light shower had turned to a drizzle by the time she stopped at Java Jim's and got a second afternoon latte for herself and a large black coffee for Dez.

Waiting for the drinks, she grabbed a handful of paper napkins from the dispenser on the counter. They stuck to her wet hand. Fenway made a disgusted face and sponged her soaking slacks, but the napkins were no match for the soggy clothes. The first napkin disintegrated in her hand, and the next two weren't any better. She lifted her hand with the wet napkins and saw that balls of wet white paper had been left on her pant leg. *Ugh*.

After the barista called *Joanne*—she'd briefly considered *Samara* but figured it was just as hard to spell and explain as *Fenway*—she hurried through the drizzle to her office building.

She wished she could shake the water off herself like a dog. She carefully opened the door to the coroner's suite while balancing the coffees and her purse with one arm. Sarah looked up and smiled.

Shit. "I totally forgot to get you a coffee," Fenway said. "I'm so sorry."

"Oh, you don't need to get me anything," Sarah said. "Besides, I can't have caffeine this late or I'm up all night."

"Me, on the other hand," Dez said, appearing behind the counter, "I wouldn't mind taking that large coffee off your hands."

"It's the Brazilian Peaberry," Fenway said.

"It's a little cup of heaven." Dez reached out with both hands, and Fenway passed her the coffee.

"Can I see you at your desk?"

"Sure, Fenway. Everything okay? You've been gone awhile."

Fenway followed Dez to her desk at the back of the room. "Yeah, for now." She lowered her voice. "I know my mom's real name. Samara Godwin."

"Really? Piper found her real name?"

"She did."

"Even if McVie screws up every other aspect of his business, hiring her sure was smart. Did she find anything else?"

Fenway exhaled loudly. "Bad-news boyfriend who wound up dead about two months before my mom showed up in Estancia."

Dez cocked her head as she sat down. "Think the boyfriend's death is related to your mom's disappearance?"

"Piper's still working on that—but listen, that's not why I wanted to talk."

Dez put her hands behind her head and leaned back. "I'm all ears. What do you need?"

Fenway pulled the side chair around the side of Dez's desk and sat down. "I just spent about fifteen minutes with the private investigator who Amy hired to follow her husband around. She fired him yesterday."

"Fired him? Why?"

"I think the prosecution will claim that because the P.I. couldn't find proof, Amy took matters into her own hands. So she lured her husband to the hotel where he took the women he cheated with, and she killed him."

"It sounds like you're finding more evidence against Amy," Dez said. "With the footage from the parking garage and now this, I think we should take this to ADA Pondicherry. See if there's enough evidence to arrest her."

"Yeah," Fenway murmured. "Except…"

Dez paused. "Except what?"

Fenway sighed. "Well—there are a couple of things I want to check. Particularly after talking with the private investigator."

"Like what?"

"The P.I. said Rick flirted with one of his customers at the Subaru dealership. He assumed that Tonnick made plans to see her that night at the Phillips-Holsen."

"That was Sunday night?"

"No, no—Friday night. Three days ago."

Dez scoffed. "Women who are attracted to men are living proof that sexuality isn't a choice."

Fenway laughed. "Guilty as charged." She scooted to the edge of her seat. "I think the hotel property manager was going to email us the footage of the parking garage. We should see if we can get it from Friday night, too. See if a new Subaru with new paper plates goes into the garage. Then we can check DMV records and get a name."

Dez clicked her tongue. "Even if we could do that, Fenway, what would that prove?"

"By itself? Probably nothing."

"But?"

"Well—Amy's the main suspect, but there are things that just don't make sense to me. For instance, how did Amy lure Rick to the hotel?"

Confusion washed over Dez's face. "How Amy lured—"

"Sure. He's not going to show up at the Phillips-Holsen in the penthouse suite waiting for his wife, is he?" She tapped her fingernails on her knee. "I mean, yes, it's possible they have some role-play thing going on, but I don't think that's likely. This is the hotel he uses to cheat on his spouse, not the romantic hotel he goes to with his wife."

Dez said, "I don't know. I don't think the prosecution would have an issue with that."

"Maybe not. Just hear me out, Dez. If we see this baby-blue Subaru Crosstrek on the footage from the garage on Friday night and then again on Sunday night, that could support a theory of how Amy lured Rick to the hotel."

"We already saw the footage from the garage on Sunday night."

"But we weren't *looking* for a Subaru Crosstrek."

"No, no, no," Dez said, shaking her head vehemently. "We saw all the cars coming and going—I didn't see a Subaru. And besides, your theory is too damn complicated. Next thing you know, you'll be creating some sort of Rube Goldberg machine in your head to catch Amy in the act. It's simple—Amy finds the online dating profile Rick uses, she pretends to be another woman, and she shows up at his hotel room."

"But that doesn't make any sense," Fenway said. "He's drunk. She's slipped pills into his scotch. He's naked in bed. How does that happen with Amy in the room if he's expecting another woman?"

"Maybe she had the key to the room, and he was already in bed?"

"But she didn't," Fenway said. "She certainly didn't come into the lobby to get it—and how else would she have gotten it?"

Dez tapped her chin thoughtfully. "What if Rick Tonnick went down in the penthouse elevator, met the woman in the Subaru, and then *she* leaves the door slightly open when they go into the penthouse?"

"That's another way I think it supports the theory too. The Subaru woman is in cahoots with Amy."

"Okay," Dez said.

"And what happens when Rick Tonnick is naked in bed and sees his wife? He's expecting the beautiful Subaru customer, and instead his wife shows up?"

"Then she attacks him."

Fenway shook her head emphatically and held up her index finger. "One, there was no sign of a struggle. No skin under his fingernails, nothing. He was already passed out when she put the pillow over his head."

"The tests haven't come back from San Miguelito yet."

"Doesn't matter," Fenway said. "For her to do it properly, he'd have to be unconscious. He's sturdy, built like an athlete. He'd need to be incapacitated for Amy to be able to smother him."

Dez was quiet.

Fenway held up a second finger. "Two, how did he get the sleeping-pill-and-whisky cocktail if it was Amy at the door?"

"Maybe she wanted to talk things through, and she made him a drink."

"Really? That's what you think happened?"

"*You* obviously don't think that's how it happened."

"I have some major questions about how she did it," Fenway said. "The only thing that makes sense to me is that she lured him there. Possibly with another woman. Possibly with the *same* woman he'd had sex with two nights before."

"And this mystery woman—she's the one who gets Rick Tonnick to drink the whisky with the sleeping pills?"

Fenway nodded. "And then Amy comes in, mystery woman leaves, and Amy puts the pillow over her husband's face, with his naked, unconscious body there for everyone to see."

"She covered him up."

"Not that much." Fenway paused. "Are there any other scenarios you can think of?"

"At least a dozen," Dez said. "A robbery gone wrong. A prostitute who didn't get paid. A serial cheater who forgot that he invited *two* of his mistresses to come over. But I haven't had time to think them all through." She pointed at Fenway. "Quite honestly, neither have you."

"Fair enough," Fenway replied. "Still, it probably makes sense if the new Subaru was caught on camera in the hotel parking garage. I hope that the property manager takes a view that we don't need another warrant."

"The Phillips-Holsen is a stickler for warrants. And their property manager—Brianna, right? She won't look the other way." Dez thought for a moment, then snapped her fingers. "There's a much easier way. I'll search the DMV records and see who bought a baby blue Crosstrek from Tonnick Subaru on Friday. I bet that narrows it down quite a bit."

Fenway nodded. "I bet it will."

Dez looked at Fenway. "You're still dripping on the floor," she said. "Why don't you go stand under the hand drier in the bathroom for a while?"

Fenway laughed and rose from the chair. She squished when she took a step and looked down at the seat of Dez's guest chair. The upholstery was soaked.

Dez shook her head. "I'll make sure to offer that seat to the mayor when he comes in."

Fenway's wet clothes stuck to her. She grunted. Maybe the hand drier —or at least some paper towels in the restroom—*would* be a good idea.

Sarah raised her head as Fenway squished past.

"Fenway?"

"Hi, Sarah. How's your first day going?"

Sarah smiled. "No complaints."

"Not even when your manager forgets to bring you coffee?"

"Hey, it's great if you're going to let me hold this over you for a couple of weeks." Chuckling, she turned her monitor to face Fenway. "I know you were busy this afternoon with interviews. I don't think he's one of your top suspects, but I was able to pull Grant Tonnick's financials. I hope that's okay."

Fenway cocked her head. "You didn't tell me you were good with financial research in your interview."

"I did some, uh, asset monitoring when I was working at the law firm. Sometimes people would come to us with stories that didn't, shall we say, exactly align with their financial situation. Especially in divorces or bankruptcy negotiation." She paused. "I was trying to be proactive."

"As long as what you're doing won't get any evidence thrown out by the judge, keep doing it." Fenway thought of Piper. "We need someone with that skill set."

"Happy to do it." Sarah pointed at the screen. "Cantle & Pommel was pretty deep in debt last year—about two point three."

"Two point three what? Million?"

Sarah nodded. "Right. Then in November, Rick Tonnick paid off all Grant's creditors and injected a little over a million dollars into the business."

"Three and a half million. Quite a chunk of change."

"And then moved everything to Amy in his will—except for the profit share and a million bucks each going to Grant and Noreen."

Fenway narrowed her eyes. "I wonder what a review of Noreen Tonnick's finances would find."

"I can see what I can dig up."

"Thanks. And I'm going to go dry off." Fenway tapped the counter with her open hand a few times and gave Sarah a smile before exiting.

Fenway walked into the women's restroom, where she surveyed her options. The hand dryer had no outward-facing blower; it was the new kind where a person's hands went in the top. It looked like it had been installed recently. Fortunately, the bathroom still held a touchless paper towel dispenser, and Fenway moved her hand in front of it. It spat out about eighteen inches' worth of paper.

She tore it off and blotted her trousers, and the towel immediately soaked through.

Fenway sighed. She'd have to go home and change before going to the hospital.

There was an active homicide investigation, and she was going to leave work to go sit next to her comatose father, reading *Gulliver's Travels*. Who knew if what she was doing was even helping?

Maybe she should stay.

Then she heard Dez's voice in her head. And Rachel's voice. And Craig's voice. You don't have to do it all yourself. Delegate. You work with talented people. You're more valuable when you're not burned out.

And she felt the water drip off her slacks into her shoes.

Dez could track down the Subaru owner while she was sitting with her dad. Sarah could get the available information on Noreen Tonnick's finances. Mark could go to San Miguelito and get the toxicology report when it was ready. She took a deep breath and left the restroom.

And almost ran over Barry Klein.

"Oh—sorry, Barry," Fenway said.

"It's *Mayor*," Klein said, malice dripping from his voice. "And just what the hell do you think you're doing?"

Fenway sized up the mayor. He was in a black suit with a red tie, such an obvious attempt at a power move. She took a step back. "Doing? Going to the bathroom?"

"You know what I mean." He clenched and unclenched his fists.

Fenway cocked her head. "I actually *don't* know what you mean."

Klein scoffed. "I didn't think you were as stupid as your father, but maybe you just had me fooled." He pointed a finger in Fenway's face. "I thought I made it clear that I wanted to be kept informed of what's going on in the Tonnick case."

Had he said that? Fenway furrowed her brow, fighting the urge to slap his hand away. "It's been four hours since I saw you last. We've been conducting interviews. Getting judges to sign warrants. Reviewing security footage."

Klein lowered his hand. "And you haven't told me any of this."

"There's nothing to tell. We've identified a few persons of interest. We've looked at Tonnick's will, and we're reviewing his financials."

"What about the security footage?"

"Whoever visited Tonnick last night managed to avoid the cameras."

"So you have nothing."

"I didn't say that. I said we've identified some persons of interest."

Klein shook his head. "That's not real progress. I expect you to be working on this case until you make an arrest."

Ugh. "You know my father's in the hospital, and you know I visit him every day."

"Not today. Not before I see something happen in this case."

Fenway folded her arms. "We're exploring several different avenues. I have multiple people in the department working on this case. It's my top priority."

"It needs to be your *only* priority."

Fenway pushed past him toward the coroner's suite, making a damp spot on his black suit jacket.

"I mean it, Fenway. I don't want to hear that you were anywhere near the hospital tonight."

"You're not my boss," Fenway said over her shoulder.

"You report to the people of this county," Klein said, "and I can call a press conference to tell the public how the incompetent coroner is ignoring all the evidence pointing to your boyfriend's ex."

Fenway stopped in her tracks.

Was someone in the office tipping Klein off?

It couldn't be Dez or Mark—they both hated Klein as much as she did. Maybe even more. Migs was taking the week off—some family reunion thing in Phoenix.

Sarah?

What was it that Klein had said about her? That Fenway had just hired her as a stain on City Hall or something ridiculous like that? Maybe Sarah was a plant—maybe that's why she was so overqualified.

Fenway shook her head. *Assumes facts not in evidence.* She turned to face Klein once more.

"So if my office hasn't been keeping you informed, Mayor," she said evenly, "it seems like you're doing a pretty good job of getting the information you need anyway." She took a step forward. "And the last time I looked, the sheriff's department was in charge of arrests, not the mayor. How do you think it would look to the D.A.'s office if I arrested someone before I had enough evidence to be confident of a conviction?"

"How do you think it will look to the people of this county if *certain things* got out?"

Fenway paused. He wasn't talking about telling the world that Fenway wasn't arresting Amy Tonnick. He was referring to the decade-old video.

She felt her knees weaken, but she took a deep breath and steadied herself. "You know you obtained those recordings illegally. That possessing them is a crime. You don't want that to get out."

"You don't want those recordings to get out either," Klein said.

"I'm not risking jail time," Fenway said, "just my reputation. And I can move away." She turned back to her office. "Not my ideal state of affairs, no. But you don't want to push me too hard on this, Mr. *Mayor.*" She pushed the door to the coroner's suite open and looked over her shoulder at Klein. "I'll go to the hospital this evening, and you're not going to hold a press conference."

She walked past Sarah's workstation, and the door slammed behind her. In her office, she grabbed her purse and her thin coat, and after a moment's hesitation, she undocked her laptop and put it in her shoulder bag. She stomped out from behind her desk. "I'm heading to the hospital to see my dad," she announced. "I've got my laptop and my phone, so let me know if anything happens. Dez—is Mark picking up the toxicology report from San Miguelito?"

"They're backed up," Dez said. "Won't be ready for another few days."

Fenway shook her head. "Great. Would you tell the mayor he can go yell at Dr. Yasuda?"

Dez stood up from her chair and hurried over to Fenway. "Okay," she said. "What just happened?"

"In my office," Fenway said. She turned back and dumped her purse, laptop bag, and coat on her desk. Dez shut the door.

"Klein is up my ass," Fenway said. "He told me not to go see Dad tonight. He wants an arrest, and he implied it should be Amy. Said he'd hold a news conference informing everyone of my conflict of interest."

Dez set her jaw. "One of these days, Klein will figure out that he can't win the game he's playing."

"It's gotten him elected mayor."

"This too shall pass," Dez said. "I've got some research to do, but you tell your dad we're all pulling for him, okay? I read that sometimes people in comas can hear what's going on. Maybe it'll help."

Fenway nodded.

<hr />

When Fenway walked into Room 317 of St. Vincent's Hospital in jeans and a Seattle University sweatshirt, Charlotte was already there, sitting next to Nathaniel Ferris's bed.

"Hey, Charlotte."

"Hi, Fenway."

"I'm really sorry about this afternoon. I was in the middle of reviewing security footage. It took a lot longer than I thought."

Charlotte nodded. "I know your job can be a bear when there's a murder investigation. Honestly, I thought that after the arrests with all those people involved in the money laundering scheme, we'd be seeing a lot fewer homicides in the county. That it would go back to normal."

"Yeah, well, at least I'm better at telling Barry Klein no."

"Oh no. What did he want?"

"He wanted me to stay at the office until we made an arrest. Or he wants me off the case because of my conflict of interest."

"Conflict of interest? Oh—like you had to recuse yourself when I was arrested."

"Right."

"You know the suspect in this case, too?"

"Not well. But everyone else in the department has the same conflict of interest. We could bring another department in, but this close to the beginning of the year? Besides, it's my call whether I stay on the case or not."

"You don't want anything thrown out of court, though."

Fenway nodded. "My point, though, is that I was getting a lot of pressure to stay at work tonight. And I came here."

Charlotte nodded.

"Which, you know, is a different decision than the one I would have made even three months ago."

Charlotte was still silent.

Fenway leaned against the door frame. "Is something wrong, Charlotte?"

Her stepmother put her head in her hands, and her shoulders started to shake.

Fenway hesitated for a moment, then hurried over to Charlotte, dropped her purse, and knelt down, wrapping her stepmother in an embrace. "I'm sorry," she whispered. "I'm sorry you're going through this."

"It's been eight weeks," Charlotte murmured, then hiccupped. "Do you think he'll ever wake up?"

"I don't know."

"The doctors don't know either. And he's just—he's just withering away. He's down almost thirty pounds. He's going to have such a hard time even if he does wake up. Physical therapy is going to be brutal. He's used to getting what he wants through his negotiating skills and his strategic mind and his ability to read other people. What's he going to be like when he has to learn how to walk again?"

"He's tough," Fenway said. "He'll figure out how to do what he needs to do."

"He's a tough negotiator," Charlotte said. "He's clueless when it comes to emotional work. And his business—if he wakes up and I've lost Ferris Energy, he'll be devastated. I don't want him to lose the will to live."

"He won't—" Fenway began, but her voice caught in her throat. She had been wrong about her father for the last twenty years. She'd thought he cared so much about his money and about his hatred toward Joanne that he was willing to let his daughter go hungry, to let her miss him at graduation and every important event in her life. And it had been her own mother who had redirected that ten thousand dollars every month, not toward feeding and clothing and housing her own daughter, but to somewhere else.

And he had to jump in front of a bullet for Fenway to see it.

"I'm scared too," she whispered, and the tears welled in her eyes.

She and Charlotte cried together for a moment.

Charlotte caught her breath first. "I got a letter from Sierra Madre Fuel. They're 'reevaluating their supply chain.'"

"Is there a chance it's just a routine letter? A chance for an audit? Maybe one of the salespeople can use it as an opportunity to expand their order."

Charlotte shook her head. "It didn't come from an auditor. It came from Archie Pendergrass himself. The CEO of Sierra Madre. We're supposed to respond by Wednesday."

Fenway let Charlotte go. "The day after tomorrow?"

"Yes." Charlotte got to her feet and walked behind the chair to stare out the door. "It's a ton of paperwork, and I've asked a couple of the vice presidents to delegate some of the research, and filling out the forms and things like that, but I'm almost positive that the embargoed oil issue will come up. I've asked the board to make it clear that we've fired everyone who was involved. But it went on right under Nate's nose for two years, and he didn't even notice."

"But the people he put in place for oversight were the same people who were in on the whole scam."

Charlotte shook her head. "I'm scared that won't be good enough for Sierra Madre."

"How important are they?"

"They're our biggest customer. Responsible for about fifteen percent of our revenues last year. If they leave, it'll hurt, but we could survive." Charlotte looked at the floor. "But I'm afraid their leaving will start a chain reaction. Archie is the one who recommended us as a customer to Transport Northwest. And if they follow Sierra Madre out the door— well, Ferris Energy will be in a bad spot." Charlotte turned to Fenway, who was still crouched next to the hospital bed. "That's why it's so important for us to have community involvement. Ferris Energy has a foundation, but the work we do—the Boys & Girls Clubs, the Estancia Food Bank—we have to increase the visibility of that work, so companies like Sierra Madre aren't looking for excuses to get another supplier."

Fenway nodded. "But you know your environmental record is weak. I know most of your customers don't support those causes, but they do care about environmental protests that disrupt their businesses. You could buy carbon offsets or donate money to the Dominguez Open Space Land Trust. That could go a long way toward making your customers aware that your efforts will keep the environmentalists off their backs."

"See?" Charlotte pointed at Fenway. "This is why we need you. You see the bigger picture. No one on the board wants to make any environmental donations at all."

Fenway smiled. "Funny, I expected you to call me cynical when I suggested donating to those organizations just to keep them off your customers' backs."

Charlotte frowned. "Well, it's not like I was going to take out an ad saying that." She folded her arms. "Besides, unless I'm mistaken, those are a couple of your favorite charities."

"Maybe." Fenway gripped the chair and hoisted herself to her feet. "But if anyone wants to look at my taxes, they'll be able to see that my donations and my words—assuming I get in front of the press—are pretty consistent."

"Can I have our P.R. team call you tomorrow? Maybe we can call a press conference?"

"You know," Fenway said slowly, "Ferris Energy owns about sixteen acres of undeveloped land next to the refinery on the other side of Ocean Highway from the beach."

"How do you know that?"

Fenway rolled her eyes. "Uh—because I followed Dad in the news back in Seattle. Ferris Energy has been fighting environmental groups for years about developing that open space. Donating that acreage to Dominguez Land Trust would be newsworthy—we could probably get reporters to show up to a press conference."

"By tomorrow?"

Fenway shrugged. "I guess there's a lot of legal stuff that would take a lot more than twelve hours to wrangle."

"Let me see what we can do," Charlotte said. "I might be able to see if we can at least get the ball rolling so we have something to announce."

"Okay." Fenway cleared her throat. "I—um, I was planning to read to Dad tonight."

"Do you mind if I sit here too?"

"You're welcome to stay." Fenway pulled out the leather-bound *Gulliver's Travels* from her purse. She found her bookmark, sat on the bench at the side of the room, and, while Charlotte leaned back in the chair by the side of the bed, started to read.

Fenway left the hospital with Charlotte a few minutes past eight. They were both silent out to the parking lot and bade each other cursory goodbyes. Fenway's throat was a little sore from reading, but it had felt good to get away from the investigation for a while. Not exactly *good* —but it was where she needed to be.

She unlocked her car, and her phone rang. It was Dez.

Crap. She hadn't told her father that the whole team was pulling for his recovery. She'd do it tomorrow.

"Hey, Dez."

"Hey, Fenway. I thought you might want to hear the results of my research."

"Uh—sure. As long as it doesn't piss off Mayor Klein even more."

Dez started giggling.

"What the hell are you laughing at, Dez? Is my frustration funny to you?"

"You need to tell the mayor to go fuck himself."

Fenway got into the Accord and closed the door. "What? Why?"

"Because," Dez said, "Tonnick Subaru sold exactly one baby-blue Crosstrek on Friday."

"To whom?"

"Catherine Klein."

PART THREE
TUESDAY

CHAPTER NINE

Fenway poured the bold, dark coffee into the large white porcelain mug as she squinted against the harsh morning light. She emptied the last of the cream into it and sipped without stirring. It was half past eight, but she could barely keep her eyes open. She'd slept badly.

McVie had texted around nine thirty last night—just when Fenway was getting home from the hospital—that he wouldn't make it over. Too much to do.

She noticed the phone on the counter next to the coffeemaker. *Ugh.* She hadn't plugged it in the night before, and now the battery was below twenty percent.

She carried the phone over to the kitchen table and plugged it in. Would it charge enough before she left to be worth it? Yawning widely, she poured cereal and milk into a bowl, then ate as she pulled up messages from the night before.

MCVIE: *sorry i wont make it over tonite*
STEVENSON: *Will Amy be okay?*
MCVIE: *shes worried and she thinks shes about 2b arrestd*
STEVENSON: *Are you okay?*

MCVIE: *dont worry abt me*
STEVENSON: *Is Megan there?*
MCVIE: *shes ok too — just concerned*
MCVIE: *something doesnt feel right*
STEVENSON: *Are you sure you can't come over when you're done?*
MCVIE: *i dont want 2 put u in awk situation*
MCVIE: *its weird enough that my ex is now my client*
MCVIE: *u shouldnt give me details abt the case*
MCVIE: *and i dont want to ask*

And that was the last she'd heard from him.

She put the phone down and paced around her small apartment. She was busy with the case and with figuring out what she would say at the press conference for Ferris Energy.

As much as she hated to admit it, it was a good thing that McVie hadn't come over. It had given her time to learn more about oil companies' land use rights and customer contracts, about Ferris Energy's assets, the price of used supertankers, and the cost of refinery maintenance. She wrote and deleted paragraphs about Ferris Energy's commitment to the environment before going to bed at midnight.

Then she'd tossed and turned for another hour. Every fifteen or twenty minutes, she thought she heard the phone ding with Craig texting her, maybe changing his mind about coming over that night. She'd finally fallen into a fitful sleep around two in the morning, only to be wakened by her stomach growling at two thirty.

She'd completely forgotten about dinner. And that wasn't like her at all. She'd gotten up and eaten a frozen pasta entrée, playing a game on her phone while it cooked in the microwave. She felt a little queasy after she ate, but she got into bed anyway—and had gone to sleep for all of three hours.

Now she was about to go to work, waiting for her phone to charge and holding her mug of coffee.

She groaned. She should have put her coffee in the travel mug. It was going to be one of those days, and she had way too much to do. She had to be on top of her game.

The phone rang as she was pouring the coffee from the porcelain mug to the travel mug, and she spilled a little on the counter. Setting the coffee down, she looked at the screen: *McVie Investigations*. She grabbed the phone and pushed ANSWER.

"Hello?"

"Hi, Fenway, it's Piper."

Disappointment flooded over Fenway. Why was she hung up on this? She knew McVie wouldn't go back to Amy. She knew Amy was much more worried about an impending arrest than any sort of rekindling of their romance. She knew McVie was there mostly for the mental health of their daughter.

"Hi, Piper," Fenway said with as much enthusiasm as she could.

Piper paused. "Everything okay? You don't sound great."

"Remind me not to eat alfredo sauce after midnight ever again."

Piper laughed as Fenway's stomach lurched. "So I haven't found out anything about Eddie's death yet."

"Eddie?"

Piper hesitated. "You know, Eddie Drake, your mother's boyfriend from 1985? Died in February 1986?"

Fenway's mental tracks shifted and clicked into place. "You called, and I immediately assumed it was information about the murder case."

"Rough night?" asked Piper.

"I sat with my dad again."

"Oh." A pause. "I'm sorry."

"It wasn't anything worse than usual. Just—it's starting to hit Charlotte hard. That he might not come out of it. Or he'll really struggle when he does come out of it. And she's putting a lot of pressure on herself to save the company."

"And you're putting pressure on yourself too."

Fenway stopped pacing and considered this for a moment. "I guess."

"Well, as I was saying, I didn't find out any more info on Eddie Drake —in fact, you might have more luck with that, since you've got access to the police files now. It'll save you a couple of billable hours, too."

"So is there any update at all?"

"I found your—uh, your grandmother, Samara's mother."

Fenway's knees felt weak, and she grasped the counter for support. "My grandmother?"

"Her name is Nell Godwin, née Joliboix."

"Joliboix?"

"With a silent X on the end. Don't ask me to spell it. She was born in New Orleans. She's eighty-one."

"Oh."

"I also found your grandfather's obituary. Maurice Godwin. Worked at BBL Printing for almost forty years. Died about eight years ago of a stroke. Nell moved from their house into a retirement home in Los Angeles about a year after that."

Eight years ago. That would have been the time that Fenway was getting her BSN from Western Washington University. She wondered if her mom had known that Maurice Godwin had passed away. Her mother had been in a better financial position by then. If she'd found out, she might have gone to the funeral. Maybe. If she'd even been able to show up safely. Did Fenway's grandparents even know that Samara had still been alive?

"She's at a retirement home?" Fenway asked.

"Yes. I've got the phone number. I'll text it to you. Rolling Meadows. On La Cienega."

"Is she—is she okay?"

"I can't work that fast, Fenway. Not without access to a police database, anyway. There are patient confidentiality agreements. But I'll text you the phone number. Maybe you can call her."

Fear gripped Fenway. Call her grandmother? What in the world would she say? "Thanks, Piper," she squeaked out. "I'll tell Craig you need a big raise."

They said their goodbyes, and Fenway screwed the lid onto the travel mug, put the phone in her purse, and walked out the door.

She didn't expect the brightness of the January sun after the overcast of the day before, and as she fumbled through her purse to get her sunglasses, she felt hungover even though she hadn't had anything to drink. She drove to the office in a daze, needing a honk from the car behind her at a green light between the freeway exit and the downtown parking garage.

She stumbled through the door to the coroner's suite a few minutes before nine, holding her traveler mug in one hand and her purse in the other. Sarah was concentrating hard on her screen, but Dez popped her head up and rushed over with a short sheaf of papers in her hand.

"Okay," Dez said, "after you talked through the potential scenarios with Amy, and after I reviewed the notes you had from that law office where Sarah used to work, I decided I needed to do some more digging." She handed Fenway the short stack of papers.

"What's this?"

"These," Dez said, "are the court filings where Rick Tonnick was named as a defendant. If we're opening up the suspect list beyond Amy, we need to explore other avenues."

"Even if we come back to Amy," Fenway said, "the defense is going to want to see that we did our due diligence."

"Exactly," Dez said. "And I don't have another good explanation as to why Amy's car was in the parking garage if Amy wasn't jamming a pillow over her husband's face, but I bet the defense will have one by the time we go to trial."

"So what do we have?"

"A few lawsuits regarding breach of contract over some extended warranties that customers say they never agreed to. I've got Sarah tracking down the current addresses of the plaintiffs. Although she's spending time right now on"—Dez pulled out a sheet from the middle of the pile—"this one."

Fenway looked at the sheet, California form CH-100, REQUEST FOR CIVIL HARASSMENT RESTRAINING ORDER. Richard Wayne Tonnick was listed under PERSON FROM WHOM PROTECTION IS SOUGHT. The name under PERSON SEEKING PROTECTION was redacted.

"This must have been serious," Fenway said.

"Maybe," Dez said. "Sometimes these are misused in divorce cases. And Tonnick *had* just gotten divorced. But the timeline matches more with a wrongful death lawsuit from two years ago."

"So, in this hypothetical, are you thinking that Tonnick kept violating the restraining order?"

"Maybe. A restraining order doesn't come with guaranteed enforcement."

"So the complainant may have decided to take things into her own hands."

"That's what I thought, too." Dez pulled out several other forms. "Now, about the lawsuit itself. Ishikawa represented Tonnick in a negligence case regarding airbag safety recalls. Resulted in three accidents and six deaths."

"Right."

"The plaintiffs won, so that reduces any of their motives—"

"No, no," Fenway said, shaking her head. "The jury did find for the plaintiff, but the amount was considerably less than what they were asking for. Barely covered the medical bills."

Dez nodded. "Then it's worth looking into the three families," she said. "The lawsuit was brought years ago, and the trial ended in April."

"About when I got here."

"Right." She pointed to the top page. "This one: a fifty-six-year-old high school teacher. Her husband and adult children brought the suit, but her husband passed away during the trial. I'm looking into what he died of."

"Hmm. Maybe the adult children did something? To the guy responsible, in their eyes, for killing both their parents?"

Dez shook her head. "It's possible, but the children both live out of the area. Andrew Benedict, 26, lives in San Jose. Software engineer. Chloe Benedict, 29, lives in Vegas, works in IT at one of the airlines out of McCarran. No spouse listed for either one. I can call them today, see if they've been traveling."

"Estancia is only a four-hour drive from San Jose."

"Point taken. Okay—next, a family of four killed. The sister of the mother killed in the accident brought the claim forward. But she lives in Boston."

"Harder to kill someone from across the country, for sure."

"Right. The last victim was a mechanical engineer who worked at a firm downtown. She was a local—I think her family is still here. I think she's the one who—" Dez scanned the form again. "Yes, she's the one who was pregnant."

Fenway winced. "And the families got—what, seven hundred thousand each?"

"A little over that," Dez said.

"After lawyers' fees, that would be a little under half a million."

Dez snapped her fingers. "I remember something being in the paper back in the spring—how a local man had sued someone for his wife's wrongful death, but the whole settlement was taken by the health insurance company who covered the treatment of the woman and fetus after the accident. He didn't even have enough left over for funeral expenses."

Fenway shook her head. "That's sounds like what happened here."

Dez shrugged. "So it's possible that we're looking at the killer in one of these pages."

"We still have to explain how Amy's car got in that parking garage."

Dez nodded. "I was able to track down Judge Miller last night and get her to sign the warrant for the Phillips-Holsen to give us video footage from Friday night. Right now, we have an eyewitness who saw flirting, a new Subaru in the mayor's wife's name, and a hotel reservation in the name of Frederick Ginn. That's not even enough for reasonable doubt."

"Okay," Fenway nodded. "I'll make you a deal. We'll follow these other leads today, and if we come across any other evidence that points Amy's way, we'll talk to ADA Pondicherry and see what he wants to do."

Dez was silent.

Fenway took a step back. "You've already done it."

Dez gave a small nod. "I met with him an hour ago. He agrees that the evidence is circumstantial, but he says that unless we come up with something else compelling enough to cast doubt on Amy's involvement by the end of the day, he'll be asking us to arrest her for murder."

"He thinks he can convict on what they have?"

"The evidence of cheating, the timing of the death, and the video footage of Amy's car? I didn't ask about trial, but he's sure he can get a grand jury to indict, given that she doesn't have an alibi."

Fenway set her jaw. "I guess we have our work cut out for us, then."

Sergeant Mark Trevino walked into the office, greeted Sarah with a wave, and came over to Dez and Fenway.

"No luck with the forensics yet?"

Mark shook his head. "They're still swamped. They say Thursday, but I think that's wishful thinking. Kav and Melissa are both doing all kinds of fingerprint work on the meth lab near Lake Serenity that they raided over the weekend."

"They know this is a murder investigation, right?"

Mark shrugged. "Half a dozen people have died of meth overdoses in the last two weeks. That's more of a public health crisis than some rich guy getting asphyxiated because he couldn't keep it in his pants."

"Save your soapboxing, I get it." Fenway said. "Okay, fine. Who wants to interview the mayor's wife?"

"Let's see if her car is on that recording first," Dez said. "And I think a political football like that is above both of our pay grades."

"You're abandoning me, is what you're saying," Fenway said.

Dez looked at Mark, who grinned. She turned back to Fenway. "Yes. That's exactly what I'm saying."

"Fine," Fenway said, rolling her eyes. "I'll take the bomb. You divide the litigants. Call the two adult children. See if they have alibis for Sunday evening and night."

She pulled off the top paper. "And this one—the pregnant woman." She read the sheet. "Katrina Perriman. Husband brought the suit against Tonnick Auto Group."

"They have any other kids?" Mark asked.

"I don't know," Dez said. "We can look into it, though." She went to her desk, then returned with a folder. "Your warrant, my liege," she said.

"Great," Fenway said. "I can't wait to get the evidence so I can interview the mayor's wife. Do they sell body armor at the hardware store on Second Street?"

Mark chuckled. "The Tractor Supply over on 326 might stock beekeeping equipment. That's close."

Fenway looked longingly at her office chair. "I'm headed out, Sarah. See if you can make life really hard for Dez and Mark while I'm gone. And I'll get you a coffee today."

Sarah looked up and smirked. "I kind of preferred the unreasonable guilt," she said. "But a hot chai latte will work too."

Fenway left the building before she realized she'd left her travel mug, still over half full, on the counter in the suite. She muttered to herself all the way to the parking garage entrance, then walked past it to Java Jim's.

Charlotte was slumped on one of the overstuffed chairs, a coffee on the small short table next to her.

"Charlotte?"

"Hi, Fenway," she said, sitting up straight.

"Is something wrong?"

"I—I was just coming over to see you. I spoke with the chief counsel this morning."

Fenway took the overstuffed chair on the other side of the table. "That doesn't sound good."

"No. Now Sierra Madre is citing an ethical breach of contract. They're up for renewing their contract in April, but they're trying to get out of it now."

"What do the lawyers think?"

"The lawyers think we can beat the breach of contract suit. But that's not the problem. The problem is, unless they back out of it soon, the damage will be done. We have three other big customers whose agreements are up before April. If we're in the middle of litigation, they'll leave for sure."

"That's not a given, Charlotte."

"Well—maybe not, but without someone with the experience of your father, it's a lot more likely." Charlotte sighed. "Look, they don't want someone like me as the interim CEO. I don't know the business well enough. I know just enough to be dangerous to the board and just enough to lure the workers into a false sense of security."

"It's not like I know any more than you."

"No," Charlotte said, "and I'm not asking you to. But we've asked others to step in as interim CEO. No one who's qualified wants to take the chance that Nathaniel will wake up and come back, leaving them without a job."

"There's always the chief operating officer position."

"Everyone who'd be willing to settle for COO when Nate comes back is not qualified to be the interim CEO. We're basically in crisis mode right now, and we need someone to steer this ship."

"What about a recently retired energy CEO who's willing to step in just until things settle down?"

Charlotte shook her head. "We've tried. There are two kinds of retired CEOs: the ones who Nathaniel forced out and the ones who he simply pissed off."

Fenway was quiet for a moment. "Charlotte, I am totally up for a press conference if you want me to do it. But I don't have any time to devote to moving the land donation forward."

"I've already asked our legal team to look into it. The lawyers say we might be able to transfer it to our foundation today and then do an asset transfer, nonprofit to nonprofit. Better for our taxes. And we could make *that* announcement today." She sighed. "But I spoke with a couple of board members this morning. They don't think it's going to stop Sierra Madre from the breach of contract suit, and that means..." She trailed off, her eyes staring unfocused across the room.

"You'll have to sell the company," Fenway whispered.

Charlotte closed her eyes and nodded.

Fenway leaned back in her chair. "Dad will understand, Charlotte. He'll realize that you're in an impossible situation." She sighed. "Besides, you two have an insane amount of stock in the company, don't you? I mean, you're poised to make millions and millions of dollars out of this. It's not like you'll be thrown out on the street."

"No," Charlotte said. "And there's a trigger clause for that kind of thing too—a golden parachute of sorts." She shrugged. "Money's not the issue. It's that your dad built this company up over his whole life. It's his dream."

Fenway felt the familiar bite of annoyance. "He can have other dreams, Charlotte. He's run this business for, what? Thirty-five years? Maybe it's time for him to learn to paint. Or write another business book. Or, hell, work on some sort of project feeding the hungry or building up infrastructure in developing nations."

"When he's ready to walk away, that's different," Charlotte said, smoothing her blue-gray dress down over her legs. "He shouldn't be *forced* into retirement."

Fenway felt a catch in her throat, then coughed lightly. "My dad's not a young guy anymore. Maybe when he wakes up, after he's strong enough, you should travel the world. See all the sights. A proper vacation, like they do in Europe. Six weeks. Not Paris for a weekend on the heels of one of his business trips. Or maybe you could pick a pet project for Dad. There are a million things that you and he can do. Stressing out over the future of Ferris Energy isn't one of them."

"Okay," Charlotte said. "I get it. I know Nate wouldn't necessarily be angry with me if I had to sell the company. But if I don't do everything I can, if I don't exhaust every possibility, I'm going to hate myself. I'm going to feel guilty for the rest of my life. What if I had just tried a little harder? What if I had done just a little bit more?"

"Dad will understand."

They sat in silence for a moment, then Fenway stood up and ordered a large chai latte to go.

CHAPTER TEN

After saying her goodbyes to Charlotte and dropping the chai latte off to a grateful Sarah, Fenway drove to the Phillips-Holsen. She parked in the garage, mindful of the camera, and walked up the staircase to the back door, where she entered and wound around a short hallway to the security office. She knocked and opened the door.

A man with skin the color of terra cotta and a long black beard, his head wrapped in a burgundy turban, looked up from a row of screens with a bit of surprise in his eyes. "Can I help you?"

"I'm County Coroner Fenway Stevenson," she said. "I'm here to view security footage from Friday night."

"I'm sorry," the man said. "I'd like to cooperate, but our corporate policy—"

"I have the warrant right here," Fenway said, holding the signed paper up.

He stood up from his chair. "May I examine the warrant, please?" He held his hand out. Fenway showed him the paper but kept her hand on it.

"I'm sorry," he said. "I'll need to check with—"

"No," Fenway said firmly. "You actually don't need to check with anyone. The warrant says you'll provide me with those recordings, and you'll do it now."

The man bowed slightly. "Of course." He sat back down, then rolled his chair to a different bank of monitors. "Friday night? What time?"

Fenway put the warrant back in the folder and looked at the sticky note that Dez had written with Frederick Ginn's check-in time and the Subaru temporary license plate number. "Let's start about nine o'clock," she said. "I'd like to see the footage from the parking garage."

He typed rapidly at a computer keyboard, and the image of the parking garage appeared on the large screen.

"Thank you," she said. "Should I ask you to fast-forward it, or is there a way for me to do it without messing everything up?"

"This dial," the man said, pushing a video controller in front of her.

She didn't have to wait long. She saw a Subaru Crosstrek whose temporary license plate had the same numbers as the ones in the DMV database for Catherine Klein. She double-checked what Dez had written on the sticky note.

Crap. Now she *had* to interview the mayor's wife.

Just like the Mustang convertible had passed without the driver ever appearing on screen, the same was true of the Crosstrek driver. She rewound to the car passing in front of the camera, but the glare from the ceiling lights was angling off the car, making it impossible to be sure that the woman driving was Catherine Klein. Same dark hair as Catherine had, and the woman was white.

Fenway fast-forwarded until the Crosstrek left again. It was 12:27 A.M. Rick Tonnick hadn't been a wham-bam-thank-you-ma'am lover, but neither was he a fan of cuddling all night. She rewound, slower this time, and a woman cut in front of the camera at 12:22 A.M. Fenway paused, advancing one frame at a time, until Catherine Klein's face was clear. It was a three-quarters profile, but it was enough. Fenway took her phone out and quickly snapped a picture of the screen, the date and time clearly visible.

She figured she was done, but she let it play a little longer. About twenty minutes later, Rick Tonnick walked in front of the camera as well, his gym bag in hand. She raised her phone and took a picture of that too.

"I'm going to need this footage forwarded to the same place where your manager forwarded Sunday night's footage."

"My manager?" the man asked, confusion in his eyes.

"The property manager. Brianne?"

"Brianna?"

"Right, Brianna."

The man wrote a note on a slip of paper and handed it to Fenway. It contained a file name and two timestamps. "Brianna Harlow is down the hall, second door on the right. Give this to her along with whatever email you have. I don't have access to anything like that in here, but she can get you whatever you need."

Fenway nodded. "Thank you."

The man grunted. "Don't mention it."

Fenway let herself out of the video room and followed the directions the man had given. She knocked on the property manager's office door and opened it.

Brianna was behind the computer where Dez and Fenway had viewed the footage the day before. She looked up, startled. "Coroner Stevenson? What can I do for you? Did you forget something?"

"I actually needed more footage," Fenway said. "I need the parking garage recording from Friday night."

"Well, as you know, Miss Steven—"

"Way ahead of you," Fenway said, holding up the warrant. "And throw in the recording of the hotel lobby with the same timestamps."

"Did you say Friday night?"

"I did," Fenway said.

Confusion bloomed on Brianna Harlow's face. "What do you, uh, need the Friday video for?"

Fenway cocked her head and smiled at Brianna. She wondered if there was something on the Friday recording the property manager didn't want Fenway to see. "Evidence," Fenway said. "Mr. Tonnick was here that night too."

Brianna nodded. "Same email address as yesterday?"

"That's right."

"I'll get right on that."

"Thanks." Fenway began to turn toward the door, then stopped. "Were you working here on Friday?"

"Oh—uh, no. I took Friday off. Had a Vegas weekend with a friend from college."

Fenway nodded. "You said your shift started at six on Monday morning. So—you must have gotten back late Sunday night."

"Oh—no, I actually took the first plane back Monday morning. That's why I looked so tired yesterday—I came straight here. I'm ashamed to say I have a hard time saying no to a ten-dollar blackjack table."

"Did you win anything?"

"I look at it as a night of entertainment," Brianna said. "I'll spend two hundred dollars on tickets to a musical down in L.A., and another two or three hundred on a tank of gas, a hotel room, a nice dinner, a few cocktails. Even a concert over at the Event Center will be a couple hundred bucks. I figure if I lose three or four hundred dollars playing blackjack, I'm about even on a night of entertainment. And frankly, I'd rather sit at a blackjack table than take in another *Phantom of the Opera* rip-off."

Fenway nodded. "So you left when? Thursday evening?"

"Right. And I flew back Monday morning. The Coastal Airways 4:15 nonstop. Landed just before five."

"Wow, that's early. You didn't have any bags to check?"

"Not for three days. I pack pretty light." She shifted in her seat. "Um, why all these questions about my whereabouts? I didn't even know the guy who was killed."

Fenway nodded thoughtfully. "I guess it's sort of in my nature when I'm doing these investigations. In this case, though, it's tough to get ahold of anyone who's seen Mr. Tonnick—or Mr. Ginn, I suppose except for entering and leaving the hotel. Which he did quite a lot."

"Well," Brianna said, "we're a high-end hotel. Our customers have a right to privacy. They expect it."

"But this is a murder investigation."

"And we're cooperating as much as we can," Brianna said. "You'll notice I haven't talked about involving any lawyers or bringing corporate leadership into the conversation. But if you want to interview our staff as to who they've seen in the halls, we might have to have a separate warrant for that."

Fenway opened her mouth to argue—but paused. It occurred to her that Brianna had something to hide about the hotel's services. Did the Phillips-Holsen not only provide a hush-hush location for trysts but perhaps deliver the evening's entertainment for certain clients as well? Her mind first went to high-end prostitutes, but there were many illicit services the posh hotel might connect the right clients to. She'd have to check with a few of the deputies in the sheriff's department who worked vice. Maybe Gretchen Donnelly. Maybe she could ask McVie too.

But arguing wouldn't be constructive. So instead: "Did you ever meet Mr. Ginn in the course of your duties here?"

"I don't think so."

"Not once?"

"Well," Brianna said, "he's a frequent guest. So it's possible, I suppose. But certainly not that I remember."

"How have you worked here for so long and never talked to him?"

She shrugged. "I usually work the day shift. From everything you've told me, he checks in after I go home and leaves before I come in. I wouldn't recognize him."

"But you know he's an important client."

"I know he's been staying here for longer than I've worked here, but you should ask Luz. She works the night shift. She'd be here when he checks in."

"I see."

Fenway waited for Brianna to continue. Instead, the property manager smiled, showing her brilliantly white teeth. "Will that be all?"

Fenway pulled the phone out of her purse. "How about this woman?" Fenway raised the phone to show Brianna the photo of Catherine Klein.

Brianna's face was blank. "She looks familiar, but I can't say for sure if I've seen her in the hotel."

Fenway put her phone back in her purse and took the folder with the warrant. "Okay, that'll be it for now. I really appreciate your help."

"You're welcome. Any time."

"You have a good rest of your day."

Fenway walked out of the office and turned to go out the back entrance. She sighed.

Mayor Barry Klein was going to have a fit when Fenway called his wife for an interview. But she had to review the Sunday night footage again for the baby-blue Subaru. Or maybe for a Catherine Klein-shaped passenger in the Mustang. She had to know if Amy had lured Tonnick to his death with the mayor's wife.

Of course, maybe Tonnick had been promised a prostitute or drugs. Without the camera on the penthouse level, there was no way to tell for sure.

As much as she didn't like Amy, and as much as she hated what Amy had put Craig through, she didn't think Amy had killed him. There were too many moving parts. There were too many other opportunities to kill him and make it look like an accident—they lived together after all. This was the only guaranteed way to call attention to his massive infidelity—which only served to make Amy look guilty.

She didn't walk down the stairs to the garage where she'd parked but instead walked along the tiled footpath to Fourth Street. She needed to walk to think, to clear her head. Maybe she'd see if McVie was in his office, offering her words of comfort about only wanting to protect his daughter from everything that was going on.

McVie knew Amy better than Fenway did—a lot better than Fenway did—and Fenway realized that McVie knew Amy didn't do it. She might not be very good at monogamy, but that didn't mean she killed her husband.

But the last thing Fenway needed right now was a distraction from the case. She should have figured out her feelings about McVie by now. She didn't think she was in love with him—not yet, anyway—but this wasn't helping. If Amy had done it, she needed to have a clear theory to provide to ADA Pondicherry. Or at least be able to offer a semi-coherent narrative.

She looked at the clock on her phone. Ten forty-five.

Oh, there was one interview she hadn't remembered to hand off—Noreen Tonnick. She looked around. She'd walked all the way to First Street, and Hair of the Dog Software was just four blocks east, closer to the freeway.

Roughly ten minutes to come up with some questions. She could do this.

Really, any reason to postpone calling the mayor's wife was good enough for her.

She pulled the door open to the full-block building of Hair of the Dog Software and was immediately hit by a sonic wall of death metal. The lobby was large, all dark sharp edges and bright reds. Artwork, all splotches of paint and untethered shapes, dotted the walls, hung at aggressive angles. One wall was a massive video screen playing a first-person shooter heavy on the blood and mayhem.

The alabaster-skinned receptionist had delicate features and a completely shaved head and wore a Darkness T-shirt and large black plastic gauges in her earlobes.

"Can I help you?" The receptionist's voice was thick with disgust, and she sneered at Fenway, who was reminded of the documentaries she'd flipped past on the white supremacist movement. She carried her identification badge in her purse, and this was perhaps the first time she'd felt like digging it out. She showed her ID to the receptionist, who snickered.

"I'm here to talk with Noreen Tonnick," Fenway said, trying to keep her voice calm while still being heard over the music.

"I take it you don't have an appointment."

"No. Is she in today?" Fenway suddenly realized that it was more than likely that Noreen was taking a few days off after the murder.

"I'll let her know you're here."

The receptionist lifted a hand to indicate an uncomfortable-looking silver-and-rust-colored slab. Fenway stepped back toward it, stared at it for a moment, then touched her hand to the rusted section. It was dry. She stood anyway.

The music changed to a mid-1990s rap-rock song with aggressively sexual lyrics. Fenway looked around. She and the receptionist were the only ones in the large lobby. She smacked her lips together. Her mouth was dry, but there didn't seem to be a water cooler or a vending machine in the expansive lobby.

The door next to the receptionist desk opened, and an Asian woman, about fifty-five years old, a skull visibly tattooed on her neck, smiled at Fenway. "I can take you to Noreen, Officer."

Fenway didn't correct her, and she found herself staring at the woman's angular haircut, her salt-and-pepper hair pushed to the right side of her head and draping over her ear. The door to the lobby closed behind them, and it was suddenly quiet. A sense of relief washed over Fenway.

The Asian woman led Fenway up a metal staircase in the middle of the office space. Fenway found herself in a large loft area with floor-to-ceiling windows. Sunlight filtered through the clouds outside and dappled the gray concrete floor.

Fenway looked up. Exposed pipes flowed from one side of the space to the other; a few pipes snaked down past the loft to the ground floor. Everything that wasn't glass or concrete was painted black.

Fenway turned around and surveyed the office. The otherwise open floor plan had a set of perhaps fifteen small enclosed pods on the ground floor. She turned around and had to hurry to catch up to her tour guide.

In front of her, a glass-enclosed office stood with its door propped open. The woman inside looked to be in her late twenties or early thirties. Her hair, a jet-black, chin-length bob, was both professional and slightly edgy. She wore a tailored business suit in olive green. The desk in front of her was glass, as was the wall behind her, giving the illusion that the office was open to the outside.

The woman who had led Fenway here stepped to the side, and Fenway walked in.

"Onyx said you're with the police?"

"I'm the county coroner," Fenway said. "You're Noreen Tonnick?"

"Oh, yes," she said. "You spoke with my brother yesterday."

She nodded. "I did. Onyx? That's the name of your receptionist? With the shaved head?"

"It is." Noreen cocked her head at Fenway. "I assume you have similar questions for me as you did for Grant. Where was I on Sunday night?

How much am I getting from his vast fortune? How much do I hate his latest wife?"

"We can start with those, sure."

"All right." Noreen smiled and leaned back. The chair was bright white and had a mesh back, almost invisible as the sunlight dappled the corner office. "Sunday night—I went to dinner with a girl from Paso Querido. We went to Quixotic, that Spanish restaurant on Santa Anita Street in P.Q. Do you know it?"

"I've heard of it. I haven't eaten there."

"I had the paella; my dinner companion had the lamb. We had some excellent conversation. We were at the restaurant until at least ten o'clock, probably later. I stayed over at her place. She's in the luxury apartments on Rio Mundo, about three blocks off the freeway."

"So you were there until..."

"Monday morning. I believe I woke about five thirty so I could make it to my Pilates class at seven and then to the office by eight thirty."

"This girl you stayed with—what's her name?"

"Hetty."

"Hetty. Does she have a last name?" And a time travel device from the 1950s?

Noreen smiled and batted her eyes at Fenway. "I'm sorry to say, I didn't get her last name. I have her phone number, however. And her Snapchat."

Fenway nodded. After the death metal assault in the lobby, talking with Noreen seemed like a walk in the park. "That's good—I don't need a last name, just a corroborating story."

Noreen's face fell. Perhaps she was disappointed that Fenway didn't register shock when Noreen said she didn't get her lover's last name. "Between roughly two o'clock and three thirty in the morning, were you both asleep or were you both awake?"

Noreen blinked. "We weren't really paying attention to the clock, to be honest, Coroner."

"Understood," Fenway said. "Let's move on to the next question." She looked up at Noreen and waited.

Color rose to Noreen's cheeks. "I'm sorry—you'll have to jog my memory."

"I believe the question you thought I would ask is how much you're getting according to Rick Tonnick's will."

"Right." Noreen cleared her throat. "I believe I will receive one million dollars, as well as what amounts to a twelve-and-a-half percent share of annual profits of the Tonnick Auto Group."

"Do you know approximately how much that is?"

Noreen laughed. "It's more than a million dollars a year, I'll tell you that much." She ran her fingernails over the glass tabletop, both hands, almost as if she were a cat scratching on carpet. "My father set us up pretty good. Even if most of it's going to that skank."

"That skank? Ah—that would answer the third question."

Noreen nodded. "She and my father were hooking up a long time ago. Definitely before he divorced Victoria. Hell, maybe even before Brigette dumped him."

"Brigette was the third wife?"

"Right. She cheated on *him*. With my calculus teacher. They moved to Boise as soon as the ink was dry on the divorce papers." She snickered. "At least he didn't have to pay alimony for very long."

"So you and Grant are brother and sister?"

"Half-siblings. Grant came from Lucy—that's Dad's first wife—and my mom was Aphra."

"Second wife?"

"Actually, mistress during the second wife. She kept me. They lived together for about three years after the second wife kicked him out." She sighed. "Would have been better for her if she'd said yes one of the ten times he asked."

"Were you angry at all about the way he treated your mother?"

She snickered. "No. She's a horrible person. She's gorgeous, always has been. But I don't blame him for leaving her—she's a manipulative little bitch."

Fenway nodded.

Noreen smiled with her mouth but not her eyes. "And Amy was almost as manipulative as my mother was. They have a lot in common—I definitely could see what Dad saw in her. I wasn't surprised that most of his fortune goes to her—twenty-five percent of the profits, the houses, the tens of millions in liquid assets. He changed his will in a similar way whenever he got married."

"You seem pretty successful here."

"Video games can be big business, but a lot of companies don't know how to have operational efficiencies," she said. "I've got my MBA from USC, and I know what I'm doing. Some of these companies are nothing more than two bros playing Grand Theft Auto, smoking a bowl and thinking they'll get rich off some awesome video game idea one of them had the last time they took mushrooms."

"That's a very 1970s way of looking at things."

"Everything old is new again," Noreen said.

"So you don't like Amy. And all the money is quite a motive. Do you think she could have had anything to do with his death?"

"Only if she did it by accident."

"Why do you say that?"

"That girl lives in the moment. Everything is done without consideration for how it's going to affect anything or anyone beyond tomorrow morning. That's why she gets so much play. When Dad goes on a business trip, it's like it doesn't even matter that she's married. I bet she doesn't even think of it as infidelity."

Fenway hesitated. "Are you saying that she's cheating on your father too?"

Noreen rolled her eyes. "Of course she is. With Tommy, for one."

"Tommy?" Fenway cocked her head. "Tommy Kinsella? Your father's second-in-command? The one who's getting the biggest chunk of the business?"

"The same." Noreen smirked. "There are a lot of things my dad would tolerate, or maybe look the other way. But he and Tommy—they go back. If he found Tommy sleeping with his wife? That would be the end of both of them." Noreen looked at Fenway out of the corner of her eye. "I mean metaphorically. And financially. Dad would have divorced Amy on the spot, and he would have donated Tommy's portion of the business to charity or something. Probably a charity Tommy really hates, just to get under his skin."

Fenway chuckled. "Did your father have any enemies?"

"Probably some of the customers who got a raw deal from his car sales," Noreen said. "Oh—and there were those people who sued him for not performing the safety recall stuff. There were a few people who died. I bet they have families who wouldn't mind my father's head on a stick."

Fenway paused. "You know, I've talked to a lot of people who knew your father and who were knowledgeable about the safety recall. Why did he do it? I heard he just didn't want to pay the mechanics?"

"He was going through his third expensive divorce," Noreen said. "He doesn't know I know this, but he thought, since his third wife was the one who cheated, that he wasn't going to have to pay alimony. But California is a no-fault state, and my father—who was intelligent in many ways, especially when it comes to selling you a Ford or a Subaru—was very dumb about other things. The law applying to him, for example. If a law didn't make sense to him—like no-fault divorce—he just thought it didn't apply."

"But he was rich enough to cover it all, wasn't he?"

Noreen chuckled. "There's a big difference between being able to pay and agreeing to pay. He moved most of his liquid assets into offshore accounts—and that includes assets from his car dealerships. But then the safety recall came. He didn't have the cash on hand to pay for the equipment he needed for the recall work. He couldn't even send the mechanics to training."

"Wouldn't he get reimbursed from the manufacturer?"

"Eventually—but he couldn't front the money. With all his dealerships, we're talking five million dollars. To the courts, he looked broke, so he didn't have to pay much alimony. Unfortunately, to the banks, he looked broke, too. He couldn't even get a line of credit."

"He didn't just send the customers to a different dealership? One where they could do the recall service?"

Noreen shook her head. "Stubborn son of a bitch couldn't look weak. So he took the recalled cars in, kept them overnight, had them detailed, and gave them back the next day. To be honest, he was lucky so few people died. It could have been much worse."

"I see." Fenway had more questions. How did the manufacturer react? Did the other cars ever get fixed? But Noreen looked at her watch.

"Oh—I'm sorry," she said. "I've got an 11:30 meeting. I hate to rush you out—but did you get all the information you needed?"

"For now." Fenway nodded. "I may have more questions later."

"I'll be here."

Fenway cleared her throat. "Any particular reason you're not taking time off for funeral preparation or anything like that?"

Noreen gave Fenway a tight smile. "Probably because I'm a cold, heartless bitch who hated everything about my father. And if I had to hang around my house and think about what a horrible person I am for not feeling an ounce of sadness, I'd probably go insane."

Fenway nodded and stood up. "Thanks for meeting with me on such short notice."

"Don't worry about it. January is the slowest month in video game land. We had a killer—uh, I mean, an excellent December. So I'm happy to meet with you."

The receptionist appeared as if by magic at the door to Noreen's office. "I can show you out, ma'am."

CHAPTER ELEVEN

Fenway began to walk the ten blocks back to the Phillips-Holsen where her car was parked. The morning was threatening to turn cloudy and cold again, and a slight smell of ozone was in the air, as if a lightning storm was imminent.

So Tommy Kinsella had not only inherited a huge chunk of a very successful business, but he was also sleeping with the dead man's wife.

Fenway stopped and closed her eyes and tried to remember if anything was visible through the Mustang convertible's windshield. She was almost positive that it had been a woman driving. She wasn't sure if anyone was in the passenger seat. But it was possible that the killer was Tommy Kinsella, not Amy McVie. Maybe Tommy and Amy and had worked together with someone to lure Tonnick to the hotel. Maybe Tommy had left Amy asleep at his house, then made off with Amy's car and killed Rick Tonnick himself. With Tonnick out of the way, he'd get the money and the girl.

She opened her eyes. Divide and conquer indeed—Fenway was getting better at delegating. She took her phone out of her purse while she walked and dialed Dez's number. It went to voicemail. She dialed Mark, too, and again, it went to voicemail.

Huh. If they were talking with the widower of Katrina Perriman and not picking up their phones, either it was going really well or really poorly.

She called the Tonnick Auto Group main office line, and the operator transferred her.

The line picked up. "Thomas Kinsella's office, this is Vivian." Vivian had a smoker's voice, but she sounded crisp and efficient nevertheless. She didn't sound like the kind of person who had ever referred to him as Tommy.

"Hi, Vivian. This is County Coroner Fenway Stevenson. I have some questions for Mr. Kinsella regarding the passing of Mr. Tonnick. Is he in the office today?"

Vivian sniffed. "He is. Wants to put on a brave face for the employees, I suppose." There was the sound of fingernails clicking on a computer keyboard. "He's got about fifteen minutes at noon, if you're available."

"Noon? Not too close to lunch time?"

Vivian clicked her tongue. "It won't be today, I don't think." She paused.

Fenway let the pause stay for a beat, then pressed. "Is there something you wanted to tell me?"

"Well—it's just that Mr. Kinsella isn't his usual self today."

"I understand. As the coroner, I talk to a lot of people in the grieving process."

"Very well. Please check in and get a visitor's badge at the front desk. They'll let me know you're here."

As Fenway continued to walk toward the Phillips-Holsen, she turned everything around in her mind. She'd been in a few corner offices and interviewed many people who were the heads of their own businesses—both Grant and Noreen Tonnick, Gordon Knapp at the law firm, and now Tommy Kinsella. It made sense that Tonnick would keep company with so many other people of his same status, but Fenway wondered if the lens she was looking through was blinding her to other possibilities.

She got to the parking garage and drove her Accord out of the lot. Heading to the big purple office building where the dealership officially had its headquarters, Fenway searched for a radio station to brighten her mood, but every station played a commercial. She even heard an ad for Tonnick Ford.

She turned it to the classical station for some relief from the advertising, but the lilting sounds of Mozart were annoying rather than uplifting, and she turned the radio off, driving the last six blocks in silence.

She sat idling her car in a visitor's space in the expansive parking lot, the only Honda in a sea of Fords and Subarus, sprinkled here and there with the occasional Toyota or Lexus. Probably lots of company cars, and probably lots of incentives to be seen in a Tonnick dealership vehicle. The clock on her dashboard read 11:53. That was close enough not to be awkwardly early for a noon appointment. Any lobby that was free of death metal and white power tattoos would be an improvement.

Unlike the garish violet of the building, the lobby was clean and sterile, practically devoid of personality. A dozen or so bright blue plastic chairs dotted the right side of the room, and the low beige industrial carpeting dampened the sound, making the lobby oddly quiet. Three vending machines stood on one side of the lobby, making Fenway think that the interior designer was more inspired by a car dealership's waiting room than the lobbies of other successful companies.

She strode to the reception desk, where a short Black woman was seated, tapping on her computer keyboard. "Coroner Fenway Stevenson here to see Tommy—uh, Thomas Kinsella. Vivian asked me to get a visitor's badge?"

The woman smiled, never taking her eyes off the monitor, and handed Fenway a sign-in sheet on a clipboard and a lanyard with VISITOR printed on a laminated business card on the clip. "Sign and date," she said in a monotone. "Someone will be here shortly."

Fenway took a seat on one of the plastic chairs, and about five minutes later, a short, stocky woman in her late forties appeared at the opening to a hallway about ten feet from the reception desk. "Coroner Stevenson?" she said in the smoker's voice.

"That's me," Fenway said, rising. "You must be Vivian."

"Correct," Vivian said, hurrying along the corridor. "Thomas's last meeting ran a little late. I hope you still have time to get what you need."

"Did you know Mr. Tonnick?" Fenway said.

"Me? Not really." Vivian shook her head. "I'd met him a couple of times—he sometimes came into the office to get Thomas for a board meeting. At the company holiday parties, of course, and at all-hands meetings. He seemed like a nice man. Easy on the eyes, too."

"A real silver fox, huh?"

Vivian smiled as they turned a corner. "Some women in the office made the same observation."

"How long have you worked with Mr. Kinsella?"

"Oh—I've been his assistant now for about eight years."

"How long has he been waiting in the wings to take the mantle?" Fenway tried to make that statement sound as nonchalant as possible, but Vivian scoffed.

"I can assure you Thomas is quite happy where he is. He knows that Mr. Tonnick is under a good deal of pressure. Those frivolous lawsuits, all those women fawning all over him? Thomas doesn't want that life. I suppose he was happy with the confidence that Mr. Tonnick has shown in him, but Thomas was expecting Mr. Tonnick to be around for another twenty years."

Fenway nodded. Vivian had Tommy on a pedestal—and she probably believed every word that just came out of her mouth.

They arrived at a door reading *Thomas Kinsella, Corporate Vice President*, and Vivian opened it and went in first.

A desk on one side of the room in front of a closed door led Fenway to believe that this was Vivian's office, and she was the gatekeeper, allowing access to Tommy's door. The office was tidy and neat, bookshelves with the spines all aligned, and several well-cared-for plants in visually pleasing spaces around the room. Vivian strode to the door, knocked lightly, and announced, "Mr. Kinsella? Coroner Fenway Stevenson is here to see you." She opened the door and stepped back.

The office had none of the opulence of the other executive offices Fenway had visited in the last two days. The large desk dominating the center of the room was oak, but there were deep scratches in the front. A large monitor sat on the corner, and a tower sat on the floor next to the desk, wires exploding out of every possible port. It reminded Fenway of biology lab during her freshman year at Western Washington, when she had dissected the fetal pig and her initial incision made the intestines burst out.

Seven or eight bookcases lined the walls, some covering part of the window looking to the parking lot. Fenway could see her car. In contrast to the neat bookcases in the anteroom, these bookcases had manuals, business books, binders, and a few cardboard boxes shoved in haphazardly.

Stacks of papers were everywhere: on the desk, on the bookcases, on the floor. A few of the stacks had slid, fanning across the floor like a card deck at a casino before the dealer shuffles. Fenway tried but failed to read the titles of some of the reports in the stacks. This mess must be like nails on a chalkboard to Vivian—what had she been doing with him for eight years?

And then Fenway turned her gaze to the man behind the desk.

As messy as his office was, the man himself was put together nicely. Tommy was white, with just a kiss of tan to his skin, suggesting exposure to natural sun through work outside rather than the artifice of a tanning booth. A square jaw with a light shadow of stubble, broad shoulders under a tight tailored French-blue dress shirt, a haircut short on the sides but just long enough on top to showcase the natural wave in his dark brown hair. Large, enticing gray eyes—rimmed with just a hint of red.

She knew Tommy Kinsella was in his late thirties, but he could have passed for twenty-five. Amy was a beautiful woman—but this guy was way out of her league.

Fenway's mouth went dry. If Tommy had this effect on her, even surrounded by the filth he'd allowed his office to wallow in, he must have been irresistible to Amy.

Walking from the door to his desk, Fenway became hyperaware of the sway of her hips, of her pantsuit not pressed quite well enough, of her sensible black flats. She tamped those feelings down and nodded professionally. "Mr. Kinsella, my name is Fenway Stevenson."

"Hello." His voice had an undercurrent of sadness but was buttery and soft.

She blinked and cleared her throat. "I'm sorry to bother you at a time like this, but I'm afraid I have to ask you some questions about Mr. Tonnick."

Tommy nodded. "Of course." He rotated his chair and looked out the window across the parking lot. "I—I can't believe he's gone."

She couldn't bring herself to start with where he was on Sunday night. "How long have you worked for Mr. Tonnick?"

"Almost twenty years." The word caught in Tommy's throat, but he soldiered on. "He gave me my first job." He turned his head to look at Fenway and gave her a sad smile. Fenway had the urge to run her fingers through his hair. "He saw something in me that I didn't even see in myself. I was a screw-up. I barely graduated high school, and I just dicked around for about six months after that. Right after Christmas—I think I got drunk at Christmas dinner—my mom told me I had to move out. And Rick Tonnick hired me. Paid for me to go to mechanic school. I'd done pretty well in auto shop, so I figured, why not? And then, as I started getting better with customers, he started showing me the ropes of the business itself. He taught me about financing, about invoicing, then about compound interest, and then next thing I know, I'm taking night classes in business management."

Fenway nodded. "So the two of you were close?"

Tommy leaned forward, elbows on his knees, head in his hands. "I loved him like a father," he said. "We didn't do a whole lot on the weekends or anything—didn't go to bars together or have dinner. Maybe a couple of times a year. But when it came to the car business, he raised me here." Tommy wiped his eyes with the heel of his left hand. "Sorry. Sorry."

Fenway waited a moment for him to catch his breath, then leaned forward and softly said, "Mr. Kinsella, I'm sorry to do this, but I'm investigating his homicide, and I need to ask you some difficult questions."

"Ah, shit," Tommy said, his voice breaking again. "You know about me and Amy."

"I do."

"Look—I know it wasn't the right thing to do. I know they were married and all. I was here late one night a couple of weeks ago, trying to squeeze a few more sales out before Christmas. Rick and Amy had come back from their honeymoon, I don't know, maybe the week before?"

"So this was what—the second week in December?"

"That sounds right. A Tuesday. Maybe a Wednesday. And she was— well, dressed to impress, I guess you could say. But Rick wasn't here. He'd told her he was working late, but he wasn't."

"Do you know where he was?"

Tommy bobbed his head, neither a yes nor a no. "I mean, he didn't tell me where he was going, but I could guess what he was doing. You know they call him the Silver Fox around here?"

"That's what I've heard."

"Rick's never been too good at resisting temptation. He's got four ex-wives to prove it."

"I hear you're not great at it either, Tommy."

He shrugged. "What was I supposed to do? She knew what he was doing. I knew what he was doing. The next thing I know, we're kissing, and before you can say abracadabra, she's walking out of my apartment at midnight and I've gotta put condoms on my shopping list again."

Fenway leaned back. Now that he had opened his mouth, his considerable physical charms were less affecting. "Do you know where your boss preferred to meet the women he was hooking up with?"

Tommy shook his head. "I know it's some fancy hotel downtown. We have a Ritz-Carlton here? That's where Rick likes to stay in L.A. during the auto show."

Fenway folded her arms and put her chin in her hand, tapping on her lower lip. Was this an act? She couldn't tell. Maybe she should cut to the chase, see what he had to say. "And Mr. Kinsella, we're asking everyone this question: Where were you late Sunday night, early Monday morning, around two A.M.?"

Tommy's whole face scrunched up in thought.

"The truth, Tommy. That's a whole lot easier in my experience."

"I was at my place."

"Asleep?"

"Uh... well, not at two."

"Were you alone?"

"No."

The silence stretched between them.

Fenway shook her head. "Are you going to make me pull this out of you?"

"I was with Amy. She was with me. We were—we were being intimate."

"I see." Fenway paused. Amy had said she'd stayed at home, so their stories didn't align. "And you're sure this was at two?"

"Yes." Tommy nodded emphatically. "She called me late, maybe eleven thirty. She asked me to pick her up because her kid was home. She said if she started the engine of the Mustang in the driveway, it would wake her kid up."

"Was that a common request?"

"I'd picked her up before, if that's what you mean."

"But using the Mustang as an excuse?"

He shrugged. "Usually she liked driving. I think her daughter caught her last week."

"I see. So you picked her up—when? Midnight?"

"About then."

"And you got back home..."

"Twelve fifteen. Maybe a little later."

"And you were still up at two?"

"We—uh, yes, we were still up at two. I remember Amy looking at the clock when we were done and freaking out because it was past three. She thought for sure Rick was going to catch her. She talked about what excuse she would make. She was in yoga pants and this, uh, kind of sports bra top, and she figured she could just say she couldn't sleep and she went out for a run, and then they'd fight about whether it was safe to go running in the middle of the night and not where either of them were. She talked about it from the time she saw the clock at three fifteen until I dropped her off two blocks away at, I don't know, three forty-five? Maybe four?"

That's why Amy looked so exhausted on Monday. "And you never went to any hotel downtown?"

"No, I swear, we were at my house the whole time."

Fenway nodded. "Did you happen to see Amy's Mustang convertible when you picked her up?"

"I drove by her house and then picked her up a couple blocks away. Yeah, I saw it. Fire-engine red, with the Estancia High Concert Choir sticker, the black canvas top—it was closed, since we'd had so much rain lately."

"Not in the garage?"

Tommy smirked. "Too far for Amy to walk in the mornings. She leaves it in the driveway by the front door. So because her kid might've gotten suspicious, I spent an extra half hour driving to get her and drop her off. No wonder she doesn't get home by two. And then she's mad at me."

Fenway nodded and looked into Tommy's expressive eyes. She wasn't sure if his story or Amy's story was the true one, but Tommy seemed genuine. Maybe he was really good at playing naïve—he was a talented salesman, after all—but Fenway couldn't see how Tommy could be lying.

But still, his story didn't match hers—and didn't fit the evidence either.

"Tommy," she said, "what would you say if I told you that Amy's Mustang was recorded—on video—entering and leaving the parking garage at the hotel where Rick Tonnick was murdered during the time you say you were with Amy?"

Tommy blinked hard. "Uh," he said, "is that what you're saying?"

"I'm asking you if your story would change."

"I mean—no. I'll swear on a stack of Bibles that I was with Amy from midnight to three forty-five. If Amy's Mustang was in that parking garage, someone must have stolen it."

Fenway stood up and stretched herself to her full height, towering over Tommy. "You're telling me that even though we see Amy's car in the parking garage—on the recording, with time code—that it wasn't Amy? That it was someone else?"

Tommy's eyes went wide, and his lower lip trembled slightly. "I don't know what you want me to say." He scooted his chair back. "I'm telling you the truth. Amy and I were together from midnight to three forty-five. Give or take ten or fifteen minutes. I don't know who drove her car, but it wasn't her. And it wasn't me, if you're thinking I had something to do with it."

"Then who—" And Fenway had a sinking feeling in her stomach.

"I don't know," Tommy said, grimacing. "I just know that Rick is dead and Amy won't return my calls and I have no idea what to do." He looked like he was going to cry again.

"Okay, okay," Fenway said, backing up a few steps.

"Just—are we done? Can you leave now?"

Fenway nodded. "Good luck with everything, Tommy."

She walked out the door, and Vivian looked up from her laptop. "Everything okay?"

"You were right," Fenway said. "He's having a hard time. I think I pushed him a little too much."

Vivian shook her head, closed her eyes, and exhaled a long breath. "Thank you for telling me, Coroner," she said, glancing from the door leading to Tommy's office to the door leading to the hallway and then back, a pained look on her face.

"I'll see myself out," Fenway said.

She made a wrong turn but eventually found her way out of the office and stood outside blinking in the sunshine. She looked around the parking lot and headed for a bench in the middle of a small grove of trees about a hundred yards away.

Was there another explanation? If Amy and Tommy had been together that night, leaving the Mustang in the roundabout of her long driveway at midnight, who else could have taken it?

The answer was jumping up and down in front of her, and although it made Fenway sick to her stomach, she had to acknowledge it.

All the pieces fit.

Seventeen-year-old Megan McVie was at home when Amy left.

Megan had access to Amy's Mustang. It was parked outside.

Amy hadn't taken the Mustang, so she may not have taken the keys for it. Or even if she had, there was probably a backup set in a kitchen drawer or hanging on a hook next to the back door. Megan could have easily driven the Mustang.

Rick Tonnick had likely gone downstairs to meet the killer in the private penthouse elevator. Rick had let the killer into his penthouse suite. Rick had drunk some whisky that he hadn't realized had crushed-up sleeping pills in it. Rick had taken off all his clothes and gotten into bed, probably raring to go for a night of pleasure.

None of that made sense if Amy were the killer.

But—Fenway closed her eyes and fought the urge to throw up—it all made sense if it had been seventeen-year-old Megan in the penthouse.

Not Amy.

Megan killing Rick Tonnick didn't make sense if that had been Megan's first time with him.

But if Rick Tonnick had been sexually abusing Megan for months?

And if Megan had finally fought back?

Yes. Then it all made sense.

Then it all fit together.

Fenway's head swam.

She set her purse down on the bench next to her and put her head between her knees. After a moment, the wave of nausea passed.

She sat back up, the taste of bile in her mouth.

Fenway stood, her feet unsteady, and then took several quick steps toward the trees and vomited.

CHAPTER TWELVE

As Fenway drove back to the office, her breaths still hitching in her throat, she kept telling herself she didn't know the whole story. That she was leaping to conclusions.

But her heart was heavy.

Rick Tonnick had been fifty-eight years old.

Megan was seventeen.

Fenway hated herself for thinking it, but she was glad Megan wasn't Black. Megan might have a chance that way. For the system to look kindly on her, for the judge to think she might have a future, for her to be tried as a juvenile.

She couldn't see a way out of it, though. Case law was pretty clear that Megan couldn't claim self-defense. Not if she lured him to the hotel. Not if she knocked him out with the sleeping pills first. Not if she put the pillow over his face and leaned on it with all her weight until her stepfather stopped breathing.

And how much did Amy know? Did she look the other way? When did it start?

She wanted to talk to Craig. She didn't know if that was okay or not, but she wasn't sure she cared. McVie would do everything he could to make sure his daughter was okay. Maybe even send her out of the country. Maybe with Amy.

Fenway shook her head, trying to calm down again. In spite of the chilly day, she was sweating in the car, and she turned the air conditioning on and rolled down the windows.

Her phone rang, and she clicked the answer button on the steering wheel. She cleared her throat and tried to keep her voice even.

"This is Fenway."

"Fenway, where are you?"

"Hi, Dez. I'm just driving back to the office now."

"Well, hurry up—and come to the sheriff's office."

"The sheriff's office? Why?"

"Mark went to talk to Duke Perriman—that's the widower of the pregnant woman who died after the safety recall on her Ford wasn't done properly. He didn't want to tell us where he was on Sunday night, and then he had some words for Mark, and so now Mr. Perriman is in the interrogation room at the sheriff's office."

"Lovely. Great work building community relations."

"Hey, don't look at me," Dez said, chuckling. "You know my bedside manner is unimpeachable."

"Okay, I should be there in five minutes. Ten minutes, tops."

"All right. He's starting to get restless, but I think that's because he's sobering up."

"Sobering up? It's only twelve thirty!"

"It's five o'clock somewhere," Dez said. "Mark and Sheriff Donnelly are conducting the interview."

"Sheriff Donnelly?"

"She knows him from way back. Her sister babysat him or something. She thinks Duke will listen to her, maybe be more cooperative. Gotta go."

Fenway clicked off right after Dez hung up. The city garage was in front of her, and the siren song of an early afternoon Java Jim's latte called to her. But her stomach gurgled—she hadn't eaten lunch, but after leaving her breakfast in the grove of trees next to the Tonnick Auto Group parking lot, she didn't think loading any more ammunition into her stomach was a good idea.

She walked across the street to the sheriff's office, passing the coffee cart in the lobby but staring at the espresso machine longingly. Wending her way down the hall, Fenway came to the interview room. She knocked lightly on the observation room door, and Dez opened it quietly and beckoned her inside.

She saw the backs of Sheriff Gretchen Donnelly and Sergeant Mark Trevino. Handcuffed to the table across from them was a Black man, heavyset and heavy-lidded. He had his hair clipped close to his head and stubble that was trying hard to become a beard. He wore a blue-and-black tartan overshirt with gray sleeves. His eyes slid lazily between his two interrogators, then up to the ceiling and back.

"You okay?" whispered Dez. "You look like shit."

"Aw, Dez, I bet you say that to all the girls."

"Just the ones who look like shit."

Fenway rolled her eyes. "Are we sure he's sober enough to interview?"

"Breathalyzer," Dez said. "Just this side of sober-enough-to-interview. And that was about fifteen minutes ago, so we're all good."

Fenway watched Sheriff Donnelly shift her weight in the chair and then lean forward. "It's good seeing you again, Duke," she said.

"Not really under these circumstances though," Perriman slurred.

"Are you sure you don't want coffee?"

He glared at Mark. "I know what you guys do. You load me up with coffee and energy drinks until I have to pee like a damn racehorse, then you make me say I killed someone I never even met just so I don't piss myself in front of you. Y'all can go fuck yourselves."

Sheriff Donnelly shook her head. "Hey, Duke, come on now. It's me—Gretchen. I'm Ulrich's older sister. You know Ulrich. From Camp Abercrombie."

Duke's look of confusion slid off his face into recognition. "Oh. Oh. You're Uli's sister! I'm sorry. I didn't recognize you. Damn. It's been a long time. You were what, sixteen back then?"

Donnelly nodded. "I was. I'm a little older now."

"And a cop." Duke barked out a laugh that made Fenway jump. "I never thought you and Ulrich would be cops."

"Oh—no, Duke, Uli moved to New York about fifteen years ago."

"New York? No shit?" Duke shook his head. "What's he doing there?"

"Designing sets for Broadway shows," Donnelly said.

"Aw man," Duke laughed. "He was really good at getting us to do the little camp musicals."

"Right," Donnelly said. "It was great to see those."

"So," Mark said, "we're not trying to do anything but ask you a few questions."

Duke tensed up.

Sheriff Donnelly turned to Mark. "Sergeant Trevino, why don't you go have Miss Stevenson bring in a coffee for Duke?"

Mark hesitated and furrowed his brow, but then he nodded.

"How do you take your coffee, Duke?" Donnelly asked.

"I like my coffee like I like my women," Duke said. "White and sweet." He barked a laugh and didn't seem to mind that no one else laughed with him.

Mark got up and left the room.

"Oh, great," Fenway said.

"Suck it up, buttercup," Dez said. "This is why you get the big bucks."

Fenway opened the door and saw Mark at the coffee machine, pouring a generous amount of coffee into a large ceramic mug with the Dodgers logo on it.

She walked up next to him. "You okay?"

"It's fine," Mark said. "I've had plenty of people tell me they don't like cops. I'm just glad the sheriff knows him."

"You making that white and sweet enough for LL Cool J in there?"

Mark smiled, tearing three sugars open and emptying them into the coffee. "He has a bunch of Dodgers stuff in his apartment. I figured we'd at least play to our strengths."

"Sure," Fenway said. "What does our friend do for a living?"

"Bartender." Mark dumped four singles of half-and-half into the mug.

"Oof. And I take it that he gets high on his own supply."

Mark laughed, handing Fenway a stir stick. "I appreciate the N.W.A. reference. And I appreciate it more that you think I'm cool enough to get it."

"Maybe it was a *Scarface* reference." Fenway elbowed Mark in the ribs. "Time for a pinch-hitter," she said, holding the mug and carrying it into the interview room.

Duke sat up straight as soon as Fenway entered. His shoulders relaxed visibly. Fenway tried not to tense up as she set the coffee down in front of him.

"Four creams, three sugars," Fenway said, taking the chair Mark had vacated. "White and sweet enough for you?"

"Aw, now, don't be like that, girl," Duke said, smiling at her. Fenway could smell the whiskey on him—American and cheap. "I was just playing."

"Well," Sheriff Donnelly said, "we're here because of Katrina."

"Everyone just called her Trina," Duke said. "She hated her full name. Named after some racist-ass aunt of hers who refused to come to our wedding." And Duke's whole body changed, sagging in the chair, folding in on himself. "Trina, that's what everyone called her."

"I'm really sorry," Fenway said. "I heard about that asshole who cared more about hiding money in his divorce than he did about keeping his customers safe."

"I hope he rots in hell," Duke mumbled.

Fenway nodded. "He's a piece of shit," she said, and her stomach gargled again as she felt the blood rise to her face. "And what he did to your wife isn't even the worst of it."

"She didn't deserve that," Duke said softly. "Roberta neither."

Fenway felt a pang of sadness and had to blink back tears. "Roberta was…"

"The name me and Trina picked out," Duke said. "I still have the ultrasound picture on the fridge. We'd picked out designs for the nursery." His eyes focused for a moment. "I had a good job. I worked in HVAC, I made good money. Trina was a mechanical engineer. She was real smart. That mother—" He stopped and stole a glance at Sheriff Donnelly. "That *monster* took everything away from me," he said.

"I hear you," Fenway said.

Duke narrowed his eyes at Fenway. "I recognize you," he murmured. "Where do I know you from?" Then he snapped his fingers. "Coroner. I voted for you. I was proud to vote for you." He blinked, once, twice, and then several times in rapid succession. "Oh," he said. "You're the coroner."

Fenway nodded.

Duke Perriman took a deep breath and held it for a moment. "And you've been talking about Rick Tonnick."

Fenway nodded again.

Duke pressed his lips together. "Tell me he suffered, Miss Stevenson. Tell me someone took hours and hours to kill him. Days, weeks, even. Tell me you found his tortured body somewhere by the train tracks where he died a horrible, painful death."

Fenway shook her head.

"Well, then, you've got the wrong man. If I'd done it, I'd have stuck ice picks under his toenails. I would have cut his face open. I would have ripped his eyes out. I would have made sure he suffered. He would have been begging for death at the end. And then I would have marched right into this sheriff's office and told you I tortured and killed the man who ruined my family."

Fenway nodded. She knew where Duke was coming from. If her gut was right, and Rick Tonnick had done anything to Megan McVie, Craig would have administered all that torture and then some—Boy Scout or not.

"Well, you wouldn't be asking me if he weren't dead. So come on, when did he die? What time do I need to, uh, account for my whereabouts?"

"Sunday night," Sheriff Donnelly said. "Between two and four in the morning."

"I was working," Duke said. "The bar closed at two, and then I had to clean up."

"Anyone else working with you?"

"No, it was just me, but I had five or six customers all the way till last call."

"What did you have to do after the bar closed?" asked Fenway.

"Get some stock ready for Monday morning. Settle a couple of tabs. There were two credit cards that got left at the bar." He snapped his fingers. "I ran them for the open tab amounts. I bet the computers can prove I was at the bar."

"What time was that, approximately?"

"Well—probably about two forty-five. Maybe as late as three. I set the alarm when I left, so I bet the alarm company could tell you when I was out of there. I got home and fell asleep, but I don't remember what time it was. Probably three thirty."

"Where's the bar?"

"It's downtown," Duke said. "Place called Valhalla."

Donnelly nodded. "I know it. We've had to break up a couple of fights there." She looked at Duke. "That's only a block from the Phillips-Holsen."

"We serve a, uh, slightly less upscale clientele than the Phillips-Holsen," said Duke, "but it's all right. Some decent beers on tap. Good burgers. We've got a nice pecan pie, too. The cook's from Pascagoula."

Fenway looked at Sheriff Donnelly, who was tough to read. She and McVie used to have some unspoken looks where they could get on the same page right away. Gretchen Donnelly was harder to understand. Especially since she seemed to keep to herself more—not as much of a partnership as it was when McVie ran the sheriff's office. Finally, Donnelly sighed, getting up and unhooking the keychain from her belt. "You're free to go for now," she said, unlocking his cuffs. "But don't leave town. Thanks for your candor."

He rubbed his wrists. "That's it?"

"That's it," Donnelly said. "Next time, keep your hands to yourself around our officers and you won't need the fancy bracelets."

"I apologize," Duke said. "It's been hard. I don't—"

"Don't apologize to me," Donnelly said. "Go find the guy you took a swing at."

Duke hesitated, nodded, then left the room.

"You don't even want to check out his story before letting him go?" Fenway asked. "It's a block away. He could have easily gone over there and been back in time to run those receipts."

"But he's not on the videos," Donnelly said, "and I don't see Rick Tonnick letting him in the penthouse elevator, do you?"

"Maybe Tonnick has the occasional affair with a man."

Donnelly laughed. "Maybe, but you saw Duke, right? Not exactly a

Chippendale. If Tonnick was inclined that direction, I think he'd be more apt to invite Tommy Kinsella than Duke Perriman."

"You're saying Duke is too ugly to be our murderer."

"Duke's a good kid," Donnelly said. "He wouldn't have said all that unless he could back it up."

"And you're all right with all that talk about torture and painful death?"

"Come on, Fenway, I'm not asking the guy to speak to my fifth-grade reading class. I'm trying to figure out if he killed the man who ruined his life. If the guy looked like he'd been tortured, I'd keep him overnight, at least, for assault on an officer. But no. Rick Tonnick's death was relatively painless."

"Any other relatives? Parents? Siblings?"

"Duke's got a couple of older brothers. We haven't looked into her side of the family yet—I actually thought Duke was a decent suspect."

Fenway's stomach flipped. "Sheriff—I have to tell you, we've got another suspect as well."

"Really?"

"Yes. But you're not going to like who it is."

"I don't like the sound of that." She sighed. "But you better tell me anyway."

Fenway opened her mouth to say Megan McVie, but she just couldn't pull the name off her tongue.

Then she remembered: the baby-blue Crosstrek.

"Catherine Klein."

"Catherine Klein?" Sheriff Donnelly said, aghast. "The mayor's wife? Uh oh."

Fenway nodded adamantly. "Politically, it'll be a shitshow, but it's true. She bought a Subaru on Wednesday from Tonnick. They flirted when she bought the car, and then both his truck and her new Crosstrek entered the parking garage of the Phillips-Holsen on Friday night."

"Friday night? What does that have to do with his murder on Sunday?"

"We're looking at the parking garage recording from Sunday to see if she's in it," Fenway said. "But there's a back door, a private elevator that goes straight to the penthouse floor. And there are no cameras up there." She paused. "We should at least question Catherine Klein, right? She cheated on her husband with the deceased forty-eight hours before he was killed?"

"Do you really think she has valuable information about it, or are you just trying to be a pain in the mayor's ass?"

Fenway crossed her arms. "The mayor's been cagey. He's been pushing me to get Amy McVie—I mean Amy Tonnick—arrested for this murder ever since he found out about it."

"Me too." The sheriff put her hands on her hips. "That's why I haven't been more involved—I've told him that your office deals with all suspicious deaths." She shook her head. "But Klein is trying to get back at McVie for daring to run against him for mayor."

"So what do you think?"

"Well," Donnelly said carefully, "it's your case, like I said. But I would be very careful about throwing rocks at the hornets' nest. If you think Catherine Klein can help you solve this murder, then by all means interview her. But do it discreetly. And if you don't, then you better stay away from it. Barry Klein isn't a nice guy, as you know, and he holds a grudge. You don't want to give him any reason to come after you."

Fenway nodded.

As she turned to leave, walking down the corridor and out the main doors of the sheriff's office, she felt a pang of guilt for not mentioning Megan McVie. But she'd feel so much worse about it if she didn't talk to Craig.

First things first. She had to draw conclusions from the evidence, not coincidences or gut feelings. Another visit to the Phillips-Holsen was in her immediate future.

"You caught me just in time," Brianna Harlow said. "I started my shift at six, and I was just about to go on my afternoon break."

"Lucky me," Fenway said, standing in the doorway of the property manager's office.

"You have another warrant for footage? Wednesday night? Last week? Something from 1972? Maybe something from the Watergate break-in?"

"Ha ha," Fenway said. "Actually, it's not camera footage I need this time. It's the check-in record for Frederick Ginn."

"From Sunday? I think you have that already."

Fenway shook her head. "Not from Sunday. I'm looking for his check-in and check-out times every time he's stayed here."

Brianna looked out of the corner of her eye at Fenway. "Every time he's stayed here?"

"That's right." Fenway nodded.

"Well, I'll have to talk to our lawyers—"

"This isn't hard," Fenway said. "I have probable cause to suspect that criminal activity took place."

"Well, sure," Brianna said, "on Sunday night. But surely, a jealous wife taking her revenge—"

Fenway interrupted. "Why do you think we're looking at his wife?"

Brianna's eyebrows knotted. "Well, I mean, isn't the spouse *always* one of the main suspects in a murder investigation?"

Fenway nodded but cocked her head at the property manager. "And— I'm not just talking about Sunday night. I'm looking at criminal activity during multiple stays. Not run-of-the-mill infidelity either. We're talking, at the very least, statutory rape."

Brianna's jaw dropped open. "What?"

"You heard what I said, Brianna." Fenway took two steps forward and closed the door behind her. "I have reason to believe that at least one of the many special visitors Mr. Tonnick invited to his room was a minor. A minor with whom he had several encounters."

"A minor?"

"Look," Fenway said, "I'm willing to avoid looking under certain rocks, okay, Brianna? If you let certain visitors in the back way so as to not embarrass your rich and famous guests, I don't have a problem with that. If you procure the evening's entertainment, I'm not going to go root out what escort service you use. I don't like it when anyone is taken advantage of, so if I hear you're dealing in human trafficking or underage women, then I'll come after you. But I haven't heard anything like that."

Brianna had a fake smile plastered to her face.

"But I've got probable cause to believe that Mr. Tonnick forced a minor to have sexual relations with him in your hotel, Miss Harlow, and that really gets under my skin."

"But—but we had no idea! If it even happened—I mean, it's a private elevator. We don't see who comes in or goes out."

"Maybe it didn't happen here," Fenway said, inwardly seething but forcing her forehead and jaw to relax. "I hope that our information is incorrect and it didn't happen at all. But one way you can help us—one way you can help yourself—is to give us the information on Mr. Tonnick's visits here. Whether he's used Frederick Ginn or another alias."

Brianna paled, and her smile faltered. "Yes. Of course. I can give that information to you in—uh, I think I need about twenty or thirty minutes. I'll need a little time to find the files."

"I'm not leaving until I get it, Brianna," Fenway said. "I'm not kidding."

"Right, right, of course." Brianna clicked onto a database search. "Can—can I offer you anything while you wait?"

"You have a restaurant here, right?"

"Award-winning."

"Save the marketing spiel, Brianna. I'm not in the mood."

Brianna flushed scarlet all the way to the tips of her ears. "I apologize—force of habit."

"I'll be waiting in your restaurant," Fenway said. "If you have any delays, come talk to me. If I find that you're trying to cover anything up or that you've left, I will find you, and next time, I won't ask nicely."

Brianna nodded, a worried look on her face, and Fenway let herself out.

The restaurant was a typical expensive but not high-end American bistro with hamburgers, steaks, chicken, and fish entrées. The dishes were unimaginative, the descriptions vainglorious. Fenway's phone buzzed as she looked at the insipid menu.

It was McVie.

"Hi, Craig."

He cleared his throat. "I'm sorry about last night, Fenway. But I—uh, I found out some new information." His voice cracked. Barely controlled rage. And grief.

Fenway was silent. It was clear that Amy had come to the same conclusion as Fenway. Amy hadn't been in the car, but someone had. Someone with access to the car. And no one had access to the car but Megan. And Fenway knew that Amy had gone down the same rabbit hole about Megan's motive.

And Amy had told McVie.

"It's okay," Fenway said.

"I wish I could talk to someone about it. But—you're the investigator. I can't tell you."

"I know, Craig."

"You know? You know what?"

"I know that Amy wasn't driving the Mustang on Sunday night. I know she's not the one who pulled into the parking garage at two in the morning. I know she's not the one who killed Rick Tonnick."

There was silence on the other end of the line.

"But I know that it *was* the Mustang in the parking garage. License plates don't lie. So someone who had access to the Mustang must have been driving it."

Fenway heard McVie's breaths, a little deeper than normal. Like when he was trying to stay calm.

"And that person must have had a motive for killing Rick Tonnick." She pressed her lips together. "Someone who Rick was expecting."

More silence.

"Have you talked to Megan?" Fenway asked gently.

"She says—" McVie started, then hesitated.

"What?"

"She says she didn't do it. She says she doesn't know what we're talking about." His voice wavered.

"Of course she doesn't," Fenway said. "Because that would mean admitting some things to you and Amy that she doesn't want to deal with."

McVie let out a breath. "I don't know, Fenway. Megan has a tell when she's lying. She always looks down at her hands. Her first boyfriend, when she was a freshman and he was a senior—I knew what they were doing and what they weren't. Even studying for tests. She'd look down at her hands. 'Yes, Dad, I studied,' examining her fingers as if she'd just spent two hundred bucks on a manicure."

"And?"

"And she said she went to bed about midnight and fell asleep and she has no idea what we're talking about. And she's staring in my eyes, looking pissed off and annoyed, sure, but looking right in my eyes the whole time. I don't know what to think." McVie's breaths became more ragged, like he was pacing. "I'd strangle that asshole myself if he were still alive."

"You really didn't think she was lying?"

"I really didn't." McVie paused. "But I can't see how it could have—"

Fenway waited for McVie to continue. Finally, an uneasy exhalation.

"How could I let this happen, Fenway?"

"He screwed everything that moves, Craig. Doesn't matter who it hurt or what it cost him. He thought he was invincible, and he thought he deserved it, and he thought the rules didn't apply to him."

"But not her. I look in her eyes, and I don't believe he touched her." McVie hesitated again. "Maybe I just don't *want* to see it. Do we get her into therapy?"

"You *better* get her into therapy. And Amy better pay for it with all the money she's got coming to her."

McVie was quiet—dead quiet.

"Craig?"

Still silence.

"Did I lose you, Craig?"

"I'm here." A pause, not quite so long. "Uh, Fenway, I don't know how to tell you this, but Amy's decided to confess to the murder."

Fenway felt her knees lock.

"Fenway, are you still there?"

"I didn't hear that," Fenway said, and she ended the call.

CHAPTER THIRTEEN

THE BLTA SANDWICH THAT FENWAY FINALLY DECIDED ON FOR LUNCH had too much mayonnaise and not enough salt. The avocado was hard—though what did she expect for January?—but the sourdough was fresh, even though it was toasted just enough to tear up her mouth when she bit in.

Charlotte had texted right after Fenway had gotten off the phone with McVie, needing to see her at a moment's notice. She wanted to order a cocktail. Maybe a Moscow mule or a whisky sour. Something to get the images out of her head, the bad taste out of her mouth.

The problem was, she would do the same thing for someone she loved. If her mother had been accused of murder, Fenway would have sacrificed herself in a heartbeat. Even if she'd been dating McVie. They could still have conjugal visits in prison.

Fenway was so lost in her own thoughts that she jumped when Charlotte slid into the booth in front of her.

"That was fast," Fenway said.

"I was at the lawyer's." Charlotte pulled a set of papers out of a messenger bag and began to leaf through them.

"What was so important that you had to drop what you were doing and meet me in Estancia's blandest restaurant?"

"Be nice," Charlotte said. "Not everything can be a hole-in-the-wall Mexican place."

"I feel like you don't appreciate Dos Milagros like you should."

Charlotte nodded. "I guarantee you that's true." She pulled the top set off the stack and held it in front of Fenway. "The offers are coming in. Petrogrande. About five hundred fifty million."

Fenway took a bite of the sandwich and chewed thoughtfully. "You know," she said, swallowing, "I did a web search for the multiplier for the oil and gas industry in California last week. It's over three—and Ferris Energy's revenue was over four hundred million last year. Any serious offer should be at least one-point-two billion. They're lowballing you."

"Of course they're lowballing us," Charlotte said. "I just had one of the other board members explain DCF valuation to me. Apparently that's what they used."

"I don't know what that is," Fenway said.

"I just had it explained to me, and I still don't know what it is." Charlotte slammed the stack of papers on the table. "The point is, they're lowballing us because they think our cash flow is untenable. Or it will be soon."

"The assets alone are worth more than five fifty," Fenway said. "The land you own—the refinery equipment, the ports, the shipping lanes, the tankers? Come on, Charlotte."

"But we can't survive if Sierra Madre goes away," Charlotte said, "so it really pissed me off when I got the second offer." She handed the papers to Fenway, who took them between her pinkie and her palm so she wouldn't get grease on them.

Fenway set them on dry part of the table, then wiped her hands on the napkin. She began to leaf through them. "I'm sorry, Charlotte," she said, "but I don't understand any of this. It might as well be written in another language."

"Page five," Charlotte said. "They break it all down."

Fenway flipped to page five. And there were several valuations. One was with all current customers of Ferris Energy, one was with all current customers except for Sierra Madre, and one was for the company without Sierra Madre and also without several other large customers—ones that Fenway knew were under Sierra Madre's thumb.

Fenway saw the offer price at the bottom. "Five seventy-five."

"It's an insult," Charlotte said. "If Nathaniel were awake, he'd be entertaining deals for a billion and a half, two billion."

"How much of that five hundred seventy-five million does Dad get?" Fenway asked.

Charlotte was quiet.

"One-fifty?" Fenway ventured. "Two hundred? Come on, Charlotte. That's more than enough for you to live on for the rest of your days without ever touching anything else. You can get new cars every month. Keep one of your private planes if you want. Probably not the jet."

"But if Nathaniel—"

"If Nathaniel nothing," Fenway said. "If Dad cared about the difference between five hundred million and one-point-two billion more than he cares about your health and the stress you're under—"

"He'll never look at me the same again," Charlotte whispered.

"Then blame me," Fenway said. "Tell him that I forced your hand. That I gave away some idiotic information that I shouldn't have."

"Fenway." Charlotte's tone was sharp. "I can't let you do that. Not when you and he have just started to repair your relationship."

"He took a bullet for me," Fenway said. "It's why he's in a coma right now. Do you know how much effort it takes—how many times in the last eight weeks I've seen my therapist—so that I'm not racked with guilt about this every single minute of my waking life?"

Charlotte was quiet.

"You really can't take a lowball offer that's going to make you hundreds of millions of dollars?" She took the last bite of the first half of the BLTA.

"They're taking advantage of me, Fenway. They're doing this because they don't think I can handle it."

Fenway swallowed with difficulty. "But you *can't* handle it!" She took the top piece of sourdough off the second half and began to scrape the mayo off with a knife. "I sure as hell can't handle it. I can barely handle my own investigation right now. How do you see a way forward? A way to win? That you get what you want?"

Charlotte glared at Fenway. "They're betting that Ferris Energy isn't well liked in the community. That we're looking for an escape hatch."

"Aren't you?"

"No," Charlotte said. "I'm looking for time. Time to get Nate into recovery. Time to get him back in fighting shape. I don't mind losing one or two customers. I don't mind my legacy being that I barely held the company together while my husband was in a coma. There aren't many spouses of CEOs who can say that. I think I'll be proud to join that small group."

Fenway shook her head. "You're not seeing the big picture. It's not worth it. My dad isn't going to wake up and think, 'Oh, no, my wife took over my company, saving it from everyone who wanted to destroy it, and only made me two hundred million dollars.' He's going to be glad to be alive. He's going to want to spend time with you. Travel to all the places he couldn't in the last thirty years because he was too busy with work. Maybe even spend time with me without having to call Japan after hours. Believe me, I saw it so much when I was a nurse practitioner. People wake up from trauma, and they're completely different people."

Charlotte blanched.

"I didn't mean their personalities change—I mean their *priorities* change. Workaholics spend more time with their families. Adulterers stop messing around. Deadbeat dads change their tune. It happens all the time. Don't kill yourself for five hundred million dollars that won't matter." She paused. "Man, when I was on food stamps in Seattle, I never thought I'd be telling you that five hundred million dollars doesn't matter."

Charlotte folded her arms. "Well, we did it."

"Did what?"

"We moved the land into conservancy. Signed the papers about an hour ago. It will belong to Dominguez Open Space Land Trust after thirty days." She paused. "The press release is being drafted, and with your permission, we're going to set up the press conference for four o'clock."

Fenway raised her eyebrows. "You're moving forward with this?"

"It's a last-ditch effort," Charlotte said. "Maybe no one will pay attention. Some of the lawyers said it won't make any difference, that people are so jaded about Ferris Energy it will look like a cheap stunt. Not only that, we're donating an asset worth literally millions of dollars."

"Only on paper. There are no water rights on most of that land."

Charlotte smirked. "If I didn't know better, Fenway, I'd say you've done your research on this."

Fenway shrugged. "Okay, maybe I care a little about it too. And, yeah, okay, it's easy for me to say to just sell it for a fraction of what it's worth, especially since I don't have a financial stake in it."

Charlotte stood up and stacked her papers. "The PR agency will be calling you in the next hour or so. Make sure you pick up."

Fenway finished her lunch alone and checked the clock on her phone. It had been more than thirty minutes. She settled the bill—another five minutes, as the service left a lot to be desired—and walked down the mazelike corridor to Brianna's office.

Brianna didn't answer the knock, and for a moment, Fenway thought she might have skipped town because of human trafficking. When she opened the door, however, Brianna was sitting in her task chair, her arms folded, staring vacantly.

"Did you get the information?"

Brianna looked up, startled. "What?"

"The check-in and check-out information for Rick Tonnick and all his aliases. Did you get it?"

Brianna pursed her lips. "Uh—yeah. I got it." She looked visibly upset.

Fenway squinted. "Are you okay?"

Brianna hesitated and then nodded. "I—I went through some of the data. Some of it I'm *sure* I can't give you without a warrant. But it's not just Rick Tonnick. We have—I mean, this place isn't..." She folded her arms and stared at the floor.

"Ah," Fenway said. "Just because the Phillips-Holsen doesn't rent rooms by the hour—"

Brianna looked up, eyes wet, a quizzical look on her face. "What?"

"You found evidence that the hotel connects your guests to high-class call girls, right? That's why you're upset?"

Brianna hesitated and seemed to catch a sob in her throat. "It makes me sick."

"Well, my father owns an oil company that's probably going to be at least partially responsible for the death of the human race," Fenway said, "so I wouldn't worry too much about your hotel pimping high-class call girls." She paused for a moment while Brianna regained control. "I'm sorry to ask you about the information I need—"

"Oh," Brianna said, startling, "I emailed it to you. Three different aliases. About a hundred nights over the last two years. If you need information before that, I'll have to fill out an information request form. And that will probably require a warrant."

Fenway nodded. "Thanks."

She let herself out and left through the back door, then walked down the steps to the parking garage.

Turning the Accord right instead of left out of the garage, she realized there was still the issue of Amy's lover adamantly insisting that Amy was with him. She'd see what he had to say after hearing that Amy planned to confess. She expected him, if he were telling the truth, to stick to his guns. She pulled up the phone app on her dashboard and called the Tonnick Auto Group again. She got Vivian on the phone.

"Thomas Kinsella's office, how may I help you?"

"Hi, Vivian. This is Coroner Stevenson. Is Thomas all right?"

"He's still not himself," she said. "But I don't think what you said upset him much more."

"I just need to confirm a couple of things about his statement," Fenway said. "Is he available?"

"He's actually with a client at the Lexus dealership. He'll be back around four, if that works for you."

Oof. The same time as the press conference.

"I'll just catch up with him tomorrow."

She hung up and tapped the steering wheel a few times. "No," she murmured, hanging a U-turn. "I'll go see him now."

When Fenway arrived at the Lexus dealership, she wandered around the lot, rebuffing the salespeople's aggressive tactics until she walked into the showroom itself. Tommy was talking to a tall, thin white man with a deep tan and a fitted black pinstripe business suit. He wore an olive turtleneck sweater underneath the suit jacket that gave his skin a gray hue.

Fenway caught Tommy's eye, and he raised his hand slightly. But his companion noticed and turned his head.

"Sorry to interrupt," Fenway said. "I just have to ask you a couple more questions when you're done." She turned to the tall man. "Sorry—I'll let you get back—"

"You're Fenway Stevenson," the man said.

"Uh—yes, that's me."

He turned to Tommy. "Make it an even ten for that price. Draw up the paperwork while I'm talking to Miss Stevenson."

"Oh—sorry, I actually needed Tommy—"

"Well, I hope Tommy can wait because I've got to head back over the pass," the man said. He stuck out his hand. "Archie."

"Hi, Archie," Fenway said, shaking his hand. The name sounded familiar, but she couldn't place it. "Can you tell me why you're stopping me from questioning a witness in a murder investigation?"

Archie put his hands over his mouth. "Oh, goodness—I forgot. You're a coroner."

Fenway cocked her head. "What did you think I was?"

"The new community liaison for Ferris Energy, of course."

"Oh—that. Yeah. I haven't really started my duties there yet. Just appointed yesterday."

He cocked an eyebrow. "So it doesn't sound like you recognize my name."

"I'm sorry, Archie, I'm afraid I don't."

"Does the name Sierra Madre Fuels mean anything to you?"

Fenway folded her arms and stared him down. "Oh, *you're* the Archie who gave Charlotte that insulting lowball number."

Archie tilted his head and blinked twice.

He hadn't expected to get any pushback at all. He'd expected to waltz in and steal the company out from under them.

She saw Charlotte in her mind's eye, across the table at lunch, trying to hold it together.

Charlotte at the side of Nathaniel Ferris's hospital bed, trying to hold it together.

Charlotte at the meeting yesterday at two o'clock, all by herself, trying to hold it together.

Fenway didn't want to hold it together anymore. She didn't know what it would get her, but she was sick of playing games. "Did you get Petrogrande to lowball her, too? Because I believe," she said, raising her voice and pointing a finger at his chest, "that collusion like that is an SEC violation. It's hard to run a company from jail, even if it's one of those country-club prisons like I see on those cop shows."

Archie raised his hands. "Now, hold on, wait just a second."

"I don't have time for this, Archie. You may get off on talking down to women, trying to trick them out of hundreds of millions of dollars, but I don't think it's very amusing." She poked him in the chest. The sweater was cashmere. "There was a dead body in a hotel room yesterday morning, and I have to solve that case. And when you give Charlotte Ferris, who's doing a better job running Ferris Energy than anyone expected, a lowball number like that, it wastes my time. It wastes *her* time." Fenway dropped her hand, took another step closer to him, and wished she had spent the extra dollar on garlic fries at lunch so her breath would have the same sting as her words. "You never would have done that to my father."

Archie shrugged. "I'm not going to apologize for trying to strike while I have a tactical advantage," he said. "It's common knowledge that Mrs. Ferris doesn't have experience in the energy industry. It's not personal—I'd do that to anyone who I think is green enough to accept."

And to think she'd tried to talk Charlotte into taking his lowball offer.

"You're using your position as a customer of Ferris Energy to force us into a sale that's bad for the organization."

"Don't say you wouldn't do the same in my position."

"I wouldn't, but that's why I'm not a CEO."

Archie laughed.

"Oh, you don't think I could have gotten my master's in business administration rather than forensic nursing? I bet you don't even know how to perform CPR. Whereas *I* know about five different ways to provide company valuation. And you're off by a factor of three. At least."

Archie gave Fenway an appraising smile. "I see I've underestimated my opponent," he said.

"Let me tell you something else, *Archie*," she said. "You require a complex mix of material in your fuel. You're not going to get one of the big boys to customize orders or provide the short turnaround times you need. You'll be a number to them. You won't even make the top fifty in terms of customer size. You're getting boutique products and boutique customer service at grocery store prices. Even though you'll pay more anywhere else you go, you'll get treated like you're in the ninety-nine-cent store, begging for someone to help you try to figure out the difference between two crucially different but identically labeled products."

"I see you've also figured out product differentiation." Archie stepped back.

"Look, I get it," Fenway said, taking another step forward. "You want to control more of your supply chain. Maybe as good as we are, we still can't provide the kind of just-in-time service you need. Maybe it makes a lot of business sense for Sierra Madre Fuels to buy us. And yeah, Charlotte Ferris is no Nathaniel Ferris. But I'll be damned if I'm going to let you run all over us just because you think you can get away with it."

Archie was silent. His brow furrowed as he sized Fenway up.

Fenway was breathing heavily, her nostrils flaring. It was a bluff—Fenway was riding the ragged ends of her knowledge about oil company valuation—but she wasn't bluffing her anger, and she wondered if Archie was counting his attorney's potential billable hours in his head. He might win this, but she'd make it as expensive as possible.

Archie nodded. "I was going to ask if you'd seen our offer letter," he said, "but I obviously have my answer. I'll talk this over with our people and see if we can send you a revision in the next day or two."

"Sign a customer extension for the next two years," Fenway said, "and I promise I'll treat you a lot nicer next time."

Archie turned and walked away, pausing briefly at an office where Tommy Kinsella sat, filling out paperwork. "Tommy, good to see you. Get those couriered to our office by tonight, and they'll be on your desk tomorrow." He looked over his shoulder at Fenway. "I think Miss Stevenson has something important to discuss with you."

Fenway clenched and unclenched her fists as she walked into the guest office.

Even though she told him that Amy would be confessing to the murder, Tommy wouldn't budge on his story. Some part of Fenway found it admirable.

"I don't believe she'd confess," Tommy said, his handsome jaw set hard in determination. "I've heard cops will lie to get people to say things. But even if she *did*, I'd say Amy was being blackmailed or threatened. Because she was with me. And unless someone says they're going to kill me or someone I love, I'm going to keep telling you—and I'll testify to it—Amy was *with me*."

If it hadn't been clear to Fenway before, it was now: Amy was planning to confess to protect her daughter. And Fenway couldn't stand by while Amy perjured herself. She'd have to look up the law on it and see exactly what her duty was here. Sometimes justice wasn't served by following the law or telling the truth.

Fenway thanked Tommy for his time and walked out of the Lexus showroom frustrated. She needed to talk to McVie.

Her phone dinged. It was a text from Piper—the address and phone number of the assisted living facility on La Cienega Boulevard where Nell Godwin lived.

Her grandmother.

She got to her car and sat staring at the phone. How "assisted" was the assisted living? Did her grandmother just have trouble getting around, or did she have Alzheimer's or dementia?

If it was Alzheimer's, would Fenway even want to go see her? Would it be worth it to just look in someone else's eyes and know there was a shared genetic history? Or would it be too painful? Too much of a reminder of missed opportunities?

Fenway shook her head to clear her thinking. She'd never even thought this was an option before—she always wondered what it would be like to have a relationship with a grandparent. For twenty years, it had really just been her and her mother. But pushing her father aside had been a choice her mother made, not him. Her friends at school or at college had whole families. They had their siblings visit, or they would leave for the weekend to see their cousins, or they'd complain about a family reunion. Their Thanksgivings had more than two people around the table. Their Christmases had real trees, tall trees, trees perhaps not as grand as the first eight Christmases she had in Estancia when her parents were still together and everything seemed okay, but trees. Not the two-foot-tall plastic tree with the ornaments permanently affixed that her mother had purchased for three dollars in mid-January at a yard sale.

She hadn't even realized the grandparent-shaped hole in her heart was there until—when? Yesterday? Just now?

She tapped on the phone number in Piper's text message.

The line clicked on, and the prerecorded message, a booming baritone, was so loud she had to pull the phone away from her ear.

"You have reached Rolling Meadows. If you know the person you are trying to reach, please enter the room number or extension now. Visiting hours are—"

She tapped 0 on the keypad, and the phone rang. A woman's voice, high and enthusiastic, answered.

"Good afternoon, Rolling Meadows! This is Julia. How may I help you?"

"Hi, Julia," Fenway croaked. She was tense all over, calling without a plan of what to say. "I—I think my grandmother is a, um, resident there."

"Sure, hon," Julia said brightly. "What's her name?"

"Well," Fenway said, "it's kind of a weird situation, so I think I need some—I don't know—guidance on the best thing to do."

"Okay," Julia said, a note of uncertainty in her voice. "Can you give me a little more to go on?"

Fenway took a deep breath. "You have a resident there named Nell Godwin. In, uh, let's see, 1986, Nell's daughter, Samara, disappeared. And yesterday, I found out my mother, who passed away last year, is probably Samara Godwin."

Julia paused. "Well, now," she said, "that is an unusual situation."

"I mean," Fenway said, feeling like she was rambling, "until yesterday, I had no idea that's who my grandmother was. I found out she was in your, um, residence, and I don't know what I need to do to be able to visit her." She swallowed hard. "Is she—would she be able to understand who I was, or who I might be? I don't want it to be traumatic for her if she thought her daughter died over thirty years ago, but maybe she'd be okay meeting a granddaughter she never knew she had."

Julia was silent for a moment. "Honestly," she said, "I don't know what our protocol is in a situation like this."

"If she has dementia or something—"

"I'm not allowed to discuss patients' health conditions over the phone," said Julia, "so let me get a piece of paper and write this all down. Are you here in Los Angeles?"

"Estancia," Fenway said, "but I could drive down, be there in a few hours."

Julia asked Fenway to repeat everything, then asked for contact information, the spelling of Samara, and told Fenway she'd need to check with a supervisor. "Expect a call back by tomorrow morning. I don't want to promise anything. We'll see what our management says. Maybe we can let Nell know a little bit about it, see how she takes it."

An idea popped into Fenway's head. "Do you have an email or text where I could send a picture of my mother? And maybe of me? Then Mrs. Godwin could see her. Maybe she'd recognize her daughter—maybe she'd see the resemblance in me, too."

"It couldn't hurt to send it," Julia said. "But if Nell reacts badly if we tell her about her daughter, I may not show it to her."

"I understand." Fenway put the phone on speaker and typed in the email address Julia gave her. "Are you in front of your email now?" Fenway said, scrolling through her photos and picking one of her favorite pictures of her and her mother having dinner at Matt's at the Market, the window behind them showing Puget Sound, a sailboat going by, the gray cloud cover a little depressing but diffusing the light well. It had been Joanne's—Samara's?—birthday, and the snapper curry had been especially good. Fenway remembered worrying about whether she could afford to take her mother out to dinner on her salary, but she'd saved up for a couple of months to get the three hundred dollars to go all out.

Both Fenway and her mother were facing the camera and smiling. It had been about a year before her mother's diagnosis. Fenway was glad she'd saved up and glad that she'd overridden her mother's insistence that it was too much, that Fenway should be saving for her own place.

She hit the arrow, selected e-mail, and a second later, the swoosh sound told her the photo was on the way.

"I just sent the photo," Fenway said quietly. "I'm on the left, my mom is on the right."

"Okay," Julia said. "I'll just refresh—all right, there it is. Oh, look at that."

"What?"

"I see Nell's eyes. Your mother and you both." She cleared her throat. "I don't usually get to connect long-lost relatives. I hope this works out."

"Me too."

Julia promised a call by the next morning, and Fenway thanked her profusely, then ended the call and tapped her phone against her chin.

An afternoon latte would help her think. And it would get the taste of that mediocre sandwich out of her mouth.

There was a Java Jim's at the exit for Highway 326, just a mile away from the Lexus dealership. The dreary January day had apparently put many people in a similar mood for an afternoon pick-me-up, and the line was nine or ten people long. But now that the idea of the latte was in her head, she had to brave the wait.

After five minutes in line, she texted McVie.

Can you talk?

Three dots appeared, then disappeared, then reappeared again.

ok come by the ofc

The queue moved quickly, and now only four people stood in front of her. Fenway let her gaze wander around the room to the coffee-themed art and the black-lacquered wood furniture.

At a table next to the door sat a thin white woman in a cream-colored business suit, her straight black hair flowing to her shoulders. Catherine Klein.

She sipped a cappuccino from a Java Jim's ceramic mug. Fenway strained to see how much she had left—did she have time to order before—

"Next," the cashier called.

"Large latte," Fenway blurted. "Name of *Joanne*." She threw a ten-dollar bill at the cashier and walked as effortlessly as she could toward Catherine Klein.

Fenway pulled the chair out across the table from Catherine and sat. Catherine looked at Fenway with wide eyes.

"Hi, Mrs. Klein," Fenway said. "I know your husband doesn't want me talking to you in any official capacity, but I saw you sitting here."

"I don't think this is appropriate." Catherine set her mouth in a tight line and sat up ramrod-straight.

"Oh, you're right," Fenway said. "Given the footage we found at the Phillips-Holsen Hotel of Friday night's festivities, I should definitely take you down to the station. Make it official. Parade you in front of all the sheriff's deputies." She smiled. "But I know your husband wouldn't like that, and I just happened to run into you. So let's just have a chat."

"Just *happened* to run into me?"

Fenway shrugged. "I just need to know the nature of your relationship with Mr. Tonnick and where you were on Sunday night."

"It's none of your business."

"I'm investigating Mr. Tonnick's death, Mrs. Klein. It's *definitely* my business."

Catherine Klein looked down at the table for a moment, then raised her eyes and spoke in a low voice. "I saw Rick Tonnick on Friday night. My understanding is that he was killed on Sunday night." She cocked her head slightly. "Do you have any evidence—any at all—that I was anywhere near the murder scene on Sunday night?"

Fenway shifted in her seat. "You've now been involved with two people who have wound up murdered. First Jeremy Kapp, now Rick Tonnick. It's like you're a mantis who eats the head of the male after mating."

Catherine rolled her eyes. "You see, this is why I didn't vote for you, Miss Stevenson. You're accusing me of wrongdoing without evidence. You don't even have circumstantial evidence. My social calendar may be full, but that's no reason to make such grotesque comparisons."

"Sorry," Fenway said quickly. "That was out of line." She leaned back. "But you see why I have to ask you."

Catherine put her elbows on the table, her forearms flat. "I see no such conclusion. Although I suppose my husband has been leaning on you pretty hard not to interview me."

Fenway nodded.

"And that made you think I was hiding something." She sighed. "The mayor and I would like our private life kept private, that's all. Barry and I were home Sunday night, Coroner. I doubt you'll find anything or anyone to cast doubt on that statement, but if you do, I'm sure my husband will make me available for an interview."

"Joanne!" the barista called.

Fenway stood up. "I won't take up too much more of your time. I just have one or two more questions."

She hurried to the counter to grab her drink, but the barista took a long time putting the lid on the paper cup.

When Fenway turned around, the table was empty, the double glass doors were swaying slightly, and a baby-blue Crosstrek was reversing out of a parking space. She shook her head.

Catherine Klein was right, though. There was no evidence that put her at the scene of the murder. Perhaps Barry Klein was just an overprotective jackass.

Fifteen minutes later, Fenway was parking on the street around the corner from McVie Investigations. She smelled the Indian spices as soon as she got out of the car and admonished herself for wasting lunch on the subpar sandwich at the hotel.

She walked up the stairs and knocked on the door for suite 202 before turning the handle. McVie sat on the desk next to where Piper had been working, his head in his hands. The corners of his mouth and eyes drooped, and the lines on his face stood out more than usual.

"Hey," he said.

"Hey. Piper here?"

He shook his head. "I told her to go get a coffee. She took her laptop —she'll be gone at least a half hour."

"Ah. Because I was coming over."

He sighed. "You have to realize, Fenway, I don't want Amy to do this. I believe in our court system. If Megan hasn't done it, and she insists— and continues to insist—that she was asleep, that she never took the Mustang, that she definitely didn't go to the Phillips-Holsen—well, I have to believe her. And I have to believe that justice will be done." McVie looked down at the floor.

"But you don't believe it," Fenway said.

"I believe that Amy was with that boy toy of hers."

"You know about Tommy?"

"I told her if I was going to help her, she had to tell me everything."

Fenway nodded. "I just talked to him, in fact. Tommy is adamant she was there. I came at it from a couple of different angles, and he says if she's saying differently, she must be getting blackmailed or something." She paused. "Or protecting her daughter."

McVie rubbed his chin. "Amy and I talked about it at length. There's no one else we can think of who had access to those keys."

"Maybe Rick's other kids?"

He shook his head. "They don't have keys—not to the cars, and not to the house." He pulled himself up. "Do you want to go for a walk? I'm going a little stir crazy."

"Sure."

Fenway walked down the stairs first, and Craig came down with heavy feet, slowly.

"I can't get my head around it," McVie said in a low voice as they left the building. "I can't think of how someone would get Rick to let them into the penthouse suite, how they'd get access to put the sleeping pills in Rick's whisky, how they'd get him comfortable enough to get him naked in bed. Not unless he was expecting to have sex with whoever came in." He dragged his feet, scraping the soles of his shoes on the concrete. "And if Amy wasn't driving her Mustang, I can't think of anyone else but Megan who could have been behind the wheel."

"It was parked in the driveway," Fenway pointed out. "Maybe someone stole it."

"Occam's razor," McVie murmured. "I'm trying like hell to think of another explanation that fits all the evidence where it's not that bastard lying in bed waiting for my daughter—"

"Okay," Fenway said a little too loudly. "Maybe we just can't see it." Fenway remembered a walking path along the river which she thought would be a little quieter and more secluded than walking along the street. She got a step ahead of McVie and turned to head toward the path.

McVie followed, fuming.

"Maybe Amy *is* the killer," Fenway said.

McVie shook his head. "No way. Rick would have seen her and immediately been on his guard—explaining that it wasn't what it looks like."

"I heard a theory that Amy and Rick were roleplaying, maybe."

McVie scoffed. "That's what Amy plans to say in her confession," he said, "but I know that's not what happened."

"And that probably leaves out Rick's children, too," Fenway said. "Unless something really unusual is happening. But I don't see it— certainly not in the way Grant and Noreen were behaving."

The path led off to the left, and Fenway stepped ahead of McVie.

"Where are we going?"

"We'll take a walk along the river. It's usually more secluded, especially in January. You and I aren't supposed to be talking about this, remember."

McVie nodded. "I'm sorry. I'm putting you in a bad situation."

Fenway smiled. "And here I thought you were such a Boy Scout."

He grunted. "Turns out I have different rules where my daughter is concerned." The wind whipped up, and he crossed his arms. "Don't get me wrong. If she had killed someone for money or because she was jealous, I'd get her a good lawyer, but I wouldn't stand in the way of her getting arrested. But we're talking about a fifty-eight-year-old man pressuring my seventeen-year-old daughter into having sex for who knows how long. And if this was the only way she thought she could get out of it? No way is she going to jail for that. Not if I can help it."

"Rick Tonnick slept with a lot of other women, though. Catherine Klein visited him on Friday night—forty-eight hours before he was killed."

"Catherine Klein? Barry Klein's wife?"

"Right."

He shook his head. "Wow. She certainly gets around."

"They've got some sort of understanding," Fenway said. "It's not my business. But Barry Klein doesn't seem to want it to get out." She cleared her throat. "Anyway, I haven't talked to any of these other women. I got a list of all the nights in the last two years that he stayed at the Phillips-Holsen."

"Oh. So you could maybe find out who a couple of these women are?"

"Maybe." She screwed up her mouth. "Um, Craig, you know that, uh, Amy was…"

He grunted. "Yes. I know she was sleeping with Rick Tonnick when she was married to me. Look, I've found out a lot about Amy in the last few months that has been very hard for me to hear."

"I'm sorry."

"Yeah, thanks. But whatever. I'm just worried about Megan."

"And you're willing to let Amy confess?"

Faintly, Fenway heard a radio. Led Zeppelin—possibly the classic rock station. It was getting slightly louder as they walked.

Craig shrugged. "I'm not sure. I mean, on one hand, I don't want Megan to go to jail. On the other hand, I don't like this. I don't like it at all. I wish I could just wake up and this would all be different. That Rick Tonnick had never raped my daughter."

"Yeah," Fenway said, setting her jaw, closing her eyes and flashing back to her Russian lit professor's office at Western Washington. She blinked. "I know what you mean."

The path led into a little clearing with picnic tables. Three teenagers were sitting at the table, one of them smoking a cigarette, an open bag of Doritos and a pack of Coke on the table between them. An old-school boom box sat on the ground next to them with the deejay announcing that they'd "get the Led out" at seven that evening.

"I wonder if this is how it started," Craig said. "If he took Megan to a secluded place like this and promised her—"

"Don't," Fenway said sharply. "You don't know what it was like. In fact, all we have that makes us think that this is the way it went down is a process of elimination. We can't think of another set of plausible circumstances, so our minds all jumped to this conclusion."

"I went over there to pick her up a couple of weeks ago. Amy wasn't there, but Rick was. And Megan looked uncomfortable. What else could—"

"No," Fenway said, stamping her foot. "We just haven't found the right answer yet." She looked at McVie. "Do you honestly think your daughter is capable of luring him to a hotel room, dropping sleeping pills in his drink, and then suffocating him with a pillow?"

Craig was quiet.

"You told me yourself that she has a tell when she lies. And you asked her, and you didn't think she was lying."

"Look, Fenway, I was blindsided by Amy's cheating. Maybe I can't see what Megan was—is—capable of, too." He looked down at the path and kicked hard at a small rock, which careened into the river with a splash. "Besides, your office is building a pretty solid case against Amy, which can only go south if Megan gets put in the crosshairs."

"I don't want to arrest either of them, Craig."

He grunted.

"I don't! You think I do?"

"I think you like the puzzle, Fenway, and I think you like the truth. And I think you've dug so far and uncovered so much that now the truth will get out. And I'm terrified for my daughter, all right?"

Fenway nodded.

"Look—I'm sorry to drag you into this. I shouldn't have asked you to come over. I understand what you have to do. I know it's your job, and I know that there's a very clear line between lawful and unlawful on this."

"Craig," she said, disliking the tone of his voice, "we can work—"

"Until this is over, I don't think we better bring this up again," Craig said.

Fenway stopped. "What does that mean?"

Craig ran his hands through his hair. "It means my family is about to blow up. And I can't have my feelings for you complicate things."

"Are you—are you breaking up with me?"

"No," he said quickly. "No. But right now, until I figure some things out, I need a little space."

"How is that not—"

"I don't want to see other people, and I don't want you to see other people. We're still boyfriend-girlfriend or whatever this is. I just have to make the best decision for my family, and when you're around, I have a big conflict of interest. And I can't deal with that right now."

Fenway stopped in her tracks. "You can't deal with me right now?" Her phone dinged in her purse. McVie continued to walk, turning up a concrete path toward the road.

Reminder: press conference at 4:00 P.M.
Ferris Energy HQ
in 30 min

"Dammit," Fenway muttered. She looked down and kicked a rock at her feet. It spun off to the side and landed in a bush.

CHAPTER FOURTEEN

She pulled out her phone on her way to the Accord and tapped the Maps application, noting that Gateway of India was open until nine o'clock. A nice baingan bharta for dinner was exactly what she needed to improve her day. She tapped Charlotte's name.

"Charlotte Ferris."

"Hey, Charlotte, it's Fenway. I've been wrapped up in the investigation, but I wanted to tell you I'm on my way. Still at the headquarters?"

"Actually," Charlotte said, "there's a place right off Ocean Highway, just south of the Belvedere Terrace Hotel, that has a great overlook to the property. Our PR folks just scouted it and said it's got plenty of room, and there's a power source we can use for the public address system."

"I hope it's the part of the property that looks nice."

"They texted me photos. It's definitely picturesque. Apparently, there's kind of a funny smell."

"Probably the petroleum," Fenway said. "From all the drilling Ferris is doing offshore."

"Great," Charlotte said. "Let's hope the reporters don't mention that in their articles."

"I'm sorry, but I haven't been able to work on any kind of announcement or speech at all. Will I have time?"

"The PR folks insisted on writing it for you."

Fenway laughed. "I hope you told them what I was like. You know I'm not putting any bullshit in there. I'll embarrass myself in front of everyone before I put out something I know is a lie."

"They were properly warned," Charlotte said. "I understand that a couple of them even voted for you."

"Will miracles never cease," Fenway said flatly.

After hanging up, Fenway turned onto the Ocean Highway exit and wished she were still driving her father's Porsche.

She thought she knew where the overlook was and pulled into a parking lot. The Channel 12 news van was already in the lot, so Fenway figured she was in the right place. Walking about five minutes to the clearing, she saw the podium, the microphones, and Charlotte, looking stunning and professional in a black pinstripe suit and a candy-apple-red blouse with the suit skirt just above her knee. Fenway looked at her own outfit—the charcoal gray pantsuit over a white polyester tank. Good enough for a press conference, she supposed, although she was sure her hair was a mess. She caught Charlotte's eye and waved.

Charlotte rushed over. "Are you okay?"

Fenway nodded. "Sure. Why wouldn't I be? I'm here with a good ten minutes to spare."

Charlotte called over her shoulder. "Debbie? Has anyone seen Debbie?"

"I'll get her," said a faint voice.

Charlotte turned back to Fenway. "You look like you've been crying. Your eyes are puffy, your skin is a little blotchy—what happened?"

"Oh—well, it's the investigation. It took a turn. There are—there are some things that were kind of, uh, tough to think about."

"Don't worry, don't worry," Charlotte said offhandedly. "Debbie can fix you right up." Over Charlotte's shoulder, Fenway saw a white woman with a brunette ponytail, a plaid shirt, and blue jeans head over. She was holding a large kit that Fenway assumed was full of makeup. "Is that Debbie? She's the one who's going to fix me?"

Charlotte followed Fenway's gaze. "Oh, Debbie. Yes. Don't look at her fashion sense; look at her face. Do you see the masterful application of makeup?" Charlotte cocked her head at Fenway. "Well, maybe you don't. But that's okay. I do. And the cameras will, too."

Debbie came up to them. "Yes, Mrs. Ferris?"

"Fenway came right from work, Debbie. Think you can work your magic?"

"Of course." Debbie smiled at Fenway. "Follow me to the trailer."

While Fenway sat on a high stool in the trailer, trying to keep her face still, another woman shoved a piece of paper in Fenway's hand—the text of the speech. The tone of the words was a bit stiff, and Fenway might trip over a couple of the turns of phrase, but she started reciting it to herself. It wasn't bad. Charlotte may not know the energy industry, but she knew how to make a good impression. And if Fenway was going to help Charlotte save her father's company, she'd do what she was told.

Five minutes later, she stood on a makeshift dais in front of cameras, the Ferris Energy Public Relations Vice President introducing her. "And now, the Ferris Energy Community Liaison, Fenway Stevenson."

Her legs felt heavy as she stepped forward in front of the microphones. She held the paper on the top of the podium, hopefully out of the view of the cameras, and she smiled as warmly as she could, looking over the top of the crowd, not in their eyes. It was a trick she had learned in a public speaking class in college. A black Lincoln Town Car stopped at the side of the highway. Looky-loos, probably.

"Thank you," Fenway said. She was pleasantly surprised that her voice was clear and confident. "It gives me great pleasure to announce that Ferris Energy Corporation has begun the process to transfer the dozens of acres you see behind me to the Ferris Land Foundation. This is the first step in transferring this ecologically valuable parcel to the Dominguez Open Space Land Trust."

She saw a man in a suit get out of the back of the limo, waving his arms angrily and heading toward them. Ugh. Was this one of Archie Pendergrass's vice presidents trying to keep the buying price for Ferris Energy down? She focused her attention slightly to her right, above another reporter's head. "As the newly appointed Community Liaison, it's my goal for Ferris Energy to become the valuable partner that my hometown needs. We've been the largest employer in Dominguez

County for years, but a valuable partnership requires more than paychecks."

"I said *stop!*" the man screamed, his voice now audible to everyone in the small group. "I will not allow the coroner to sully the reputation of my office—"

Fenway squinted. Barry Klein. She should have recognized his gait.

"This whole thing is a sham! Everything out of her mouth is an unsubstantiated lie!"

The reporters all swung their heads toward Barry Klein. The television camera from Channel 12 did, too.

Barry Klein stopped running and miraculously didn't even seem out of breath. "The coroner has been following several leads that are not currently panning out," Klein said, "and while she doesn't report to me, she doesn't speak for what the county—and what the Sheriff's Office—is doing to catch the killer of one of our beloved pillars of the community—"

Fenway clenched and unclenched her fists. "Mayor Klein," she said loudly, her face closer to the microphone, and her ears were greeted by a slight squeal of feedback. "I'm announcing an initiative—"

"I know exactly what you're doing," Klein barked.

"—to donate Ferris Energy land to a large open space preserve in the county."

Klein stopped.

"I'm not announcing anything about the murder investigation, Mr. Mayor," she said, trying to keep her voice calm and even. "I'm here in my capacity as Community Liaison for Ferris Energy, not as Dominguez County Coroner."

Klein's eyes narrowed. Fenway expected him to perhaps be embarrassed, but instead he appeared to double down on anger. "My office. Tomorrow morning." He turned and started walking back to the limousine.

Fenway bent down to the microphone.

I can assure you, Mayor Klein, that your wife's infidelity with the decedent has not yet been confirmed to be relevant in the investigation of his murder.

That was on the tip of her tongue, but she closed her eyes and counted to ten in her head instead.

Shouts of "Mr. Mayor! Mr. Mayor!" "Care to comment on your feud with the coroner?" "What are the specific lies you're referring to?" followed him all the way back to the side of the road, where he opened the door and got in. The limo immediately drove off.

"Our mayor, everyone," Fenway said. "We may not see eye to eye on the way to conduct a murder investigation, but I think you'll find we both agree that this open space donation is a great thing for both the monarch butterfly population and the city of Estancia."

After the announcement, the reporters harassed her for five minutes about her feud with the mayor. "I assure you," she said, "that wherever significant progress is made, it's because the people involved have looked at all sides of a situation and have worked through their differences. Conflict makes a strong process—and that's especially true with something as important as a murder investigation."

"What do you believe the mayor is accusing you of lying about?" one reporter asked.

"I don't want to speculate," Fenway said, "but I would like to take questions regarding the donation of this land—and the many monarch butterfly waystations we have here. We've got butterfly experts from the Dominguez Land Trust, and we've got Ferris Energy's controller here if anyone has questions on the effect of this on our bottom line. Anyone?"

A reporter from an environmental magazine raised his hand, and Fenway, relieved, called on him. His question was about butterfly migration patterns, and she gratefully ceded her spot on the dais to the butterfly expert.

She stepped down, and Charlotte walked up to her, arms crossed and brow knitted. "What in the world was that about?"

"I found out that his wife slept with the dead guy last week," Fenway said. "I guess he thought I was announcing that instead."

"How dare he," Charlotte said, seething. "Can we sue?"

"For what?" Fenway replied. "And even if there was something to sue over, it wouldn't be a good idea. It'll just throw more light onto the mayor and none on the initiative."

Charlotte craned her neck. "They're calling on the reporters from the environmental and the industry publications, so that's good. Our financial numbers look pretty good on this, too—just the tax savings alone are making our bottom line improve this year."

"Doesn't really affect the EBITDA," Fenway said.

"The what?" Charlotte said.

"The bottom line before all the deductions, like taxes," Fenway said. "But if your controller spins it so that the industry publications frame this well, it doesn't really matter if the EBITDA is unchanged."

"I thought you said you didn't know anything about economics."

Fenway shrugged. "Not enough to be CEO, that's for sure. But I couldn't sleep last night. Read a little background on the industry."

Charlotte nodded. "Are you and Barry Klein ever going to put this behind you?"

"Who knows? He's the one who has the problem with me. And with Dad." Her phone buzzed. It was a call from the assisted living facility. "Oh, Charlotte, I have to take this. Will you be all right?"

"Sure," Charlotte said. "Thank you for making the time to do this."

Fenway snorted. "This was a disaster. I hope I just didn't damage anything too badly." She clicked ANSWER and started walking toward the Accord.

"Fenway Stevenson."

"Miss Stevenson," said a low, no-nonsense voice. "This is Pascal Beauregard with Rolling Meadows. I'm the supervisor here."

"Oh, yes. Thank you for getting back to me." Fenway had to watch her feet; the sun was about to dip below the horizon, and the gray light was getting dimmer.

"I must say, this is quite an unusual request."

"You're telling me. A couple of months ago, I thought my mom was just my mom. Now I find out she had this whole other life with a whole other name."

"Our care facility will accept any visitor that our residents want to see," Beauregard said.

Oh, good. That meant Mrs. Godwin still had power of attorney over herself. She probably didn't have dementia or Alzheimer's.

"I've reviewed what you communicated to our staff, and I saw the photograph. We are, of course, concerned about the safety of our residents, and about them providing financial assistance to persons claiming to be related when they are not."

"I understand." Fenway was at the end of the path where it met the parking lot. "I'd be concerned, too. What can I do? Do I need to get some sort of court declaration about Samara? Maybe a blood test to see if I'm related to her?"

"Well," Beauregard said, "we spoke to her about you, and the staff would be comfortable with supervised visitation."

"Oh—that's good." Fenway opened her car door and sat in the driver's seat with the door open. "Do—do I need to make an appointment to come see her?"

"If you let us know you're coming, that would be best. That way, we'll make sure she's not on one of the sponsored excursions here."

"When can I see her?"

"Oh—well, it's almost five o'clock now. Our suggested visiting hours end at eight—that's when many of the residents start to fade."

"I can't get down there tonight—not through traffic," Fenway said. "But I think I can come down first thing tomorrow. If I leave around seven and traffic's not too bad, I can get there at maybe eleven? Take her to lunch? Supervised, of course."

"We can make that work," Beauregard said.

"How—how much did you tell her about me? About the whole situation with my mom?"

"She knew Samara had to go away for a while," Beauregard said. "But she assumed it would be a couple of months. She didn't hear from her again."

"Did you show her the picture?"

"Yes," Beauregard said. "She recognized her daughter right away."

Fenway felt a tear run down her cheek. "Does—does she know..."

"We didn't want to cause her too much stress," Beauregard said gently. "She—well, she was quite excited. We told her we didn't know much yet. She insisted we call you back tonight."

"Can I talk with her?"

"She's resting right now," Beauregard said. "I don't want to strain her too much this late in the day. If you can call tomorrow and let us know when you'll be here, we'll let you talk to her then. She's got more energy in the mornings."

They said their goodbyes, and Fenway was fairly bursting with excitement.

She started the car and tapped the phone icon to call McVie. Then she stopped. McVie didn't want to see her—not right now. True, it was mostly about the case, but she'd seen him only an hour or two ago. Maybe she'd tell him later.

Rachel's phone went right to voicemail. Oh—as the county public information officer, she was probably getting inundated with calls regarding the mayor's meltdown. In fact, maybe the coroner's office was being hit too. She called Dez.

"Sergeant Roubideaux."

"Hey, Dez—is the office all clear of reporters?"

"What did you say to Barry Klein? There are about four reporters camped out in front of the entrance."

"I didn't say anything. He screamed at me and called me a liar in the middle of my press conference, then he stalked off and said he'd see me —oh, crap."

"What?"

"He said he'd see me tomorrow morning. And I was going to L.A. first thing."

"What's in Los Angeles?"

"My grandmother."

"Your grandmother? I thought your—oh, that's right. Your mom's secret identity. You have a grandmother you didn't know existed?"

"Right. She's in a nursing home in L.A. And I'm going to drive there tomorrow and see her."

"In the middle of a murder investigation?"

"Dez, I didn't know I had a grandmother until yesterday. And yes, in the middle of an investigation. I have a feeling we're about to get to the end of it anyway."

"What makes you say that?"

"I think we're going to have a confession by tonight. And that means the mayor will want to take a victory lap, and I can let him do that for twenty-four hours before I start figuring out how to disprove the confession."

"Do you want to tell me what's going on, Fenway?"

"I wish I could tell you," Fenway said. "But I'll be having lunch with my grandma." She paused. "Should I get her something? What do you get for the grandparent you didn't know you had?"

"Are you washing your hands of this whole investigation, or are you still up for an interview or two?"

"I'm still up for an interview. I'm not leaving till tomorrow morning."

"Okay," Dez said. "You know where Valhalla is, right?"

"I assume you mean the bar a block away from the Phillips-Holsen and not the Viking afterlife."

"No, no, Fenway, I'm inviting you to a secret Scandinavian death ritual. Will you bring the Rumple Minze if I grab the lutefisk?"

"You're hilarious, Dez," Fenway said flatly.

"Meet me there in fifteen minutes."

The sun was long gone at about half past five when Dez pulled up in front of Valhalla. They walked in. Two white men in plaid shirts were playing pool in the back. A man and a woman in business casual dress were at a small table near the front window, a Querido Springs beer bottle in front of each of them. And two men, one large and Asian, one skinny and black, were at each end of the bar. The large man had a fizzy clear drink, and the skinny one had a glass of light-colored beer in front of him. Duke Perriman stood behind the bar and walked to the side closest to the entrance.

"Thanks for coming," Duke said. "Can I get you anything?"

"We're still on the clock," Fenway said, "although that does sound tempting." Especially with the last interaction with Mayor Klein.

"I'll get right to the point," Duke said. "You asked if I was here on Sunday night. Yeah—I was. But then I remembered that Gretchen—uh, I mean, Sheriff Donnelly—said this was on the same block as that fancy hotel."

"Okay," Dez said.

"Well, it made me remember this blonde who sashayed in just before closing time. I'd already done last call, but she was pretty, done up real nice, and dressed to impress, if you know what I mean."

"I think we get it," Fenway said.

"Well, anyway, she seems real nervous, and I'm trying to put the moves on her—figure, a hot white girl in this part of town? Maybe she had a date end bad. Doesn't mean her evening can't get better."

"You're real smooth," Dez said. "Almost makes me wish I didn't play for the other team."

Duke laughed heartily. "You know, I don't usually like cops, but y'all are all right down there." He put his hands flat on the table. "Anyway, I come into the bar today, and the news is on, talking about the guy that got murdered."

"Yes?"

"And the news shows a photo of the dead guy and his new wife, right?"

"Yeah?" Dez said, perking up.

"Well, that was her. That was the woman who came into the bar."

Fenway blinked a few times rapidly. "Wait—the woman who was here at the bar just before two in the morning—that was the dead man's new wife?"

"That's what I'm saying."

"How late was she here?" Dez asked.

"She did a tequila shot. No salt or lime. Not a girl lookin' for a good time, I guess. Some bad dates are like that. Anyway, she paid—ten bucks on a six-dollar shot, and she let me keep the change."

"Cash, not card?"

"Right."

"Did you get her name?" Dez asked.

"Naw. I asked, but she was on some kind of mission, you know? Then she walked out the door and across the street. She was hurrying, but she had these big high heels on. Couldn't run too fast."

"Did you see where she went?"

Duke put his elbows on the bar. "Now, see, if I told you I watched her go across the street and then go into that little walkway there between the hotel and the building next to it, you're going to accuse me of being some kind of pervert or something. Nothing wrong with watching a nice-looking woman walk across the street. I didn't wolf whistle or nothin'."

Fenway felt both relief and sickness come over her. Tommy Kinsella must be a great actor, and Amy must be one too, to convince McVie that she was going to confess even though she hadn't done it. Fenway couldn't yet figure out how Amy had gotten into the penthouse elevator, much less the suite, but with an eyewitness—one who wasn't involved romantically with the suspect—it was all but assured that Amy Tonnick would be arrested for the murder of her husband.

They asked Duke to go down to the station on his dinner break and make a statement.

As they left the bar, Dez set her mouth in a line. "What do you think? Do you think she did it now?"

"I don't see how we can ignore Duke's account," Fenway said. "I could have sworn that Tommy Kinsella was telling the truth, but he's got a reason to lie. Duke doesn't."

"I think it's time," Dez said. "I'll call Sheriff Donnelly. Maybe we can arrange for Amy to give herself up."

Fenway had a bad feeling in the pit of her stomach. "I should go and prepare them," she said. "I bet Craig is over there, too, and I want him to hear this from me."

Dez looked at Fenway out of the corner of her eye. "Don't get too involved in the emotional politics of this," she said. "He's your boyfriend, but remember, he's got a daughter he's trying to protect."

"Oh," Fenway said, "believe me, I'm aware of the daughter he's trying to protect."

"I'll text you after I tell Donnelly," Dez said. "I hope we can negotiate something so we don't have to embarrass Megan."

"Right."

Dez got into her Impala and drove off. Fenway swallowed hard, got out her phone, and texted McVie.

There's a witness who saw Amy go into the hotel just before Rick was murdered
There's enough evidence to arrest her

*I'm headed to Amy's house and will try to convince her to give herself up
tonight*
Can you help me or are you already there?

Fenway walked to her car, but Craig hadn't returned her text. She started the engine and punched the Tonnick house address into her phone.

CHAPTER FIFTEEN

Fenway pulled up in the long driveway behind the red Mustang with the black top, the license plate frame reading "Estancia High Mom," and the Estancia High Concert Choir sticker on the bumper below the three vertical taillights on the left. Like Tommy Kinsella had said, she parked it on the right side of the roundabout that split the driveway toward the rear of the house and toward the garage.

Amy opened the door to the sprawling house in gray yoga pants and a red tank top. She looked partially like she was about to work out and partially like she was coming from a photoshoot where models were only pretending to work out. Fenway suppressed her jealousy.

"Amy—hi. Are Megan and Craig here?"

"Megan's here, but Craig's at work, I think."

"I don't have a lot of time," Fenway said, stepping inside. "They're preparing an arrest warrant for you right now."

Amy closed the door, then crossed her arms and sighed. "No, you must be mistaken. I talked about this with Craig last night—I'm waiting to turn myself in until tomorrow. I was just off to Pilates."

"I don't think they'll let you do that," Fenway said.

"You don't have to worry," Amy said. "I can turn myself in without actually confessing."

"Are you saying that you did it or not?" Fenway asked. "Because Craig says you insist that you did it."

"What's the alternative?" Amy snapped. "I can't have Craig thinking that Megan is guilty."

"Is she? Tommy's ready to swear on a stack of Bibles that the two of you were together."

"He's the sweetest guy," Amy said. "My lawyer says if I turn myself in without confessing, not only will Megan be in the clear, but the prosecution will have to make the case against me in court. And they can't prove anything. They may have my car, but there isn't anyone there who saw me go in or who saw me take the elevat—"

"Yes, there is," Fenway said. "There's an eyewitness who watched you go into the walkway off Fourth Street that leads to the back of the Phillips-Holsen."

"There's an—an eyewitness?"

Fenway nodded. "It's enough to arrest you, and I don't think they'll be too concerned about your yoga class."

"Pilates."

"Focus, Amy," Fenway said. "Megan's here? It's going to be rough on her to see her mother taken away in cuffs. I think if you call the sheriff's office and tell them you'll turn yourself in, you can buy a couple of hours. Get Megan settled."

Another car pulled up outside.

"Were you expecting anyone?"

"I wanted to talk to Grant and Noreen about helping with Megan while I sorted this all out." She frowned. "I told them to come in an hour. Not now."

"You've certainly packed a lot into one evening."

"My lawyer wanted to meet with me tomorrow morning and negotiate me turning myself in then," Amy said. "I have a lot of stuff to take care of first." She reached out and opened the door again. Grant and Noreen Tonnick were walking up the driveway. A Jaguar coupe was parked behind Fenway's Accord.

The corners of Grant's mouth were turned down, but there was a mischievous delight in Noreen's eyes. Fenway's mouth went dry.

"Guys," Fenway said, "I appreciate you being here, but Amy actually needs some time to take care of a couple of things."

"We'll definitely help take care of things," Grant said.

Amy was taken aback. "What does that mean?"

"It means," Noreen said, "that under California law, you can't profit from your bad action. As soon as they take you in, we're taking over this house."

"I'm innocent," Amy protested. "They've got the wrong person, and my lawyer—"

"I hope you're using your own money for the lawyer," Noreen said, "because I don't think Daddy would like you using his money to help you get away with killing him."

Amy's eyes went wide. "You promised you'd help Megan—"

"We promised we'd come over and help *you*," Grant said, "but really, we're just going to help you get your stuff out of the house." He set his mouth in a hard line. "You killed my father, and I'm not letting you stay in his house or use his money for an expensive defense attorney." He turned to his sister. "What do you think, Noreen?"

"I think Amy should be glad we're just kicking her out," Noreen said. "Believe me, when we heard she'd done it, I was in favor of junking it all," Noreen said. "Grant convinced me that the courts would probably like it a little better if we moved their shit into storage first."

"Which wing do you want, Noreen?" Grant said. "Me, I've always been a little partial to the in-law quarters. As long as I get the game room and the extra space in the garage."

"The master suite is fine by me," Noreen said. She took a framed art photo off the wall. "I don't remember this being here before you moved in, Amy."

"That's mine," she said. "I had it before—"

Noreen dropped it onto the floor with a crack of breaking glass. "Oopsie."

"Stop," Fenway said, raising her voice. "You don't have any right to be in here yet." She took her cell phone from her purse and turned the video on, then hit the RECORD button. "This is Amy's property. You don't have the right to come in here yet."

Noreen wheeled around and faced Fenway. "She murdered our father, and she's living in his house," she said through gritted teeth. "What the hell would you have us do?"

The sound of a door opening and slamming in the back of the house, then footfalls stomping up the hallway. "I'm trying to study!" Megan shouted. "Mom, if you want me to—" Then she stopped short when she saw Fenway. She glanced at Grant and Noreen's angry faces.

"I'm sorry," Fenway said. "I came over to try to get her ready before the sheriff—"

"You put them up to this?" Megan shouted. "I know you're fucking my dad, but do you have to ruin *my* life too?"

Fenway jumped back. "Listen, Megan, I don't know what's going on, but I didn't—"

"Coroner, we need to get them out of this house," Grant said. "I'm having my lawyer file a motion to freeze my father's accounts. I don't want her spending his money to find an attorney who'll get her off on a technicality." He pointed at Megan. "And when Amy vacates, her daughter needs to get out, too."

"Innocent until proven guilty," Fenway said.

"We'll see what happens with the lawyers," Grant growled.

"Grant and I aren't leaving," said Noreen. "And since you're recording, Miss Stevenson, make sure you get footage of everything on the walls. If Amy sells one thing of my father's, we'll be suing."

In the distance, sirens.

"I thought you said I could negotiate turning myself in," Amy snapped at Fenway.

"*That's* what you're worried about?" Fenway said. "I come give you a heads up, your stepkids tell you they're kicking you out—"

Megan stomped off into the hall and slammed the door.

Fenway stopped recording and called McVie. His phone rang three times and went to voicemail. "Craig, your ex is being arrested, and Grant and Noreen are throwing Megan out as soon as they can. Get your ass over here." The sirens grew louder.

"I'm not turning myself in until—"

"You don't have a choice!" Fenway roared. "You're not married to the sheriff anymore. You don't get special treatment. There's an eyewitness,

Amy. You're in trouble. Call your lawyer now. Give him a heads-up on Grant's motion to freeze your accounts."

"This isn't what—"

"You have about two minutes to get as many of your affairs in order as you can," Fenway said. "I'll stall the police as long as possible, but you better come out with your hands up and go willingly."

Amy looked defiantly at Grant, then Noreen, then Fenway—and her face fell. She turned and hurried into the back of the house—the master suite—hopefully to make as many arrangements as she could.

"You two"—Fenway turned to Noreen and Grant, bringing her video back up on her phone—"aren't coming back until a judge weighs in."

"When Amy vacates, the law says—"

"Not until a judge weighs in," Fenway said, "and I'll stay here myself if I have to."

Grant narrowed his eyes, and Fenway saw that he had no intention of keeping away for that long.

The sirens grew louder, ending in the driveway behind the Jaguar coupe. Fenway glared at Noreen until there was a knock on the front door. "Police," came the call. It was Gretchen's voice.

Fenway walked over to the door and opened it. Sheriff Gretchen Donnelly stood with three uniformed sheriff's deputies.

"Fenway?" Donnelly said.

"Amy wanted to negotiate turning herself in," Fenway said. "But I guess you all had other plans." She motioned to the half-siblings. "Would you tell Grant and Noreen here when they can take over their father's house now that their stepmother is being arrested for their father's murder?"

"Is that why they're here?" the sheriff said.

"Yes. They've told Megan she has to get out as soon as Amy is taken away."

"Folks," Sheriff Donnelly said, "I don't know what television show you watched that made you think you can evict your stepmother, but that's not how it works. She's got to plead guilty or be convicted, first of all, and then the court will give her a reasonable period of time to vacate." She tapped her holster. "I would suggest that perhaps you think about leaving the premises before my deputies make some assumption about you trespassing on Mrs. Tonnick's property."

Grant threw a hateful look at Fenway and stomped out the door, Noreen following.

"They're going to be back as soon as we're gone," Fenway said to the sheriff.

"Then we'll post a deputy here overnight," Donnelly said. "I've got a couple of 'em jonesing for some overtime. Christmas hit their credit cards hard this year." She looked around the foyer, peering into the kitchen and great room. "Exactly where is the grieving widow?"

"Getting her affairs in order," Fenway said. "I can go get her if you like."

The sheriff grinned and shook her head. "I don't know many people who would go to these lengths for their boyfriend's ex-wife."

"It's true," Fenway said. "I *have* done some pretty idiotic things when it comes to relationships."

Sheriff Donnelly laughed.

Fenway walked to the master suite through an entertainment room that had cinema-style seating and the biggest screen Fenway had ever seen—even larger than the one at her father's house. She came to a door she assumed was the master bedroom and rapped on the heavy walnut three times. "The police are here, Amy," she called, "and it's time to go."

Fenway heard tentative steps on the other side of the door, then the knob turned and the door opened. Amy was dressed in a brown pantsuit with a cream-colored blouse. No jewelry adorned her fingers or neck except a gold band.

"Were you able to get things in order?"

"I called my lawyer," Amy said. "I don't really know what's happening next." She cleared her throat. "Will you take care of Megan?"

Fenway blanched. "Take care of her?"

"Make sure she gets to Craig's safely. Take as much stuff as you can out of her room. I don't trust those kids."

Fenway nodded. "I can do that. There's going to be a deputy here all night."

"Good," Amy said. "Maybe most of my things will still be in one piece when I get out on bail."

Fenway nodded. "Are you covering for Megan?" she said in a low voice.

"I don't know," Amy said. "I didn't do it, but I don't believe she did either. But nothing else makes sense."

Amy walked through the entertainment room, and Fenway followed a few feet behind her.

"Amelia Renée Tonnick," the sheriff said, "you are under arrest for the murder of Richard Wayne Tonnick. You have the right to remain silent. Anything you say can and will be used against you…"

Fenway closed her eyes for a moment, wondering if Megan would willingly go with her. She had no idea how to talk to teenagers. She hadn't even known how to talk with them when she was one herself. She opened her eyes and watched the sheriff lead Amy to the squad car, but not in handcuffs. At least there was that small gesture.

Fenway heard the police car start up and back down the driveway. Two of the other deputies got into a second car, and they swung around the roundabout before driving out. The third deputy watched the others leave, then walked to the fountain in the lawn in the middle of the roundabout and stared down the driveway.

Fenway was alone in the house with Megan, and Megan had to get out.

How much trunk space did her Accord have, anyway? And did the inside of the car still smell like tacos?

She walked down the long, dark hallway until she got to a door with light coming from underneath it. She knocked firmly, but, she hoped, kindly.

A moment passed, and then the door swung open. Megan, her dirty blonde tresses falling to her shoulders, had tear tracks staining her cheeks.

"They really took her away," Megan said.

"They really did."

"I hate you."

Ouch. Her tone stung. But Fenway just nodded. "I'm sorry. I didn't want it to happen this way."

"Yes, you did."

Fenway sighed. "No, I really didn't. Your mom and I might have our differences, but I didn't want it to go like this."

Megan crossed her arms and sniffled. "So why are you still here?"

"Because," Fenway said, "your mom wanted me to get you to your father's house safely. She doesn't trust Grant or Noreen. She thinks they're going to come back. There's a deputy stationed here tonight, but it'll be safer with your dad."

Megan eyed her suspiciously. "You're not going to stay over at my dad's, are you?"

Fenway ignored her. "Do you have things that are valuable to you? Things you don't want Grant and Noreen to destroy?"

"My bed," Megan said.

"Your bed can be replaced. I mean sentimental stuff. Yearbooks. Scrapbooks. Awards. Your favorite sweatshirt. Stuff like that."

Megan thought for a minute. "Um, yeah. I have some stuff like that. My concert choir trophies, for one thing. And I want my yearbooks."

"Do you have some boxes?"

"I think so. Probably in the spare room down at the end of the hall."

For the next two hours, Fenway helped Megan pack her important items—books, trophies, friendship bracelets from sixth grade, photos of her friends at the Dominguez County Fair, pictures of her boyfriend. When Megan was out of the room trying to locate a photo album, Fenway emptied Megan's nightstand drawer and found a diary and a partially used box of condoms and placed them both in a box that she started to label PERSONAL, then thought better of it and labeled it FEMININE HYGIENE. Megan didn't talk to Fenway unless she pointed at things to have her pack.

"Where's your Jeep?" Fenway asked.

"In the shop. Mom was going to drive me to get it tomorrow afternoon."

"I'll give you a ride. We can take my car."

Fenway carried most of the boxes out to the Accord and folded the rear seats down. Megan wanted to take her skis, and Fenway said no. She whined about it, saying that the skis were special, they didn't make them anymore, and Fenway finally gave in, moving the boxes in the trunk so that the skis stuck all the way up between the driver's and passenger's seats.

Craig hadn't responded to Fenway's texts—she tried again about an hour into packing, telling him she'd bring Megan and a lot of her stuff over. It was past nine o'clock when they finally got out of the house. They walked past the deputy keeping sentry—Fenway said goodbye to him, and he just nodded in response—and Fenway steered the Accord around the fountain and down the driveway.

Megan pulled her phone out and put her earbuds in, then slumped in her seat and turned her head toward the window. Fenway thought she heard sniffling and turned the radio up.

Fenway pulled into Craig's apartment complex fifteen minutes later and parked in a visitor's space. She texted *we're here come help us,* then loaded Megan up with boxes and grabbed a couple herself. Megan made a beeline for the elevator, and Fenway hurried to get in behind her.

The doors closed, and Megan hit the 2 button. They stood in silence for a moment.

"Did you reach your dad?" Fenway said.

"I thought you were texting him."

"He didn't respond to me."

Megan smirked. "You guys fighting?"

"Sort of."

Megan flinched. "You are?"

"Yes."

"What about?"

"The way I'm handling this case."

"Really?"

"Yes." Fenway paused, debating how much to tell Megan. The doors opened on the second floor, and Megan took the boxes out of the elevators. Fenway followed her.

"Kind of sucks that you and Dad don't get to work together anymore."

"Yeah," Fenway said. "I liked working with him."

Megan got to the door and unlocked it, turning the lights on in the living room, and dumped the boxes next to the sofa.

When the two of them got back out to the Accord, Craig was standing next to the car. "Hey," he said. "What happened?"

"They arrested Mom for murder," Megan said, flipping the hair out of her face.

"Are you okay?"

Megan shrugged. "I'd rather stay in that big mansion than in your tiny apartment that smells like cheese," she said, "but whatever. I'm supposed to see Jack in an hour anyway."

"Maybe you better not see Jack tonight," McVie said. "You've had a lot going on today."

"I finished all my homework, which wasn't easy with all the drama in the house."

"Right," McVie said, "but it's late, and you've got to—"

"Can't I just deal with the boxes another time?" Megan said. "Besides, when this is all over, I'm just going to move the boxes back into Rick's house anyway."

Fenway popped the trunk with her key fob, and they took more boxes. Craig pulled the skis out of the trunk, and Fenway thought she heard scraping—the skis scratching the leather upholstery. She told herself she didn't really care about the interior that much anyway.

Megan and Craig took the elevator, and Fenway took the stairs. By the time she got into the apartment, they were yelling at each other.

"Jack gets what I'm going through."

"Really? You're telling me his parents are divorced? Was his mother just arrested?"

"Come on, Dad, you know what I mean."

"I don't, Megan. You've got a bedroom here. You've got school tomorrow. You've got your choir concert on Friday night. Your boyfriend would understand if you just—"

"Ugh!" Megan rolled her eyes. "Come on, Fenway. Tell my dad that I need to see Jack tonight."

Fenway looked from Megan's eyes to Craig's and back again. Is this what she had missed out on by not having Nathaniel Ferris in her life growing up? Dumb fights about going over to her boyfriend's house? She remembered the partially used twelve-pack of condoms in the FEMININE HYGIENE box.

"Let me talk to you for a second, Megan."

She rolled her eyes again. "Okay, fine, I won't get you in the middle of this. Sheesh. So much for girls sticking together."

"Outside. For just a second."

Fenway stepped out into the chilly January night. When she'd been moving the boxes, it hadn't seemed like it was so cold, but now, without the physical exertion, the cold almost stung her skin. Megan stamped her feet as she followed.

"You don't have to say anything," Megan said. "If you—"

"Shut up and listen for a second," Fenway snapped. "There was a bunch of stuff in your bedside table drawer. Stuff that looked like it was private. There's a box labeled FEMININE HYGIENE that has all of it."

"So?"

"So? So there's a box of condoms in there, and if you're going to go see your boyfriend Jack, you might need them. That's the 'so.'"

Megan hesitated. "You're not going to rat me out to Dad?"

Fenway shook her head. "You're obviously having sex with him, and that means you need to protect yourself, and that means condoms, and I'm telling you where I put them. End of story."

Megan cocked her head. "You used to be a nurse, right?"

"Nurse practitioner, right."

"So, uh, I've heard you can't get pregnant if you have sex on your period. Is that true?"

"It's less likely. Ovulation usually occurs about two weeks after your period. But it's still possible. So use a condom." Fenway hesitated. "Are you on the pill?"

"Yeah. Dad doesn't know." She paused. "And don't you dare tell him."

"What? Why doesn't he know?"

"He thinks Jack is an idiot."

"I can *guarantee* you he knows that the two of you are having sex. If he knows you're on the pill, at least he won't think you'll get pregnant with an idiot's baby."

"Whatever." She tapped her foot. "We done with today's lesson?"

Fenway opened the door, and Megan went back inside.

CHAPTER SIXTEEN

Fenway followed Megan in. Immediately, Megan started in on Craig again. "I can't believe you're going to stop me from seeing my *boyfriend* on the most traumatic night of my life."

Throwing the keys to her Accord on the kitchen table and grabbing her purse, Fenway turned down the short hallway into the master bedroom. "I'm peeing," she called. "You can get the last load of stuff from the car."

She went into the master bathroom and shut the door, turning on the modesty fan, and closed the toilet lid and sat. Fenway hadn't had a lot of interaction with Megan before, but the divorce had obviously not been great for her. She wondered, too, how serious McVie was about the "pause"—or even what it meant. Fenway had never even been in McVie's apartment when Megan was over.

Amy had been adamant about her innocence in front of Fenway, but then—according to Craig, anyway—she'd been adamant about her guilt, too.

Her phone rang in her purse.

She looked at the screen. Mayor Klein's cell phone.

She debated letting it go to voicemail, but considering he insisted she meet with him tomorrow morning, she decided she'd better take it. She tapped ANSWER.

"Fenway Stevenson."

"I hear we arrested Amy McVie without incident."

"You mean Amy Tonnick, Mayor," Fenway said gruffly.

"Right, sure." He coughed. "I understand there's an order for overtime for one of the deputies."

"The decedent's adult children threatened to come back and destroy Amy's possessions, Mayor. It's literally the very least we can do to make sure her things stay safe."

"I'm not made of money."

"There's overtime in the police budget," Fenway said, "and besides, that's not in your purview."

"Don't tell me what is or isn't in my purview," Klein said.

Fenway was silent.

"I called to make sure you'd be in my office tomorrow at nine o'clock," he said.

"Regarding what?"

Klein exhaled. "Regarding the stunt you pulled today."

"Regarding the press conference that you interrupted?"

"You are *not* to hold press conferences without my approval, Fenway. Or things like this happen. I think you're hiding something from me—"

"Since we started working together, Mayor, when have I hidden anything from you?"

"You know you've been giving your father and his company special treatment—"

"Unless you're complaining about how poorly I've been treating them when literally half the arrests I've made have been Ferris Energy employees—"

"I'm not having this conversation at ten at night. I wanted to congratulate you on arresting the murderer and tell you to get your ass into my office at nine tomorrow morning."

"Sorry, Mr. Mayor," Fenway said, "but I've got to be in Los Angeles tomorrow."

"You're going to L.A.? For what purpose?"

"A personal matter. We've arrested the killer, and I've put in quite a few hours."

"You can postpone a personal matter. This is more important."

"I can be in your office at four thirty in the afternoon."

"Nine o'clock, Fenway."

Then he hung up.

He wasn't her boss, and he couldn't make her show up in his office. A *normal* person would let it go, or perhaps ask if it were important enough to postpone the meeting. Or better yet, have a valid, helpful, relevant reason to have a meeting. But he just wanted to yell at her.

She got up and looked in the mirror, expecting to see a defeated expression. Instead, she was pleasantly surprised. Debbie the makeup artist had done a masterful job on her face. She looked both more youthful and more professional at the same time. She'd have to ask Debbie what color of blush was on her cheeks. Seeing herself in the mirror made her a little upset that she wasn't going to be the focus of the news stories—that instead it would be about the dysfunction in City Hall. And of course Barry Klein would find some way to make it her fault even though he was the one who'd interrupted her, who'd yelled at her, who'd baselessly accused her of lying.

Fenway's stomach rumbled. She hadn't had dinner—they'd been packing Megan's stuff, and Fenway had intended to stop and get something for the two of them on the way to McVie's apartment but hadn't.

In spite of the loud whir of the modesty fan, Fenway heard both Craig and Megan's voices escalate, then a door slam—that would be Megan's bedroom.

Fenway listened carefully but heard no voices. She debated flushing to complete the ruse, but Megan and Craig both had their minds on other things. She washed her hands anyway, then left the bathroom.

McVie was in the living room, sitting on the beige sofa.

"Hey, Craig," Fenway said.

He looked up at her. "You're not going to start, are you?"

Fenway took a seat next to him on the couch. "It was a bad situation all around. I don't know what's going to happen now."

"I can't believe she was planning to turn herself in, and instead they arrested her in front of Megan."

Fenway shook her head. "The situation changed. We found an eyewitness who put Amy at the scene. Apparently, she parked in the garage, ran across the street to a bar, put down a tequila shot, then went to the hotel."

"How does the eyewitness know where she went once she left the bar?"

Fenway snorted. "He was staring at her ass the whole time." She kicked her shoes off and sat cross-legged on the sofa. "Her car on tape, an eyewitness seeing her cross the street—it's enough to arrest her."

Craig was quiet.

"I'm sorry, Craig," Fenway said. "I know it's tough."

"It's tough for Megan," McVie said, "and she's in complete denial that it's even affecting her."

"You were seventeen once, too," Fenway said. "Wasn't your girlfriend more important than your parents back then?"

McVie grunted.

"I know there are some holes in the logistics of the killing, for sure, but unless you can explain the car and the eyewitness, I don't know what else I can do." She stretched her arms above her head. "So—uh, listen, you and I didn't end things very well this afternoon."

"I'm sorry about that, Fenway. I—I just couldn't think about Megan having killed someone. And what Rick would have done to her to *make* her kill him. My brain—it just didn't want to process that. I don't want us to, uh..."

"Pause?"

McVie gave a slight nod.

Fenway rested her chin in her palm. "I'm relieved that it wasn't Megan." She hesitated. "Look, since I've never stayed over when Megan's here, maybe I won't start tonight."

"Yeah," Craig said. "This has to be a hard time for her, what with me not letting her go over to Jack's."

"Did you get everything in from the car?"

"Yep." He elbowed her lightly in the ribs. "I even put up your rear seats. Because that's the kind of boyfriend I am."

"Oh, goodness me," Fenway said, affecting a Southern accent and a fainting posture. "I must go get a trophy fashioned for this moment. It's almost as selfless as you taking out my trash the other day!"

Craig rolled his eyes. "All right, fine."

"Oh—before I forget, Megan's Jeep is in the shop. It has to be picked up tomorrow."

"Oh, great," Craig said. "Something *else* I have to pay for that Amy was supposed to take care of." He sighed. "Give Megan a day, maybe two, maybe the weekend. Let's see what happens when Amy gets arraigned."

"She'll have to spend the night in jail, but surely they'll arraign her first thing tomorrow, right?"

"Right. Then it'll probably be an insane amount of money for bail."

"Gotcha." Fenway stood and slipped her flats back on. "Just so you know, I don't think Megan had dinner. I got over there at almost five forty-five, and after the arrest, Megan and I packed like crazy. Maybe she's a little contrary because of low blood sugar."

McVie stood up and pulled Fenway into him with his left arm around her waist, kissing her. She put her hands through his hair and kissed him back, hard.

She broke from the kiss first. "Don't make me manipulate you into letting me stay over," Fenway said mischievously, "because you know I can." She spun, as if dancing, out of his embrace and walked over to the kitchen table. "Hey, what did you do with my keys after you emptied the car? Did you put them in my purse?"

"I put them back on the kitchen table."

"You sure? They're not here."

"Well—I thought so." Craig emptied his pockets onto the coffee table, but Fenway's keys weren't in the pile of keys and change.

Fenway walked into the kitchen and searched on the counter, then she and Craig went into the master bedroom and searched on the dresser, then the nightstands.

"That's weird," Craig mused. "I could have sworn I put them on the kitchen table."

"Maybe they got knocked off onto the floor?"

Fenway hurried out of the master bedroom, then stopped so suddenly that Craig ran into her.

"What is it?" Craig said.

"I was seventeen once, too," Fenway said. She took a few steps to Megan's door and knocked. "Megan, have you seen my keys?"

No answer.

Fenway knocked again. "Megan?"

Still no answer.

Craig reached past Fenway and tried the door. It was locked. "Dammit," he muttered.

Fenway went to the kitchen and dug around in her purse before coming back with a U-shaped bobby pin. There was a small hole in the center of the doorknob, and she stuck one of the sides of the U in it, twisting it and pushing, feeling around for the trigger, until she heard a soft popping of metal. The doorknob turned.

The window in Megan's room was open, and the screen had been popped out. Two boxes of clothes had been opened, as well as the box reading FEMININE HYGIENE. Fenway looked in the open box. The condoms were gone.

Fenway sat on the sofa holding a glass of red wine. Her Accord was gone as well, and Craig was livid, pacing in front of her.

"I can't believe she'd do that. It's unacceptable."

"I don't know what to tell you, Craig—except it's not really that surprising. She wanted to be with Jack tonight, so she's with Jack tonight."

"But she stole your car! She could be pulled over and sent to jail for grand theft auto!"

Fenway watched Craig pace back and forth. "Are you sure that nothing happened with her and Rick?"

"She says it didn't."

"Because this kind of behavior is kind of a classic cry for help."

"Her mother was just arrested for murder, Fenway. You don't think that's enough explanation for this kind of behavior?"

Fenway was quiet. She should be furious at Megan, but she just couldn't bring herself to get angry.

"We're going to go over to Jack's parents' house, and we're going to get your car and bring her home."

"No, we're not," said Fenway. "She's pissed off and confused, and she's lashing out at all the wrong people, and if you go get her and embarrass her in front of her boyfriend, it's just going to make it worse."

"What the hell is wrong with Jack's parents that they'd let a seventeen-year-old girl stay over?"

Fenway shrugged. She'd seen a lot of odd parental behaviors when she was working in the ER and at the clinic, and this didn't come close to odd. Jack's parents might have thought it was better for Jack and Megan to be safe under their roof than in the back of Jack's car—or Fenway's Accord. Craig was making assumptions.

"You know, we have no evidence that they *are* at Jack's house. For all we know, they might be camping on the beach or at another friend's house or in a motel for the night."

Craig shook his head. "That doesn't make me feel any better."

"Sorry, but it's true." Fenway paused. "You know, when people are going through a tough time like this—when she's essentially been abandoned by one of her parents—it's important that you make sure she's okay and that she has the help she needs. And that she doesn't feel like you're attacking her."

"She stole your car, Fenway. That's not okay."

"No, it's not, but how is tracking her down going to help?"

"It'll get your car back." He paused. "Why are you so calm? She stole your car."

Fenway smiled. "Maybe I'll use it as an excuse for you to buy me dinner. And breakfast."

Craig shook his head. "My daughter is missing, and *that's* what you're thinking about."

Fenway rolled her eyes.

"And now you're rolling your eyes at me?"

"I'm trying to show you how *not* to make the situation worse."

"By letting her know that her behavior—her *illegal* behavior, by the way—is just fine by me? All hunky-dory?"

"I don't want to fight, Craig. I know she's not my daughter, but—"

"Yeah, that's right. She's *not* your daughter."

Fenway stood. "I should go."

Craig turned toward the door. "I should go, too. Bring her back here."

"Do what you want, Craig," Fenway snapped. "I may not have a daughter, but *you've* never been abandoned by a parent. You've never had someone ask you, 'Oh, so where's your dad?' and had *no idea* how to respond." She pulled her purse over her shoulder. "Tomorrow at school, when some of the kids have seen that Amy's been arrested, what do you think Megan's going to say?"

Craig was quiet.

"Right now, she's with someone who—I hope to God—will let her talk and let her cry and tell her that everything is going to be okay and that she doesn't have to worry about where she lives or what those dickheads at school say because he'll be right there with her."

"Jack's an asshole," Craig said.

"Maybe he's got just enough good guy in him to make things a little easier for Megan tonight," Fenway said. "Not someone who's bugging her about her homework or what TV shows are inappropriate for her. Someone who's just *there* for her."

Craig stopped in his tracks, then kicked at the carpet.

"If I were you," Fenway said, "I'd text Megan, and I'd tell her that I love her and that I'm sorry she's going through this, and that you're sorry you didn't talk with her about it before she left."

"And to bring your car back."

Fenway shook her head. "Give me my apartment key," she said.

"What? Fenway, I don't want to—"

"Not permanently, Craig. Your daughter has my keys. I need to get into my apartment."

"Let me at least drive you home."

"You need to deal with Megan." Fenway took out her phone and tapped the screen. "There's an Uber a couple of minutes away. I'll be fine."

McVie took Fenway's apartment key off his keychain and handed it to her. Fenway bent down and kissed his cheek, then walked out the front door, shutting it firmly behind her.

PART FOUR
WEDNESDAY

CHAPTER SEVENTEEN

FENWAY WOKE TO A NOISE AND LIFTED HER HEAD. IT WAS STILL DARK. What time was it? Oh—that was her mobile phone. She reached her arm out and smacked her headboard.

Grimacing in pain and shaking her hand, Fenway sat up. Somehow, she'd turned sideways in bed, her feet drifting off the side.

Her stomach gurgled. The Uber ride home the night before had been uneventful, but she'd gotten all the way to her apartment before she remembered she hadn't had dinner. She'd mistaken her hunger pangs for the guilt or pain of fighting with Craig. The frozen burrito she'd eaten left a lot to be desired, and the beer she'd washed it down with wasn't a good choice after the two glasses of wine she'd had at Craig's. She wasn't hung over, but her stomach was not happy about the mixture.

She picked her phone up on the fourth ring, clearing her throat. "Fenway Stevenson." It came out as a croak anyway.

"Hey, Fenway, it's Craig."

"Oh. Hey."

"Sorry it's early, but I wanted to let you know that Megan didn't come home last night. She didn't respond to any of my texts except to tell me she was okay and she was safe."

"Well, at least that's something."

"And I don't know if she was okay *or* safe. She could be lying. I just—I just wanted you to know that I wouldn't be able to get your car back to you by the time you have to leave for work. But I promise, you'll have your Honda today."

"Maybe you could pick me up and drive me to work?"

"Sorry—I wish I could. I have a client who got arrested for murder yesterday. I've got to get to San Miguelito to view the autopsy results, and I want to make sure I'm back in time to meet with my client later this morning."

"You're going to San Mig but you'll have my car back today?"

"I'll be back by ten. Don't worry—the Accord will be at your house by the time you get home."

"Gotcha."

"Have a good day."

"You too."

They hung up.

Have a good day? What was that about? That was like a business call.

Fenway shook her head. She still hadn't been able to tell Craig that she loved him. He'd said it, but only once—or, depending on your interpretation, maybe twice. And he was under a lot of pressure with the new business, with his ex-wife and client arrested for murder, and with his daughter's world turned upside down. Really, Megan's life had gone through many changes a few times in the last nine months or so.

So maybe this was to be expected.

Fenway had thought that this time *she* was being the mature one. Her car, her almost-brand-new car with less than ten thousand miles on it, was stolen by her boyfriend's daughter, and she was understanding and nice. Wasn't she?

Of course she was understanding. She saw a lot of herself in Megan.

She looked at the clock. 6:02 A.M. Ugh. McVie got up at an ungodly hour. But she supposed if he had to get to San Miguelito and back by nine or nine thirty, he'd need the time. She had another thirty minutes before her alarm would go off.

She tried to go back to sleep, but her bladder was screaming, and then her feet got cold on the tile floor.

Then she remembered.

Los Angeles. Meeting her grandmother. Her heart leapt. She didn't know what she would say, but she hopped in the shower and put on a cute granddaughterly dress and thought about meeting Nell Godwin. She didn't care if she was going to catch ten different kinds of hell from the mayor upon her return.

She was digging through her purse before she made the connection that because Megan had taken her car, that meant she didn't have a way to get to Los Angeles.

Fenway picked up her phone and called three rental car companies at the Estancia airport. Their rental counters all opened at eight thirty. That would be too late to get to Rolling Meadows in time to take Nell to lunch.

She pulled up the rideshare app on her phone, only to find out that an Uber there and back would be upwards of five hundred dollars.

Sighing, she scrolled through her recent calls and selected the assisted living facility, where she requested the operator.

"Rolling Meadows, this is Julia."

"Julia—hi, it's Fenway Stevenson. From yesterday."

Julia gasped with enthusiasm. "Oh, hello again! I'm so glad you were able to work things out. Mrs. Godwin is really looking forward—"

"I have to postpone my visit," Fenway said.

"Oh no—why?"

"I don't have my car today. And I can't rent one until it's too late to get down there. Plus, I have a—um, co-worker who insists on meeting me this morning." She sighed. "Can we do it tomorrow instead?

"Tomorrow? You're sure?"

"Yes. Definitely tomorrow."

Julia exhaled. "Nell is going to be so disappointed."

"Believe me, I'm disappointed too. I was really looking forward to meeting her." Fenway tapped her fingers on the kitchen table. "Do you think maybe you could put her on the phone?"

"Oh," Julia said. "Oh, yes, I think that can be arranged. She's usually up this early—do you mind holding for a few minutes?"

"Sure," Fenway agreed, "I can do that."

Especially if there were two hours to kill between now and the time she had to face the tongue-lashing in Mayor Klein's office.

She considered walking down to The Coffee Bean to get a coffee and a pastry. *What flavor muffin goes best with the dread of knowing you're going to be yelled at for something you didn't do?*

Julia came back on the line. "I'm going to have to call you back," she said. "Nell's not quite ready for the call. Can we get your phone number?"

Fenway gave it to her and pressed END.

She wanted everything to go back to normal, when she and Craig were dating and his ex-wife's dead husband wasn't hanging his existential dread between them.

Her heart beat fast as she dumped coffee into the coffeemaker and filled the glass carafe with water. She had two hours, and while she didn't usually drink more than two cups, today felt like a half-a-pot day. Maybe more than that.

She pushed the start button before she realized she'd planned to go to the coffee shop.

The coffeemaker seemed to take forever to brew, and Fenway paced around the apartment, trying to figure out something to keep her busy while she waited for Rolling Meadows to call her back.

She poured her coffee, looking at her phone to see if somehow she'd gone out of service range—when it rang.

It was the Los Angeles number.

"This is Fenway Stevenson," she said, expecting either Julia or Beauregard on the call.

Instead, a pause, then a tentative voice. "Hello? Is this Fenway?"

Fenway's voice caught in her throat. "Oh—hi. Is this Nell Godwin?"

"Yes, ma'am," Nell said.

"I'm not sure how much they told you, Mrs. Godwin, but you had a daughter who disappeared in 1986, right?"

She sighed. "Yes. My beautiful Samara."

"I've been doing a little research on my mother," Fenway said, "and I can't find anything about her before April of 1986. She used the name *Joanne Stevenson*. I found out a couple of days ago that her name, social security number and birthdate all belong to a little girl who died in a car accident in 1965."

There was silence on the other end of the line.

"Mrs. Godwin?" Fenway asked tentatively.

"Julia showed me the picture," Mrs. Godwin said. "I—I didn't know what to say. She said the picture is of you and your mother at a restaurant. I can't believe it."

"You—um, you think it might be her?"

"I'd know that smile anywhere. Her eyes, too. Yes, that's my Samara. I thought for sure that all those people who Eddie owed money to had killed her."

Fenway wasn't prepared for the rush of emotions that hit her. She steadied herself, grabbing the kitchen counter for support, and felt a tear run down her cheek.

"You're almost the spitting image of her when I saw her last, too. A little different, but for a minute I thought *you* were her instead."

Fenway hadn't ever had a grandmother. For nine months now, she thought her father was the only family she had left.

"I can't believe she's alive," Mrs. Godwin said softly.

Fenway's stomach sank. "Oh—Mrs. Godwin, I guess I didn't tell Julia. My mother passed away last year. Pancreatic cancer. It took her really fast. In fact, her death was the only way I was able to get access to some of this information. It's the only way I was able to find you."

Mrs. Godwin was quiet for a moment. "Well. I just—I thought I was going to see her again. After all this time. I was worried about what I'd say. I didn't know what I'd—"

Fenway just heard the sound of Mrs. Godwin breathing for a moment, a hollow sound, almost strained.

"I'm so sorry," Fenway said. "I—I didn't want you to find out like this."

"It's a real hard thing, not to know what happened to your baby," Mrs. Godwin said softly. "I couldn't bear to accept that she was dead. I kept thinking, maybe today will be the day she comes back. We never moved from that house, not when the neighborhood got worse, not when it got better again. Only when I needed too much help, only when I couldn't take care of myself, when my heart wasn't strong enough to keep me going all day. And I still feel guilty for moving. What if she came back?"

Fenway listened to her breathing again. *That sounds like congestive heart failure.* Piper's great-grandmother had it too, diagnosed in her seventies, and she lived until she was ninety-two.

"I kept the forwarding address as long as I could. And then I thought, Nell, you're going to have to face it. Samara is never coming home."

A tear ran down Fenway's cheek. "I'm so sorry. I didn't mean to—"

"Now, now, child," Nell said, her voice gaining strength. "I never thought I'd ever see a grandchild. It's nice to know that Samara was alive for so long, anyway. I don't know why she ran away, but I'm glad she had a life."

"I really wanted to drive down there today and meet you."

"Oh, now, Julia says you'll come tomorrow. That's plenty soon. I've been waiting since 1986. Surely I can wait one more day."

"Do you want to know what my mom—what Samara—did after she left?"

"I think so." Nell paused. "I'll let you know if it's a little much."

Fenway sniffled. "Okay. So it looks like Joanne—I mean, Samara, reappeared up the coast. Estancia. About two and a half hours north."

"Oh, yes," Mrs. Godwin said. "Maurice and I drove up to that Cameron Castle there for our anniversary one year."

"That's not too far from here." Fenway topped off her coffee. "Anyway, she was a painter."

"A *painter?*"

"Yes—she was quite good. She got a showing in a gallery here in Estancia. My dad was walking by one day and came in. He liked her work so much, he wanted to buy three paintings for his new office building. My mom showed him all the paintings, and then they got to talking, and then they fell in love."

"And then you were born." Nell coughed again, a dry wheeze, two short barks, then cleared her throat. "So Samara kept painting?"

"Well—yes, mostly. When I was eight, though, she left my father and took me with her."

"Oh. Do you know why?"

"Because my father—" Fenway stopped and shifted in her seat. "You know, I always thought it was because my father was self-absorbed and didn't really let my mom have a life outside of his work circle."

Mrs. Godwin clicked her tongue. "Maurice was married to his job, too. You'd have thought the print shop was his mistress." She laughed, and Fenway heard the hollow sound inside the laugh, confirming a symptom of heart trouble.

I wonder if Mom left Estancia for the same reason she left Los Angeles. Maybe trouble followed her here.

"Where did you go?"

"I'm sorry?"

"You said your mother took you away when you were eight…"

"We went to Seattle. For years, it was just my mom and me. We were poor at first, but Mom worked two jobs and eventually managed to sell about a dozen paintings every year. She even bought a house a few years ago."

"Good," Mrs. Godwin said softly. "Good for her." She cleared her throat. "And what about you? What do you do? Let's see—you must be right around thirty?"

"Twenty-nine." She paused. "I became a nurse practitioner for a few years. I worked in the ER for a while, then went to a clinic. Better hours, less stress, but less pay, too."

"Do you still live in Seattle?"

"No, after my mom, uh, passed, I moved back down to Estancia. I couldn't keep the house, and I wasn't making enough money to get my own place *and* pay back my college loans."

"What's in Estancia? Is that where your father still is?"

"Right," Fenway said. "Oh—have you heard of Ferris Energy?"

"The oil company? Who hasn't heard of Ferris Energy? It's up that way, isn't it?"

"It sure is. My dad owns it. Well—he's the largest shareholder. And the president and CEO."

Mrs. Godwin laughed. "Oh, I've seen him in some of the magazines. He's got one of those old literary names. Edgar or Alfred or something."

"Nathaniel."

"Nathaniel, that's it. How about that? My daughter, marrying a white boy."

"Yeah," Fenway said. "He's okay. He has his moments."

There was silence between them for a few seconds.

"I'm so sorry I can't drive down to see you today," Fenway repeated. "I'm going to do my best to come tomorrow."

"Problem at the hospital?"

"Oh—actually, I'm the county coroner now. I'm in the middle of an investigation."

"Coroner? So you cut up dead bodies?" Nell cackled. "First one in the family to go to college, and she studies to cut up dead people."

Fenway thought about explaining the structure of the coroner's office and how she was assigned the investigation of all the suspicious deaths, but it wasn't worth it. "It's strange but fascinating work. I kind of love it."

She sighed. "Oh, that was Samara, too. Strange but fascinating."

"What was she like growing up?"

Mrs. Godwin hooted. "She was stubborn when she was little, I'll tell you that much. Constantly wanting her own way on things. But she was smart. Best in her class at math and reading and science." She sighed. "Until high school. She discovered boys, and when she was a junior, she started dating Eddie Drake."

"Right, Eddie Drake. I saw that name when we connected my mom to Samara's name. He died of a knife wound, right? A couple of months before Samara disappeared?"

"He was a dangerous boy. A sweet talker, though. He was a handsome kid, and my Samara fell for him pretty hard. He always had an angle on everything. It was always a friend of his who knew someone who could get him a sweet deal on this or that. He was always on the cusp of a big payday, some get-rich-quick scheme that never panned out. You know the type. When something went wrong, it was never his fault. It was always everyone else who didn't know a good thing when they saw it, or who wouldn't ignore the rules for him." She sighed. "I don't know. We told her we didn't like him. But maybe that just pushed her more into his arms."

"I'm sorry." Fenway thought of Megan and the advice she'd given McVie.

"Heh—I bet you were on the receiving end of Samara's stubbornness more than once yourself."

Fenway smiled. "We were in a clothing store once, and my mom had picked out a few outfits for me to go back to school. Clothes I really needed. And then the sales staff started making, you know, rude comments about us. She left the stack of clothes on a table, and we just took off. She didn't want to reward the store for hiring people like that. Even though I really needed the clothes."

Mrs. Godwin laughed. "Yeah, that sounds like Samara, all right."

"So," Fenway said, "I—um... I'm wondering when you last saw Samara."

Silence on the other end of the line. Then, finally: "Samara had moved in with Eddie Drake right after New Year's. I couldn't say anything to change her mind. She was working as a cashier in the art supply store over on La Cienega. Heh—in Ladera Heights, *everything* is on La Cienega. I don't think Eddie had a real job. Samara kept saying he was running his own business, but I think that was just an excuse to hang out with his friends all day."

Fenway couldn't remember her mother dating after they moved to Seattle. She hadn't thought anything of it when she was younger. Maybe the experiences with Eddie and Fenway's father had soured her on relationships in general.

"So at the end of January, Samara called us and said Eddie had a client fall through and was a little short on the rent."

"Uh oh."

"You know it. Samara had most of it—I think she only asked to borrow a hundred dollars. Of course, a hundred dollars was a lot more back then. I think the rent on their whole place was only four hundred or so. Anyway, she came to pick up the money, and she had a black eye."

Fenway set her jaw. "A black eye?"

"We near about lost our minds, Maurice and me. She said she'd gotten hit by something that fell at work, but of course we didn't believe her. Maurice said Eddie was no good, and of course she stormed out of there. With our money, of course, but she was angry. I tell you, I definitely expected Eddie to have some emergency where he was short the next month too. But we got a visit from the police around the twenty-first. Asked if we knew Eddie Drake. We told them what we knew. Told them about his friends who always seemed to have money but never seemed to have a job. They were interested in talking to Samara."

"Why did they want to talk to her?"

"They wouldn't tell us. I assume it's because she was a suspect." Mrs. Godwin sighed. "We had to wait almost a week to post a missing persons report. We picked up Samara's furniture from the apartment at the end of the month—and we found her purse there with all her identification. Her wallet was empty, but the place had been trashed—all the drawers gone through, the sofa cushions everywhere. We tried to get an update from the police—I think they were under the impression that Eddie owed his friends money, so they killed him and took everything that was valuable."

"That's awful."

"The worst part is, we didn't know if Samara had been killed, or if they'd kidnapped her and wanted ransom, or if they were, you know, forcing her to work for them."

As a prostitute. Yeesh.

"Anyway, one of the police detectives assigned to the case came by and kept asking questions about Eddie's friends."

"What?"

"It was all I could do not to strangle the detective. He said it like he didn't care about what happened to Samara at all. Like they were just washing their hands of the whole thing." She sighed. "I'd forgotten about that detective's smug face and his greasy hair. He never had an update on Samara, though. In fact, he kept coming back accusing us of hiding her."

"I'm sure that would have looked really good with public relations."

"You've got to understand, Miss Stevenson—"

"I'm your granddaughter," Fenway interrupted. "You can call me Fenway."

Nell chuckled, "Well, Fenway, you need to understand that the L.A. cops didn't care about public relations back then. This was before Rodney King. This was before the O.J. chase."

That had been over thirty years ago. Maybe the detective was still alive. Maybe there was something more concrete about why Samara Godwin had left.

Yes, she could have been kidnapped, maybe forced to work as a prostitute, and then escaped. But why not go back to her parents?

There was always the possibility that Samara had been the one to kill

Eddie Drake. Domestic violence was just starting to enter visibility then—maybe Samara/Joanne felt that no one would believe her and that she'd have to spend the rest of her life in jail.

And maybe someone had followed her to Estancia.

"Oh, dear," Mrs. Godwin said.

"What is it?"

"I haven't thought about that detective and his horrible attitude in years. The way he looked at Maurice and me as if it was *our* fault that Samara fell in love with the wrong man. Like I was wasting his time. Maurice said he had half a mind to record the conversations he'd have with the detective and go complain to his precinct." She scoffed. "As if it would've done any good." She began to cough, then took a minute to catch her breath, inhaling with a hollow sound. "I'm sorry, dear, but I'm feeling a little tired."

Congestive heart failure.

"I certainly didn't mean to upset you." Fenway paused. "Can I still take you to lunch tomorrow? I swear I'll only talk about my mom's paintings—I've got photos of several of them on my phone. And I'll answer any questions you want to ask."

"Lunch tomorrow sounds lovely," Mrs. Godwin said. "Here—I'll put Julia back on. I have to rest for a bit."

The sound of the phone being passed.

"Hi," Julia said. "I'm so sorry, she got a little worked up—I should have stopped her from going through all of that emotional stuff."

"I didn't know," Fenway said.

"That's all right. Don't you worry about it. Did I hear you say you'll be taking her to lunch tomorrow?"

"Yes—I hope that's okay."

"You'll be here for sure?"

"My investigation is wrapping up today, so I'm sure I'll be able to come down. I'm really looking forward to meeting you."

"It's not every day you find a granddaughter you didn't think you had," said Julia. "You have a safe trip tomorrow."

CHAPTER EIGHTEEN

IT TOOK FENWAY ALMOST AN HOUR TO CALM HERSELF DOWN ENOUGH to leave. How did people usually deal with meeting their grandmother for the first time? She found herself going through her closet, looking at different pieces of clothing, judging whether they were grandma-worthy.

Finally, a few minutes after nine, she called for an Uber. She was opening the door to the coroner's office suite when she remembered she was supposed to be in the mayor's office.

Sarah looked up from her typing and tilted her head. "You didn't already see the mayor, did you? If so, that was awfully quick."

"I've got a lot on my mind this morning," Fenway said, going into her office and dropping off her laptop case next to her desk. "If I start walking over there now, I'll only be a few minutes late. Doesn't seem like he can get any angrier with me than he already is."

"Shall I let him know you're on your way? Maybe invent some reason you got waylaid?"

"Doesn't much matter," Fenway said, tapping her fingers on the counter in front of Sarah as she passed. "He can fume for a few minutes."

Dez prairie-dogged up. "You leaving already?"

"My super-important meeting with the mayor," Fenway said. "I'm sure he's giving me some sort of commendation for arresting the murder suspect so quickly."

Dez smirked. "Yeah, in your dreams. I've got some information. Can I walk with you?"

"Is it about the Rick Tonnick murder?"

"Just tying up loose ends. Thoroughness is my middle name."

"Sure, come on."

Dez hurried around the counter, and Fenway held the door for her.

"So," Dez said, "I was following up on a couple of leads. I saw in the arrest report from last night that we have a couple in the drunk tank. They were picked up in front of Valhalla at two fifteen this morning—they're regulars there. Police report mentioned the two of them are in that bar almost every night. I guess last night they were fighting, neither one of them in any condition to drive. I know Duke said he saw Amy Tonnick in his bar. I thought maybe—if they've slept it off by now, and if they have any memory of Sunday night at all—we could get corroboration of Duke's story."

"Thoroughness," Fenway said, looking at Dez out of the corner of her eye as they stepped into the crosswalk. "Just like you'd do in any murder case."

"I've asked for corroboration for witness statements before," Dez said. "Particularly when the witness has a reason for wanting the victim dead."

"And this is for McVie's ex."

"I'm just being thorough. I don't even like Amy, remember?"

"I remember." The two of them arrived at the door to City Hall. "Anything else?"

Dez crossed her arms and tapped her foot.

"What is it, Dez?"

"Something isn't hitting me right about those lawsuits," Dez said. "Duke Perriman's wife is dead from Rick Tonnick's negligence, and suddenly he's the star witness against Tonnick's wife."

Fenway nodded. "It's not hitting me right either. If it were the only thing tying her to the murder, I don't think she'd be sitting in jail. But you saw the video of her car just as well as I did."

"Maybe the video was faked. I've seen security footage with fake timestamps."

"We can call the security company when I get back. Make sure it wasn't tampered with." Fenway opened the door. "If the drunk couple saw Amy too, that'll go a long way toward my confidence that we got the right person."

"What's wrong, Fenway? Usually you'd be overjoyed with the chance to corroborate a witness statement."

Fenway shook her head. "I've got a feeling in my gut that I'm not putting something together. Like I've seen something important, but I just haven't figured out what it is." She sighed. "But my gut reactions aren't always right, and they sure won't stand up in court."

"What do you think you might be missing?"

Fenway shrugged. "I wish I could put my finger on it. Maybe something about the other victims of the airbag recall problem."

"I checked out the families of the other victims. The ones who brought suit. The one where the widower died during the trial? The son stayed in San Jose, and the daughter stayed in Vegas. No one traveled anywhere. And the sister of the other woman *was* traveling. She was on a train to New York for a conference on Sunday. Checked into her hotel at 10:00 P.M. Eastern Time, about seven hours before the murder."

"I guess we need to focus our efforts locally, then," Fenway replied. "Okay—I've got to go face the executioner now. Wish me luck. If I survive, I'll see you later. Maybe you want to grab some lunch?"

Dez cackled. "It's been almost two weeks since I went to Dos Milagros with you. That must be some kind of record. But no, I've got plans with my nephew. Maybe we'll go to that Indian place by McVie's new office."

Fenway nodded and walked inside the City Hall building.

The coffee cart seemed to call to her. Anything to postpone this meeting with Barry Klein. She felt as if she were moving through quicksand, picking up her legs one at a time until she got to the door to the mayor's office suite.

The admin at the reception desk looked up. "He's expecting you," he said in a hushed tone, as if speaking to an unruly student in the principal's office. Fenway straightened her posture and walked through the reception area to a heavy wooden door with the nameplate reading MAYOR BARRY KLEIN. She took a deep breath and knocked.

The voice on the other side of the door was firm and terse. "Enter."

She turned the handle, seeing everything in slow motion. The door creaked open, revealing the large office, neat and uncluttered, with photography of Estancia in ornate gold frames on the wall. As spotless as the room looked, there was a faint fetid smell of sweat tinged with cortisol and adrenaline. Barry Klein was, in spite of his scowling face behind his large walnut desk, nervous.

"Sit," Mayor Klein instructed, holding out a hand to indicate the wooden straight-backed chair on the other side of the desk from where he sat in his fancy, cushy, tall-backed brown leather Executive Seating Solution.

I hope my chair isn't sitting on a trap door above a shark tank. Fenway glared at Klein but took a seat. The floor stayed still.

Barry Klein looked down his nose at Fenway. He leaned back, putting his elbows on the arms of the chair. Silence.

Fenway was well-versed in the art of using the silent treatment for intimidation. She focused on a spot on the wall above Barry Klein's head. *Mom's painting of Estancia Pier would look good up there.* There was no way she was going to speak first.

It felt like she was staring at the wall for hours, but it was probably only a minute or two before Barry Klein spoke.

"You and I," he said, "have to get along better."

"I agree," Fenway said. "Yesterday wasn't a good look." She almost said *for you,* but she held her tongue.

"I can't have you undermine me like that, Fenway."

"Undermine you? How exactly did I undermine you?"

"You held a press conference without my permission."

"Without your permission? It didn't have anything to do with you!"

He leaned forward. "When a representative of local government appears at a press conference, I expect to be briefed ahead of time. I don't care if you're announcing the launch of a charitable organization or the adoption of a giant panda by the Estancia Zoo. You come to me first."

Fenway tilted her head. He wasn't screaming at her, which was unexpected. Maybe because Amy Tonnick had managed to be arrested without bringing Klein's wife into the spotlight. Which Fenway knew was the reason he'd wanted to stop the press conference—he thought Fenway was going to announce his wife as a person of interest in the case.

She opened her mouth to push back—she didn't report to him. She felt the secret about their open marriage on the tip of her tongue. About her spending the night in the hotel with the murder victim.

But she shut her mouth. She and the mayor could spend an hour or two screaming at each other about protocol and department collaboration and the best interests of the city and county. But she was tired of fighting. Would it have been that hard to pick up the phone to give him a heads-up that she'd be speaking at a press conference that had nothing to do with the murder?

Besides, if the tables had been turned and Fenway had been worried that Klein would be publicly accusing Craig McVie or Nathaniel Ferris— or even Charlotte—of wrongdoing, she knew she'd be furious, and she'd probably rush to the press conference too. And she'd be embarrassed if it turned out to be something completely unrelated.

"I'm sorry," Fenway heard herself say. "It didn't even occur to me that you'd have any interest, let alone any problem, with me speaking at a Ferris Energy press conference. You had a delicate situation. I see now that I should have let you know."

There. That was perhaps the most mature thing she'd ever said to Barry Klein.

But Klein's eyes narrowed. "What, exactly, is this 'delicate situation' you just referred to?"

Fenway sighed and rolled her eyes. "I have no interest in embarrassing you or your wife, Mr. Mayor."

"You better not bring my wife into this—"

"Are you angry that our investigation uncovered something potentially troublesome for you, Barry?" Fenway asked sharply. "You realize that I could have done a *lot* by now to make your life difficult. But your wife has an alibi, and I didn't have to drag her into the station to get it. If the evidence had pointed to her, that would have been a different story, but I'm not going to announce embarrassing rumors that hold no bearing on your ability to fulfill your duties as mayor." Fenway raised her eyebrow. "You're not going to let that affect your work, are you?"

"You *talked* to my wife without telling me?" Barry's ears turned beet-red.

Fenway rolled her eyes. "You don't need to worry about it. You and I don't like each other, but name-calling and one-upmanship make us both look bad." She leaned forward, putting her palms down on the desk, and raised up slightly. "And don't you *ever* again accuse me of lying in public. Especially when I've made a conscious choice to protect you and your wife."

Barry Klein snarled. "Don't you threaten me."

"You are batshit insane if you think I've done anything *close* to threatening you," Fenway said.

"You breathe a word of my wife's involvement in this, and it'll be the last thing you do."

Fenway scoffed. "Now *that's* a threat." She sat back down in the chair. "So exactly what were you going to suggest for us to *get along better?*"

"You accept whatever position your daddy's company offers you, and you resign as county coroner," Klein said. "I'm mayor. I can get enough signatures for a recall election for you."

"You're out of your mind."

Klein stood and pointed a finger in Fenway's face. "Don't test me," he said evenly. "You know I'll win. Here's the deal—get out of the county government, and you can leave with your reputation, such as it is, intact. Otherwise, I'll rain terror down on you."

Fenway slapped his hand away, then stood and stomped out of the office.

"Don't you walk away when I'm—" Klein said before the door slammed shut behind her.

Fenway seethed as she strode past the shocked admin and out of the mayor's suite. She hurried past the coffee cart to get out of the City Hall building.

The morning had turned cold, with low clouds sweeping over the downtown area. She felt the dampness on her hair and could smell the ocean as the wind picked up.

Her insides were in knots, and she didn't want to stop walking. It was about a block and a half to Java Jim's, then probably another four blocks to the French bakery next to the Phillips-Holsen. The French bakery was about the right distance for her to calm down a little.

The dampness in the air settled into a mist, making Fenway's hair frizz, and she had a sheen of water on her jacket and her skin when she reached the patisserie. It was almost ten o'clock, and as Fenway ordered her latte, she noticed many of the baked goods were gone—no more pains au chocolat, no more croissants. She pointed to an item with rectangular layers of alternating pastry and cream with sliced strawberries on top—out of season, for sure, but they still looked pretty decent. "Is that a strawberry Napoleon?"

"Mille-feuille," the woman behind the counter said with a paper sleeve in one hand.

"I'll take one of those."

Fenway sat at one of the bistro tables and let her eyes lose focus. Could Barry Klein really force her out? She knew a couple of things Klein knew that she didn't want to get out, but she had more on him.

Maybe he'd thought of a way to discredit her. Fenway tapped her chin as she sat. She had won the election to the coroner position in a landslide, but she knew the public was fickle.

The woman behind the counter caught her eye, and Fenway got her latte and mille-feuille, grabbing a fork and napkins on the way back to her seat.

The delicate pastry crumpled immediately when the fork touched it, making a mess, but the first bite was heaven. A little sweet for a mid-morning snack, but so tasty.

The door opened, and a man and a woman wearing Phillips-Holsen polo shirts came in. The man had on a navy-blue turban. Fenway turned her attention to the pastry, trying not to think of what Barry Klein could do.

"They're out of croissants," the woman said.

"Then just a coffee," the man replied.

A shadow fell on the table, and Fenway looked up to see the man standing above her—the security guard she'd talked to in the video surveillance room on Monday.

"I thought I recognized you," the man said. "I don't mean to interrupt. Did you get everything you needed the other day?"

Fenway nodded with a mouthful of pastry, cream, and strawberry. "Yes." She chewed quickly and swallowed. "The property manager's been very gracious. Thanks for asking."

"Poor Brianna," the woman said.

"What do you mean?"

"It's just—" The woman looked furtively at the man. "With everything she's been through."

"You shouldn't talk of others like that, Lisette," the man said quietly.

"No," Lisette said, shaking her head. "I just worry about her, is all. She's such a sweet girl. She reminds me of my daughter."

Fenway tilted her head. Something was here—she could feel it. Something about what Brianna had been through. But she didn't want to press Lisette any further. The security guard would certainly shut her down.

But maybe there was an excuse she could give to talk to her. Oh—she could ask to see the tape of Catherine Klein coming in again.

But then again, that might get back to Barry Klein.

Fenway opened her mouth, then shut it again. "You're so nice for thinking of Brianna's feelings like that. She's lucky to have a co-worker like you."

Lisette shot the man a self-satisfied look.

"Are you quite sure you got everything you need?" the man said.

"Well," Fenway mused, "now that you mention it, maybe I'd like to talk to Brianna one more time. Just a couple of follow-up questions."

The man nodded. "She gets in at noon today."

"Eleven thirty," said the woman.

"Well, yes," the man said, "but she has the managers' meeting then. So if this young lady shows up at eleven thirty, she's going to have to wait half an hour."

"Thanks," Fenway said. "I'll come in this afternoon." She put another forkful of mille-feuille in her mouth as the two workers from the Phillips-Holsen left the patisserie.

Wiping her hands, she reached for her purse and pulled her phone out of her handbag.

"This is Sergeant Roubideaux."

"Dez—hey, it's Fenway. You doing anything right now?"

"I was just about to head to the jail to interview Keith and Karen."

"Keith and Karen?"

"The two drunks—the regulars at Valhalla. They'll be released in about an hour, and I want to be sure I interview them before they leave."

"You haven't gone over there yet?"

"There's this thing called paperwork, Fenway. Plus, Mark and I paid another visit to Grant and Noreen Tonnick. The judge denied the injunction this morning—Rick's accounts won't be frozen."

"Ha. They must have been livid."

"They were."

Fenway cut another piece of pastry and let it sit on her plate. "So I was just talking to a couple of co-workers of Brianna Harlow."

"Brianna Harlow?"

"The property manager at the Phillips-Holsen. The one who showed us the video footage of Amy's Mustang."

"Oh—right."

"Can you do a little digging on her? She's been awfully important to this investigation, and I want to make sure she's on the up-and-up."

"You suspect her of something shady?"

"Maybe it's nothing."

Dez sighed. "It might soothe your brain to know that I called the video storage company. They sent over their cybersecurity logs. They can assure me the video hasn't been tampered with. The original files were backed up within an hour of being shot, and all versions of the footage match in terms of timestamps."

Fenway nodded. "That's good to know."

"I recognize the tone in your voice. You're still not satisfied."

"Humor me?"

"I can ask Mark if he has time—or I can do it when I get back from the jail. Do you want to meet me over there?"

Dez insisted on keeping the tone casual and light, so they met Karen Chan in the common area of the jail where family members sat at round tables with their incarcerated loved ones. Fenway wasn't sure it was a good idea, but Karen Chan had been remorseful. Still, she looked warily from side to side as the guard walked her in and sat her down at the chair.

"What is this?" Chan said. "Who are you?"

"I'm County Coroner Fenway Stevenson."

"And I'm Sergeant Dez Roubideaux," Dez said. "We just want to ask you a couple of questions about the bar on Sunday night."

"Not last night? That's when we—"

"Nope," Dez said. "Sunday night. Were you and your husband there?"

"Yes," Chan said. "We're regulars there. Sunday is trivia night."

"Did you win?" Dez asked.

Chan laughed. "Not even close."

Fenway leaned forward. "When did you leave the bar?"

"We closed it down."

"Do you remember much?"

"Sure. Duke was bartending. The guy does *not* know how to make a good Manhattan. I wound up having Jack on the rocks. At least there's nothing for him to screw up."

Dez tapped her fingers on the table and shot a sideways glance at Fenway. Was it time to do what they were here for?

Fenway nodded slightly, and Dez began her question. "Did a woman come in around one thirty? Right at last call?"

"A woman? What kind of woman?"

"A well-preserved forty-something," Fenway said. "Blonde, fit. Maybe a little Botox."

"Coming into the bar at one thirty in the morning?" Karen asked. "I might not have noticed her, but I bet Keith would have. And I would have for sure noticed Keith noticing her. Woulda kicked his ass."

"Maybe he was too drunk to notice."

Karen shrugged. "He only had a couple of shots. He likes to stay sharp for trivia."

"What time was trivia over?" Dez asked. "It couldn't have lasted much past ten."

"I didn't check the time, but that sounds about right."

"So Keith had a good three and a half hours to get drunk enough not to notice a pretty woman walk through the door."

"I guess. I still think someone who walks in that close to closing time is going to get noticed. Duke never misses a chance to make a sale, and he was chatting with us. Reciting lines from our favorite movie. He thinks he's hot shit because he knows all the lines to *Napoleon Dynamite*."

"That sounds impressive."

"Not when you're watching the movie with him. It's annoying as hell." She crossed her arms and leaned back. "At least he's not running trivia anymore. There would always be a couple of quotes from *Napoleon Dynamite* every single week."

"So you *didn't* see a blonde come into the bar about one thirty."

Karen shook her head emphatically. "I mean, my back was to the door, but Keith and I were joking around with Duke for, I don't know, maybe ten or fifteen minutes before last call. We ordered a couple of drinks right *at* last call, and Duke drank a seven and seven with us. There might have been a couple of people in the back corner, but we shut the place down."

Dez cocked her head. "You were talking with Duke the whole time?"

"Definitely from before one thirty until closing."

Fenway nodded. "All right, thanks."

Dez motioned the guard over.

Karen leaned forward as the guard walked up. "And you'll put a recommendation to release me without bail?"

Fenway nodded. "Sure. I don't see any reason for bail." She got up from the table and turned.

There, across the room, was Craig McVie. Sitting across from Amy Tonnick, in an orange prison uniform that made her skin look sickly.

Fenway stopped in her tracks. Straining her ears, she could barely make out what Amy and Craig were saying. Neither of them noticed Fenway as she took a seat at an empty table a few feet closer, turning her back to them and slouching down.

"I'm innocent, Craig."

"I believe you. I do. And I'm looking into how we can prove your innocence."

We. Fenway frowned.

"I never took the car anywhere that night."

McVie exhaled sharply. "But you weren't home then, either, were you? Not like you told the police."

"No. I was with Tommy."

McVie sighed.

"Okay," Amy said, a note of determination in her voice. "I don't need that. You don't need to judge me right now."

"I didn't say anything."

"I saw that look enough when we were married. Megan is seventeen now. She can stay home alone. I see her the same amount of time if I'm over at Tommy's or if I'm at the house."

"It's just that she *sees* what you're doing. She knows you're lying to her. And lying to me, and to—well, everyone."

"You don't get to tell me how to parent, Craig. Megan chose to live with *me*."

McVie was silent for a moment. He probably hadn't said anything to Amy about Megan not coming home the night before.

Amy's voice softened. "I'm sorry. I know you're just trying to help."

"Yes, I am," McVie said.

"It was a mistake."

McVie clicked his tongue. "*What* was a mistake?"

"Marrying Rick." She lowered her voice. "And getting divorced."

"Oh," McVie said. He hesitated a moment. "I thought you were going to say it was a mistake to kill him."

All the wind went out of Amy's voice. "You *don't* believe me."

"Can you blame me, Amy? I feel like an idiot. I'm supposed to be the town sheriff, the guy who people trust. I don't even know how many affairs you had."

"They didn't mean anything," Amy said.

"Yes, they did," McVie said. "I know Dylan meant something to you, and I know Rick meant something to you. Maybe most of them didn't, but those two did." He whispered something to Amy that Fenway couldn't hear.

A tug on her sleeve almost pulled Fenway off the chair. "What the hell are you doing?" Dez hissed at her.

She looked up into Dez's narrowed eyes and knit brow.

"I—I was just—"

"Amy has an expectation of privacy with McVie," Dez said. "Just because she's your boyfriend's ex-wife doesn't mean you can listen in on their conversation."

"But—but there's no attorney-client—"

"You want us to get thrown in front of a judge during an evidentiary hearing?" Dez asked. "You better not get off on the wrong foot with the new ADA. Even if the judge rules for the state, you're damaging relationships. Come *on*."

Fenway got up from her chair and followed Dez out the door of the common area. Amy and McVie never even glanced up.

CHAPTER NINETEEN

"I don't know what to tell you," Charlotte said, looking at the leather-bound menu. "Pendergrass said he wanted to meet with both of us."

Fenway tapped her fingers on the table. She was itching to get to the Phillips-Holsen Resort Hotel. There were some possible scenarios in which Duke Perriman might have exaggerated what he saw. Maybe he *did* see Amy walking into the hotel, but perhaps she hadn't actually walked in. But with Karen Chan disagreeing with Duke Perriman's version of events, it was hard to see how Perriman's testimony would hold up in court.

She looked around the restaurant. Maxime's was only open for lunch Wednesday through Sunday, though Sunday was technically brunch.

"I don't see their pheasant," Charlotte murmured.

"I think they only serve pheasant for dinner."

Charlotte sighed and set the menu down. "Do you even know what today is, Fenway?"

"Uh... is this a trick question? January seventh?"

"Your father took controlling ownership in both Wallace Fuels and the Dominguez Star Petroleum Company on this day thirty-four years ago, turning two failing local oil companies into the biggest employer in the county and one of the top five energy companies in California."

You were a year old. Fenway bit her tongue and opened the menu. "They've got an ahi tuna sandwich that looks great."

"Your father and I," Charlotte continued, "came to Maxime's on our first date. And he comes here every year on January seventh and orders the pheasant."

"The pheasant is delicious here," Fenway admitted.

"I was planning to come down here tonight," Charlotte said, "so even though Nathaniel wouldn't be with me, I wouldn't break tradition. But then when Pendergrass said he wanted to meet with us—well, I know you're on a case, and I thought we might not be able to squeeze in dinner at Maxime's." She looked around the restaurant; it wasn't quite full. "They certainly don't do the business at lunch that they do in the evenings." She closed the menu. "Maybe I can just order it off-menu. They sometimes let me do that."

"I found my grandmother," Fenway blurted.

Charlotte looked up, confused. "What?"

"My grandmother."

"I thought she died years ago."

"Not Grandma Ferris. My mom's mom."

Charlotte's eyes widened. "Oh—wow. I didn't—I didn't realize, uh, much of anything really. I didn't know you were looking for her."

"I wasn't, really. My mom said her parents both died in an accident when she was in her early twenties. But she didn't—I mean, my grandmother didn't die. Neither did my grandfather. I mean, he's dead, but—" Fenway stopped and took a deep breath. "I'm sorry. It's a long story."

The server appeared in a fitted white shirt and black slacks, her black hair pulled back into a ponytail. "Have the two of you decided?"

"If you could just give us another minute," Fenway started to say, but Charlotte talked over her.

"You have the most incredible pheasant at dinner," Charlotte said. "Is it possible to get it for lunch?"

"I'll go check with the chef," the server said, and she turned and disappeared.

Fenway sighed. One of the most important discoveries of her life, and Charlotte was more concerned with whether or not she could get a roast pheasant dinner at lunch.

"So remember in the courtroom," Fenway began, "when Dad told me that he'd actually been paying my mom ten thousand a month in child support and sending her tuition checks?"

"Um," Charlotte said, "yes. Not all the details. A lot of stuff happened that day."

"Right." Fenway looked down at the menu. Maybe it wasn't such a good idea to bring this up. "Never mind. I can tell you later. With the Pendergrass meeting coming up, you must have a lot on your mind."

Charlotte nodded. "Thanks. I mean, I do want to hear the story, but I'm not sure how well I can concentrate. If we lose Pendergrass as a customer, that will be the first domino, and I don't know if I can keep the rest of them from falling." She paused. "Maybe I can put off the meeting until tomorrow morning. I work better in the morning."

"I'll be in L.A.," Fenway said.

"What?" Charlotte's head snapped up.

"The investigation is close to done—or at least, we've arrested some-one. And my grandmother is in a nursing home down there. I want to go visit her." She set her jaw. "I was *supposed* to go this morning, but Craig's daughter borrowed my car last night and didn't return it."

"Why did you let her borrow your car?"

"I didn't. She—she was having a tough time with her mom getting arrested right in front of her. She sort of borrowed it without asking."

Charlotte nodded. "I see."

"Plus, I had to deal with the mayor at nine this morning—although I was definitely prepared to blow off that meeting."

Charlotte rolled her eyes. "I feel so gross just saying 'Mayor Barry Klein.'"

"You and me both."

The server appeared again. "I'm so sorry, but the chef does prepara-tion work on the birds between the lunch and dinner seatings. We don't have any pheasant prepared."

Charlotte's lips twitched. "What do you have that is just as wonder-fully inventive as the pheasant?"

"For lunch?" the server asked.

"Yes," Charlotte replied, a little icily.

"One very popular dish is the bacon and brie sandwich with the garlic and butter Brussels sprouts."

"Hmmm." Charlotte's mouth twitched. "I think I'll just get the salmon, as rare as you can make it. And a cup of the pozole."

"Oh," the server said, "the pozole is only available after four."

Charlotte blinked. "A house salad, then. Vinaigrette on the side."

The server nodded and turned to Fenway. "And for you?"

"That bacon and brie sandwich sounds great."

The server took both menus and left as stealthily as she'd come.

Charlotte shook her head. "Well, now I know why it isn't nearly as crowded for lunch."

"What time does Pendergrass want to meet with us?"

"He didn't specify a time."

"I'm not sure I can get away before six o'clock."

"Six it is, then. Perhaps we can meet you at your office, so you won't have to drive all the way to the Ferris Energy building. And being in your office will keep Pendergrass on his toes." She took a sip of her iced tea. "What do you think he wants?"

"I—uh," Fenway said.

"What is it?"

Fenway paused. "I ran into him at the Lexus dealership yesterday."

"You did? Why didn't you tell me?"

"Well... I might have told him off. So he might be—*might be*, I must stress—coming back to us with a higher offer."

"What did you do?"

"A little research into where else he could go for the product he needs, for one," Fenway said. "I know what our margins are, and I know where we've gotten good prices in our supply chain."

"What does that mean?"

"It means I pushed back. If he goes somewhere else for the mix of products he's buying from us, he'll be paying twice what he is now. Maybe he can get away with that for a couple of weeks before it starts significantly affecting his bottom line, but I don't think it's a risk he wants to take."

"You got all of this from meeting him yesterday?"

Fenway paused and looked down at her hands. "When I was working in the ER, there'd be all kinds of people coming in with weird injuries, and none of them wanted to tell you how they'd done it. It was always something embarrassing or stupid. But I'd have to find out because it was important to diagnose the injury correctly." She sat back in the booth. "Then when I became coroner and started to investigate the suspicious deaths, I also had to deal with people who lied all the time about what happened. Sometimes they did something embarrassing or stupid, and their friend overdosed or fell off a ladder and died, and they don't want to tell you. But as you know, I've dealt with my share of murderers, too. And they definitely didn't want anyone to know what they'd done."

"So you're bragging that you know when to call someone's bluff." Charlotte smirked at Fenway, who grinned back.

The food came, and the server made a flourish with the pepper grinder. Charlotte declined to put anything on her salad.

Fenway realized Charlotte was still waiting for an answer about what Pendergrass wanted, and she leaned forward. "I think he's going to make you a significantly higher offer for the company. And I think it'll be in line with the valuation the rest of the board expects."

Charlotte paused, chewing, and then put her fork down. "It was easy to know what I *wanted* to do when he was lowballing me. I wanted to do everything in my power to keep him out. But if this is a fair offer—well, Fenway, I don't know that I can say no to it. Not with your dad in the hospital, and not when we have no idea when he'll come out of the coma."

Fenway nodded. "That's the right decision."

Charlotte took a bite of the salmon.

"How is it?" Fenway asked.

"The pheasant is better."

"Maybe the meeting will be short. You could still make the reservation."

"It's possible, I guess."

"Are you going to the hospital tonight?" Fenway asked, then took a bite of her sandwich. The flavors were phenomenal—the smokiness of the bacon might usually have conflicted with the tang of the brie, but there were thinly sliced apples—Granny Smith, if she wasn't mistaken—and honey. Not too much—just a touch of sweetness. And red pepper flakes. Amazingly, the sweet-and-spicy combination pulled the whole sandwich together. Fenway pushed the plate slightly toward Charlotte. "You have to try this."

"Bacon and brie? Ugh. No thanks. That sounds like a disgusting combination."

"One bite."

Charlotte gingerly picked up the half that Fenway hadn't touched yet and took a tiny bite.

"No," Fenway said. "A *real* bite."

Charlotte tilted her head but took a medium-sized bite. "Oh," she said through the mouthful, her eyes closing.

"Right?" Fenway said.

"It's—it's so unusual."

"The red pepper flakes and the honey. I know. But it's perfect, right?"

"I mean, the apples and honey and brie combination is classic, of course. But the bacon and red pepper flakes? I don't know whether to call that inspired or insane." She set the sandwich down on the plate. "And when you look at it, it just looks like an ordinary sandwich."

Fenway blinked. "It just looks ordinary."

She'd missed something.

She closed her eyes and pinched the bridge of her nose.

"Uh oh," Charlotte said. "Nate always does that when he's figuring out a big problem."

"I'm missing something," Fenway murmured.

"What?"

"I—I don't exactly know. I saw something that looked ordinary. Plain. And it didn't register with me at the time that I was missing something."

"Is this for the murder investigation?"

"Yeah—oh, sorry, Charlotte. I know we were talking about the company and what Archie Pendergrass is going to do."

Charlotte leaned back and shook her head.

"He's going to give you another offer, based on an actual valuation but still not that favorable to you," Fenway said. "And Tonisha, one of the analysts in your research department, has more up-to-date valuations you can use in negotiations. You can start with the most favorable, of course, but those are the valuations that—in my opinion—overvalue leveraged positions and undervalue cash on hand. Where we are right now, that's favorable to us, but I don't think it's reflective of the market dynamics today."

"So what does Pendergrass want?"

"He wants to control more of his supply chain," Fenway said, pulling her plate back in front of her and picking the sandwich up. "He's worried that whoever gets control of the company is going to start charging a lot more for the unique mix of fuel he needs, and that could force him to raise prices, which will affect the upcoming earnings announcement— which won't be good for his stock options. And he's coming up on his five-year anniversary with the company, so he has, I don't know, tens of thousands of shares vesting. For him, the ability to control the supply chain is worth maybe ten or fifteen million dollars personally to him."

Charlotte's eyes went wide.

Fenway shrugged. "It's right there in the financial reports on the web. It's boring as hell, but I had to do *something* at Dad's bedside when my voice got tired."

"Did Piper help you with this?"

"She told me where the bodies were buried, sure. I did some of it myself."

"I didn't know you were good at math."

"I know how to use a calculator. Don't go thinking I know how to figure out compound interest or anything." Fenway leaned forward and tapped her fingers on the table. "Ask Tonisha to get you those figures. Pendergrass won't want to go as high as the top valuations, but his position is much weaker than he let on."

"When did you do all this?"

"Tonisha told me a couple of weeks ago that Sierra Madre was dragging their feet about paying their quarterly invoice. So after I got home last night, I did a little digging."

"Well," Charlotte said, a smile touching the corners of her mouth. "That was worth the price of a bacon and brie sandwich." She placed her fork and knife on top of the salmon plate. "See you tonight?"

"Six o'clock," Fenway said. "Unless the investigation blows up." Fenway's phone buzzed, and she started to dig for it in her purse.

"I thought you said you had everything wrapped up. You even said you were going to Los Angeles tomorrow."

Fenway nodded, finding her phone. "I'm definitely going to see my grandmother. But I've got to figure out what I'm missing." She pulled the phone out and looked at the screen. The text message was from Dez.

Brianna Harlow's sister is Trina Perriman

Duke Perriman's wife, who died in the car crash. Whose family Rick Tonnick had lost the negligence case against.

And whose family didn't get nearly enough money in the judgment against Tonnick, either.

So much for having a sixth sense for what people were hiding.

An hour later, Fenway and Dez walked into the Phillips-Holsen and saw Brianna Harlow's beaming smile from across the lobby.

"Ah, Coroner! It's nice to see you again." Brianna held her hand out as Fenway and Dez approached, and they both shook her hand. "Is there additional footage you need to see? I've talked to corporate, and they've agreed—"

"Could we actually talk to you in private, Ms. Harlow?" Fenway asked.

"Oh," Brianna laughed. "So *formal.* Call me Brianna, please." She turned and walked down the corridor, Fenway and Dez hurrying to keep pace. After the labyrinthine hallway, Brianna opened the door to the property manager's office and followed Fenway and Dez in.

"I might still have the video cued to the same place it was the other day," Brianna said. "I know you're supposed to turn the computers off every night, but when there are two of us sharing this office, it doesn't always happen." She woke the computer and clicked over to the video surveillance application. Sure enough, the video was paused on the red

Mustang convertible leaving the parking garage, Amy Tonnick's license plate clearly visible onscreen.

"You didn't tell us you were Trina Perriman's sister," Fenway said.

Brianna's forehead crinkled. "What? I don't understand—what does my sister have to do with this?"

"The man who your brother-in-law sued for negligence in her death? Rick Tonnick, the dead man in the penthouse suite."

Brianna shook her head as she took a seat in front of the computer. "I'm sorry. I'm not following you."

Dez took a step forward. "The man who's responsible for the death of your sister is found murdered in your hotel. In a property that *you* manage." She crossed her arms. "My boss doesn't like coincidences. I don't either. It might be one thing if you had *told* us about your sister, first thing. But you didn't."

Brianna's head snapped up. "Wait—you're saying that I might have had something to do with his death?"

"You certainly had a reason to want him dead," said Fenway.

Brianna set her jaw. "It took me a year and a half of therapy and some pretty dark places to deal with my sister's passing." She stood up from her chair. "I don't appreciate you bringing that up again."

"We're just saying—" Fenway began.

"You're suggesting I killed him," Brianna said, raising her voice. "First of all, I didn't have any idea it was him. He signed in under an assumed name, remember?"

"But paid with his real credit card," Dez pointed out.

Brianna rolled her eyes. "How in the *world* was I supposed to know that? I don't work the front desk or the payment system. I had no idea he was staying here."

"He's on commercials all the time," Fenway said. "You could have seen him in the hotel."

Brianna shrugged. "I suppose I could have, but I already told you I didn't recognize him. Besides, I paid for years of therapy to deal with my sister's death."

"Did the therapy include wiping your memory?" Fenway said. "You didn't mention *anything* to us when you found out what his real name was."

Brianna scoffed. "Really? You expect me to just offer up that my brother-in-law sued the dead guy?"

Fenway stared at Brianna, unblinking. Neither of them said anything.

Dez broke the silence. "Just out of curiosity, where were you on Sunday night between 2:00 and 4:00 A.M.?"

"Making increasingly poor decisions at a blackjack table in Vegas," Brianna said. "I had a girls' weekend, like I told the coroner. I was on the first flight from Vegas to Estancia at 4:15 on Monday morning. That's why I was so tired when you talked to me on Monday, remember?"

Two days before seemed like a lifetime ago, but Fenway vaguely remembered her telling part of this story.

"I've got my plane ticket stub still in my travel suitcase if you want to see it."

"Can anyone corroborate your story?" Fenway asked.

"My friend Uschi was with me until Sunday night. She left for the airport around seven o'clock. I went to the tables right afterward, and I rode hot hands for about five hours. Then I lost almost everything." She shook her head. "Five hours winning, thirty minutes losing, and suddenly I looked down and only had about a hundred bucks in chips left. I cashed out and went to some all-night greasy spoon for breakfast. Then I took a cab to the airport."

Fenway tilted her head. "Any receipts?"

"If I had known I'd need receipts, I wouldn't have paid with the very little cash I had left," Brianna said.

"You paid for both dinner and your cab ride to the airport in cash?" Dez asked.

Brianna nodded. "So I wouldn't waste the rest of it on the slots at the airport."

"I see." Dez tapped her foot. "Can anyone verify you were in the casino?"

"Well—only about a thousand of my closest friends. But I didn't know any of them."

"Why didn't you come back with Uschi?"

"The first flight Monday morning was about two hundred cheaper than Sunday night." Brianna's smile faded slightly. "And, uh, because I guess I wanted to gamble without my friends judging me."

"I get that," Fenway said. There weren't evenings of solo gambling for Fenway, but there were definitely nights in college where Fenway went clubbing by herself. It wasn't safe, but meeting someone who didn't know her and who wasn't judging and who didn't want to see her ever again— the idea was sometimes intoxicating.

"I *do* have the long-term parking receipt from Monday morning," Brianna said. "I think I do, anyway. I drove straight here from the airport. It's probably in my car."

"All right," Dez said, then exhaled loudly and pressed her lips together before speaking again. "The man found dead in the penthouse suite was legally responsible for the death of your sister, but you're saying you didn't know that was him."

"I didn't."

"And you were in Las Vegas Sunday, gambling all night, coming back early Monday morning."

"That's correct."

Dez looked out of the corner of her eye at Fenway.

Fenway cleared her throat and looked at the screen, freeze-framed on the back of the Mustang convertible. Amy's license plate and telltale "Estancia High Mom" license plate frame were clearly visible.

Fenway blinked.

And when you look at it, it just looks like an ordinary sandwich.

What was her brain trying to tell her?

She looked at the license plate. At the frame. At the bumper. At the trunk. At the silver horse silhouette directly above the license plate. At the three vertical taillights on each side. She squinted. She tilted her head. She blinked hard.

Then it hit her.

It looked like an ordinary bumper.

Without the Estancia High Concert Choir bumper sticker.

That might have been Amy's license plate, but it definitely wasn't her car.

CHAPTER TWENTY

"A missing *choir* sticker." Dez tapped her chin thoughtfully.

"I don't know how that Mustang got Amy's license plate," Fenway said from the passenger seat, "but without that choir sticker, that's not Amy's car."

Dez frowned as she put the Impala into gear. "Back to the office?"

Fenway hesitated. "Could you drop me off at St. Vincent's? I want to see my dad."

"Going against Barry Klein's wishes again, are you?"

Fenway shrugged. "Yep. I'm hoping that seeing him will clear my head."

"Sure." Dez turned toward the freeway. "Are you sure Amy didn't put the sticker on the car after Sunday night?"

Fenway folded her arms. "Not entirely, but I can double-check." She bit her bottom lip. "If Amy *had* put the choir sticker on after the murder, though, wouldn't she have mentioned it before now? Try to at least add some reasonable doubt into the equation?"

Dez stared straight ahead. "Maybe. Or maybe she was waiting until the discovery phase after her arrest, so it would look like she'd only thought about it after her lawyer requested the recording. It might make her look more innocent."

Fenway chuckled. "The prospect of spending a night in jail—never mind a couple of weeks—would have horrified Amy so much that she'd have said something by now."

Dez clicked her tongue. "License plates are easy enough to steal."

"And Amy doesn't put her car in the garage. Her Mustang would have been in the driveway."

"There goes our main suspect," Dez said. "Amy wouldn't have switched license plates to an identical Mustang."

"That also means Megan isn't a suspect. Not if she didn't take her mother's car." Fenway looked out the window as they turned onto the freeway. "We've been going down the wrong path since the body was found."

"Barry Klein isn't going to like this."

Fenway laughed. "Remind me to tell you what happened this morning in his office. If he could fire me, he would."

"If Barry fired everyone he wanted to fire, there wouldn't be anyone left in the county to do any work," Dez said. "And we still have suspects. We have Duke Perriman and Brianna Harlow."

"Right." Fenway tapped the arm rest on the door. "Duke lied about seeing Amy that night."

"And he had a strong motive for wanting revenge on Rick Tonnick."

"So it follows that he's working with someone."

Fenway nodded. "Maybe the other plaintiffs."

"Maybe. Although Trina Perriman's sister works at the hotel where he was found dead. And that coincidence is hard to swallow." Dez checked over her shoulder and moved to the right, into the exit-only lane for San Vicente Boulevard. "What do you think of Brianna's story?"

"That she didn't know that Rick Tonnick stayed in the hotel? She usually worked the day shift, didn't she? And Rick usually came in around ten at night and would leave by four or four thirty in the morning. I suppose it's plausible that she didn't know—but like you said, it's another coincidence."

Dez nodded. "Worth digging into her alibi, for sure."

"Right." She thought about the role of Brianna, one of two property managers, who usually—but not always—worked the day shift. "It's possible that she never saw him, but given that they're both at the

Phillips-Holsen so much, I find it hard to believe that their paths never crossed."

"Innocent until proven guilty," said Dez.

"So, yeah, I agree with you, Dez. Let's dig into her alibi. In fact, let's do more than that. We can check her hours at the hotel against his credit card bills and against his check-in and check-out times. I'll put Piper—" Fenway paused. It had been months, and she still wasn't used to Piper not working for the county. "Uh—I'll talk to the IT team. See who they'd like to put on this."

"You've never even talked to the new guy, have you, Fenway?"

"No. I keep meaning to go over and introduce myself. I just haven't done it yet."

"You should really give him a chance."

"I know." Fenway paused. "I wonder if I should give the new ADA a heads up on this. I don't want his first murder trial to go off the rails because of something we found out post-arrest."

"Right," Dez said, nodding. "We've still got a copy of the video recording. Do you have a picture of Amy's Mustang?"

"With the choir sticker visible, right?"

"Right."

"I don't think so," Fenway said. "I suppose I could drive over to her house and get it. Or I could see if Megan has it on her phone." *If she's even talking to me.*

"I suppose we don't really need it for the initial meeting," Dez said, "but I can go get a photo of it too. Especially since I'm out."

"I really appreciate you dropping me off at the hospital," Fenway said.

"No worries." Dez set her jaw. "Whoever did this worked really hard to set Amy up. I wonder if they've got something against her, too."

"So you think Brianna Harlow was working with Duke Perriman?"

Dez shrugged. "The sister working with the widower? I've seen stranger things, I guess. We might be talking a murder for hire. Or maybe Trina's parents are involved. It's even possible that *everyone* who was involved in that lawsuit contributed something."

"Brianna does have an alibi, though."

"Not an alibi," Dez corrected. "She's got a decent *explanation* for where she was."

"Right. She was in another state and has the plane ticket to prove it."

"But there's still a lot of time unaccounted for in her timeline."

"We should definitely talk to her friend. What was her name? Utley?"

"Uschi," Dez replied. "Yes. That's why I went back and got her friend's information. I'll call her and confirm the story."

"We should talk to her right now. The longer we wait, the more time Brianna has to call Uschi and get her to confirm whatever story Brianna wants to tell."

Dez dug her small notepad out of her pocket and tossed it at Fenway. "You give her a call."

Fenway pulled her phone out of her purse while flipping open the small notebook. She landed on the last page and dialed the phone number scrawled there.

"Matson Architects, this is Uschi Berglund."

"Hi, Uschi. I'm sorry to bother you at work, but this is Fenway Stevenson from the coroner's office."

"The coroner's office? What happened?"

"I have a question about your friend Brianna Harlow."

Uschi let out a sigh of relief. "Oh. Of course. The dead rich guy in the penthouse of the hotel. What can I tell you?"

"Was she in Las Vegas with you last weekend?"

"Yes. We had a girls' weekend. A good show, some expensive meals, a little gambling."

"What time did you leave for the airport?"

"About seven o'clock Sunday night. I was catching the eight forty-five back to Estancia."

"And Brianna was planning on catching a flight the next morning?"

"That's what she told me. She was planning on staying out all night, partying or gambling or something. For all I know, she could have slept in the airport." Uschi sighed loudly. "I don't know about you, but I'm not in college anymore. I can't stay out all night without serious repercussions the next day. I don't know how Brianna does it."

"Did she say what she'd be doing all night?"

"Well, honestly, she was a little evasive. I think she was planning on either gambling or—" Uschi hesitated.

"What?" Fenway pressed.

"I really hate to say this, but Brianna was seeing a guy a couple of years ago, and they broke up. He got married and moved to Vegas, and I kind of had a feeling she was going to see him."

"And you think she did that instead of spending all night at a black-jack table?"

Uschi paused. "I—I don't know. Brianna loves blackjack, so I definitely think she could have gambled until her flight in the morning. She missed a Cirque du Soleil show once because she was on a roll. Wound up winning six thousand dollars, though."

"But you were in Vegas with her on Sunday until about seven o'clock."

"Yes."

"Were you with her the whole time?"

"She went out for a run on Sunday morning. She was gone for about an hour and a half. And Saturday afternoon, I went down to the pool by myself, but she said it was too cold. I hate to admit it, but she was right."

Fenway looked up from her phone at Dez with a questioning look on her face, but Dez shook her head.

"Thanks for your time," Fenway said. "We'll be in touch if we have anything else."

They said their goodbyes, and Fenway ended the call.

"What do you think?" asked Dez. "Did she confirm Brianna's alibi?"

"I think it's pretty likely Brianna was at the casino at seven o'clock," Fenway said. "But I'm not so sure she was playing blackjack all night."

"Why not?"

Fenway leaned back in her seat. "She could have gotten on an earlier flight from Vegas to Estancia," she said. "Assuming she knew where the Tonnicks lived, she could have driven there, switched out the license plates, gone to the hotel, killed Rick Tonnick, switched the plates back, and gotten to work in plenty of time to start her shift. She might have even gotten a couple of hours of sleep."

"Need I remind you she checked into her flight?" Dez pursed her lips. "Besides, when you asked me to look into her, I checked her DMV records. A black Dodge Charger is registered in her name, not a Mustang."

"She could have rented a Mustang from the Estancia airport," Fenway said. "That would have been easy enough to do."

"She rented the car while in midair?"

Fenway crossed her arms. "Humor me. Just look into it. It'll take you fifteen minutes."

Dez sighed. "Okay, you're the boss—but there are plenty of other people who wouldn't have minded Rick Tonnick dead. And a lot of those people would have been jealous of Amy, too. Ex-wives, ex-lovers, ex-business partners. Plenty of them could have had access to a red Mustang convertible." She exited the freeway. "You were right not to hyperfocus on Amy. But now we shouldn't hyperfocus on Brianna Harlow or Duke Perriman either."

Fenway considered this for a moment. "But we *should* keep looking into Duke Perriman. As if it weren't enough that a regular disagrees that Amy ever came into the bar, it's now very clear that he was intentionally trying to mislead us."

Dez turned into the St. Vincent's Hospital lot.

"Thanks for giving me a ride," Fenway said.

"You need me to pick you up?"

"No," Fenway said, "I need to talk to McVie. Megan is still missing, and my car is still gone, too. We've got a lot to talk about."

"All right," Dez said. "I'll go talk to ADA Pondicherry. Then I need to look into Duke Perriman."

"Why don't you call the new guy in IT? See if he can research who rented a red Ford Mustang before Sunday night and returned it."

"It doesn't matter if the Mustang's been returned," Dez pointed out. "The killer could be biding his time, not wanting to put us on the scent." Dez turned her head toward Fenway and grinned. "And I think *you* should contact IT. You have to establish some rapport with the new guy eventually."

Fenway frowned. "Does it have to be today?"

"Yes, it does," Dez replied firmly. "You'll have time when you get back from seeing your dad to talk to the newbie. Just tell him what you need. Yes, he's not a mind reader like Piper was, but he's decent."

"Fine," Fenway said. She got out of the car and walked into the hospital.

Fenway hadn't been in to see her father much in the mid-afternoon, especially if it wasn't on the weekend. The quality of the light was different somehow, and she lost interest after just a couple of pages of *Gulliver's Travels*. She was just setting the book down when she looked up and saw a short Indian woman in a white coat standing in the doorway of the room.

"I'm Dr. Ogrireddy," the woman said. "I've been assigned to Mr. Ferris on most weekdays. I haven't seen you before."

"Fenway Stevenson," she said, standing. "I'm, uh, his daughter."

The flash of surprise on the doctor's face vanished as quickly as it came.

"Of course," she said, scanning her electronic tablet. "It's nice to hear you read. I wish more of my patients had visitors read to them."

"You must deal with a lot of comatose patients," Fenway said. "Well, when my dad comes out of it, we'll see how much of *Gulliver's Travels* he actually remembers."

Dr. Ogrireddy hesitated.

Uh oh. Fenway knew that hesitation. The specific way medical workers carried themselves when something was wrong. Fenway had done it herself after car crashes, boating accidents, severed limbs. She wasn't used to being on the receiving end of a conversation like this.

"Your father—" Dr. Ogrireddy began, and Fenway held up her hand.

"I used to be a nurse practitioner," Fenway said, "and I started out a lot of conversations almost the exact way you did just now. The patient's relative would say something hopeful, I'd hesitate, and then I'd try to figure out how to deliver the bad news."

"It's not definite," Dr. Ogrireddy said, "but your father hasn't responded for weeks. We're not sure why he's still in a coma."

Fenway nodded. "I know modern medicine doesn't have a lot of hard answers about comatose patients. But there's still hope, isn't there?"

"I don't want to say he'll never recover," the doctor admitted, "but if he hasn't responded by now, experience has shown that it's rare to wake up. He's been in this condition over sixty days, and this is about the time we see things taking a turn for the worse."

"But—people have been in comas for years and woken up."

Dr. Ogrireddy nodded. "But as you know, Miss Stevenson, there's a reason they make movies about those people. Because most of them *don't* recover. Especially those your father's age."

The doctor continued to speak, but Fenway could only hear the sound of her own heart beating. She looked at her father, his body withering from lack of use. Even if he woke up today, he'd have months of physical therapy ahead of him. Sometimes, she knew, these incidents would cause lasting damage with no visible signs that something was wrong.

Fenway's mouth went dry.

Her father had jumped in front of the bullet to save her. And now *he* was the one who wasn't going to wake up. He was leaving Charlotte to fight battles about the business where she was outgunned.

Fenway had found out, two months ago in the locked-down courtroom, that her dad wasn't nearly as vindictive as she'd thought. Something else was afoot—which led her to find that her mother wasn't who she said she was.

Everything she knew about her parents six months ago wasn't true.

And it looked like her dad was going to die before she could heal their relationship.

CHAPTER TWENTY-ONE

Fenway stepped out of the hospital into the weak, dappling sunlight of the chilly January day. The wind had picked up and swept across the drop-off area in front of the entrance. Fenway's curls smacked her in the face as she walked across the parking lot—and then she stopped and looked around. Where had she left her Accord?

Oh, that's right. Megan still had it. She frowned. If Megan had been anyone *except* Craig's daughter, Fenway would have had her arrested and charged with grand theft auto by now. If Fenway had pulled a stunt like that when she was seventeen, she'd have spent a few days in juvie. If not longer.

She trudged to a concrete bench in a long, narrow planter area that separated the visitors' lot from the staff lot. Exhaustion overwhelmed her, and she slumped forward, her elbows on her knees, covering her face with her hands.

Her father, the doctor had said, would likely never wake up. Had she told Charlotte? Had Charlotte known and not told Fenway? Fenway didn't even know how she felt about it. She vaguely remembered happy times with her dad before her mother took her away.

Fenway had always assumed that her mother hadn't gotten along with her father. That maybe he'd been emotionally distant, or maybe even abusive. Her mom hadn't talked about Nathaniel Ferris at all, though, unless it was to tell Fenway that he couldn't come to the school play, or to the volleyball playoff game, or to her graduation.

Maybe, this whole time, she'd been angry at the wrong parent.

But it did no good to look in the rearview mirror. Her mother was dead, and Fenway would find a way, come hell or high water, to get down to Los Angeles to see her grandmother. She might even unravel more of the mystery behind why her mother had changed her name and left her life in Los Angeles—and, if Fenway was lucky, provide a clue or two for why she'd left Estancia, too.

And there was nothing more she could do for her father, either, except for visit his bedside and talk to him. She had no idea if he could hear her in his state—the doctors weren't even sure why he didn't wake after his surgery, so how could they be expected to know whether he could hear her read *Gulliver's Travels*?

She set her jaw. *Gulliver's Travels* was for her, not for him. It was her way of using the expensive books in the library to be more than decoration. But that's not what he liked. He'd prefer a history of Fenway Park, or maybe a biography of Ted Williams or Wade Boggs. Hadn't one of the outfielders from the nineties written a series of spy novels? Or maybe even find some of the YouTube videos of old Red Sox games that the two of them watched together when she was little.

Even now, more than twenty years after Joanne Stevenson Ferris had taken the eight-year-old Fenway to Seattle, Fenway could still remember some odd Red Sox trivia, some of the playoff matchups from the seventies and eighties, even the nineties. There were huge gaps in her knowledge—to her father's chagrin, right when they started winning those World Series after the eighty-six years of heartbreak.

The phone in Fenway's purse buzzed. She sighed. Would this be Mayor Barry Klein again, yelling at her for finding exculpatory evidence on Amy Tonnick, or for spending part of the afternoon at her father's bedside? Or maybe McVie was calling to tell her that Megan had crashed her Accord. Fenway opened her purse and pulled out her phone.

It was Charlotte.

She cleared her throat, tossing her hair back—the wind immediately blew it into her face again—and answered.

"Hi, Charlotte." She turned her back to the wind so the whistling made as little noise on the phone as possible.

"You're brilliant, Fenway."

"Oh." Fenway sat up straight. "Thanks. What am I brilliant for this time?"

Charlotte chuckled. "I took your advice on how to deal with Archie Pendergrass. I got the numbers on all the valuation exercises from that woman in accounting you pointed me to."

"Tonisha."

"Yes. I had pages and pages of information. I wanted something in case Pendergrass pushed back on the valuation in our meeting tonight. And you're right, his costs will triple if another company buys us."

"Oh—Charlotte, keep that information in your back pocket! Only if he threatens to use the escape clause in his contract! Not if another company—"

"No, Fenway—look, you're brilliant, but as soon as I got back to my office, I read the fine print in Sierra Madre's customer contract. A sale of the company is one of the things that triggers the ability to either party to end the contract. I made sure to run it by legal—and it's true."

"No way. Customers *never* agree to that."

"Maybe not, but your dad made sure that trigger was in every customer contract that went out the door. Customers usually insisted on deleting that language, but Sierra Madre never made that request. And you'll never guess who showed up right as I finished reading it."

"Archie Pendergrass."

"Right you are. Without an appointment. He waltzed into my office and said he hoped he wasn't disturbing me, and I said no, I was just reviewing Sierra Madre's customer contract." Charlotte chortled. "You should have seen his face! He knew exactly what I was referring to."

"So what did he do?"

"He more than *tripled* his offer. One-point-eight billion."

"Oh—one of the high valuations, then."

"That's right. The second-highest."

"What did you say?"

"I asked him if that was the best offer he could provide."

Fenway chuckled. "Oh, I wish I'd been there."

"Then he asked if I had a higher offer on the table. I told him I had to give time for others to counteroffer. He almost lost his mind. He bumped his offer up by fifty million. That's twenty million higher than the top valuation."

"He's done his homework, I guess," Fenway said. "My guess is that he knows owning Ferris Energy is worth more to Sierra Madre as part of his directly-controlled supply chain than it would be to anyone else. Twenty million isn't a lot when you're talking about buying an oil company, but it would give a competitive bidder pause if they knew another investor was overvaluing the company."

"Particularly without—" Then the words stuck in Charlotte's throat.

The wind died down for a moment, and Fenway heard Charlotte inhale deeply, her breath catching.

"You talked to Dr. Ogrireddy, too," Fenway said.

Charlotte was silent for a moment, then said, "Yes."

"I'm really sorry, Charlotte."

"Well," she said, getting a professional tone back in her voice, "it certainly makes it easier to make a decision. If Nathaniel isn't going to be back as CEO, we may as well maximize the value we get for the sale, don't you think?"

Fenway was about to agree, but a horrible thought struck.

"Do you know," Fenway said, "what Sierra Madre is going to do with the employees? With the land and the company and everything?"

"Honestly," Charlotte said, "we didn't talk about that."

"It's the largest employer in the county," Fenway pointed out. "If Sierra Madre buys Ferris just for the parts of the supply chain that *they* need and eliminates everything else—well, that's thousands of people out of work. That'll throw the county into chaos."

Charlotte was quiet for a moment. "Do you think that's possible?"

"Of course it's possible," Fenway said. It happened to a couple of her friends when they took a job at another clinic—a large pharmacy chain bought the clinic and laid off half the staff, including all the nurses with advanced degrees. *Shareholder maximization*, they called it.

"I told him," Charlotte said, "that I'd need twenty-four hours. What do you suggest we do?"

"There are CEOs who are more strategic," Fenway said, "and you could be one of them. You could hire people with industry experience to run the business, make it just as strong as it was when Dad was running things."

"I don't know how to hire the right people," Charlotte protested.

"You have some good people on the board of directors," Fenway said. "They'll have some say in how to staff things."

"Will someone even *want* to come run things if they can't be CEO?"

"Hire someone smart and hungry but without experience. Or someone who's been passed over."

"Passed over?"

"You know what an old boys' club the energy industry can be. There must be someone who's smart and talented enough for it, but who hasn't gotten the opportunity."

Charlotte was silent.

"Then you could put a succession plan in place. Maybe three or four years—chief operating officer now, CEO when you step down. Businesses do it all the time."

"A few days ago, you were suggesting that I sell for a third of this price. Now you don't want me to sell when the offer is fantastic?" Charlotte paused. "I don't *want* to be CEO of an energy company, Fenway. These last two months without Nathaniel have been exhausting. I can't imagine doing this for three more *weeks,* let alone three more years."

"Maybe you can gauge where Pendergrass is with things, then. You could ask him what he plans to do with the business."

Charlotte scoffed. "If I'd suggested that, you'd tell me that Pendergrass would just tell me what I want to hear to get what he wants."

"Oh. Yeah, you're right." Fenway shook her hair out. The wind was bad today. "I don't know, Charlotte. If Pendergrass won't gut the company, I say you take the offer."

"Can we extract that promise from him in the contract?"

"I guess you'll have to talk to legal. That's above my pay grade."

There was silence on the phone.

"Charlotte, are you still there?"

"I want you on the hiring team, Fenway."

"Excuse me?"

"The hiring team," Charlotte said. "If I'm going to hire someone young and hungry and not a member of the old boys' club to run things, I need you on the hiring committee."

"Well," Fenway said, "I guess that makes sense."

"Try not to sound too enthusiastic about it." Charlotte laughed a little nervously.

"I keep telling you, I don't know the energy industry," Fenway said.

"But you know when people are bullshitting you," Charlotte said, "and I absolutely cannot hire a liar."

"All right," Fenway said, "I'll do it."

"And you need a seat on the board of directors."

"What?"

"You heard me, Fenway. We need a voice like yours. Someone who has the best interests of the community at heart, not someone who wants to, uh—"

"Maximize shareholder value?"

"That's not how I'd put it. Someone who understands that the stakeholders include more than just the investors."

"I don't know, Charlotte."

"Four meetings a year. You'd get a six-figure stipend. You could still solve murders as part of your day job."

"Doesn't the board need to approve another member joining?"

"After you handled yourself so well at the press conference, the board members are pretty impressed with you, Fenway. I don't think it would be unanimous, but I bet I could get the votes to get you approved."

Fenway smirked. "Now you sound like Dad, wheeling and dealing to make nepotism sound like competence."

The line was silent for a moment. Then Charlotte said, "Look, I know we haven't always gotten along, but you know I only want your dad to be happy. And if he won't"—she caught her breath and coughed —"come back to work, then I guess I agree that we owe it to him to do right by the community he loved."

"There are still all the apartment buildings Dad owns. And the commercial properties."

"I'll deal with those later," Charlotte said. "Right now, it's just been a matter of collecting rent and dealing with the property management companies. Ferris Energy is the biggest ball of craziness I have to deal with." She sighed. "And besides, who's going to pay rent if everyone at Ferris Energy gets laid off? Who's going to pay for the shoes and the pizza and the haircuts in those commercial properties if no one has money?"

"I guess you're right," Fenway said. "I—I don't really want to be on the board, but I know Dad would want us to take care of this town."

"We don't have to decide right now," Charlotte said.

"No," Fenway said, snickering. "We've got a whole *day* to respond."

"Yes, but you're wrapping up your murder case, right?"

Fenway sighed.

"Uh oh," Charlotte said. "That doesn't sound good."

"I mean," Fenway said, "it's good for the person we arrested because we found out someone's trying to frame them. But it's not good for the timing of the investigation—and the mayor's going to do everything he can to force me out."

Charlotte was quiet.

"Are you okay, Charlotte?"

"No," she said, and her voice cracked. "No, not really. These last two months have been really hard. And now I hear that he's never going to wake up—and when I hear that, I have to defend his business against a hostile takeover and save everyone in the town from getting laid off? It's too much."

"Yeah," Fenway said. "You're right. It's too much."

"Why do *I* have to be the one who's responsible for this town's economy?"

"I don't know," Fenway said, "but you are. That's how the dominoes fell."

"Well, if I get hit by a bus tomorrow," Charlotte said, "this will all be on *you*."

"I'm helping you, Charlotte."

"I know that. I'm not mad at you. I'm mad at the entire situation. I'm mad that Nate was shot."

Fenway's stomach dropped, and she tasted copper.

"Nate would be able to take care of all of this," Charlotte continued. "He loves this kind of stuff. He'd relish the chance to fight Pendergrass, and at the end of it, he'd end up more powerful, and he'd extend the contract with Sierra Madre for another five years."

Fenway was quiet. She was way out of her comfort zone on this, but she'd been the same way when McVie first offered her the chance to be appointed coroner. In fact, she'd felt the same way when she abandoned her literature major for nursing at Western Washington. But she had done it. In fact, she'd thrived.

So maybe she'd thrive at this, too. With a little elbow grease, a lot of research, and maybe a few weekends spent at the Ferris Energy building, she might be successful. Besides, a six-figure salary to fall back on if she couldn't take the heat from the mayor wouldn't be a bad thing. And she'd have a lot of free time to... uh, to what, exactly? She didn't have hobbies. Maybe she'd need to find something. Maybe she'd learn to play guitar.

"I've got to figure out what I want to do," Charlotte said. "I'll sleep on it tonight and call you tomorrow morning."

"Sure," Fenway said.

"I never cancelled my dinner reservations at Maxime's," Charlotte said. "Do you want them? Maybe take Craig there? Celebrate the opening of his new private investigation business?"

"What time?"

"Six. I wanted to go visit your dad afterward and didn't want to be too late."

It would be expensive, but maybe it was worth the splurge. And maybe it could be an olive branch between them. Fenway had been seventeen not that long ago, and she remembered how mad she could get at her mother. Her father, too. Just like Megan.

"Sure," Fenway said. "Thanks for thinking of us."

"And," Charlotte said, "the Porsche is just sitting in the garage, collecting dust."

"Dad's Porsche?"

"Right," Charlotte said. "It needs to be driven. And I don't like driving it. I haven't taken it out in over a week. The clutch is too fussy."

"If by 'too fussy,' you mean 'a joy to use,' then I agree."

"See?" Charlotte said. "You should take it."

"I should take it? I don't even know if I can afford the insurance on it."

"A long-term borrow," Charlotte said. "Come by and get it this afternoon."

Fenway paused. She didn't have her Accord. She didn't have a good way to get up to the mansion. And the Porsche was so impractical. "I can't—uh..."

No. Those reasons were just excuses. There were three taxis waiting at the curb in the visitors' lot behind her and rideshare services a click away. She needed a car tomorrow morning anyway—she wasn't sure if Megan would get the car back to her tonight or if the car was even still in one piece. And there was a nice stretch of oceanfront highway between Estancia and her grandmother's assisted living facility.

Plus, she thought with a grin, there was no way to make the mayor angrier than showing up in a fancy car that he thought she didn't deserve.

Ha.

"I can't think why not," Fenway finished. "What are you doing now?"

The Porsche 911S hurtled down the winding road from the mansion. Charlotte seemed happy, even relieved, to let Fenway borrow the Porsche for the long term. Fenway tried not to let the giddiness in her stomach override the sadness in her heart. Even though they both promised a return of the Porsche as soon as Nathaniel Ferris returned from the hospital, Fenway and Charlotte knew it was unlikely. This was a gift, and although Fenway didn't feel she deserved to be driving such an expensive sports car, she knew her dad would have loved for her to have it. Plus, it was so much better than gathering dust in the garage.

As Fenway got off the freeway at the Broadway exit, she wondered if she should broaden the search for Rick Tonnick's murderer beyond Trina Perriman's widower. She and Dez hadn't put all that much work into Tonnick's kids' background. They seemed to lack financial incentive, but people were murdered for more reasons than money.

As she turned onto Main Street, she realized she hadn't asked Darren Ellsworth everything she could have. She'd asked the P.I. plenty of questions about Rick Tonnick's mistresses and the Phillips-Holsen Hotel but hadn't even asked if there were other persons of interest that Tonnick met with. Some businesspeople were good at making it look like they were successful even if they owed money to loan sharks. If Ellsworth had followed Tonnick around for a whole week, only stopping a couple of days before he was killed, she could only imagine the various people he'd met. With any luck, perhaps Ellsworth had even snapped a photo or two of Rick Tonnick meeting his killer.

Fenway turned down Second Street, away from the city center buildings, on the way to the warehouse district. As she turned onto La Crescenta, she thought she saw Craig's beige Highlander turning away from her. It was too far away for her to be completely sure.

She felt uneasy leaving the Porsche parked in front of the building—it was out in the open, and it wasn't a good neighborhood—but she wouldn't be very long. She walked in the front door, and just like on Monday, the front desk was unoccupied. This time, she didn't bother to knock on the door to the back office.

Both Ellsworth and the blonde assistant jumped up from their chairs as Fenway walked in.

"Shit!" Ellsworth shouted, knocking over a bottle of whiskey on his desk. The woman quickly reached across and righted it—only a splash came out of the bottle.

"Good catch," Fenway said.

"First the sheriff, and now you?" Ellsworth said.

"Sheriff Donnelly was here?"

"No, no, the other one. The new P.I."

"McVie?"

"That's it."

"What did he want?"

"Probably the same thing you want," Ellsworth said.

The blonde grabbed the whisky and ducked past Fenway, out the door.

"And, Mr. Ellsworth, what is it that *I* want?"

"Information," Ellsworth said.

Fenway nodded. "On the Amy Tonnick case. I talked to you about the cheating and the affairs. But you followed him all week long."

Ellsworth narrowed his eyes. "Yeah."

"Did you see Rick Tonnick with anyone?"

"With lots of people."

"I mean anyone who looked like they had an argument with him. Someone he owed money to, maybe. Or someone he'd cheated. A used car transaction gone wrong. Something like that."

Ellsworth laughed. "You've obviously never hung around car dealerships," Ellsworth said. "Or—not around Tonnick dealerships, anyway. Lots of people came in to complain. They were mad as hell when they got there, but after Rick Tonnick talked them off the ledge, almost all of them walked away looking pleased."

"Any photos to go along with that?"

"I already gave you the information on the woman he flirted with," Ellsworth said. "You're saying nothing came of that?"

"I'm saying we're investigating it," Fenway lied smoothly, "and I'm asking if there are more people we should be talking with."

Ellsworth sat back down. "I'm a pretty good judge of when something's up." He counted on his fingers. "The people in the neighborhood. The places they go. The times they go there." He held up the three fingers in a W shape and wiggled his digits in front of Fenway's face. "I know when people fight about money. I know when it turns ugly. And I know when it turns violent." He shook his head. "A few of those people said some things they ordinarily wouldn't have, maybe, but no one got to the point where they were angry enough for a physical altercation. Not last week, anyway."

Fenway nodded.

Ellsworth looked at her, then raked his eyes down her body. "You know, you keep showing up unannounced," he said, "and I'm going to start thinking you might want something from me besides information."

She rolled her eyes. "I investigate all suspicious deaths, Mr. Ellsworth," Fenway said. "And if I wind up getting called out here, taking your liver temperature after finding you with a broken Jack Daniels bottle sticking out of your neck, I might take pity on your assistant and pretend I couldn't find any evidence."

"My assistant knows what's up," Ellsworth said.

"There's nothing up here except my time with you," Fenway said, turning on her heel and walking out the door.

She passed the assistant, who stared at her all the way to the exit, as Fenway silently pleaded with the universe to have her father's Porsche be in one piece.

She opened the front door, and the 911S was still there, untouched. She let out the breath she'd been holding, unlocked the car, and got inside, her heart beating fast.

McVie had been talking to Ellsworth just minutes before Fenway's arrival. He might have been pressing him for information about what else Ellsworth saw or photographed. Sometimes, McVie and Fenway would think similarly on cases and reach similar conclusions. Now that he wasn't the sheriff anymore, Fenway felt a hole in her work life. She tapped McVie's name in her phone list before backing out of the parking space.

His voice came over the Porsche's Bluetooth system. "Hey, Fenway."

"Hey. You were just visiting Darren Ellsworth?" Fenway turned onto La Crescenta toward the office.

A pause. "Maybe."

"Because he said you'd just visited him. But I got the feeling you weren't asking about Amy's case."

"Ellsworth is a fraud and a liar."

Fenway waited.

Finally, McVie sighed. "All right. I was visiting him to get information for *you*."

Fenway frowned. "I don't think I need your help on the Rick Tonnick murder."

"Wrong case," McVie said. "I thought it was unusual that your mother changed her name, moved to Estancia without telling her family, then pulled up stakes again and moved to Seattle."

"But she didn't change her name the second time."

"I know," said McVie, "but it's still strange. I was doing some digging on Amy's case, trying to figure out if he'd found any information about Rick Tonnick that he didn't share. When I looked at Ellsworth's registration records, I found that he moved to Estancia about two months before your mom took you to Seattle."

"Two months?"

"Think it's just coincidence?"

"Lots of people move here all the time."

"But not many private investigators do."

Fenway turned onto Fourth Street, the city center parking garage looming on her left. "So you asked him... what?"

"If he'd been following Joanne Stevenson when he moved to Estancia."

"Do you know if he's from Los Angeles?"

"I'm still searching. Business records from the eighties were on paper, or worse, computerized files that are incompatible with the current system. Piper can't get into a lot of the county records from before 1994. But if he was a P.I. in Los Angeles, my money is on her to find out."

"But you think he could have been involved with her disappearance?"

"I don't have any proof. Just a feeling. If Ellsworth tracked her down in Estancia, maybe she thought her boyfriend's killers wouldn't be far behind."

"And Seattle was far enough away?"

McVie paused. "I don't know. I guess it depends. Estancia is a three-hour drive—longer in traffic, but doable. Seattle is three days. Two if you drive in shifts and sleep when you're not driving. That might be too far if Eddie's killers weren't big time. Which they may not have been."

"Was Eddie in a gang?" Fenway pulled into the parking garage.

"We're looking into it. I asked Ellsworth about that, too. All through it, though, he said he didn't know who Joanne Stevenson was. Said he didn't know Samara Godwin either. Didn't say much of anything after that."

"So we're no closer to knowing where the money went."

"No. I'm sorry. We're working hard to get this done, but I've got another client, too."

Fenway pulled into a space on the third floor, set the parking brake, and closed her eyes. *Another client who regrets leaving you. Another client who's the mother of your child.* "Speaking of which," Fenway said, opening her eyes, "she should be getting some good news soon."

"Really?"

"Exculpatory evidence just came to light," Fenway said. "Talk to her lawyer, maybe—the ADA is getting briefed right now."

"Thanks, Fenway."

"Yeah."

A pause. "Is something wrong?"

"No," Fenway said.

"Are you sure?"

"No. Yes. Something's wrong." Fenway cleared her throat. What could she possibly say? That the doctor said her father would never wake up? That her livelihood was being threatened by the mayor? She opened her mouth, and the words spilled out. "Amy wants you back, and she's the mother of your child, and I'm fourteen years younger than you."

"Oh." McVie sighed.

Fenway paused, waiting for McVie to continue, but he said nothing. "That's all you have to say? 'Oh'?" She turned off the engine.

"I actually thought you were pissed off about the Accord."

"Yeah, well, Charlotte let me borrow the Porsche, so getting the Accord back isn't at the top of my list. But it's pretty shitty that your daughter stole my car."

"I'll get it back."

"It's a good thing I like you," Fenway said. "Not a lot of girlfriends would be cool with grand theft auto."

"I know. I'm sorry."

"Hey," Fenway said, "since the mayor's going to rip me a new one anyway once he finds out that we have to release Amy, how about we go out in style?"

"In style?"

"Charlotte gave us her reservation at Maxime's tonight."

"Ouch."

"Ouch?"

"Well—I'm trying to get this business off the ground. A four-hundred-dollar dinner isn't going to help that."

"My treat."

"I can't let *you* do that, either."

"Come on, I'll be your sugar mama."

"My what?"

"Your sugar mama. I'll come pick you up in my Porsche, buy you a nice expensive dinner, get you a little tipsy on wine, bring you home, and take advantage of you."

"That sounds—uh, really excellent, actually."

"Great. The reservation is at—"

"But I have to deal with Megan."

Fenway hesitated. "She's not staying at her boyfriend's house again?"

"Not if Amy's getting out of jail."

"Right. You have a point."

"Can I get a rain check?"

"The next time Charlotte gives me her reservation? Yeah, absolutely."

They said their goodbyes and hung up.

Fenway hadn't told him about all the stuff that was going on with her. Nothing about her father never emerging from the coma. Nothing about the threats from the mayor. She supposed he couldn't do anything about those things. The issue with Amy declaring her desire to get back together with him? Now that was something he could take action on.

Fenway took a deep breath and opened the door of the Porsche. She could deal with McVie later. She still had work to do if she wanted to catch Rick Tonnick's killer.

CHAPTER TWENTY-TWO

Walking into her office building, Fenway went past the coroner's office suite and opened the double doors to the Information Technology division. At the desk about ten feet in front of the door, sitting in the cubicle where Piper used to sit, was a rail-thin Asian man with thick glasses, the lenses full of water spots. He looked over his shoulder at her, the screen covered with a dashboard for what looked like router configurations. She took a deep breath and stepped into his cubicle.

"Hi," Fenway said. "I'm the county coroner. Fenway Stevenson. We haven't met properly." She stuck out her hand.

"This is not a good time," the man said. "I will be available in one hour."

"Oh—I'm actually investigating a murder, and it's rather time-sensitive—"

He looked up at her. "Hello. I work for Jordan Daniels. Due to the volume of requests, we have recently implemented an IT work order form. Please fill one out, and Jordan will prioritize it a put it in my queue."

"An IT work order form?"

"Yes. It's improved efficiency. The form has been available for over a month. It's on the sheriff's office intranet."

"Ah," she said, "well, you see, I don't work for the sheriff's office."

He blinked up at her. "You don't? I thought you said you were investigating a murder."

"I'm the county coroner. We're a different department."

"I'm sorry," said the man, who had not introduced himself. "You can talk to Jordan about how you can get access an IT work order form. My job is to deal with the prioritized work orders in my queue."

It took every ounce of self-control for Fenway to back out of the cubicle without screaming, but she did, then poked her head into Jordan Daniels' office.

"Jordan?"

A Black man with jowls and hair cropped close to his head looked up from his phone. "Fenway, hi! I haven't seen you for a while."

"Yeah." Fenway leaned against Jordan's doorway and scuffed her foot on the carpet. "I guess it was hard to accept that Piper's gone."

"Patrick is great, though," Jordan said.

"His people skills could use some work."

"Oh, for sure." Jordan chuckled. "I go to this vet's office over by Cherry Island. Recommended by a friend of mine. Well, the first time I take Casey over there, I meet the vet. My first impression? The vet is *weird.* She looks like she cuts her own hair. She can't look me in the eye; she talks so quietly I can barely hear her."

"What'd you do?"

"I figured I was already there, so what the hell. Then she gets down on the floor with Casey, and he *immediately* starts wagging his tail. She's talking gibberish to him, but he sniffs her, and then he lays on his side and lets her prod and poke him for about five minutes. It seemed like forever. But she diagnosed him correctly and saved me a ton of money."

Fenway tilted her head. "I'm glad you got a good vet. Those can be hard to come by."

"My point," Jordan continued, "is that when you're looking for a good vet, you want someone good with animals, not people. And when you're looking to replace Piper, you want someone good with computers, not people." He sat back in his chair. "Yes, Piper was good with both people *and* computers, but give Patrick a chance, okay?"

She nodded. "Deal." She took a step forward. "Patrick said I needed some new form."

"Right. It's on the intranet."

Fenway shook her head. "Not the one the coroner's department has access to."

Jordan rolled his eyes. "Ah, geez. I can't believe I set it up like that. Sorry, Fenway. I'll post it to the coroner's intranet right away."

"Can I give you the request in the meantime?"

"Sure. What do you need?" Jordan pulled a notepad toward him.

"I need a list of all the rentals of red Ford Mustang convertibles."

Jordan picked up a cheap black pen. "What's the time frame?"

"The murder was committed early Monday morning. Any rentals where the car was on loan at that time."

"Oh—this is for a murder?" Jordan wrote quickly on the pad. "Did you tell Patrick that?"

"Yes."

Jordan grunted. "I assume you want us to search the rental agencies at the Estancia airport?"

"Yes. Every rental place in the county, in fact."

"Okay. Every rental of a red Ford Mustang convertible. Got it."

"Thanks, Jordan. Think you can have it by the end of the day?"

Jordan looked at his watch. "Um—no, sorry. Midday tomorrow okay?"

Fenway nodded. "Call my cell. I'll be out of the office."

Jordan finished writing and crossed his arms. "I thought you arrested McVie's ex for that murder. Doesn't she own a Mustang convertible?"

"Yep," Fenway said. "And if you breathe a word of this to the mayor before I have another suspect, I'll never get another americano for you from Java Jim's."

Jordan held his hands up as if he'd just fouled another player in soccer. "Hey, not a word."

Fenway walked through the IT office, passing Patrick's cubicle but not glancing at him, then to the coroner's office suite.

She nodded at Sarah, who was typing on the computer, and strode to Dez's desk. Dez typed in a search box on an airline database page.

"What did the ADA say?"

"He's putting the case on hold until tomorrow," Dez said. "We need to come up with some additional information by then. If it's exculpatory, then he'll drop the charges."

"Did you tell him the car wasn't the same?"

"I did." Dez clicked her tongue. "He was reluctant to release a suspect based on the existence of a choir sticker. He wants to see a picture of the car with the sticker that was taken before Sunday night."

Fenway nodded. "I just hope one exists."

Dez grunted.

"Now what are you doing?" Fenway asked.

"I'm looking at the Coastal Airways report for flight 7331 from Vegas to Estancia. Seeing if Brianna actually checked in at the gate."

"You still suspect her?"

"Yep. Too many coincidences."

Fenway folded her arms. "What does it say?"

Dez blinked. "I don't believe it. Says she scanned her ticket at the gate. 4:05 A.M. I would have put money on her not being on that plane."

Fenway patted Dez on the shoulder. "I hate it when my gut isn't right, too."

"Maybe we should check her financials. See if she's made any payments to anyone. She could have been on that plane and still hired someone."

Fenway thought about the form that Jordan needed to post to the coroner's office intranet. "Yeah. There's a new process. I should be able to make the request tomorrow morning." She took a step away, then stopped.

"What is it?" Dez asked.

"So—I know we're basically restarting this investigation," Fenway said, "but I talked to my grandmother this morning."

"Oh—you talked to her?"

Fenway nodded. "Yep. She saw a picture of my mother and me. Said it was definitely her—and said I look like she did when she was younger."

"What's your mom's real name? Sahara?"

"Samara. Samara Godwin." Fenway looked at the floor. "I've never met my grandmother before. I didn't even know she was alive until this week."

"Did your grandmother say something that bothered you?"

Fenway smiled. "Well, I was going to go visit her today. Take her out to lunch. Except, well, Megan took my car without asking."

Dez cackled. "Right."

"Craig is lucky I'm such an understanding girlfriend."

"This was after Sheriff Donnelly arrested Amy, right?"

"Right." Fenway shifted her weight from foot to foot. "We were moving her into Craig's apartment. Rick Tonnick's kids were threatening to throw her stuff out. She didn't feel safe there."

"Or *you* didn't feel safe with her there."

"Whatever. Megan went to Craig's and moved a bunch of her clothes and stuff there. The next thing we knew, she'd taken my keys and driven off with my car."

"I hope she returned it in one piece."

"I haven't gotten it back yet."

"Then how are you getting to L.A.?"

Fenway smiled. "Charlotte let me borrow the Porsche."

Dez shook her head. "You better do the speed limit on Ocean Highway. They've got speed traps just past Carpinteria, and if you get pulled over and your name isn't on the registration—"

"I'm a peace officer, Dez."

"You better have your badge visible, then. Driving an expensive sports car that isn't yours for a couple of hundred miles? Not the best idea."

"That's actually what I wanted to talk with you about. Whether I should go." Fenway sighed. "I thought for sure it would be fine once we made the arrest. I thought things would be light. But now that we know Amy didn't do it—and we know the defense can prove it—we've got to get moving."

"So reschedule."

Fenway bit her lip. "I've already pushed it off once."

Dez cocked her head and dipped her chin. "If meeting your grandmother for the first time is that important to you, Fenway, then go. Delegate the work to your team."

Fenway shook her head. "The mayor won't accept that."

"The mayor won't be happy no matter what you do. If it were *his* grandmother, you better believe he'd be there."

Fenway looked up at the ceiling and sighed. "The problem is, we're back at square one. We have people to interview. We should look at all the people from the lawsuits again—the grown children, the woman in Boston—see if anyone can place them in their cities on Sunday night."

"We're not at square one. We've still got a couple of suspects floating around." Dez grinned. "We should talk to the ex-wives. Just because Amy is the *current* wife doesn't mean she's the only one who's a suspect."

"Right. So I'll stay."

"Absolutely not, Fenway. It's one day. I can cover for you. So can Mark. You said you're waiting on some results from IT anyway, right?"

"Right," Fenway said.

"So go. If Mayor Klein storms in here looking for you, I'll tell him you went to San Mig to get the toxicology report and view the fingerprint analysis in person."

"The toxicology report isn't back yet."

"I know that. I put a rush on it, so if we're lucky, we'll hear something Friday. But the *mayor* doesn't know that." Dez leaned back. "As someone who didn't always get along with her family, I know how important it is to make connections, even if things don't go the way you want."

"Like with me and my dad."

Dez smiled. "Yes, like you and your dad. I guess I don't have to tell you."

Fenway leaned back against the desk.

"You know what you have to do, Fenway. I think you're just scared of finding out more about your mom. You've thought about her in one particular way all your life, and now that's being threatened."

"Yeah," Fenway whispered.

"Go down to L.A. and talk to your grandmother," Dez said. "And if you need to take another day off, just let me know."

Fenway blinked hard. "Thanks, Dez."

"Anytime."

Fenway turned and walked back to her office. Sarah looked up and gave her a slight smile before Fenway closed the door.

She sat heavily in the leather chair behind her desk. When would Mayor Klein find out that Amy had been exonerated? And what fresh hell would he rain on Fenway's head as punishment? Maybe ADA Pondicherry would wait a day or two before informing him, and if so, Fenway had a stay of execution—she could find another suspect in that time.

But the avenues of inquiry were spread too thinly. Tonnick's son and daughter had been interviewed but not researched. Besides, their attitude at the house—the house they so clearly wanted to be theirs and not Amy's—gave away a motive that they didn't reveal in the interview. Not just for killing their father, but also for setting Amy up to take the fall. Maybe Mark could reach out to them again.

She woke her computer up and launched her browser, typing in the address of the coroner's office intranet. As Jordan promised, he'd posted the new IT form to request research and financial forensics.

Fenway pulled out her notes and brought up the online files of Grant Tonnick and Noreen Tonnick. Neither had records, but their bank accounts might reveal secrets. Fenway sat back in her chair. She should also ask Mark to look into their alibis—or lack thereof. It was very possible that one of them had rented the Mustang—although perhaps they had been too smart to use their own name. Maybe the security systems at *their* houses would reveal comings and goings.

Fenway's stomach rumbled. She looked at the clock on the computer and was surprised to see it was a quarter to six.

Oh—Fenway hadn't told Charlotte to cancel the reservation since McVie couldn't go. And it was too late to cancel now. Charlotte would have to pay the no-show fee.

Well, maybe. Nathaniel Ferris was still the most powerful man in town, even in a coma, and Maxime's might not charge Charlotte.

But that was bad form.

Fenway stood up from her desk and opened the door to her office. Sarah was standing too, putting on a light pink windbreaker.

"Sarah," Fenway said, "do you have dinner plans?"

Maxime's wasn't busy on Wednesday night, and the maître-d' seated Fenway and Sarah immediately. The short, balding, impeccably dressed man led the two women to Nathaniel Ferris's table, an out-of-the-way booth in the back. Sarah walked behind Fenway, looking around at the dark wood and the leather booths, mouth slightly agape. She'd had a similar reaction to the Porsche, which Fenway had found herself apologizing for.

Fenway took a seat in the U-shaped booth first, then watched as Sarah, her cheeks flushed red, slid into the booth on the opposite side of the table.

"This place is *really* swanky," Sarah said.

"Swanky?"

"Uh—yeah. I mean, not to sound like a flapper or anything, but that's the only way to describe it. These seats are *plush*."

"Order whatever you want. I'm paying."

"I can't ask you to do that." Sarah shook her head gently, her blonde curls swaying.

"I'm the one who had the reservations and the boyfriend who couldn't make it. I'm paying."

Sarah picked up the menu and opened it. Her eyes went wide.

"Do you want wine?" Fenway asked.

"Are you getting some?"

"Yes." Fenway smiled. "Thought we could split a bottle. Do you want red or white?"

"I—I don't know."

"What are you going to order?"

"Honestly? I have no idea."

Fenway nodded. "Did you ever go to restaurants like this when you worked for the law office?"

Sarah chuckled. "Not on your life."

"How about when you were a network admin?"

Sarah visibly stiffened.

"Oh—sorry. I didn't mean to bring up a sore subject."

"No, no, it's okay. It was just—it was *before*."

Fenway squinted—before? Then it clicked—before Sarah's transition. She changed the subject. "Yeah, I know the feeling. My dad is pretty rich, so I was in restaurants like this when I was little, but when my mom and I moved away, we didn't have a lot of money. It was a *long* time between visits to nice restaurants for me."

"You've been here a lot?"

"It's my dad's favorite place."

Sarah tilted her head. "Your dad is Nathaniel Ferris, right?"

"Right."

"I heard—" Then Sarah clamped her mouth shut.

"What?"

"Nothing."

Fenway nodded. "You were going to say that you heard he was shot in the courtroom lockdown a couple of months ago."

Sarah looked down at the menu. "I'm sorry. I didn't think before I opened my mouth."

"It's okay," Fenway said. But was it? When she'd just found out that the doctors held little hope for his recovery?

"Ah," Sarah said. "So is this your favorite restaurant, too?"

Fenway shrugged. "It's nice for a special occasion, but truth be told, I'm more of a hole-in-the-wall taquería girl. Give me a nice lengua taco with a lot of cilantro and onion, maybe some guacamole and chips."

Sarah chuckled. "I don't know about lengua, but I like this one place downtown, not too far from work. You ever been to Dos Milagros?"

Fenway tilted her head and smiled widely. "You're just saying that to get in good with the boss."

"What? No—I eat there at least once a week. Really."

"Me too. I'm surprised I haven't run into you there. I eat there all the time." *Way more than once a week.*

"I live right above Dos Milagros. I usually just run down and get a to-go order for dinner."

"What's your favorite?"

"So—I know the tacos are the specialty there, but I like the tortas. The torta ahogada is amazing."

Fenway frowned. "I don't even think I know what that is."

"It's a special pork sandwich dipped in hot sauce. Kind of vinegary, too. Really good."

Fenway opened her menu. "I better see what *this* menu has before my stomach starts thinking it's getting Dos Milagros." She scanned the appetizers. The mushroom bisque was usually good. The pheasant with roasted apples was always a hit with her taste buds, and she'd been thinking about the pheasant ever since lunch. Even as good as the bacon and brie sandwich was.

She glanced up. Sarah's face was full of confusion.

"What kind of food do you like?" Fenway asked. "Aside from the tortas ahogadas, that is."

"Oh," Sarah said, "I like all kinds of stuff. Put it in front of me, and I'll eat it."

"You had pheasant before?"

"No, but I've had roasted apples. Let me guess—pheasant tastes like chicken?"

"Sort of. A little bit of a different flavor, and a lot *more* flavor. It's their specialty."

Sarah closed her menu. "Sold."

The server appeared, and Fenway ordered for them both—the mushroom bisque, the pheasant, and a carafe of the house red—even though a bottle of the Blue Jay Estate Sauvignon Blanc was the suggested pairing. Without the signature sommelier experience her father usually insisted on, Fenway thought she could keep the damage below two hundred.

Sarah was polite but reserved and didn't offer much about herself. Her apartment above Dos Milagros was a small studio, and she hadn't graduated from college, leaving Paso Querido Community College a few credits shy of an associate's degree, but not moving back home. She didn't talk about the network admin job or the gap in her résumé. Fenway opened her mouth to ask Sarah about it—but then closed it again. No, she shouldn't force anything.

Fenway talked enough for both of them. She told Sarah about her long-lost grandmother—though she didn't mention her mother's secret identity. Fenway talked about her racist opponent in the coroner election, relishing the story of her opponent's wife caught on camera at the George Nidever Dinner. Sarah asked questions and laughed in the right spots, but her posture was straight, her guard up, even after two glasses of red wine. Fenway stopped at two glasses as well. If she was going to make it to the hospital without falling asleep—and still in condition to drive—the last two inches in the carafe would have to stay unconsumed.

Sarah refused dessert and raved about the pheasant. Fenway thought Maxime's had shown off for a new guest well, and Sarah thanked Fenway profusely on the ride back to her apartment—she had walked to work. Sarah unlocked a narrow door between Dos Milagros and the salon next door, and she smiled at Fenway before going upstairs and shutting the door.

Fenway drove to the hospital, her post-meal satisfaction shrinking with every freeway exit. She'd be alone in the room with her father for the first time since Dr. Ogrireddy had given her the bad news. Would her dad be able to hear the fear and disappointment in her voice? Would it make him weaker to know that his loved ones were giving up on him?

Was she, in fact, giving up on him?

Walking into his room, knowing that Charlotte was probably negotiating a sale of the company, the finality of it all hit her hard. She sat in the chair next to Nathaniel Ferris's hospital bed and stared at her father.

She noticed the lines etched into his face that his youthful exuberance often covered up. She saw his left arm with the IV sticking out, the discolorations on his bicep, skin yellowed like old paper.

He'd aged twenty years in the last two months, and it was because of her.

Fenway shook her head. She couldn't allow herself to think like that. It wasn't her fault. It was the shooter's fault.

But that didn't make the ache in her heart go away.

She sighed. She didn't want to read this evening. But she couldn't watch the Red Sox game with her dad either—she'd left her laptop at work. Besides, the Wi-Fi was slow in the hospital. She'd have to figure out how to download the video to play it offline another day.

She stayed for about an hour, and just before nine o'clock, she pulled herself out of the chair and stood. Her feet dragged as if her shoes were sandbags. Maybe it was the two glasses of wine on a work night, but she felt heavy and unmotivated. Maybe she was afraid of what she was going to find the next day, talking to her grandmother. Maybe she was scared of how the mayor would react—because he would find out, and he would be angry. Especially if he found out that Fenway was visiting a relative in Los Angeles instead of working the recently blown-up investigation.

She grimaced.

She missed Craig.

He picked up on the second ring. "Hi, Fenway."

"Hi." Fenway squeezed her eyes shut. "I miss you."

"I miss you, too. Do you—do you want to come over?"

Fenway opened her eyes. "I thought Megan was there."

A pause. "No. She's staying at her boyfriend's house. I thought about arguing with her, but I need to concentrate on getting her mother back home. At least for a couple more days." He cleared his throat. "I got your car, too. I even drove it to your place."

"If I had known you'd be free, I would have taken you to Maxime's."

"The way Megan and I were arguing, I would have been late anyway. Did you go?"

"I took Sarah there. She'd never been. Not a really fancy-restaurant kind of girl."

"Oh."

Now it was her turn to pause. "The doctors told me my dad probably won't wake up," she said, a catch in her voice.

"Oh, Fenway," McVie said.

"So I need to come over."

"Of course you can come over."

"I don't have an overnight bag with me, so I'll have to leave first thing. Plus I have to get on the road early to see my grandmother anyway. But I need to be with you."

"I'm here," McVie said softly.

"Okay," Fenway whispered. "I'll see you soon."

PART FIVE

THURSDAY

CHAPTER TWENTY-THREE

FIVE THIRTY CAME AWFULLY EARLY, AND FENWAY AWOKE IN MCVIE'S embrace, almost as sad and exhausted as she'd been when she fell asleep. She felt strong enough to drive to Los Angeles, though, and strong enough to withstand whatever the mayor had to dish out.

She pulled on her clothes, drove the Porsche to her apartment, and took a shower. There wasn't time to dither about what to wear, though she almost changed out of her aqua turtleneck sweater and dark blue jeans. With a blazer, it would look respectable enough for the office. She hoped.

She debated between taking the Accord or the Porsche, and even as sad as she was, she decided to take the Porsche. She didn't know what kind of neighborhood Rolling Meadows was in, but she was counting on a decent parking lot—plus the daylight hours—to minimize her risk.

What kinds of questions would she ask her grandmother? There were so many years to catch up on. A grandchild that she'd never met—maybe Mrs. Godwin would have more questions for Fenway than Fenway had for her.

The Broadway ramp had no cars at this hour, and Fenway floored the accelerator when she got on the freeway. Her online Alicia Keys station was playing a song with a hard, driving beat, Alicia singing full throttle—

when the music paused and a loud phone ring sounded throughout the car's interior. She pushed the phone button on the steering wheel.

"Fenway Stevenson."

"Oh—Miss Stevenson, I hope I caught you in time."

"Hi, Julia. Good to hear your voice. I'm just getting on the freeway—tell my grandmother that I should be there by about ten."

"That's why I'm calling," Julia said. She sniffled. Had she been crying?

Fenway's arms broke out into goose flesh.

"Mrs. Godwin," Julia continued, her voice breaking, "passed away last night."

Fenway drove into the parking garage in a daze and shuffled into Java Jim's. It wasn't quite seven o'clock, and the sun had yet to crack the horizon. She ordered an extra-large latte and didn't even notice the quizzical look she got from the barista when she said her name was *Fenway* and not *Joanne*.

One phone conversation was all she'd gotten from her grandmother, taken away from Fenway before they'd even met.

Fenway hadn't even formulated the thoughts about her schedule when she found herself at the door to the coroner's suite. She reached for the handle, but it didn't turn.

Locked?

Oh—she was here early. Earlier than Dez, even. She set her latte down on the floor and rummaged through her purse. At the bottom, underneath her phone and her wallet, her keys lay in a crevice formed by the inside seam. She yanked on the keyring, and with it came the phone, a box of mints, a packet of tissues, and her sunglasses. Her phone hit first, knocking over the latte, and Fenway jumped into a kneeling position to right the cup, dropping her purse.

She held the now half-empty latte in one hand and her keys in the other, staring at the mess on the floor in front of her. The coffee was soaking into the carpet, and the packet of tissues had landed open side down in the spill. The mints were all over the floor, too. Her wallet and phone had a few drops of coffee on them, but it could have been worse.

Pulling the rest of the half-wet tissues out of the pack, Fenway mopped up the coffee from the carpet, wondering if there was a carpet spray somewhere in the supply cabinet.

She felt her throat constrict and immediately stood up, willing the tears to stay in her eyes. Fenway hadn't even met her grandmother. There was no way she could be this upset about her death. She closed her eyes, breathing slowly in and out, trying to stay in control. She unlocked the door, then bent over and dumped her wallet, phone, keys, and sunglasses back in her purse. Turning the handle and shoving the door open with her foot, Fenway backed into the darkened office, setting her latte and purse on the counter.

She flicked the light switch on, and the fluorescent bulbs flickered once, twice, then stayed on with a low hum that Fenway hadn't noticed before. She walked into her office, grabbed the trash can, and went out into the hall. Kneeling to pick up the sticky mints and sopping tissues, she threw the mess away.

"Hello."

Fenway jumped slightly and looked up. Patrick stood in the hallway, a blue-and-black flannel long-sleeved shirt over a *Rick and Morty* T-shirt. His khakis were pressed, a crease down the front, and his glasses were spotless, unlike yesterday.

"Oh. Patrick. Hi."

He tilted his head. "You know you can look up car rental agencies on your computer. You don't need to wait for me for that."

Fenway nodded. "I know. But you can access the credit card information that people use to pay. You can cross-reference that information with other alerts, right?"

Patrick pursed his lips. "That wasn't on the form."

"What do you mean?"

"I mean, that's not on the form. I didn't know you wanted that information."

"Didn't Jordan make the request himself?"

"He filled out a form."

Fenway, still kneeling, shook her head. "So if I say that a Mustang convertible was used in the commission of a murder and ask you to find if anyone had rented a Mustang convertible to have it on Sunday night, you're telling me that if you don't find any rentals in the county, you just stop?"

"Of course."

Fenway bit her tongue to stop her from telling him that Piper Patten used to actually care about catching criminals and that a little extra work to make an actual connection would go a long way. Patrick was no Piper, that was for sure.

"You don't expand the search to neighboring counties? You don't look for second-tier car rental agencies?"

Patrick knit his brow. "Why would I do that?"

Fenway exhaled. "Because we're trying to catch a murderer."

"No." Patrick shook his head. "That's not my job. I have users who are having issues logging in; I have router configurations to fix."

"A man is dead, Patrick."

"Jordan can recalibrate my priorities if you have an issue with my work schedule." He walked past her, then stopped and turned. "Oh. Have a good day."

Fenway stared at him in disbelief. Pushing herself to her feet, she took the trash can back into her office.

Maybe she was the one at fault for expecting Patrick to be a clone of Piper. And maybe Piper had let Fenway overstep. Piper hadn't reported to her, after all; she'd worked for the IT department. Patrick had a point —he didn't work for Fenway either, and it probably *was* unreasonable to expect Patrick to follow the same threads that Piper would have followed.

It still pissed her off, though.

She sat in the leather chair and woke her computer up. An email from Patrick showed that none of the car rental agencies in Dominguez County reported a red Mustang convertible as being rented on Sunday night. The QualiTempo Rent-a-Car at the airport had a red Mustang convertible in their fleet, but it had been returned Sunday morning. There was a Road Thrills agency in downtown Paso Querido that had a red Mustang convertible in its inventory as well, but their records showed that it had been returned the day after Christmas and not rented again. Fenway sighed. She thought it would be easier to find than this— people didn't usually rent convertibles in the winter, even on the relatively mild California coast, though there were always the tourists from the Upper Midwest for whom an overcast fifty degree day demanded shorts and flip-flops.

She had other questions for Patrick. What about the car sharing organizations? What about other car dealerships in the area—or Tonnick Ford itself? Could Tommy Kinsella have borrowed a used red Mustang convertible the night of the murder and done the deed himself? Or taken Amy out for the evening while a partner in crime switched the license plates and murdered Tonnick?

Fenway shook her head. Whoever had committed the actual murder had probably been brought up in the private elevator and let into the room by Tonnick himself. Tonnick had been expecting a night of intimacy, and whoever Tonnick had let in was most likely a woman. Besides, both Amy and Tommy admitted they were together at the time of the murder.

Still, Tommy might have hired a woman to kill him. Or, she realized, he wouldn't have had to hire a woman to kill him. He could have hired a woman to pretend to seduce Rick Tonnick, knock him out with the whisky-and-sleeping-pill cocktail, and let Tommy up in the private elevator and into the room.

She turned the possibility over in her head. A lot about it made sense. Tommy was Amy's alibi, but if he had knocked her out too—with the same sort of sleeping pill cocktail—Amy might have *thought* she was with him the entire night.

And the fact that Amy originally denied it worked in his favor—she was embarrassed to tell anyone that she was cheating on her new husband, which threw all suspicion on *her,* not him.

But he'd been in a situation where he could have made sure Amy's Mustang was parked in her driveway. Even if it was in the garage, he could have filched Amy's keys and gotten it out of the garage. He could have made sure Amy was passed out but ready to give him an alibi anyway.

Fenway heard the door open. Sarah stepped into the suite and glanced over. "Hi," she said. "You're in early. I thought you were going to see your grandmother today."

Fenway swallowed the lump in her throat. "Change of plans," she said. "Hey—you've been pretty good with getting information for me. Do you think you can see if Tonnick Ford—or, really, any of the Tonnick dealerships in the area—had a red Ford Mustang convertible in their inventory?"

"Sure," Sarah said. "I can access a couple of databases that should give me that information. Does it matter if it's used or new?"

"It needs to be late-model," Fenway said. "Either new or from the last couple of years. Thanks."

"Sure," Sarah said, then she chuckled. "You took me to a fancy dinner last night so you wouldn't feel bad about overloading me with work today?"

Fenway remembered how Julia's voice had cracked on the phone and blinked hard, trying to keep herself calm. "I don't know *what* you're talking about," Fenway said, trying to keep a lilt in her voice to sound like she was joking. "All right," she said, getting up and walking to the other side of her desk, "I'll be on the phone for a while." She shut the door and went back to her seat.

Distraction is what she needed. She had to keep pushing on this until she got a viable suspect. Dez was working on Tonnick's adult children— maybe she had found something the night before. Mark was looking into where the other plaintiffs in the Tonnick safety lawsuit were on Sunday night to see if anyone could actually place them in the cities where they said they were. And now Fenway was looking into Amy's lover and Tonnick's second-in-command. Something was bound to shake out of it all.

She picked up the phone and called Tonnick Ford. It wasn't eight o'clock yet, but the service desk picked up, and Tommy Kinsella was already in the office. The technician transferred Fenway. The phone rang twice.

"Tommy Kinsella."

"Tommy," Fenway said. "This is Coroner Fenway Stevenson."

Fenway could hear Tommy stiffen. "Coroner," he said. "I didn't expect to hear from you again. Are you calling to apologize for arresting the wrong person?"

"I am," Fenway said, then realized that she had no idea what information she wanted to get out of Tommy. She usually prepared for these sorts of calls, but she was so focused on distracting herself from her grandmother's death that she just picked up the phone with no plan at all.

Could she just wing it? People often opened up to Fenway, treating her more like a confessor than an investigator. Maybe Tommy would do the same.

Fenway cleared her throat. "I appreciate you sticking by the truth even though it didn't make you look good."

"No one wants to get caught with their boss's wife," Tommy said. "And maybe I'm a jerk for being with her, but I'm not going to lie about it."

"News travels fast," Fenway said.

"I heard from Amy's ex-husband last night. Said new evidence had come to light that exonerated Amy. As if my alibi weren't enough."

"I'm sorry to say it *wasn't* enough," Fenway said. "People lie for their friends and lovers all the time."

There was silence on the other end of the line.

"Mr. Kinsella? You still there?"

"I am," he said. "You said you called to apologize. I'm waiting for the apology."

A wave of annoyance washed over Fenway. She'd been pressured by Mayor Klein to make a fast arrest even though certain things about the scenario didn't sit right with her. And witnesses had given inaccurate statements to prop up the false narrative that Amy was guilty.

Duke Perriman. That was someone else to look into. Maybe he just wanted Amy and Rick Tonnick both to pay for what happened to his wife, but Fenway suspected he wasn't acting on his own.

"I'm waiting, Coroner."

She should at least make this apology useful. "I'm sorry, Mr. Kinsella. I apologize for putting Amy Tonnick through all of this. I should have confirmed the witness statements. I should have noticed that the Mustang convertible in the parking garage wasn't the same car."

Another pause from Tommy Kinsella. "What did you say?"

He'd been hooked. "Oh—didn't the former sheriff tell you what evidence was found?"

"No."

"I see." Fenway leaned forward. "Someone's been trying to make it look like Amy was guilty."

"She—she was framed?"

"It seems so," Fenway said. "The car on the recording from the parking garage—the recording that did the most damage to seal Amy's arrest—was a red Mustang convertible with Amy's license plates. But it looks like someone had a similar car, and they put Amy's license plates on *that* car before going to the hotel to kill her husband."

More silence.

"It wasn't obvious at first," Fenway said. "After all—same car, same plates, right? But there was a piece of identifying information missing from the car in the recording."

"The choir sticker," Kinsella said. "Megan's school concert choir."

"Oh," Fenway said, "you know it?"

"I hate that damn sticker. It's going to peel the paint off the bumper. It'll damage the resale value of the car. And for what? Megan will be graduating soon, and then Amy'll have an old choir bumper sticker, and she'll get a thousand dollars less when she sells the car."

"I see." Fenway pulled a notepad over and began scribbling. "You don't happen to have a picture of the Mustang with the choir sticker, do you? With some sort of date stamp or something?"

"Sure I do. Amy and I went to the beach just before Christmas—that day where it was in the seventies, remember?"

"Oh. Right."

"We parked overlooking the cliffs, and we had the top down. I took a picture of Amy posing behind the car. You can see the cliffs and the ocean in the background, and you can see that stupid choir sticker clear as day. It almost ruined the picture."

"Can you send it to me?"

"Sure. Aren't there time and date stamps on digital pictures like that anyway?"

"Yes. Plus, there hasn't been a sunny day at the beach since Sunday— if we can get that to the ADA, it'll be proof enough to release her."

"When do you think she'll be released?"

"It's not up to me."

Tommy sighed. "I guess if someone's been actively trying to make Amy look guilty, then maybe it's not as much of your fault as I thought."

"I appreciate that."

"Do you have any leads?"

"Whoever it is," Fenway said, "had access to a red Ford Mustang convertible that looked pretty close to Amy's. But no one in the county rented one like that."

Fenway could almost hear the wheels turning in Tommy's head.

"I have access to some Mustangs, don't I, Coroner? That's where you were going with this?"

Fenway chose her words carefully. "We're dealing with someone who's doing everything they can to make other people look guilty, Tommy. If one of the Tonnick Ford cars were used in the commission of this crime, we'd have questions for you, sure, but that doesn't automatically mean we'd arrest you."

Tommy sighed. "I can run a report for you, see what cars we had on our lot on Sunday night. I don't know if any of them were red Mustang convertibles, but I guess there's a pretty good chance that at least one of them was on our lot."

"And who has access to those cars?"

"Lots of people. The sales staff. The technicians. We lock things up at night, but the security people have keys, and if one of the sales staff— or a technician—comes in and says they need a car, the security people will open the gates up. As long as they've got their ID."

"Great. When can I expect the report?"

"I could probably have someone run it at the end of the day."

"The end of the day?"

"We're a business, Miss Stevenson, and running a full inventory report of all the dealerships takes time."

"Okay," Fenway said. "I appreciate your cooperation."

"You'll have it first thing tomorrow, I promise." Fenway heard a rat-a-tat noise—probably Tommy impatiently tapping a pen on his desk. "Is that all?"

"Just one more thing," said Fenway. "Can you think of anyone at the dealerships or in his businesses who'd gain by Rick Tonnick's death?"

"Besides me and his kids?"

"Rick Tonnick was a rich man, Tommy. You know yourself that you're inheriting the dealerships. You'll have a lot more money next year than you do right now, that's for sure." Fenway debated saying any more, but maybe Tommy would jump on a statement where she blamed others. "Plus, even though Amy got the house and all the money, his kids would get all of it if Amy were convicted of the murder. His money would go to them."

"Really?" Tommy said. "I just can't picture either of them going through all the trouble to set up Amy to take the fall. They're lazy."

"Lazy? They're both running successful businesses."

Tommy scoffed. "That have to be continually propped up by Rick. That's why he left me the dealership and not them—he wants it to succeed. He doesn't want them to run it into the ground."

Fenway blinked. He hadn't taken the bait—not on that. "Well, you get us that inventory list, Mr. Kinsella, and I'll see what comes of it."

They hung up.

Fenway sat, staring at the computer screen for a moment.

A soft knock sounded at the door, and Sarah opened it slowly and stuck her head in. "I've got some information about the Mustangs that the Tonnick dealers have in inventory."

"Oh—that was fast." She chuckled. "So much for waiting till tomorrow."

"The Toyota dealer in P.Q. is getting back to me in about an hour, but I thought I'd let you know what I found."

"Lay it on me."

"Three late-model red Mustang convertibles. Tonnick Ford has all of them. One new. They just took delivery on Friday. Two used—last year's models. One of them's a GT, though."

"Does that make a difference?"

"If you saw that the car looked different than Amy's? Yes. The GT has a big ugly 'GT' on it where the horse silhouette usually goes."

"You know a lot about Mustangs."

"I was a teenager who was into big muscle cars." Sarah looked down and cleared her throat.

"This car had a horse silhouette. So it wasn't the GT."

"There's a third car, too. It's listed as being in the shop."

"In the shop?"

"Yep." Sarah grimaced. "I'm not sure if I should have done this, but I called over there, and the mechanic was more than happy to talk about what a piece of crap this car was. Someone traded it in, but I guess there's some short-circuit issue with the controls on the passenger seat. He said they replaced the entire control board twice and it's still an issue. He went on for a while."

"Did he say how the engine runs?"

Sarah rolled her eyes. "He said 'like a dream' seven times before I lost count."

"When you say 'in the shop,' did you ask what that meant?"

Sarah smiled. "It's in the lot. They're waiting for a new fuse panel."

Fenway nodded. "That sounds promising. A car that can't be sold, can't be fixed, but drives perfectly. Someone could take it out without anyone caring. I bet no one would even notice."

"Right."

Fenway grabbed her purse. "Feel like going to check out some muscle cars?"

CHAPTER TWENTY-FOUR

Sarah got out of the Porsche in the Tonnick Ford parking lot, and immediately a salesman, wearing an ill-fitting black suit, a crisp white shirt, and a loud yellow, blue, and maroon tie shouted across the service drive-through area at her. His voice echoed off the concrete and asphalt, and his words were unintelligible.

Fenway got out of the driver's side, watching the salesman jog toward their car.

"Oh boy," Sarah said.

The salesman stopped about six feet from the front bumper of the Porsche. "How are you ladies doing today?" Barrel-chested and broad-shouldered, the man had a deep tan, odd in early January, and sparkling white teeth that showed in one of the least genuine smiles Fenway had ever seen.

"We're fine," Fenway responded.

"Did you come to trade in your 911 on a real American sports car?"

Fenway smiled, keeping her lips closed.

"Actually," Sarah said, "we're interested in a used Mustang convertible you have in the back lot."

Fenway reached in her purse and pulled out the badge holder and opened it for the man to see.

His face fell. "Oh. Of course. Let me get Raúl." He turned and walked dejectedly through the service door.

After a few minutes of waiting, a tall, lanky Latino man in slate-blue coveralls came out. "Are you the one who called earlier about the Mustang that didn't work?" As he came closer, Fenway guessed he was in his late twenties, and she could read *Raúl* on the nametag sewn on the left chest of his coveralls.

Sarah raised her hand halfway. "That was me," she said, a coquettish tone taking over her voice.

Fenway looked at Sarah, who stood up straight.

"That car matches the description of one leaving a crime scene," Fenway said. "Can you tell me if the car was here on Sunday night?"

"The service department doesn't open on Sundays," Raúl said. "We've been waiting for the fuse panel for a week or so. I know I left it in the back lot, but we get cars in and out of there all the time."

"Who has access to the keys?"

"All the technicians and the salespeople. Only during business hours, though."

"What happens after business hours? You put the key box in a safe or something?"

"We lock the doors."

"Who has after-hours access to the room with the key box?"

Raúl looked uncomfortable. "I guess everyone with a key. Everyone who opens and closes."

"Who does that include?"

"Almost everyone," Raúl said.

"Ever had a problem with theft before?"

Raúl shook his head.

"Do you get the keys back from employees who leave?" Fenway asked.

"Leave?"

"Who stop working here."

"Oh. I'm not really in charge of that, but I assume we do."

"Does Tommy Kinsella ever take any of the cars out of the lot?" asked Fenway.

Raúl squinted, thinking. "Tommy? No. He comes around to talk to us sometimes. He used to work in service, you know. Some of the technicians remember him from the old days. But no, I don't think he ever takes any of the cars out." He shuffled his feet and shifted his gaze to Sarah. "Look, I can go find the car for you if you want. I can't guarantee that no one has touched it in the last few days, but if you need to see it..."

Sarah nodded, then looked over at Fenway. "Yes. I think that would be best."

"I may have to find it," Raúl said. "Usually they're pretty good about letting me know where they leave it, but sometimes they put it back on the other side of the lot."

"I understand," Fenway said. "We're patient."

Raúl nodded and jogged back to the service area. He disappeared inside for a moment and then appeared again at an easy run around the corner. Fenway saw Sarah watching Raúl all the way.

"Maybe we should follow him," Sarah said. "Make sure he doesn't do anything foolish like drive the car out here for us." She cleared her throat. "You know, contaminate the evidence or something."

Fenway nodded, and the two women walked together around the corner of the building. They continued following the asphalt through an open chain-link gate. Sarah looked to the left and right, scanning the lot. "There," she said, pointing to a glimpse of red.

Sure enough, Raúl appeared from behind an SUV and looked at the car, then checked the paper he held in his hand. He looked up and caught Sarah's eye, smiled, and motioned them over.

"It's got a silver spoiler," Sarah said.

"What?"

Sarah pointed. "One of the options is a silver blade on the edge of the trunk," she said. "Did the recording have the blade on the trunk line?"

"Um—I don't know. I don't think I was paying attention that closely."

"If it didn't, this isn't the car."

They arrived at the car, and Raúl smiled at Sarah, who shyly smiled back.

"Do you need to look inside?" he asked. "I can get the key."

Fenway stepped to the driver's side window and peered in. The interior was black, and Fenway could see a slight but nevertheless noticeable layer of dust on the steering wheel and the dashboard.

"Hasn't been driven in a while," Fenway observed.

"No, it's in the same place I parked it a couple of weeks ago. Probably been here in this spot since before Christmas."

Fenway shook her head. "We can go back and check the video for the silver spoiler," she said to Sarah, "but I don't think this is the right car. If the video shows the spoiler, then we'll get the team from San Mig over here to take fingerprints inside."

"Everything okay?" Raúl said.

Fenway pulled her phone out of her purse and took pictures of the spoiler. "I think we're fine," she said, "but don't drive this for two more days. We might need to fingerprint the inside of the vehicle."

"I promise, no one will touch it," Raúl said, flashing a smile at Sarah. "Perhaps I should call to make sure it's okay to move, even if it's after two days."

Fenway rolled her eyes and handed him her business card. He looked a bit disappointed. "My main line rings to Sarah first," she said, "so if you need to reach me, don't be surprised if she gets on the line."

Raúl brightened.

<hr>

They stopped at Java Jim's before coming back to the office—Fenway needed a replacement for the latte she'd half-spilled on the carpet. Sarah opened the door for her to the coroner's office suite and she went inside and immediately sensed the tension in the room.

Dez sat at her desk, her lips pursed, and she shook her head slightly. Fenway turned her head toward her private office.

Mayor Klein was perched on Fenway's desk, feet on the guest chair. His face was contorted in rage, staring daggers at Fenway through the open door.

"Here we go," Fenway said, sucking in her breath.

Sarah stepped back.

"I warned you," Klein said. "I warned you not to mess around with this case. And you let her go free."

"Unless you're the one who set her up, Barry," Fenway said, "I would think you'd be happy we uncovered that she was being framed before trial. That could have been an expensive mistake."

"She's guilty!" Klein roared.

"She's not guilty," Fenway said as calmly as she could, "and you pushed me to arrest her when I thought the evidence was shaky. If I didn't know better, I'd think you just wanted to embarrass McVie. Sully him with an ex-wife who you'd get to label a murderer."

Barry Klein stood still for a moment, his mouth opening and closing.

"And if I see a decade-old recording of myself online," Fenway said, "may I remind you I still have an arrest warrant with your name on it."

Klein hopped off the desk and casually knocked over Fenway's pen cup. Pens and pencils spilled all over the desk and the floor. He walked out of Fenway's office, standing next to her, halfway between the reception counter and her office door, and spoke in a low voice near her ear. "You *will* re-arrest Amy Tonnick for murder," Klein said, "by *tonight*. If you don't, you're done. I'll start rumors. I'll make sure a recall campaign gets started before the end of the month and you're voted out by St. Patrick's Day."

"Amy Tonnick didn't kill her husband," Fenway said loudly, "and you're not going to make me manufacture evidence."

"I never asked you—"

"Get out of my office," Fenway said.

"You don't get how this works, Miss Stevenson," Barry Klein said. "You think your daddy owns this town, but *I* own this town. And he's about to die. Not as painfully as I'd like, but it'll have to do." Barry smiled toothily in Fenway's face; his breath was minty. "And I'm about to take over as town big shot. So you're going to arrest Amy McVie or you will regret it."

"Tonnick."

"What?"

"Amy Tonnick. You said McVie. That's not her name."

Klein spat in Fenway's face.

Sarah stepped between them. "Okay, Mayor," she said, nudging him gently to the side. "It's time for you to go."

"Get your hands off me, freak!" Klein shouted.

Sarah jumped back as if slapped.

Fenway felt the spit slide down her cheek.

Everything crashed onto Fenway at that moment. The taunts on the playground, the store employees following her around the mall in her teens, the guy in her organic chemistry class who'd whined that she'd unfairly taken his friend's admission spot in the master's program, the worst week of her life watching her mother die.

Every person she met being startled that Nathaniel Ferris's daughter was Black.

The look on her opponent's wife's face at the Nidever dinner.

The racial slur painted on her car.

Barry Klein's smug, entitled face during the first board of supervisors meeting.

She was watching herself in slow motion, like one of those martial arts films from the mid-nineties, and Barry Klein hadn't expected it. He knew he could get away with everything because he had always gotten away with everything.

Time stopped, as it had sometimes when Fenway was a nurse practitioner, and while the phrase *first, do no harm* flitted through Fenway's mind, her body didn't register it. She saw the target. And that's *all* she saw.

She came back to herself, breathing hard, her fists clenched.

"I told you," Fenway said evenly, "to get out of my office."

She tilted her head. Barry's nose began to bleed, and his left eyelid began to puff up.

He lifted his finger to his nose and touched the wet blood. "You'll pay for this," he said, and Fenway noticed his bottom lip split open and run with red when he pronounced the *f* in *for*.

She looked at her hands. Her knuckles were discolored.

Barry Klein turned and strode to the exit door to the office suite, opening it and slamming it behind him as he left.

Sarah narrowed her eyes at Fenway. "I don't need anyone to fight my battles for me."

"Yeah?" Fenway said. "Well, that battle was for *me*."

"You didn't do anything until he called *me* a name. You don't need to prove your ally cred by doing stupid shit like that."

Fenway shook her head. "I did that for me," she repeated. "I should have done that long before you started working here."

Dez stepped up between the two of them. "Okay—*stop*." She turned to Fenway. "I'm the one who's supposed to have the reputation of being headstrong and dangerous. You just flew off the handle." Dez shook her head. "I don't know, Fenway," she said. "You might lose your job over this."

"He spit in *my* face."

"I'm afraid a white guy spitting in a Black girl's face won't exactly resonate with a jury of your, uh, peers." She shook her head. "What the hell were you thinking? Giving him a black eye and a bloody nose."

"And a split lip," Fenway added.

"Maybe he'll be so embarrassed about getting beat up by a girl that he won't report it," Sarah said.

"He'll report it," Fenway said. "This is a golden opportunity to get rid of me." Her jaw started to hurt, and she opened and closed her mouth with quiet pops. "Did he hit me?"

Dez nodded. "He got a decent shot in."

Fenway gingerly touched her chin and the sides of her face. "Shit. That was idiotic. He baited me into it."

Dez scoffed. "Of course he baited you into it. Sitting on your desk when you walked in, knocking that pen cup off, spitting in your face? Yep. He played you, Fenway, and you fell for it."

"Dammit." Fenway looked at the floor.

Sarah folded her arms. "This has been a first week to remember."

Fenway walked into her office and started picking up the pens and pencils.

"Stop!" Dez shouted.

"What?"

Dez hurried over to the doorway to Fenway's office. She took her phone out of her pocket and started snapping pictures.

"What are you doing, Dez?"

"I'm taking pictures. That show what he did to your office." Dez looked up at Fenway. "Oh—that's good. Still some spit hanging from your chin. And the side of your face is starting to swell."

"What do you plan on doing with the pictures?"

"We need to get out in front of this. Go to HR, tell them what happened, tell them you were assaulted first."

"I'm not asking you to lie for me."

"We're not lying for you. We'll tell HR what happened. He's been pushing you to arrest Amy, and he's the one who confronted you. He asked you to falsify evidence. That's a felony."

"You heard me tell him I wasn't going to manufacture evidence—but you didn't hear him ask me directly."

"We both heard him say he wanted Amy arrested by tonight or he'd spread false rumors about you and start a recall election."

Fenway shook her head. "Does *any* of this excuse punching the mayor in the face?"

Dez took a step back. "Probably not," she said. "But it might be the difference between a sternly worded letter in your file and a disciplinary hearing."

CHAPTER TWENTY-FIVE

BY THE TIME FENWAY, DEZ, AND SARAH WERE DONE TALKING WITH the dour woman in Human Resources, each separately discussing the incident, it was almost noon. Fenway had wasted the entire morning on Barry Klein instead of finding suspects.

Fenway expected to be placed on leave immediately, but the woman just clicked her tongue and told her that she would update her on the status of the incident by the end of the week.

"Has Mayor Klein contacted you yet?"

"I can't comment on open cases, Miss Stevenson."

"Right. Sorry."

Dez insisted on going from the HR meeting right to Dos Milagros. The lengua tacos made Fenway feel a little better in spite of her bruised jaw—and she had a bite of the torta ahogada that Sarah ordered, too. She liked it, but not as much as the tacos. As Fenway dumped her trash and put the plastic basket on the top of the tray return, her phone dinged.

"It's from Mark," Fenway said. "He wants to go over the information he found out about the other plaintiffs back in the office."

"And away we go," Dez said.

Fenway had a feeling of impending doom. At any moment, she expected her phone would ding with the announcement of her suspension. She wasn't sure how it worked, actually—as an elected official, could she really be suspended? She was almost curious enough to look it up on her phone as Dez drove them back to the office, but she decided she didn't really want to know.

Sergeant Mark Trevino was at his desk when they got back to the coroner's suite. "Nice of you to finally join us, Mark," Dez said as Sarah went back to her desk. "San Mig's been taking all your time lately."

"I didn't mean for you to rush back here," Mark said, "but I wanted to go over what I found about everyone's alibi. See if maybe I missed something."

"That's anticlimactic," Dez said.

"I didn't even tell you what Sarah and I found out," Fenway said. "Klein was too busy egging me into a boxing match."

"What's this?" Mark said.

"You missed all the drama this morning," Dez said. "We'll fill you in later."

"Okay," Mark said, looking at the bruise on Fenway's jaw. "So—the plaintiff from Boston—the sister of the mother from the family of four who was killed? I talked to seven different people from the train who remember her. Apparently, she's quite gregarious. And the hotel confirmed her check-in time. She wasn't our killer."

"What about murder-for-hire?"

"I've asked Patrick from IT to look into all of our suspects' bank accounts and flag any payments over five thousand dollars coming in or going out in the last six weeks. Tommy Kinsella has had some business purchases, of course, but so far, nothing looks suspicious."

"All the suspects?" Fenway asked.

"Right. And that includes the plaintiffs and their family members."

"Brianna Harlow is on that list too."

Mark nodded. "I've included Rick Tonnick's kids and ex-wives, and—well, just to be thorough, I included Amy Tonnick and Megan McVie, too."

Dez looked at Fenway, who shrugged.

"Okay, who's the next plaintiff you want us to review?" Dez asked. "How about the family of the victim whose husband who passed away during the trial?"

"Right—the two adult children," Mark said. "For the son, Andrew Benedict, I spoke to two of his friends. They were online playing video games and chatting Sunday night. He logged off around eleven thirty. I'm checking with the internet provider, but if the IP address comes back as San Jose, I'm thinking he's not the killer either."

"What about the daughter?"

"Chloe Benedict. She works as an IT admin at McCarran Airport—works in the data center for Coastal Airways. She worked on Sunday and Monday both—from ten in the morning to seven in the evening on Sunday and then from seven in the morning to four in the afternoon on Monday."

"Did she clock in?"

"Someone with her credentials logged into her workstation during those times. I talked to a couple of her co-workers too. Confirmed her whereabouts both days."

Fenway shook her head. "It's *possible* that she took the last flight out to Estancia, rented a Mustang, killed Rick Tonnick, and flew back in time for the start of her shift, but it's unlikely."

"I agree," said Dez. "Unless someone faked her login information and convinced her co-workers to lie for her"—Dez shot a look at Fenway—"I don't think she's our killer either."

Fenway pinched the bridge of her nose and shut her eyes. *Faked her login information.* There was something there, but Fenway wasn't sure what.

"You okay?"

"There's something there. Something I'm not connecting." She shook her head. "Let me think about it for a minute."

"While you're doing that," Sarah said, "we should look at the recording of the Mustang convertible in the parking garage again." She grinned. "Some of us for the first time."

"Why?" Mark asked.

"Because," Sarah said, "there's a Mustang convertible that Tommy Kinsella has access to at Tonnick Ford. If it's got a silver spoiler, it's possible that Tommy was the one driving the Mustang convertible. He's the one who might have set up Amy."

"That doesn't make any sense," Dez said. "Didn't Tommy say that Amy was with him all night?"

"Yes," Fenway said.

"Well—what, you think he put sleeping pills in her drink too?"

"Or something like that, yeah."

"And what? Rick Tonnick just let him into his penthouse and took off all his clothes?"

"Tommy Kinsella isn't a bad-looking guy," Mark ventured.

"No, he's not, but I don't think Rick Tonnick swung that way." Dez paced around the desk. "I mean, he wouldn't be the first guy with a macho lady-killer image to visit the middle of the Kinsey scale every so often. But nothing about that room suggested he was meeting with a man. There were flowers."

"Guys can like flowers," Sarah said.

Dez paused. "Okay, I'll grant you that it's possible. But even if it were —and if Tommy really wanted to stick it to Amy—wouldn't he just take her keys and drive *her* car to the parking garage? Why go through all the trouble of getting a car that looks just like hers—but without the choir sticker—and swapping the plates?" Dez looked around. "Am I missing something? Does that make any sense at all?"

Fenway shook her head. "No. It only makes sense if the killer knew where Rick and Amy lived but didn't have access to the car keys."

"So that means Grant and Noreen Tonnick, right?"

Fenway shook her head again. "They had keys to the house, and I saw the spare keys to the Mustang hanging on a hook when we went to arrest Amy."

"Well," Dez said, "wouldn't they risk alerting Megan if they went into the house to get the key?"

"I think they'd rather do that than get a Mustang and swap license plates in the middle of the night," Fenway pointed out.

Fenway's phone buzzed in her purse. It was Charlotte.

"I've got to take this." Fenway walked into her office and closed the door.

"Hey, Charlotte."

"Hi, Fenway."

"What's up?"

"I talked with Archie Pendergrass."

"And?"

"He showed me his business plan. He's keeping all the lines of business open—not just getting his fuel mix and bumping everything else."

"Well, that's what he *says*."

"He says that his investors won't let him get this money without a plan to make it back within three years."

"He can't do that by selling pieces of Ferris Energy off?"

"He showed me his report. It's all intertwined, he says. If he sells sections off, he doesn't get his fuel mix. And he can make money on the entire business."

Fenway sat down on her desk in the same spot Klein had been a few hours earlier. "He might have just said all that and prepared all the information so you'd give him what he wants."

"Maybe," Charlotte said. "But Fenway, I'm tired. I'm not up for this. I don't know who to trust. Except you."

Fenway sighed. "And I don't want to do it either."

"We would if we had to, Fenway, and I don't know how much I can trust Archie Pendergrass, but I can't beat him if he wants to go against me head-to-head. And you're smart and tough, and you won the first round over him. But he won't underestimate you anymore."

Fenway shifted her weight. "What changed your mind? I thought you were all ready to run the world."

"We changed a couple of assumptions in our projections, Fenway. Sure, if you assume the bottom won't fall out of the oil market and if there are no supply chain disruptions, I should be able to handle things okay and learn as I go. But there isn't a lot of room for error. Change one thing that I've taken for granted, and the entire thing could change completely. Your father knows what he's doing. He can walk that line. He knows when he's inching off course and can recognize when he needs to self-correct. But I don't. And you don't either." She clicked her tongue. "And Archie Pendergrass knows what he's doing, too."

Fenway was silent.

"It's more money than I know what to do with, Fenway. On top of everything your dad and I have now. If something happens and Archie Pendergrass screws the town over—well, I can invest in some small businesses. Maybe *you'll* have a great idea for a business. Maybe we can attract more high tech to the area. My point is, we can work to replace it. And I'm more comfortable doing *that* than I am doing *this*."

Fenway nodded. "I understand."

"But you don't agree."

"It's easy for me to disagree—I'm not the one sacrificing the next three years of my life running an oil company. You do what you have to do, Charlotte. I support your decision."

"I'm calling to accept Archie's offer right now, Fenway. I've got the package in my hand, and our legal team is going over it as we speak."

"Like I said," Fenway said, "I support your decision."

"Do you think it's what your father would have wanted?"

"I know," Fenway said, setting her jaw, "that he wouldn't have chosen anything that would have made your life difficult. He would have wanted you to be well taken care of. And you will be."

Charlotte paused. "Thank you, Fenway." She cleared her throat. "And —how was your visit with your grandmother?"

All the air got sucked out of the room. Fenway slumped to the side and caught herself with her hand. "It—it didn't happen. She passed away last night."

Charlotte gasped.

"It's okay, really. I didn't know her. I never even met her before."

"Oh, Fenway," Charlotte said, "I'm so sorry."

"Nothing to be sorry about, Charlotte." Fenway stood up. "Okay— listen, I've got to get back to my investigation."

"Okay. I hope you get your murderer."

"I hope so, too."

"Let me know if you want to talk about anything."

"Will do."

She hung up and opened the door. Mark, Dez, and Sarah were watching the recording of the parking garage on Mark's computer. "There's the spoiler," Sarah said. "Not silver. That's not the car."

"Good to confirm it," Fenway said, walking up behind them.

"Maybe I should talk to Raúl and let him know it's okay to move the car now."

Fenway nodded. "Yes. That's the sensible thing to do."

"Are there any other ideas we need to toss around?"

Dez shook her head. "We can wait on the financial information from Patrick, and we can widen the net."

"We've still got Trina Perriman's widower. He lied about seeing Amy the night of the murder."

"Yeah," Dez said, "but he was with ten witnesses when Rick Tonnick was being killed. And he barely has two dimes to rub together. He couldn't have hired anyone."

Charlotte's voice suddenly echoed in Fenway's head. *Change one thing that I've taken for granted, and the entire thing could change completely.*

What if the plaintiffs weren't as separate as they'd all been assuming?

What if, with just a little push here and a little push there, one of them had gotten an airtight alibi—and pushed the magnifying glass toward Amy as the main suspect?

Faked her login information.

"Hey," Fenway said, "what airline did Chloe Benedict work for?"

"Coastal Airways," Dez replied.

"And what does she do there?"

"IT."

"But—what specifically? Is she the email administrator or is she the chief information officer?"

"Her title is 'database architect.'"

Fenway tapped her chin. "On what airline did Brianna Harlow fly back from Vegas?"

"Coastal Airways," said Dez.

"Do we still have that airline database available, Sarah?"

"Uh... give me a minute. I can get there."

Fenway sank into one of Dez's guest chairs and put her head in her hands. *Why did I have to take the bait like that? Why couldn't I just smile and nod and watch Klein leave like all the other times?*

"They're covering for each other," Fenway said. "That's what I was missing. We thought Duke Perriman and Brianna Harlow were in cahoots, but because she checked in for her flight, we didn't think she had done it."

"You think Chloe Benedict changed Brianna's check-in status in the Coastal Airways system?"

Fenway nodded. "I bet if we checked the airport cameras, we'd find out she never went through security."

"Okay," Sarah said, "what do you want to know?"

"Look for Brianna Harlow's flights—both going to Las Vegas and coming back. Anything look unusual? Anything look like her check-in was added later?"

"Well," Sarah said, "she checked a bag when she flew to Vegas, and didn't check one coming home."

"That's not that unusual," Dez said. "You check your roll-aboard on the way there but don't want to check it on the way home."

"No, it's usually the opposite," Fenway said. "Scared of not having clothes or toiletries on vacation, so you carry your bag on the plane. When you fly home, you know you have a closet full of clothes and another toothbrush at your house, so you check your suitcase."

"Right," Sarah said. "Also, she didn't have a hotel room Sunday night, and she told us she just gambled all night."

"So?" Mark asked.

"So the casinos now have a service where you check your bag directly to the plane from the hotel. It's about the same as tipping the bell service desk, and she wouldn't have to drag a suitcase around behind her."

"I don't know that it would be enough to convince a jury," Fenway said, "but it's enough for me to wonder if she rented the Mustang convertible in Vegas, not in Estancia."

Sarah was already clicking on the computer. "Rental car database is taking a minute to load. I'll start with McCarran."

Fenway rubbed her jaw where Mayor Klein had punched her. It wasn't that sore.

"So you're saying," Dez mused, "that Brianna rented a car in Vegas, had Chloe Benedict change her check-in from a *No* to a *Yes*, then drove to the Tonnicks' house in Estancia, where she switched license plates—"

"Five minutes and a screwdriver," Fenway said.

" —drove to the hotel, where she had—what? A date with Rick Tonnick?"

"Something like that."

"How did she pull that off?" Dez asked.

"There are lots of hookup apps," Sarah replied as she typed. "A guy like Rick Tonnick is probably on *all* of them."

"Rick's phone didn't have any hookup apps."

"He's not stupid," Sarah said. "You have a wife with prying eyes, you delete the app after each time you use it. As soon as she showed up, he probably got rid of it. He'd download it again when he wanted to meet someone else."

"People really do this?" Dez said, shaking her head, more of a statement than a question.

Sarah clapped her hands together. "Bingo. A red Ford Mustang convertible. Rented Sunday evening at Wayfarer Rent-a-Car at 8:03 P.M., returned at the Estancia Airport location Monday morning at 5:25 A.M." She paused and scrolled down the page.

"That's it?"

"One more thing." Sarah stopped scrolling and pointed to the screen. "Rented by Miss Brianna Harlow."

CHAPTER TWENTY-SIX

Fenway shook her head. "It still amazes me that when I asked for all the red Mustang convertibles that were shown as rented for Sunday night, you only pulled the records of the cars that were rented from Estancia, not the ones that were returned to Estancia."

"You need to be more specific next time," Patrick said.

"Well," Fenway said, "here's what we need you to do."

"Is it in the form?"

"I'm not sure we made ourselves clear enough in the form," Fenway said.

"This isn't how I work."

"Fine," Fenway said. "Here's the decedent's phone." She'd pulled it from the evidence room, the latest iPhone that, until recently, had been Rick Tonnick's.

The form had been clear: find who Rick Tonnick had set up a date with on Sunday night. Or Monday morning. Use any means necessary to open Tonnick's dating app accounts, and find his login information to any dating or hookup sites he could find.

The goal was specific, if not the way to get it. Fenway just hoped it would be enough. She turned on her heel and walked out.

Back in the coroner's office suite, Mark was on the phone with

Coastal Airways, explaining that they needed a snapshot of the database server captured on Monday morning as the plane took off. It sounded like the technician on the other end of the line grew increasingly exasperated. Until the snapshot, captured ten minutes after the earliest flight to Estancia took off Monday morning, revealed that Brianna Harlow had not boarded the flight—yet the current database server said she had.

"I know you don't understand how it happened," Mark said, the receiver pressed against his ear, "but we believe the database was changed after the fact by one of your database architects. Was Chloe Benedict on-site around seven in the morning that Monday?"

"I think it's time to pay Brianna Harlow another visit," Fenway said to Dez. "Bring her down to the station for questioning."

"Won't she get suspicious?"

"Maybe we make it something about the video. Something we say we want her expert opinion on."

"And what would that be?" Dez asked.

"Something related to the hotel property, maybe." Fenway folded her arms. "Okay—forget the video. Let's say that we found a room key on the floor, and we assumed it was his—but we want to make sure."

"And we have to bring her down to the station for that?"

"You come up with an idea, then," Fenway said.

"A lineup," Dez said. "We say we found several women that Rick Tonnick was currently dating. We ask her if any of them were in the hotel in the last several days."

Fenway nodded. "That could work. It might make her think we're on the wrong track. Maybe she'd jump at the chance to give us more incorrect information."

"That'll get her down to the station, anyway. Then we can confront her with the evidence when she's in the interview room."

"Should we pick up Duke Perriman, too?"

"Definitely," Dez said, nodding. "Obstruction of justice. Make sure we walk him through the sheriff's office in cuffs right as we're leading her into the interview room. Then she'll be off her game, wondering if Duke will give her up."

"You think they worked together on this, right?"

Dez thought for a moment. "I can't really see how it would work otherwise. Unless Duke Perriman truly thought he saw Amy. But even so —everything about his statement was false."

"Yeah."

Dez stood up. "It's almost four o'clock," she said. "Brianna will be off soon, won't she? We better get going."

Fenway nodded. "We taking your Impala? The Porsche doesn't really have a back seat."

Dez scoffed. "Hell no. We're checking out a cruiser. I'm not putting a murder suspect in the back of my car unless I have to."

"Right."

Fenway and Dez arrived at the Phillips-Holsen just after four and parked the cruiser in the valet area in front of the door. The red-vested kid's eyes widened, but Fenway shot him a look as Dez said, "Police business. We need to leave it right here for a few minutes."

They walked through the lobby, and butterflies fluttered in Fenway's stomach. She had never gone to a location specifically to arrest someone before. She looked at Dez's belt: the holster, the handcuffs tucked into the back of her work belt. She looked intimidating in a way that Fenway didn't think she'd ever be able to achieve.

They walked right between the front desk and the concierge and started down the long, winding hallway. "Can I help you?" a young white man with blond hair in a navy blazer said to Fenway.

"We know the way," Fenway said, and she smiled.

Dez went first, twisting and turning with the hallway until the back door appeared on the left and the property manager's office appeared on the right. Dez rapped on the door.

A middle-aged Latina woman opened the door. She wore a navy-blue polo shirt with the hotel logo and neatly pressed khakis. She jumped slightly upon seeing Dez and Fenway. "Oh can I help you?"

"We're looking for Brianna Harlow," Dez said.

"She's readying a suite for a VIP customer," the woman said. "But I'm a property manager, too. Can I help you?"

"I'm sorry, ma'am," Fenway said, "but I'm afraid it has to be Brianna."

"And this is a matter of some urgency," Dez added. "So it really would be best if you could point us in the right direction."

"I'll certainly call her and tell her to come meet us." The woman pulled the door open. "We can wait in here." She took the walkie-talkie off the table and held down the call button. "Brianna, come in, please."

A crackle, then a reply. "Hi, Luz. This is Brianna."

"Are you with a guest?"

"No—just making sure the suite is ready."

"Can you come back to the PM room?"

"I should be just another fifteen minutes. Can it wait?"

Luz looked at Dez, who shook her head. Fenway stepped forward and reached out her hand, motioning for the walkie-talkie.

Pushing the call button, Luz said, "Those police people are here again."

There was silence on the other end. The moment stretched into awkwardness. Finally, Luz pushed the button again. "Brianna, are you there?"

A crackle. "Oh—sorry. I must not have had the button pushed down. I asked if they can just ask me over the walkie-talkie. Or if they need to see video, you can show it to them, Luz."

Luz handed the walkie-talkie to Fenway.

"Hey, Brianna, this is Coroner Fenway Stevenson," Fenway said, trying as hard as she could to keep her voice casual. "It's nice to chat with you again."

Another pause, this one shorter. "Hi, Coroner. What do you need?"

"Well," Fenway said, as lazily as she could muster, "we identified a few women that Mr. Tonnick was romantically involved with in the past. Some of them can't provide an alibi for Sunday night. We wondered if you could come down to the station and look at a few photo arrays."

"A few what?"

"Oh—uh, photos of different people, arranged three across and two down. I call them photo arrays."

"For what? To see if they were guests of Mr. Tonnick at the hotel?"

"That's right."

"Honestly, Luz would be better for that. She's the swing shift property manager. That's when people are checking in. She'd be more likely to see them."

Fenway hadn't thought of that. Dez grabbed the walkie-talkie out of her hand.

"You're more likely to see them when they leave the hotel, Miss Harlow," Dez said. "When they get here, they're being cautious, and Rick Tonnick often took them from the back door up the private elevator to the penthouse. But when they leave, Mr. Tonnick has already left, and often they'll walk right by the concierge desk you sit at."

Dez released the button. There was a crackle, but no voice.

"Miss Harlow?" Dez asked.

Brianna's voice finally came through. "I just need another fifteen minutes to finish this room. This is the first VIP to stay with us since the murder, and we need to make sure everything is in tip-top shape."

Fenway crinkled her nose and looked at Dez. Something in Brianna's voice told Fenway that Brianna saw through their ruse. How were they going to make sure that Brianna wouldn't make a run for it in the next fifteen minutes?

Luz motioned for the walkie-talkie and took it. "Brianna, honey, you don't need to make the police wait. I can come up and finish the walk-through."

Another pause. "Okay. Thanks, Luz. The minibar needs to be restocked. I've called catering already."

"I'll be up in just a minute."

"Okay. Tell the police I'll meet them in—" Brianna hesitated. Fenway heard a catch in her voice. "In the lobby."

Luz put the walkie-talkie on her belt and opened the door into the hallway. Dez and Fenway left the property managers' room, and Luz followed them out, locking the door behind her. She stared at them until they moved down the corridor toward the lobby.

"How many ways out of here do you think there are?" Fenway whispered.

"Too many to keep track of," Dez murmured.

They arrived in the lobby, and Fenway turned to the concierge. "Does the penthouse elevator go down to the parking garage?"

"What?"

"The penthouse elevator—does it go down to the parking garage?"

"No, it stops at the ground floor."

"Any other way to get to the penthouse?"

"There's the main elevator. And the fire stairs."

"Is that exit alarmed?"

"No—but you need a card key to get from the stairwell onto the penthouse floor. Only penthouse guests and staff."

"Where does the stairway end? The ground floor, or does it go to the garage?'"

"I don't—I don't know."

Fenway turned to Dez. "Maybe there are officers in the area who can station themselves at the exits."

Dez looked at the concierge. "Can we tell the parking attendant to hold everyone exiting?"

He shook his head. "There's no attendant. It's automated. Any of the card keys will open the gate."

Fenway and Dez moved away from the concierge. "For sure," Fenway murmured, "Brianna's going to try to leave. Maybe I should go to the garage exit and stop Brianna from driving out."

"She'll run you over."

"I have to try," Fenway said. "At least I'll be able to get a license plate."

"Okay," Dez said. "I'll go to the back door on the ground floor. From there, I can see the private elevator and part of the parking garage if I look down that stairway. And the sidewalk on Fourth Street."

Fenway nodded. "Should I stand in front of the hotel between the parking garage exit and the main hotel entrance?"

Dez grimaced. "That's as good a spot as any." She turned to go back down the hallway, then stopped. She turned and threw Fenway her car keys. "Go to the cruiser and call on the radio to see if any deputies are close enough to give us any more coverage. It's a long shot—if Brianna runs, she'll leave in the next two or three minutes—but maybe we'll get lucky."

Fenway hurried out the front door, surprising the doorman, who couldn't open the door in time, and passed the valet. She ran around to the driver's side door, climbed in, and grabbed the radio. "Units in the vicinity of downtown, respond to a 10-29f on Brianna Harlow. Respond to Phillips-Holsen Hotel on Fourth Street."

She clicked off, and no one responded. Dispatch came on and repeated the request. Two deputies responded that they weren't in the vicinity. Fenway tapped her fingers on the steering wheel, gritting her teeth.

"What the hell am I doing?" she said aloud. She could block the exit with the cruiser. That way, even if they missed Brianna going into the parking garage, she couldn't escape.

Fenway had never driven a cruiser before, but she started the engine and flicked a switch to activate the lightbar. She checked the mirror and pulled out into the street, then used the turn signal half a block down and blocked the driveway of the parking garage at the corner of Third Street, lights flashing. She didn't have a gun or a weapon of any kind, but she doubted Brianna did either.

"Okay, Brianna," Fenway murmured. "You'll be coming down to the station with us soon enough."

She stared at the exit gate of the parking garage. No one appeared to be leaving. She glanced up at the traffic on Fifth Street, where a black Dodge Charger braked hard at the intersection and squealed around the corner.

Fenway saw the driver's brown hair and the burgundy-and-navy ascot.

Brianna Harlow.

She hadn't parked in the garage after all.

Fenway threw the cruiser into drive and glanced over her shoulder as she pulled into the street. The lightbar was flashing but she couldn't see where the switch for the siren was.

The Charger sped around cars, and turned hard at Broadway, heading toward the freeway. Fenway grabbed for the radio and almost dropped the microphone. She floored it through a green light at Sixth Street and squealed around the same corner to get onto Broadway.

Fenway pushed the mic button. "This is Fenway Stevenson in pursuit of a one-eight-seven suspect in a black Dodge Charger, heading east on Broadway toward Ocean Highway. Request backup."

"10-4," the dispatcher said in reply. "Careful of traffic, Fenway. If it gets crowded or you sense unsafe conditions, stop your pursuit."

"It's Brianna Harlow," Fenway said.

"She's not going anywhere. If she doesn't pull over by the first freeway exit, let us take over."

"Copy that."

Brianna was two blocks ahead, but the lights were green, and there were no cars between the two vehicles. Fenway reached her left hand back and grabbed awkwardly for the seatbelt, drifting into the left lane as she pulled it across her body and buckled it.

The red light didn't stop the Charger from making a hard right turn onto the freeway onramp. Fenway reached down with her right hand and flicked the switch next to the lightbar. Nothing happened. She flicked it back and tried the next switch.

The siren wailed happily, and Fenway felt a rush of adrenaline as she turned the steering wheel hard and the cruiser responded, tires squealing around the corner. Fenway pushed the accelerator to the floor and the engine roared, throwing Fenway back in her seat.

As the cruiser flew down the onramp, cars ahead pulled to the shoulder, and the black Charger raced past them. Not an unsafe situation. Besides, Fenway was gaining on Brianna.

The exit for San Vicente Boulevard loomed ahead. Fenway sensed that Brianna didn't know where she could escape to, and she must realize that the cruiser had a more powerful engine than her Charger.

The Dodge drifted from the left lane to the middle. Was Brianna going to pull over?

Fenway was still gaining, now only one or two car lengths behind. But they were about to pass the exit, and Fenway would have to stand down. In spite of the pulsing in her veins, and as much as she hated to see a murderer get away, letting Brianna go was the right thing to do.

She eased up on the gas.

The Charger braked hard and shot to the right.

Holy shit—Brianna was gunning for the San Vicente exit to throw Fenway off the chase.

Fenway slammed on the brakes, but it was too late.

The front bumper of the cruiser clipped the back corner of the Charger, which spun on the asphalt like an ice skater.

Fenway watched in horror as the black Charger smashed into the wall of the San Vicente overpass.

She put her blinker on—why would she put her blinker on?—and stopped the cruiser on the shoulder about a hundred yards past the overpass. She looked in the rearview mirror—no one was coming—and opened the door halfway. Then she stopped and grabbed the radio mic.

"This is Coroner Stevenson." She searched the file of radio codes in her head. "Um—in pursuit of a black Charger." Like a flash, the code came to her. "11-83. Suspect's car was in the accident, not me." Dez would probably make fun of her radio lingo, but she didn't care. "Ocean Highway northbound at the San Vicente exit."

"You okay?" the dispatcher said.

"Yeah. I'm fine. She might need an ambulance. I'm going to check on her right now."

"10-4. Ambulance on its way."

She grabbed her phone from her purse, clicked off the siren, and scampered out of the cruiser, then sprinted toward the black Charger, its front end crumpled like the nose of a paper airplane. The airbag had deployed, and the figure in the seat was motionless, slumped slightly over to her right.

Fenway opened the door, and Brianna Harlow turned to look at her, blinking incredulously.

"Brianna Harlow?" Fenway said, out of breath. Brianna had a scrape on her forehead and was covered in dust.

"I didn't think anyone would figure it out," Brianna murmured.

"You sit tight. An ambulance is on its way. Are you hurt?"

"That bastard killed my sister," she said.

"I know. I need to know if you're injured, Brianna. Can you move your arms and legs?"

Brianna cracked a smile. "I'm gonna be sore tomorrow, that's for sure."

Fenway nodded. "Brianna Harlow, you are under arrest for the murder of Richard Tonnick. Anything you say can and will be held against you..."

As she finished reciting the Miranda rights, she heard an ambulance siren in the distance, growing louder with each passing second.

"I hope Tonnick and his wife burn in hell."

"They probably will," Fenway said.

"I didn't do it. I was on that plane from Vegas."

"No, you weren't," said Fenway. "You had Chloe Benedict alter the flight record for you."

"Ah." Brianna turned her head slightly and grimaced. "Don't go too hard on her. She lost both her parents in the same year."

"She testifies against you, maybe she gets probation."

"Yeah. That's probably okay." Brianna licked her lips. "You said the ambulance is coming?"

"It's almost here. Can't you hear the siren?"

Brianna shook her head almost imperceptibly. "My ears are ringing. Probably these damn airbags."

The ambulance pulled onto the shoulder in front of the Charger, and two paramedics got out.

"This is where I put you in capable hands," Fenway said.

"Oh, Coroner," Brianna said, closing her eyes, "I hope you burn in hell too,"

PART SIX
FRIDAY

CHAPTER TWENTY-SEVEN

Fenway was filling out her fourth online form of the day—this one a vehicular incident report for the minor damage to the front bumper—and it wasn't even ten o'clock yet. Her eyelids drooped as she filled out her employee number for what seemed like the hundredth time. A knock on the door woke her out of her stupor.

The door swung open, and Charlotte leaned her head into the room. Her eyes were bright, the bags that had been under her eyes were all but gone, and her hair was shiny, almost moving on its own.

"It looks like the contract has been signed," Fenway said.

"For now, it's just a letter of intent," Charlotte said. "But barring any bad stuff the lawyers find—and I've been assured there are no longer any bodies buried there—Ferris Energy will soon be a wholly owned independent subsidiary of Sierra Madre."

"Congratulations, Charlotte."

Charlotte sniffed. "I don't know if congratulations are exactly in order. But I've made my peace with it. I was in a pretty dark place yesterday."

Fenway nodded. "Me too. It was overwhelming."

Charlotte stepped into Fenway's office, shutting the door behind her, and sat in the guest chair. "You know how far in over my head I was, Fenway."

"I was, too."

"Maybe you can fake it better than I can." Charlotte grinned, then pulled an envelope out of her purse. "Anyway, here you are. Consulting fee for your time as the community liaison."

"Thanks. Maybe it'll cover dinner at Maxime's."

"Oh, I think it'll go a little farther than that."

Fenway opened the envelope. Her eyes widened, and she gasped. "I don't think I've seen a check with that many zeroes." She looked up at Charlotte. "You must be kidding. That was literally *one* day of real work."

"Are you kidding? You're the reason that Sierra Madre increased their offer so much. Every one of the investors are getting at least triple what they would have made if you hadn't been there."

"But surely it's not worth this much."

Charlotte drummed her fingers on the desk. "My dad used to tell this really awful joke when I was growing up," she said. "This guy has a floorboard in his house that squeaks. It drives him crazy. Keeps him up at night when anyone steps on it." She laced her fingers together in front of her. "One day, he can't stand it any longer, so he calls a carpenter. Well, the carpenter can't fix it. So he calls a mechanic. But the mechanic can't fix it either. Finally, he calls a flooring specialist. The specialist arrives, hears the creak, takes a nail out, and pounds it into the offending floorboard."

Fenway nodded.

"The homeowner steps on the board," Charlotte continued. "No squeak. He steps around the board. No squeak. He looks at the floor specialist and says, 'It's a miracle! It's fixed!' And the floor specialist says, 'Glad I could help. That'll be two hundred dollars.'"

Fenway's eyes widened.

"The homeowner is aghast," Charlotte said, slamming her palm on the table. "'Two hundred dollars! All you did was put a nail in! What about that cost two hundred dollars!' And the floor specialist grins, and says—"

"'A dollar for the nail, a hundred ninety-nine for knowing where to put it,'" Fenway said.

Charlotte chuckled. "You know that story."

"I've heard it once or twice."

"If you heard it, you should pay attention to it." She reached over to Fenway's side of the desk and tapped the check. "That's for knowing where to put it."

Fenway nodded. "Thanks, Charlotte."

"And now," Charlotte said, "you can't complain that you can't afford the insurance on the Porsche."

"What?"

"Oh, come on, Fenway. You love that car. That car loves you. It would be silly to keep in my garage. Next time I see you, you're going to pay me a hundred bucks for the Porsche, and I'll give you the pink slip."

"No, I can't—"

"I insist." Charlotte stood. "You going by the hospital tonight?"

"I was thinking about going at lunch," Fenway said. "Getting some Dos Milagros, then going to see him. Dad should hear me talk about how good that place is at least one more time." She looked up. "Maybe you could join me?"

"I'm not sure I can get away for lunch," Charlotte said, opening the door. "I'll text you if I can."

As Charlotte left, Sheriff Gretchen Donnelly caught the door before it closed and stepped into Fenway's office.

"Hi, Sheriff," Fenway said. "I filled out the arrest paperwork correctly, right? I double-checked it."

"That's not why I'm here, Fenway." Donnelly sat down in the same chair Charlotte had just vacated.

Fenway's stomach sank. "Don't tell me it's Klein. If you're arresting me for assault, you better arrest him, too. He initiated everything. I was defending myself. You can ask HR."

Donnelly shook her head. "Spitting on someone is considered assault according to the law," she said, "so I was able to convince the mayor that if you were arrested, he'd have to be, too. He saw the wisdom in not pressing criminal charges." She leaned forward. "But he is asking for you to be dismissed from your position."

"I was elected by the people of this county, and I don't report to him," Fenway said. "If there are no criminal charges, there are no grounds for it."

Donnelly pursed her lips. "He's scheduled an administrative hearing and he's going to argue for your dismissal in front of the city council. He wants them to decide."

Fenway's mouth fell open. "Can they do that?"

Donnelly rolled her eyes. "Not the way I interpret the county bylaws. But who knows what Klein will say?"

Fenway set her jaw. "So he thinks that the council will punish my fists more than his spit."

Donnelly shrugged. "I don't know what to think. But according to the county bylaws, I have to put you on administrative leave."

"What?"

"With pay," Donnelly said hurriedly.

"Then you need to put him on administrative leave, too."

Donnelly smiled sadly. "I guess he knew that—he agreed. He's going on vacation."

Fenway sat back. "He's a snake, Gretchen. He'll destroy this whole county if he can."

Donnelly nodded. "Maybe you should use your time off to start a recall election. Of *him*." She stood. "If you strike first, his recall petition will look like sour grapes."

"Seriously? This office caught Brianna Harlow the same day that Klein threatened me. And he's pushing a recall campaign?"

"Out of town for at least a week," Donnelly repeated. "I bet you could do a lot of damage by the time he gets back."

Fenway looked at her screen, still full of the incomplete paperwork. "When do I need to leave?"

"I'm supposed to walk you out," Donnelly said.

Fenway grabbed her purse. "Sorry you have to finish the paperwork. If you need any information, you've got my number."

Fenway walked out of her office. Dez and Mark, like Fenway, were filling out paperwork on the computer and looked up. Fenway tapped the counter, and Sarah looked up from her typing as well.

"Because I couldn't stop myself from punching Barry Klein in the face," Fenway announced, "I'm going on administrative leave." She turned to Sarah. "It was fantastic to work with you this week. I'm sorry you had to be in the middle of all this drama. You're an asset to this office, and I hope we haven't scared you off. Migs will be back on Monday, and you can keep him busy with the legal paperwork from the warrants and the recordings." She grinned. "And maybe he can delve into the depths of the employee handbook and see if I have a leg to stand on at the hearing."

Fenway walked out of the building into the misty morning, expecting to feel sad, but instead felt strangely free. The check from Charlotte meant that she could be dismissed—if that were even possible—and she'd be fine for at least a year or two. More if she was careful, or if she moved somewhere a lot cheaper than the California coast.

She walked the six blocks to the French bakery next to the Phillips-Holsen hotel and ordered a pain au chocolat and a latte. She took her time eating and drinking her coffee, without anything to do until seeing her father at lunchtime. Fenway realized she had a free Friday night— and a boyfriend who might want some company.

Fenway parked the Porsche in front of McVie's office at a few minutes before eleven. She felt light even as she was ascending the stairs. She opened the door to Suite 202 and Piper turned her face toward Fenway.

"Hey, Piper," Fenway said.

"Hey, Fenway," Piper said. "I heard about your grandmother. I—I'm really sorry."

Fenway shrugged. "I didn't know her at all." *So it shouldn't hurt as much as it does.*

"Still." Piper said. "Let me know if you want to talk."

"McVie around?"

Piper shot her thumb over her shoulder. "Boss-man's in the next room. Getting an update for our client."

"Amy or me?"

"Well, I was talking about you, but I guess Amy's paying a little better."

"For now," Fenway said and opened the connecting door.

The adjoining room wasn't much bigger than a broom closet, and even the small desk and chair overwhelmed the space. McVie looked up from his laptop and grinned.

"Hey, Fenway," he said. "Didn't expect you to show up in the middle of the day."

"I have been cruelly forced into a life of leisure," Fenway said, setting her purse down on McVie's desk, sitting sidesaddle on his lap, and kissing him.

The kiss was good—they hadn't kissed like this in a while. Too much stress with McVie's new P.I. firm, too much anxiety with Megan, and too much conflict over the stolen Accord.

Fenway broke from the kiss first.

"What are you talking about, a life of leisure?" McVie asked.

"Oh," Fenway said, "you know how yesterday I told you about how we arrested Brianna Harlow?"

"I do."

"I may have forgotten to mention that I punched Mayor Klein in the face before that."

McVie blinked. "I'm sorry—you *what?*"

"I'm on administrative leave for a week—until the hearing, actually."

"You're on leave?"

"*Paid* leave." Fenway smirked. "He totally deserved it, though."

"I'm sure he did," McVie said. "Is it your word against his?"

"Oh, no," Fenway said. "This all happened in the office. There were witnesses. I admitted everything to HR."

McVie's jaw dropped.

"I think he's going to try to get me dismissed."

"What? The county bylaws—"

Fenway put a finger over McVie's lips. "Shh. I don't want to talk about Barry Klein. I wanted to see if you wanted to play hooky for the rest of the day. Or is your mean ol' boss going to be mad at you?"

He crinkled his nose. "Maybe this afternoon. I was about to head to an interview."

"An interview? Not for another job?"

McVie chuckled. "No, not with the chunk of change I'm billing my ex-wife for."

Fenway stood.

"It's actually for your case. One of your mother's—uh, that is, Samara's—former classmates. See what she can tell me about her relationship with Eddie Drake."

Fenway nodded. "If it's for a good cause."

He leaned forward. "Piper actually uncovered something a couple of days ago. I tried to dig into it a little more, but I keep running into dead ends." He sighed. "I wish we had more to show for our efforts."

Fenway shook her head. "I know it's a long shot. A lot of this stuff happened over thirty years ago."

McVie stood, and Fenway scooted around the desk and out to the main part of the office.

"I heard my name," Piper said.

"Show Fenway what you found on Tuesday," McVie said.

Piper nodded and turned to the screen. She clicked a few times, and a photo of a check appeared. Fenway squinted.

It was a check from her mother—Joanne Stevenson, not Samara Godwin.

And it was paid to the order of *Darren Ellsworth*.

Dated June 1, 2000. Just a few years after they moved to Seattle.

The check was made out for eight thousand nine hundred dollars.

Fenway pointed to the number. "That's odd."

"Not really," Piper said. "It's under the mandatory federal reporting guidelines."

"And that would leave a little over a thousand dollars for Mom and me to live on." Ramen for dinner, clothes at Goodwill, and a one-bedroom apartment in the bad part of town. That sounded about right.

Fenway pursed her lips. That might have been right before she started selling her paintings.

She pointed to the name. "And that's the charming local private investigator."

"Same name, yes." Piper shook her head. "But this check was never cashed. It was digitized as part of an unclaimed property exercise in the late nineties."

"Unclaimed property?"

"Some good Samaritan," said McVie, "probably found it on the ground and turned it into the lost-and-found at the local police station. The clerk obviously threw the check in a box and forgot about it until some bureaucrat decided to audit the unclaimed property a few years later."

"But a check for almost nine thousand dollars?"

McVie arched an eyebrow. "You've obviously never been through an unclaimed property box."

"Also," Piper said, "I don't know for sure if our local private investigator was this Darren Ellsworth or not."

"How many—"

"Three," Piper said. "There were three Darren Ellsworths living in Seattle at the time. I'm sure there were more if you expand the search to the entire metro area. I can't say for sure if this is the P.I. from Estancia."

"And he says he's never heard of Joanne Stevenson," McVie added. "And of course I don't have the power of the badge behind me anymore. We have to get a little more creative."

"Fortunately," Piper said, "I like being creative."

McVie chuckled. "It just takes a little longer."

"What do you think the payment was for?"

"He's a private investigator," McVie said. "My first thought was that she hired him to get information about your father."

Fenway shook her head. "She wouldn't keep us in poverty unless she had to. It must have been something else."

Piper nodded. "I agree—but we don't know if this was a one-time payment or part of a monthly thing."

Fenway's thoughts were dark—*blackmail*. "You sure you can't get into his financials?"

"Well," Piper said, "that would probably be illegal without a warrant. If one were to ignore it and do it anyway, one might find that there have been no suspicious deposits in any of the P.I.'s accounts—business or personal—for two decades. If one were to obtain his financial records."

"Which you didn't."

Piper shrugged. "That's why we didn't want to tell you. There are over a hundred Darren Ellsworths who were living in the United States in the nineties. It might seem like a coincidence, but you'd be surprised at the odds."

Fenway was silent.

***

Fenway took a seat next to Nathaniel Ferris's hospital bed. She could still taste the cilantro on her tongue from the lunch special at Dos Milagros.

"Dad," she said, "I'm going to do something different. I know I usually read to you. I *was* going to watch Red Sox games with you, but the Wi-Fi in here is too slow, so I'd have to download it—well, I couldn't figure out a good way to do it. So instead, I'm just going to tell you about my week."

Fenway set her purse down on the floor. "I won't bore you with all the details, but you know that Craig got a divorce, right? And Amy—that's his ex—is kind of a bitch to me. Probably because I'm younger than she is, although honestly, I hope to look as good as her when I'm forty. Maybe less fake. But still good."

Fenway spent the next twenty minutes recounting everything to her dad: Rick Tonnick's murder, Amy's arrest, Megan stealing the Accord, Charlotte insisting that Fenway take the Porsche.

Although she creatively left out the part where Charlotte sold Ferris Energy to Sierra Madre, it was otherwise warts-and-all. Finding out that Joanne Stevenson was really Samara Godwin. The call from Julia telling her that Nell Godwin had passed away. The pressure that the mayor put on Fenway to arrest Amy Tonnick. The horror she felt when she thought Megan had been the murderer.

The discovery of the bumper sticker. Finding that the database admin at Coastal Airways had doctored the flight information. And the car chase leading to Brianna's arrest.

"And maybe the best part, Dad." She leaned forward, elbows on her knees. "I punched Barry Klein right in his smug, entitled face. He spit on me. He's been treating me like dirt. So I didn't take it anymore." She lowered her voice to a whisper. "And even if I lose my job, his bloody nose and his split lip will be an image I'll be talking about when I'm eighty years old. It will provide me comfort in my darkest hour. I don't care if it's mean. I don't care if he pushed my buttons just so I would do it. I can *guarantee* that he didn't think I'd hit that hard. I bet he'll never push my buttons again." She chuckled. "Part of me isn't proud of it, but part of me wishes you had seen it."

She stood up and paced around the room for a moment. "I miss you, Dad. I know the doctors aren't giving you a chance. And I know I owe you my life. I just wish you hadn't had to sacrifice yourself to save me." She felt the tears well in her eyes and blinked them back. "Anyway." Fenway cleared her throat. "I've got to find a bathroom. I'll be right back."

There was a set of one-stall bathrooms down the hall in the ICU, but Fenway wanted to save those for the families. She turned down the hall and went into the cavernous women's room off the long, carpeted hallway that connected the ICU with the gift shop and the lobby. The light was off, but it was on a motion sensor and turned on as soon as Fenway stepped inside. She went into a stall, closed the door, sat on the toilet, and let the tears flow. She didn't sob or make any sound at all, but the tears came, fast and cleansing, and rolled down her cheeks. She was crying for both her grandmother who she'd never truly meet and her father who was brave enough to save her.

His last words to her were "I'm so proud of you." Her last words to him when he'd been conscious were far less flattering. Yet Fenway knew he'd seen her jump into action, try and save him, do everything she could —and she hoped that it would make up for the mean things she said when she showed everyone in that courtroom that he didn't know the name of her prom dates, or what part she played in the elementary school play, or even what sport she excelled at in high school. She hoped that some part of his comatose brain was engaged, and he had heard Fenway confess how much she missed him.

She wiped her face with the rough, one-ply toilet paper, blew her nose on it, and threw it in the toilet. She finished and wiped, stood up and buttoned her jeans—another blazer-and-jeans day for her.

The mirror didn't mince words. She looked like she'd been crying, but she also looked at peace. Her makeup was mostly gone, and a little water, soap, and paper towels took care of the rest. She didn't really care.

Fenway stood up straight and assessed herself. Nothing wrong with the natural look. Her hair was more frizzy than normal, but it was fine. Lots of people in hospitals looked like they'd been crying.

She took a left turn out of the bathroom and went into the gift shop. The ICU forbade flowers and balloons—and a comatose Nathaniel Ferris couldn't appreciate them anyway.

Sports edition of a popular crossword book series—that would do. Fenway would do the crossword and ask her dad for clues. They hadn't done many crosswords together, but that didn't matter. They hadn't done a lot of stuff together. Fenway hadn't told her dad about how her day went since she was eight. She was surprised at how good it felt—even though the conversation was completely one-sided. She bought a mechanical pencil, too.

She opened the crossword book as she walked down the hall, keeping the corridor in her peripheral vision. She opened the door to the ICU wing and leafed through the book until she found a crossword solely about baseball. Surely at least five or six of the clues would be about the Red Sox. "Nomar" always seemed to be in puzzles like this. There it was, 28 down: "Shortstop Garciaparra." Well, no points for creativity to the clue writer on that one. She turned into her father's room as she started to fill in the squares.

"Fenway." The voice was hoarse and frazzled—but achingly familiar.

The crossword book and the pencil fell from her grasp. The book landed with a dull thump, and the pencil hit Fenway's shoe and clattered across the floor.

Nathaniel Ferris, eyes open, stared at his daughter quizzically.

"Did I dream that you punched Barry Klein in the face?"

CAST OF CHARACTERS

Fenway Stevenson: A former nurse practitioner with a master's degree in forensics, she moved to Estancia in April after her mother, Joanne, lost her battle with cancer. Fenway has a rocky relationship with her father. Appointed to fill out the coroner's term, she decided to run for election—and won. Her official four-year term started January 1.

Her family

Nathaniel Ferris: The richest, most powerful man in the county, the oil magnate founded and owns Ferris Energy. After his wife took away the then eight-year-old Fenway to Seattle two decades ago, he threw himself into his work, but has hardly seen or talked to Fenway during the last twenty years. Two months ago, he took a bullet for Fenway and has been in a coma ever since.

Charlotte Ferris: The former beauty pageant winner married Nathaniel a decade ago when she was 25 and he was 50—the weekend of Fenway's high school graduation.

Joanne Stevenson: Fenway's mother, who passed away from cancer about nine months ago.

Her co-workers, past and present

Sergeant Desirée "Dez" Roubideaux: A detective in the coroner's office, Dez has worked for the county for 25 years. She's a dedicated, determined investigator despite her wisecracks.

Craig McVie: The former sheriff of Dominguez County, he lost the mayoral race in November. Recently divorced from Amy, he's now a private investigator. He and Fenway officially started dating after the election.

Piper Patten: Formerly in the county's IT department, this willowy redhead is a whiz at forensic accounting and data gathering. She likes the command line interface almost as much as she likes her boyfriend, Migs. She helped Nathaniel Ferris prove his innocence in a murder case, and now works for McVie.

Dr. Barry Klein: The former optometrist and county supervisor was expected to run against Fenway for coroner in November. Instead, he ran for mayor against Sheriff McVie—and won. His feud with Nathaniel Ferris has bled over into a caustic relationship with Fenway.

Sergeant Mark Trevino: Another detective in the coroner's office, he is nearing retirement.

Miguel "Migs" Castaneda: The legal advisor for the coroner's office, he's a paralegal studying to be a lawyer.

Sarah Summerfield: The newly hired coroner's assistant.

Rachel Richards: Fenway's former assistant, she was promoted to be the county's youngest public information officer in a century.

Sheriff Gretchen Donnelly: The new sheriff who replaced McVie when he ran for mayor.

Victims, suspects, witnesses, and persons of interest

Rick Tonnick: The wealthy owner of a string of car dealerships, he's found dead in the penthouse suite of a fancy hotel under an assumed name.

Amy Tonnick: Rick's new bride (wife #5) is also McVie's ex-wife.

Megan McVie: Craig and Amy's 17-year-old daughter; she lives with her mother and stepfather.

Tommy Kinsella: He worked his way up through the ranks from mechanic to Rick Tonnick's second-in-command. Still has the killer good looks that got him in trouble in high school.

Grant Tonnick: Rick's son from his first marriage, Grant owns a fancy beachfront steakhouse.

Noreen Tonnick: Rick's daughter and Grant's half-sister, Noreen is the president of a video game company.

Brianna Harlow: The overly-chipper property manager working for the hotel where the body is found.

Duke Perriman: The widower of a woman killed by Rick Tonnick's negligence regarding an airbag safety recall.

Andrew Benedict, Chloe Benedict: The son and daughter of another woman killed by the same botched airbag recall.

Darren Ellsworth: An established P.I. in Estancia, he worked for Amy to find out if Rick was cheating on her.

Archie Pendergrass: The CEO of Ferris Energy's biggest customer, Sierra Madre Fuels.

ACKNOWLEDGMENTS

Many thanks to my editors, Max Christian Hansen and Jess Reynolds, and Ziad Ezzat of Feral Creative, who has designed all the Fenway Stevenson covers.

Special thanks to Theresa Baumgartner, who supplemented her always-valuable feedback with an incredibly valuable first line.

Thank you to all the early readers, including (but not limited to) Jill Davies, the merry band of critics from the Wordforge Novelists group, Blair Semple, Dana Luco, Genesis Hansen, Michelle Damiani, Beverly Ange, Katheryn Mandel, and my trusted medical experts Dr. Christina Bellinger and former forensic nurse Pamela McCarty, who spent their valuable time catching errors and getting my book to be the best it could be (even if I *still* took poetic license with a couple of things that aren't completely accurate). To my advanced reader team, thank you for catching a few errors that slipped through the cracks. I'd also like to thank Cheryl Shoults and Ryan Mahan for helping my novels rise as high on the booksellers' charts as they have.

To my wife, my children, and my mother: I'm deeply grateful for your encouragement and support, without which these books would never have seen the light of day.